CRIMSON LAKE

Candice is the middle child of a large, eccentric family from Sydney's western suburbs. The daughter of a parole officer and an enthusiastic foster-carer, Candice spent her childhood listening around corners to tales of violence, madness and evil as her father relayed his work stories to her mother and older brothers.

Candice won back-to-back Ned Kelly awards for her first two novels *Hades* and *Eden*. She is also the author of the critically acclaimed *Fall* and co-writer of the latest James Patterson blockbuster *Never Never*, set in the Australian outback. She lives in Sydney.

Also available by Candice Fox

Hades
Fall
Eden

CRIMSON LAKE

CANDICE FOX

arrow books

1 3 5 7 9 10 8 6 4 2

Arrow Books
20 Vauxhall Bridge Road
London SW1V 2SA

Arrow Books is part of the Penguin Random House group of companies
whose addresses can be found at global.penguinrandomhouse.com.

Penguin
Random House
UK

First published in Great Britain by Arrow Books in 2017
(First published in Australia by Bantam in 2017)

www.penguin.co.uk

A CIP catalogue record for this book is available from the British Library

ISBN 9781784758066

Printed and bound in Great Britain by Clays Ltd, St Ives Plc

For Gaby and Bev

PROLOGUE

I was having some seriously dark thoughts when I found Woman. The only company I'd had in a month was my gun, and they can start to talk to you after a while, guns, if you're alone with them long enough. The weapon watched me with its black eye as I rattled around the bare house, saw when I failed to unpack the boxes in the hallway day after day. It lay on its side and judged my drinking. Halfway down a bottle of Wild Turkey one night, I started asking the gun what its fucking solution to everything was if it was so smart. A gun has only one answer.

The night before I found Woman, there'd been another brick through the front window. It was the third since I'd arrived in Crimson Lake, and I hadn't bothered to patch it up this time. I'd looked at the glass for a while and then gone out to the back porch and taken up residence there as the sun began to set, watched it blinking red across the wetlands, dancing on

1

the grey sand. The house was falling apart anyway, which was why I rented it so cheap. The previous inhabitants had done a good job on the back porch, though. There was a nice strong rail and sturdy stairs, and the wire fence at the bottom of the yard that kept me safe from the crocs was intact.

The fence was also very familiar. I was used to looking at the world through diamond wire.

I'd sat there in the evenings wondering if the former residents had been hiding from something too, relishing in the predictability of nightfall as I did. The stickiness. The swell of insect life. The crocs beginning their barking in the dark, hidden, sliding in the wet and smelling me up here on the porch.

Between the vigilantes out the front and the crocs out the back I felt like I was in prison again, which wasn't so bad, because it was secure. I was free from the decision to run, because I couldn't run anymore from my crime. Then the gun reminded me, sitting beside me on the dry, cracked wood, that I still had an avenue out. I was just looking at the weapon and agreeing a little and swigging the last remnants of the bourbon when I heard the bird down near the fence.

I thought she was a swan at first. The sound coming out of her wasn't like anything I'd ever heard a bird make: a kind of coughing squeak, like she had a rock in her throat. I bumbled down the hill through the long grass and, incredibly, she approached me from the other side of the fence, so that I could see a mess of little grey chicks all swirling and scattering clumsily around her as she tried to walk. The goose seemed to rethink the approach and stumbled back, hissing and flapping one great white wing.

'Jesus Christ, are you nuts?' I asked.

I do that when I'm drunk. Talk to things. My gun. Birds. She was nuts though, clearly, waddling around wounded and plump on the banks of the croc-infested Cairns marshlands. I glanced out over the water and then opened the gate.

I'd never opened the gate before. When I'd moved into the rundown house thirty days earlier I'd asked the estate agent why the previous inhabitants had even installed one. Unless they had a boat, which it didn't appear they had, there was nothing out there in the water but certain death. He hadn't had an answer. I stepped out tentatively and my bare feet sank into the muddy sand, crab holes bubbling.

'Come here.' I waved at the bird, gripping the gate. The goose flapped and squeaked. Her babies gathered together, a terrified bundle of fluff. I looked out at the water again, seemed to spy a hundred black ripples that could have been croc eyes. The sun was down. It was their time now. 'Come here, you stupid bitch.'

I sucked in a gutful of air, rushed forward and lunged at the bird, missed, lunged again and gathered it upside down in a tangle of bones and limbs and claws and feathers. It snapped at my nose, ear, eyebrow, drew blood. The chicks scattered, reformed, clicking and squealing an infantile rendition of their mother's noise. I turned and threw the goose into my yard. The chicks followed, drawn along in a frantic row by some instinctive fishing line. I slammed the gate closed, ran up the yard and grabbed a towel that had been hanging on the verandah rail, leaving the gun sitting on the step.

On the way to the vet, the big bird and her chicks stuffed into a cardboard box, the squealing got to me. It was a heartbreaking distress siren. I yelled, 'Jesus, shut up, woman!'

3

I guess her name was Woman from that moment on.

In the sterile light of the vet's office, the bird seemed smaller somehow, peering from the bottom of the box at the man who had opened the door for me. She and the chicks were revealed united, a panting mound of crooked feathers in the dark. They were all silent now. I stood back so the vet couldn't smell my breath, but from the disdain on his face as he'd watched my hack parking job and my bare sandy feet coming up the drive I was fairly sure he had me pegged. I folded my arms and tried not to take up too much of his tiny examination room with my hulk. The vet didn't seem to have recognised me yet, so I took a chance and spoke up as he lifted the struggling Woman out of the box, wincing as she snapped at his collar.

'She can't walk on that foot there,' I said.

'Yep. Looks fractured. This wing too.'

I watched as he folded the goose into her natural shape, reassembling the barely contained terror-mess that she was until her feet were beneath her thick, round frame and her wings lay flat against her sides. The bird looked around the room, black eyes big and wild. The vet squeezed her gently all over, lifted her tail and looked at her fluffy rear.

'So I'll just leave her with you, I guess?' I clapped in summation, startling the bird.

'Well, that's up to you, Mr . . .?'

'Collins,' I lied.

'That's up to you, Mr Collins, but you're aware we don't have the resources for unpaid treatment here?'

'Uh, no. I wasn't aware.'

'No, we can't treat this animal without compensation.'

I scratched my head. 'I found her, though.'

'Yes,' the vet agreed.

'Well, I mean, she's not mine. Doesn't belong to me.'

'You've said.' The vet nodded.

'So that's not my goose.' I pointed to Woman, tried to tighten up my slurred speech in case that was why I was being misunderstood. 'Neither are they.' I pointed at the chicks. 'They're . . . dumped, I suppose. Abandoned. Don't you people rescue abandoned animals?'

'We people?'

'Vets.'

He gave me a long stare. 'This is not a native Australian goose. This is an Anser. A domesticated goose. It's an introduced species in this country. I'm afraid a wildlife rescue wouldn't treat it either.'

'Well, what will you do with her?' I asked. 'If I just leave her here with you?'

The vet stared again. I blinked under the fluorescent lights. Their gentle humming filled the room like gas.

'Christ,' I said. 'Well, okay. This is a business, I s'pose. You can't just go around rescuing everything for free.' I took out my wallet and flipped through the red and blue notes there. 'How much is it to fix a broken goose?'

'It's a lot, Mr Collins,' the vet said, squeezing Woman again around the base of her long, lean neck.

Seven hundred dollars later I drove home trembling and sick and the new owner of a family of domestic geese. It wasn't the fact that I now had exactly fifty-nine dollars to my name that gave me the shakes. The vet had noticed the name on my credit card was Conkaffey, not Collins. It's an unusual name. People don't forget it. And it had only been a month since it was all over the national news. I'd watched his face harden. Watched the lines around his mouth deepen, and then his eyes begin to lift. I grabbed the box of birds and left before I could see the look on his face.

I was sick of that look.

I didn't know Sean was there until his shadow fell over me. I jolted, grabbed my gun. I'd fallen asleep in my usual place on the porch, spread out against the wall on an old blanket. For a moment I thought an attack was coming.

'This is a sorry sight,' my lawyer said. The morning light was already blazing behind him.

'You look like an angel,' I said.

'What are you doing sleeping out here?'

'It's glorious,' I groaned, stretched. It was true. The hot nights on the porch behind the mosquito netting were like a dream. The roll of distant thunder. Kids laughing, lighting fires on the faraway bank. The old blanket was about as thick as the mattress I'd had in segregation.

Sean looked around for a chair on which to place his expensively fabricked backside. When he didn't see one he went to the step, put the coffees he'd been carrying and the bag on his elbow on the wood and started brushing off a spot. Even in the Cairns humidity there was some silk in his ensemble, as always. I sat up and joined him, scratched my scalp awake. I'd placed Woman and her young in the cardboard box turned on its side in a corner of the porch, a door made out of a towel. The big goose hissed at the sound of us from behind the towel and Sean whipped around.

'Don't tell me –'

'It's a goose,' I said. '*Anser domesticus.*'

'Oh, I thought it was a snake.' The lawyer gripped at his tie, flattened and consoled it with strokes. 'What the hell have you got a goose for?'

'Geese, actually. It's a long story.'

'They always are with you.'

'What are you doing up here? When did you get here?'

'Yesterday. I'm heading to Cairns, so I thought I'd stop by. Got a sexual assault defendant who's jumped bail. I'm going to try to talk him back down. Everybody flees north.'

'If you've got to hide, it's better to do it where it's warm.'

'Right.' Sean looked at me. 'Look, good news, Ted. Not only have I brought my favourite client a delightful care-package, but as of this morning your assets are officially defrosted.'

The white-haired man handed me a plastic bag of goodies. Inside were a couple of paperbacks and some food items. I didn't have the heart to tell him about my fridgeless state. There was an envelope of forms as thick as a dictionary in the bag. He took one of the coffees and handed it to me. It smelled good, but it wasn't hot. There wasn't anything at all within twenty minutes' drive of the house, certainly nowhere that made coffee. It didn't matter. The scary forms and the cold coffee couldn't possibly dampen my joy at seeing Sean. There were about twenty-one million people in Australia who believed I was guilty of my crime. And one silk-clad solicitor who didn't.

'I imagine there's something in that envelope from Kelly,' I said.

'Adjustments to the divorce settlement. Again. Semantic stuff. She's stalling.'

'It's almost as though she wants to stay married to me.'

'No. She just wants to watch you wriggle.'

I sipped the coffee and looked at the marshlands. It was flat as glass out there, the mountains on the other side blue in the morning haze.

'Any sign of . . .?' I cleared my throat.

'No, Ted. No custody inclusions. But she doesn't have to rush, she can do that any time.'

I stroked my face. 'Maybe I'll grow a beard,' I said.

We considered the horizon.

'Well, look at you. I'm proud of you,' Sean said suddenly. 'You're a single, handsome, thirty-nine-year-old man starting all over again with a rental house and a few too many pets. You're not really that much worse off than a lot of guys out there.'

I snorted. 'You're delusional.'

'Serious. This is your opportunity for a do-over. A clean slate.'

I sighed. He wasn't convincing either of us.

'So are they guard geese?' he asked, changing the subject.

I had to think for a moment what he meant.

'The Nazis used geese to guard their concentration camps,' he explained.

'That so?'

'Can I take a look?'

I waved. He approached the box cautiously, squatted and lifted the towel with manicured fingers. He wore houndstooth socks. Probably alpaca. I heard Woman squeal from the gloomy depths. Sean laughed.

'Wowsers,' he said.

'All still alive?' I asked.

'Looks like it.' Sean glanced at me. 'You looking for work?'

'Not yet. Too soon.'

The little geese pipped and shuffled around in the box. Claws on cardboard. He left them alone.

'Would you do me a favour?' Sean said.

'Probably.'

'Would you check out a girl in town named Amanda Pharrell?'

'Would I *check out a girl?*' I looked at him, incredulous.

'A woman,' Sean sighed and gave me an apologetic smile. 'Will you pay a visit to a woman in town?'

'Who is she?'

'Just a woman.' Sean shrugged.

'What do I want to visit her for?'

'You're full of questions. Stop asking questions. Just do what I tell you. She'll be good for you, that's all. Not to date. Just to meet.'

'So it's not romantic in any way.'

'No,' Sean said.

'Then what the hell is it?'

'Jesus, Ted,' he laughed, before repeating an adage he'd used many times during my trial prep. 'I'm your lawyer. Don't ask me why. Just *do* it.'

I made no commitment.

We sat for a while talking about what he was doing in Cairns and how long he'd stay. Sean was sweating through his linen trousers. His poreless nose was burned already by the sneaky tropical sun, slowly cooking the unwary Sydney man through the wet air. I'd managed a nut-brown tan just trudging around the property for a month, walking to the nearest shops to buy Wild Turkey. I hoped I'd fit in eventually. That I'd grow safely unrecognisable from the man who had graced the cover of the *Telegraph* for weeks at a time, the broad-shouldered ghoul in a suit hanging his head outside the courthouse, pale from jail. A beard might do it, I thought. And time. I'd need plenty of time.

Here's what I remember. And it's a lie. It's a composite memory, built from things I actually remember, stuff I heard during my trial, what I read in the paper and things whispered to me in my jail cell while I was on remand. Some bits and pieces I'm sure come from my nightmares – it's possible that the storm wasn't so foreboding, or her eyes so big and pretty. But the memory of those fatal moments is impossibly clear. More fabrication than history. The narrative is woven from many colourful strings. It cannot be snapped now, even if small fibres over the years will part and coil away. I believe it. Even if I know it isn't true.

She was standing by the side of the road, exactly in line with the road barrier markers, which weren't that much shorter than her. She was thirteen. She looked ten. The girl was so pale, and her hair was so doused in flaming afternoon sunlight coming through the clouds that she almost became one of those markers; a white sentry beside the isolated highway, still as stone. I didn't see her at first. I saw the bus stop and the well-worn tracks of the great vehicles in the dry mud. I slowed, turned off the highway and pulled in to the bus stop area, parking my car somewhere between ten and fifteen metres from the girl.

A blue Hyundai Getz drove past on the highway going south,

carrying Marilyn Hope, 37, and her daughter Sally, 14. They would testify to witnessing my car pull off the highway 'suddenly' and park 'close' to the girl. It was 12.47 pm. Sally Hope testified to the exact time I pulled off the road because she glanced at the clock in the car as they went by, and she remembered calculating that they had thirteen minutes to get to her dance lesson.

I got out of the car and spotted the pale girl standing there for the first time. She was looking at me, her pink Pokémon backpack sitting on the ground beside her.

My first thought was: *Where did she come from?*

My second thought was: *Fix the noise.*

The fishing rod had been tapping against the back window of my Corolla. I opened the back left-hand door of the car, climbed halfway in, and pulled the rod and the tackle box towards me across the seat so that the handle of the fishing rod slid down into the gap behind the front passenger seat, pulling the tip of the rod away from the window.

A red Commodore drove past on the highway going north, carrying Gary Fisher, 51. Gary was the third witness. He would testify to seeing my car parked by the girl, the back passenger-side door open. The door closest to the girl.

I spotted my car insurance renewal notice, open and crumpled, in the mess of papers and takeaway containers on the floor behind the driver's seat. I picked up the pale green paper and examined it, still half-in, half-out of the door.

Truck driver Michael Lee-Reynolds, 48, drove past on the highway going south. Witness number four. He'd back up Gary's claim of seeing me parked by the girl, the back passenger door open. A tall, broad-shouldered man fitting my description, halfway in, halfway out of the back seat.

I leaned out of the vehicle, righted myself, and tucked the insurance notice into the pocket of my jeans. I looked at the girl. She was still watching me. A light rain had begun to fall and it was caught by the gentle breeze, tiny droplets misting all around her in the sunlight like tiny golden insects. She kicked the dirt with her shoe and played with the belt loops of her jeans, then turned away. She was a thin girl. That's about all I would genuinely remember about her, all I would tell the police I remembered in my initial interrogations. She'd been thin, bony, and white. The rest of my recollections of the girl who would ruin my life I would fill in from photographs at the trial. I'd see her big teeth in 'before the attack' pictures. The way her nose crinkled when she smiled.

I stood beside the highway on that terrible day and glanced at the dark purple horizon beyond the trees as I closed the car door.

'Some pretty heavy rain coming,' I said.

A red Kia drove past going south, carrying sisters Jessica and Diana Harper, 34 and 36 respectively. Witnesses five and six testified that they'd seen me talking to the girl. They were unable to agree whether my back left door was open or shut. It was 12.49 pm.

'Yeah,' the girl said.

'Your bus coming soon?' I asked.

'In a minute,' she said and smiled. Crinkled her nose. Or maybe she didn't. I don't know anymore.

'All right,' I said. Two more cars full of witnesses drove past, uncertain, between them, if when I waved at the girl it was with my right hand, palm flat, facing towards her, in a 'goodbye' type of gesture, or if in fact I was beckoning her, left hand up, palm open and turned towards me, in a 'come

14

here' type gesture. Testimony about the exact nature of the 'goodbye'/'come here' gesture would last three days.

All of them would agree, in the end, that I made some sort of gesture while I was standing by the back passenger door of my car. The door closest to the girl.

I walked around the front of my car, got into the driver's seat, started it, and drove away. I didn't look back.

At 12.52 pm, the girl's bus drove past. The exact time would be recorded on the vehicle's GPS. The Pokémon backpack was on the ground, the driver and passengers all agreed.

But there was no girl.

Claire Bingley was abducted from the bus stop at Mount Annan, on the edge of the highway, that Sunday afternoon. She was driven to a patch of bush about five minutes away along dusty back roads dividing cattle farms and vacant lots. In the dark of the woods, she was beaten, brutally raped and then strangled until she lost consciousness. Her attacker must have thought she was dead. But with the unexplainable tenacity and physical resilience possessed by some children, the girl, against all odds, didn't die. Claire lay in the dark listening to the sounds of the bush around her for several hours, terrified that her attacker was nearby. Night fell and then the horizon lit again. The girl wandered out of the bush and walked in a zombie-like daze to the highway, reappearing some ten kilometres south of where she'd vanished. It was about six o'clock the next morning. Claire had been missing for seventeen hours.

An old man driving to Razorback to help his son move house spotted her crouched at the roadside, nude. Her face was so bloody he'd thought at first she was wearing a red mask. Her throat was so damaged she couldn't explain what had happened to her.

Social media, by this time, was well into a frenzy that had begun the previous evening, about three hours after the girl disappeared. The eight o'clock news updates picked it up, right between *The Project* and *MasterChef*. The whole country saw it. Her parents whipped up the panic until it was on all news networks, and a quickly designed missing poster of Claire was shared online eight hundred thousand times, in places as far away as San Francisco. Claire had been abducted. They knew it. The disappearance was totally uncharacteristic of their daughter. Claire's parents knew in their hearts that something terrible had happened. They were right.

The first time a suspect was ever mentioned was in the comments section of one of the social media posts. Under a picture of Claire, plastered with pleas to share the image of the missing child around, one of the drivers who had been on the highway that day wrote 'I think I saw the guy.'

That guy was me.

I walked to the corner shop in the rain. It's like that in Cairns sometimes. It will begin to rain without warning, hammering downward like bullets, and there will be no shelter on the road, a strip of bare earth between stretches of yellow sugar cane six metres high, running for kilometres, the walls of a hidden city. Grasshoppers in every earthly colour sprang and danced on the hot dirt in joy. Hundreds of swallows lined the sagging wires. I inhaled steam and watched the cloud bank pass overhead for an hour, plodding slowly.

It wasn't that I'd chosen Crimson Lake as my hideaway by throwing a dart at a map. I'd simply headed north from Sydney with my belongings in the car and panic at the back of my throat, certain only that I couldn't stay where I was, and with some vague notion that I'd stop running when I felt safe, when people stopped recognising me. The five or six days I'd spent in Sydney after I'd been released from prison had been a cat-and-mouse game with the press, who hung around any hotel I stayed in, annoying the owners until they threw me out on the street. Kelly wouldn't have me at the house without a police escort, so I'd only been able to go home briefly to gather some things. The city people were fuming. I was being talked about on every television channel. Every radio station. I was on the front cover of every newspaper. I hardly ate. Half the times that I ducked into a fast food restaurant to grab something, the counter staff recognised me. The other half, I left without ordering anything, too afraid that they would.

Things were easier in the small towns I stopped in heading north. The more remote the location, the less people seemed to mind each other's business.

When I got to Crimson Lake, not only were people dis-interested in 'city news', but I seemed to have found a region stolen from the hands of time, a slice of bare-bones civilisa-tion only just managing to fight back the rainforest trying to swallow it whole. Moss and vines grew on every surface they could manage. Along the rivers, broken-down houses with yawning doorways squatted in the bush, peering out, not a brick or patch of wood that composed them showing through their cloaks of lush leaves. This was a town where the bad things about a person's life might be eaten up. The constant dampness, the regular rains, the rivers and lakes that swelled and grabbed at the roadsides could wash away histories, cleanse sins. It was a place that wanted to consume itself; a warm, green abyss. I fell into its arms.

The house I found was on the edge of the lake for which the town was named, a wide glassy mirror nestled in the tangled wetlands. The owners of the house had acquired it from an inheritance, but were too old themselves to go and live in it. It had been forgotten for years. When I'd been taken to view the property, I'd stood on the porch and looked out across the lake. The cane farmers had been back-burning on the distant shore and a heavy sun had been struggling through the smoke, a red eye making bloody patterns on the water.

Now, in sodden jeans, I stood for a while on the porch of my nearest store, examining Crimson Lake community notices. Chicken feed and wire for sale. Mobile butcher. Guitar lessons and pool cleaning services. There was a six-month-old funeral notice for a woman who'd died in a car accident. Teresa Miller, dearly missed mother and wife. A bell rang above the door as I entered and sat at the row of old, beige computers near the window. There were newspapers in a stack nearby. I avoided them.

I danced around without searching for Amanda Pharrell, the woman Sean wanted me to see, for about ten cents' worth of internet time. I'd become paranoid about what I googled on my phone, and I didn't know who she was, what 'checking her out' might mean. I hadn't pestered the old man too much to know what the suggested meeting was about. Sean and I both knew how ridiculous anything romantic would be right now. So if it wasn't that, then it had to be something I'd rather avoid. Was she a counsellor? Was someone else who had been falsely accused, dragged off to prison for eight months and then spat back into the world? Was Sean thinking I'd bond with her, that we'd share stories about fighting off rape attempts in the shower block? Was she a sex-offender employment specialist who'd find me a nice, isolated job away from people who might target me for my alleged crime? I couldn't think of anything that Amanda Pharrell could possibly be that I'd appreciate. The truth was, I didn't want to interact with anyone unfamiliar, ever again. It was too dangerous.

Nevertheless, I was curious. I plunged in and googled her. There were only newspaper reports on the first page. I brought them up and flicked through them, telling myself I wasn't interested.

Teen girl killed in Kissing Point tragedy.

One girl survives horror night on mountain top.

Police hunt Kissing Point killer.

Girl arrested in Kissing Point slaying.

I looked through the articles, minimised them, stared at the beach wallpaper on the desktop for a while, the dozens of icons. It was probably the headline font making me sick, I decided, and not the sharp snippets of a story of true terror flashing before me. The familiarity of it all. Teen innocence. Prison bars. Pleas. Families crying into their hands behind polished wooden rails. I rubbed my eyes with my palms, and it was only when I heard the creaking of the chairs on either side of mine that I stopped. The familiar smell of their leather hit me before I saw the two officers who had entered the shop. The squeaking and clanking of belts and buckles. The fattest one, hair plastered to his forehead in dark downward spikes, spoke first.

'Got to keep myself informed on the town's happenings, haven't I, Lou?'

The conversation was apparently being carried on from outside. I let a breath sneak into my lungs and opened a sports page.

'Don't think you'll find much, mate. Pretty slow around these parts,' Lou replied to his partner. I looked at him in the reflection in my computer screen. Another porker on his way to a heart attack. A tired, peach-white face.

'Well, that's how we like it, isn't it, Lou?'

'Sure is.'

'Like our town nice and quiet, nice and safe.'

I wiped at rainwater running down my temple, warm with sweat gathered in my hair. I clicked through to a sports photo gallery. Looked at cricket players, heads down, staring at grass.

'Got to keep our little old ladies and our itty bitty kiddies feeling happy and safe.'

'Don't want no surprises for our people.'

'That's right, Steve,' Lou said. 'Especially the little kiddies.' The cop gave up the charade, turned and looked at me. I cleared my throat and maximised the news pages about Amanda Pharrell, clicked them closed. One I hadn't read flashed on the screen. I hit print and closed it fast as lightning, floundering now, just wanting to be out of the chair but not wanting to have left the house for nothing.

Convicted Killer Opens PI Agency.

I twisted awkwardly out of the double barrier of police bodies, tossed some coins on the counter and grabbed the paper from the printer.

The dreams come, and when they do, there's no struggling out of them.

Morris and Davo in the tiny interrogation room, circling me like sharks. Frankie in the doorway, noncommittal, looking at her fingernails intensely like there was something on them she'd never seen before. Her eyes were anywhere but on me.

My colleagues. My work friends. These guys had drunk beers with me around my greasy backyard barbecue. We'd kicked down doors together. Hit pubs together. Stood guard over protests together, back when we were all patrollies. Frankie and my wife Kelly went out sometimes for coffee, texted each other. Our shared lives were slowly draining away. I was in the chair now, on the wrong side of the interrogation table. They were restless. Guilty. Horrified at the words they were saying, even as they came out of their mouths.

'Can you tell me what's going on?' I pleaded.

'Sunday afternoon,' Morris said. 'Mount Annan. The highway, just up from the tyre and auto place. You were driving your Corolla past there at about 12.45 pm?'

'Yes. I've said this.'

My stomach felt like a brick. It had been three hours, maybe longer, of the same questions around and around and around. What had I done the morning of 10 April? What had Kelly and

22

I said to each other? What had we fought about? How long did the fight last? Which way had I driven when I left the house? What had I seen on my way?

There was no clock, but I could feel the minutes creeping away. Two minutes for a fraud squad guy, Nguyen, to come and collect me from my desk, tell me the chief wanted to see me. Ten minutes of waiting in the chief's office, alone, until the man himself came and silently led me to the interrogation room. Forty-five minutes in there, alone, sighing, the prank or whatever it was beginning to get on my nerves. An hour is far too long for a joke. It wasn't my birthday. Was I being promoted? I'd actually sat there, imagined them all hanging bunting in the coffee room, getting an ice-cream cake out of the freezer. I'd known I was wrong when Frankie and Morris and Davo came in. Their faces had been grave. The kind of faces they wore when they did death-o-grams.

'Can you just tell me what's happening?' I pleaded. 'I don't understand why I'm here.'

'Were you driving your car on that day or not, Ted?'

'Yes, I was driving it! How many times do you want me to –'

'You didn't lend it to anyone?' Little Frankie, who'd only the last few weeks or so trained herself not to cry privately in the locker rooms after crims were mean to her during interrogations. Little Frankie, who got sore hips from the obscenely large police utility belt, the taser hanging off her, oversized, like a water pistol on a toddler. 'Think, Ted.'

'No,' I said. 'Sunday afternoon I went fishing. By myself. I'd had a fight with Kelly and I wanted to be alone. I didn't lend the car to anyone. I went through Mount Annan. That's all I did. I didn't do anything wrong. I don't know when I was on the highway, maybe it was twelve forty-five, maybe it was one o'clock. I don't know! It

23

was a Sunday, so I wasn't paying attention to the time. If you tell me what's happened I can tell you if I saw anything –'

'Ted, you're telling us you went fishing. We don't believe you. We've got weather reports. It was pouring fucking rain Sunday afternoon.'

'No. It poured with rain for about twenty minutes,' I insisted, sweat rolling down my body. 'I knew it would clear. You could see it.'

'Right. You're a fucking weather man now.'

'Jesus, Davo.'

'The fishing story doesn't fit, Ted. Come on. You didn't go fishing in the fucking rain.'

'Look, to be honest –'

'Oh, you're going to be honest with us, are you?'

'The fishing wasn't really the whole purpose of why I was going,' I said.

'What was your purpose, Ted?'

'I was trying to get away from Kelly,' I groaned. This was embarrassing. 'We'd fought. So I wanted to get out of the house. Go somewhere. Do something. Anything.'

'So you left the house in an aggravated state. Is that right?'

'Jesus,' I said, seething. 'What is going on?'

'What's going on is that you're lying to us.'

'Why would I lie to you? What's happened?'

'No one went with you?'

'No.'

'No one saw you.'

'I just said that.'

'I'm going to show you some pictures.' Morris threw himself out of his chair. His energy was painful. I winced as he snatched the envelope up from the shelf beside the door.

'Can I –'

24

'You go fishing often, do you?'

'I just said —'

'Answer the question.'

'Stop fucking interrupting me!' I was starting to get angry now. My face was hot. I'd suddenly let go of the idea that this was some sort of prank by my colleagues and the seriousness of it, whatever it was, was rushing over me. Making me tremble from my fingers to my elbows, my feet to my knees. I felt cold and fever-hot at once. Morris with his fucking interrupting wasn't helping. That was the way he talked to crims. Never let them get a word in. Cut them off whenever they open their mouths. Do it for hours, until they explode, until they'd kill someone just to finish a goddamn sentence. 'I'm trying to answer the que—'

'Did you park anywhere on the highway near Mount Annan before you reached your destination at Menangle?' Davo asked.

'No,' I said. 'I left the house, and went to Menangle. I bought bait at Menangle. At the petrol station.'

'I'll ask you again. Think about it carefully.'

'I don't need to think about it! I didn't go anywhere that afternoon but Menangle. Was there an accident? Was someone hurt?'

'Why are you asking if someone was hurt?' Morris, with a picture in his hands, using the edge to score his wrist, an anxious gesture, making the skin run bright pink with false suicide lines.

'I'm just —'

'Did you park at a bus stop at Mount Annan?'

'No.'

'I suggest that you did. I put it to you, Ted, that at approximately 12.45 pm last Sunday, you parked in a bus zone at Mount Annan and exited your vehicle. Why are you lying to us?'

I was visibly shaking now. We could all see it.

'No, no. Wait. Yes! Yes, wait, I remember.' I laughed, absurdly.
'You remember?'

'I did stop,' I admitted. 'I stopped at a bus stop. You're right. My rod was in the back. It was tapping against the back window. I stopped and shifted it away from the window, and then I got back in the car and drove off.'

'So you admit now that you stopped off on the side of the highway at the 372 bus stop at approximately 12.45 pm?' Davo and Morris glanced gravely at each other.

'Yes.'

'You're changing your story.'

I thumped the table. Frankie jolted in the doorway.

'Tell me what fucking happened!'

Morris put a picture of the child, Claire Bingley, on the table in front of me.

I woke drenched in sweat on the porch.

It was dark. The crocodiles were barking.

I was in prison for 241 days. The morning I was arrested, I kissed my wife and infant daughter goodbye and drove in to work, stopping for toast and coffee at the station cafe before I ascended the escalator to the third floor of New South Wales Police headquarters on Charles Street in Parramatta. It was overcast. Light breeze ruffling the hair of the ladies out on the smokers' balcony. Exactly a week had passed since Claire Bingley had reappeared on the roadside after her ordeal in the bush near Mount Annan. I'd seen the case on the news, but no one in my department had been talking about it. I was on drug squad. My head was buried in the mobile phone chatter of a coke-importing Lebanese gang who may or may not have been waiting for a new round of drugs to go through customs. Davo, Morris, Little Frankie and I had been watching their activity for a couple of months, trying to decide when we should raid them. It was all pretty standard stuff.

The coffee and toast would be the last non-state-issued meal I'd have for months. I started noticing some whispering and some weird looks from people around the station at about ten. At eleven o'clock Davo, Morris and Frankie were called away to interview room five. I wondered why I hadn't been asked to go with them, but I was on the phone at the time and couldn't ask. Just before lunch, another colleague, Nguyen from the fraud squad, came to my desk and told me that the station chief wanted me to go to his office. He didn't say why.

I couldn't bring myself to eat during the fourteen hours of interrogation I endured. Davo, Morris and Frankie started the interrogation. It was a conflict of interest, but my friends were so upset by the whole situation that no one stopped them barging into the room and questioning me upfront. I guess everyone thought they had that right. A couple of hours in, when they weren't getting the answers they wanted, they handed me over to homicide detectives because the charges, when they would eventually be drawn up, would include attempted murder. I slept that night in the cells at my own police station, after hours standing by the slot in the door trying to get the attention of officers I knew walking by, trying to get some answers. Everyone was ordered not to speak to me. In a single day I'd gone from friend to enemy.

I was never acquitted of Claire Bingley's rape and attempted murder.

27

That might have been the hardest part of it all. I was committed to stand trial, which told the world that the Director of Public Prosecutions thought that there was enough evidence against me that I might be convicted. Then, halfway through the trial, the DPP withdrew the charges, stating that the evidence wasn't strong enough to satisfy a jury properly instructed beyond a reasonable doubt. They weren't saying I didn't do it. They were just saying they'd changed their minds – they didn't want to keep forging ahead with a trial with the evidence they had, and risk having me acquitted, never to be re-charged with the crime again. The charges were effectively being set aside, maybe to one day re-emerge when the evidence against me was stronger.

I didn't know if anyone was still investigating Claire's case. I was no longer a cop, and none of my old friends had ever spoken to me again. I woke up every day knowing that this could be the day I was rearrested and send back to prison.

There's only one way to survive on the inside. Total physical and emotional submission. It's the most efficient way to spend time. The only way to remain sane.

The inmate follows the routine. He reads the orientation handbook and acts according to it in all situations. He keeps his cell and uniform immaculate, his papers filed, his interactions with staff and other inmates courteous and professional. Any situation that arises, from registry to rape, is outlined in the rules of the prison. So the inmate is never required to enact his own judgement.

When a fight breaks out, for example, the inmate's responsibilities are clear. He immediately drops to the ground, places his hands on the back of his head, fingers interlocked, and waits for further instruction. During a routine cell inspection, the inmate remains quiet, follows the directions of staff and makes available all personal belongings for review. The inmate stays up to date with regulation changes throughout the prison, and is accountable for his actions in accordance with changed or updated behavioural guidelines. Ignorance is no excuse.

There's comfort in being organised. Up to date. Judgement free. The inmate becomes a gear in the ever-expanding prison machine. He fits and turns, a laser-cut cog.

It's when you let your organisation slip that you start grinding, creating sparks. Some people come to prison and make a point of being a grinding cog as long as they can. But nobody lasts long that way.

I'd let myself slip since I arrived at Crimson Lake. I'd been free just over two months and didn't have anyone writing my rules anymore. I'd taken up the drink, rented a beaten-up property on the edge of nowhere, and checked out of society. Sometimes I didn't shower for days. Sometimes I just didn't eat. Forgot all about it, until I was ravenous. I was tumbling, wheeling. But now was the time to cut the bullshit. Unpack my things. Stop sleeping on a blanket like a dog.

I sat on the porch in the warm morning light, took out my phone, and found the number for a furniture store in Cairns.

I didn't order a television set. I was afraid I might see myself.

Beneath the house, a rusty Victa mower had been left by the previous owners, so I fired it up and tackled the lawn. By mid-afternoon I was drenched in sweat and the geese were traumatised, but I'd reduced every inch of the property around the house to tiny spikes of lush green carpet. I left Woman on the porch and gathered the little ones up in my hands, laughing as their webbed feed pedalled frantically between my damp fingers. They fell to pecking and plodding over the lawn. I went to Woman and tried to pat her head. She hissed and snapped at me. I didn't take it personally.

By nightfall, I had a washing machine, a fridge full of food, a freshly made bed and a nice cane lounge for the porch. It wasn't much, but it was all I'd proven to desire in my time at the house. I'd boarded up the front windows and swept away the glass. The geese snuggled together in their cardboard box for the night. I pulled the towel down in front of their box and stood looking with satisfaction at my lawn. Blessed organisation. I'd checked off the regulations of my own new life. Anything that came at me now would surely be covered by the handbook.

The newspaper article about Amanda Pharrell mentioned an office in Beale Street. I washed my face, brushed my teeth and arrived at the office at eight o'clock, wearing a neatly ironed light cotton shirt and grey trousers. It was already too humid for the town's resident wild dogs, who lounged under trees by the Crimson Lake Hotel.

When I tried to decide what this was all about, I came up blank. Sean's reasons for asking me to see Amanda were vague – the lawyer had learned during my trial that I over-worried about the small stuff and it was easier when he just told me what to do. I could only think that Sean had directed me towards this Amanda character because she was an ex-inmate, like me, and maybe she was having some trouble going about life as a pariah. Maybe he'd been involved in her case, way back when. Maybe he thought the two of us would have tips for each other on how to get through the day when nine out of ten people in the world would like to see you dead. Maybe, if she was doing worse than me (which I could hardly believe was possible), I might be spirited on in my own recovery and the two of us could get through it together.

Lying on my new bed the evening before, I'd been googling stuff about infant geese and read that if an injured baby bird won't

31

eat, it's sometimes helpful to put it in the same box as another bird its age, so that it can be led by example. One orphaned bird cheers the other one on to survive. Maybe Sean thought that two public enemies were better than one. I didn't know.

My punctuality was a mistake. I stood outside the small converted weatherboard house crammed between the bank and corner store, and looked at the drawn blinds. I thought I heard meowing behind the door. I took the article I'd printed about Amanda from my back pocket and examined it, checked the address. I found myself reading the words again, incredible as they were.

Convicted Killer Opens PI Agency

Kissing Point Killer Amanda Pharrell began trading in private investigations this week from a shopfront on Beale Street. Pharrell acquired her private detective's licence after serving ten years in prison for the stabbing murder of Crimson Lake teenager Lauren Freeman in 2004. While some district residents have expressed dismay at the business venture, Crimson Lake Local Member Scott Bosc said there are no licensing restrictions preventing Pharrell Private Investigations from investigating 'everything from insurance fraud to murder' in the greater tropical north. Pharrell indicated that the agency, which has been open three days, has already received inquiries.

There was a handwritten note in the window of the little office.

The Shark Bar was an ageing tropical-themed diner, complete with potted bird of paradise plants and hibiscus-flower murals exploding over the walls. The counter was covered in junk – cups of novelty pens, battered three-month-old magazines, pamphlets for coral dives in Cairns and miniature solar-powered Hawaiian ladies who swayed at the hips. There was a waitress wiping the counter and two people at the tables; a colourfully tattooed junkie scouring newspapers and a lady reading a crime fiction novel, grey wisps creeping from her temples into her orange curls. I went over and sat down, and she lifted her eyes to me.

'You start at ten?' I said. 'Jesus. This place really is a holiday town.'

'Excuse me?' The woman frowned.

I sat back, disoriented.

'You're Amanda Pharrell?'

'Who?'

'Sorry.' I laughed. Felt my face burning. 'Sorry, ma'am.'

I patted her novel in consolation, stood up and backed away. The anaemic-looking tattooed butterfly across the room hadn't looked up. I went over and stood uncertainly by the table. One of her hands lay fidgeting with the edge of the paper.

'Excuse me? Ms Pharrell?'

'If it ain't me, then Vicky over there is your last shot.' Amanda looked up over thick-framed red glasses and motioned to the waitress with her chin. I sat down, unsure whether to feel relieved or disappointed. There were five newspapers between

33

us, three in a stack on her right, one under her hands and one on the left. I reached out but she didn't shake my hand, just stared like she didn't know what it was.

'Edward Conkaffey,' I said. 'Ted.'

'Sean's guy.' She gave me the once-over. 'I didn't expect you to be so tall.'

'I didn't expect you to be so . . .' – I looked at the tatts – 'colourful?'

She smiled. There was a twitch to her. A repetitive jerking of her head sideways an inch or two. I told myself not to stare.

'You know Sean, do you?' I said.

'I do not.'

'Well, this is interesting. How did you come to speak to him about me?'

'He called me,' she said. I waited for more. There wasn't any.

We examined each other in ringing silence. Her arms were skinny and veined, but there seemed to be an awful lot depicted on them. Radios and microphones, birds and angels, lush jungle plants hiding gaping Louisiana-style plantation houses. Feathers and beautiful women in portrait: black, Asian, a mixture. On her left hand, a rabbit in a three-piece suit.

'Sean said you'd be able to begin work over the next week or so,' she said. 'That right? Or do you need the weekend?'

'Sean said I'd come work for you?'

'Yes,' she said.

I laughed.

'Is that funny, honey?'

'Yes,' I said, smiling. 'It's funny. It's funny and annoying and ridiculous.'

'What the hell did you think he was sending you my way for?'

'I don't know, to be honest.' I shrugged. 'I guess I didn't think too much about it. I've been following his directions mindlessly for about a year now.'

'Hmm.'

'I guess I wondered if maybe . . . Maybe he thought I could help you. Both of us being ex-inmates. I see you've been out for a couple of years, but –'

She laughed hard. 'Do I look like I need your help?'

'No.'

'I'm doing fine, sweetheart.' She patted my arm, patronising. 'It's funny that you assumed he wanted *you* to help *me*, rather than wondering if he wanted me to help you. You're the one wearing *Eau de Jack Daniels*.'

'It's Wild Turkey.' I sniffed the collar of my shirt.

'Sean wanted you to get off your arse and get to work.'

'Yeah, thanks.' I cleared my throat. 'I get it.'

She smiled. The whole thing was steadily becoming absurd, uncomfortably absurd, a joke gone wrong. A prank. I glanced towards the door.

'From what I understand, you run some homegrown private investigations firm?'

'That's right.' She twitched.

'And Sean thinks I'm just going to throw my lot in with you and start working cases like nothing ever happened?'

'I don't think he's under any illusion that nothing happened.' Amanda got bored looking at me and turned the page of her newspaper, examined the pictures carefully before letting her eyes drift to the text. 'He's well aware of what your life has become. That's probably why he thought of me. Because I'm the only person in Queensland likely to hire someone accused of what you've been accused of.'

My stomach really wasn't taking this well. I looked at the door again.

'He said you're up shit creek,' she said, smiling. 'I had a look at your case. I think he's right.'

'Christ. Look, pardon me, Ms Pharrell. But just because you're the only person in Queensland who would hire me for detective work –'

'For anything, really.'

'For anything,' I conceded, 'doesn't mean I'm interested. I mean, you yourself. You're –'

'A convicted murderer?' She looked up at me. 'Look, sugarplum. Convicted, acquitted. Guilty, not guilty. Charges entered. Charges withdrawn. It's all the same around here. If you don't get it now, you will soon. You're doing time. We're both doing time.'

I toyed with the napkin dispenser beside me.

'Think about it,' she continued. 'What's the real difference here, between you and me?'

'There's plenty of difference,' I said.

'Okay, you're still in denial.' She turned back to the paper, waved dismissively at me. 'That'll wear off.'

We sat in silence for a long time, Amanda reading the newspaper like I wasn't there at all, me staring at the top of her head, her glasses, the flaming orange roots of her dyed black locks. I couldn't believe how casually she was talking about my life. My charred wasteland of an existence. She slurped her coffee, loudly, like a child. I sat bewildered and disturbed in my seat, the passenger of a car wreck, trying to reorient my up and down, trying to understand why my forward motion had stopped.

'So how free are you to work?' she asked finally.

'Free?'

'Available.'

'I'm pretty available, I guess.'

'What's your background?'

'Drug squad. Couple of related homicides,' I said. My mind was spinning. 'I can't believe we're even having this conversation.'

'Why not?'

'I mean, is your business real?' I leaned forward, conspiratorial. 'You actually have clients?'

'It's real.' She smirked. 'What? You think it's a front or something?'

'No, I just . . . You're a convicted murderer. Don't people wonder if you're dangerous?'

'I'm a convicted murderer,' she whispered, her red lips spreading into a grin. 'I *am* dangerous.'

'So why do people hire you?'

'Dunno.' She shrugged. 'Guess they think I've got the criminal mind. I'm on the bad-guy wavelength. I can sniff out the cheaters and the dodgers and the villains using my ultra-evil senses.' She snuffled loudly.

'Huh.'

'It also helps that I'm the only private investigator this side of Brisbane.'

'Right.'

'Well, look.' She leaned back and gave the weary groan of someone resigned to doing a huge favour that could possibly sink their entire business. 'I'm willing to give you a shot. As a favour to Sean.'

'But you said you don't know Sean . . .'

'I don't.'

'But –'

'Why don't we try this out?' she said. 'We can head back to the office, and I'll set you up with your pick of the case files this morning. We can use one of those as a sort of unpaid trial. See if you're any good.'

'What case files?'

'Oh, I've got plenty that'd suit you.' Her head jerked once harder, her ear almost touching her shoulder. 'Infidelity cases. Insurance stuff.'

'That's just lovely, but I'm not interested in going around snapping pictures of bare arses in hotel rooms.'

Amanda's entire demeanour changed, cracked with open-mouthed laughter. She gave herself a little hug, like she was being cuddled by the very humour itself.

'Bare arses in hotel rooms! Oh lordy!'

'I'm not so sure this is a good idea. This whole thing.'

A long slurp of coffee. 'Well, I'm not here to convince you.'

I looked at my hands. Thought about good ideas, bad ideas, Sean. And money.

'I'm not interested in working for free,' I said. 'This is not an apprenticeship, and I'm not fourteen.'

'Well, it was worth a shot, love. You've got to admit.'

'What are you working on?'

'Oh, you're not having *my* case,' she laughed. 'I don't work well with others.'

'Neither do I,' I said. 'So maybe we ought to forget this thing altogether.'

Vicky the waitress had come and barricaded me into the booth just as I was about to dramatically exit it. She stood with her pad and pen and smiled. I looked at Amanda, and she returned my gaze passively, the choice mine. I ordered coffee with milk and sugar and Vicky went away.

'This is going to be difficult.' Amanda gave a bored sigh and stared at the windows.

'I think you're right.'

'Most people have almost forgotten who I am in this town,' she said, ignoring me. 'What I did. If they haven't forgotten, they're at least not as confronted by me as they were when I first got released. They're used to me, I guess. But you? You're going to be like a ghoul around here, once the mob finds out you're in town. I really think you should take the office. The night work and the bare arses in hotel rooms.'

'No thanks.'

She tore a corner off the newspaper and folded it into a tiny, bulging square. I watched her stick it between her front teeth, pressing it flat, before sucking it onto her molars.

'Look.' She munched the paper thoughtfully. 'I feel for you, mate. So I might let you follow me around for a little while. See if you can do more than kick down doors. But you better keep your brim down. You're going to have to be *incognito*, you understand? Like a *mosquito* in a *burrito*.'

She seemed pleased with her impromptu rhyme. Slurped her coffee with a smile. I considered whether to thank her.

'You could grow a beard, maybe.'

'I'm trying,' I said, feeling my stubble.

'So, you want to do it? Are we partners?' she asked, the long-suffering exhaustion gone and excitement of a girl about her. I rolled my eyes, and she clapped in glee.

'Tell me about your case,' I said.

Vicky brought my coffee, and Amanda pulled a couple of silver rings off her left middle finger. The two smaller rings, I realised, were holding a much larger ring on the base of the finger. It was so large that it clunked loudly on the table when she finally got it off. She rolled it towards me and I caught it before it could roll off the table.

'The local celebrity is missing,' she said.

'It's the Jake Scully case,' she said dramatically.

'Is that name supposed to mean something to me?'

'It might if you're a big reader,' she said. 'I got to be a real big reader in the can. I read everything, but the big hit going around Brisbane Women's Correctional was the Last Light Chronicles.'

'Sounds interesting,' I said.

'They *are* interesting!'

'What are they about?'

'The series kind of picks and chooses bits of the New and Old Testaments and makes them into popular stories for young people. The books are very controversial. They take place after the Rapture and include plenty of cool pop-culture add-ins that certainly aren't very biblical. Vampires and werewolves and witches and stuff. It's all the epic drama of the Bible with all the badass sex and violence young people love.'

'Actually, I think I've heard about these. The guy's sold a million copies or something.'

'Ten million. They're pretty amazing.' Amanda smiled. 'Adam and Eve, the main characters, start out as ordinary schoolkids before the end of the world comes. They finish up as these epic heroes fighting off zombies and consulting with apostles and stuff. It's total blasphemy. But Christian kids get a kick out of seeing their biblical heroes reinvented as grisly post-apocalyptic warriors. All the cool people are there. Gabriel the archangel, Saint Christopher, some very sexy demons.'

Amanda looked beyond me, out the windows, and seemed to sigh with pleasure.

'In Brisbane Women's we got real obsessed with those books,' she said. 'We made sure no one gave away spoilers. Sometimes we'd sit in the dorms and read aloud to each other.'

'And now the author of these books is missing,' I said.

'Dead, I reckon.'

'And the ring?'

'Totally biblical,' Amanda said. 'They found it inside a salt-water croc the size of a mini-van.'

'Jeez.' I held the wedding ring up to the light. She took the ring back and slipped it onto her finger.

'Interesting?'

'Very interesting,' I said. 'Who's commissioned you?'

'Jake's wife. She's sick of the Queensland Police. It's been three weeks, no progress. *Nada*. They're not keeping her updated. She's got the money, so why not bring in extra help?'

'Okay,' I said. 'So where do we start?'

'Well, don't get too excited. We have to establish the ground rules, if you're going to be on this with me.'

'There are ground rules?'

'Uh-huh.'

'All right. Lay 'em on me.'

'Number one is the most important. You don't touch me. Ever.'

'How did I know that was going to be the most important one?' I said.

Amanda's face went hard for a moment, like freckled stone.

'Don't feel so special. No one touches me. If I touch you, that's fine, but no one touches me. Or my stuff.' She drew the newspaper a little nearer to her.

'Right.'

'We don't talk about Kissing Point.'

'Sounds reasonable. I expect the same courtesy about my case.'

'What? Oh no. Come on, Ted,' she scoffed. 'Let's be real. I'm going to want to talk about Claire. That's half the reason I came here today.'

Claire burst into my mind in an agonising flash. Her lean white frame by the side of the road. The rain misting all around her. When I came back to myself I found my teeth were gritted, my hands gripping the sides of my head.

'Christ almighty,' I breathed. 'Why would you say that? Why the hell would you bring that up?'

'Because I want to talk about it. Are you kidding? I've wanted to talk about it since my old mate Sean called me.'

'Why?'

'Because you're claiming your innocence, right?' She leaned in.

'What? Yes! I'm not *claiming* I'm innocent. I *am* innocent.'

'Then wow!' She threw her hands up. 'How fascinating! Right?'

'No! It's not fascinating. It's terrible.'

'It is fascinating! If you didn't do it, then who did? And if you're lying, then how did you get the charges dropped?'

'You need to stop now.'

'Don't you want to get the guy who did it? We could do the case together. Your case. In our spare time. Like a hobby.'

'No,' I seethed. I tried to shake off the fury slowly lighting all my bones on fire. 'No, Amanda. I don't want to do the case with you in my spare time. I don't want to go anywhere *near* my fucking case with you or anyone. Can we please –'

'Urgh. All right.' She slumped back in her chair. 'So boring. Such lack of vision.'

'Can we please just –'

'Okay, okay! I get it,' she said. She slurped the rest of her coffee, slammed the cup into the saucer and got up. 'We can leave it for now. You go home and work on that beard, and I'll go home and try to get my head around what I'm going to do with you. High-five, brother.'

She put a hand up, and I did the same, still numb from the sudden intrusion of my case into the meeting. She gave my palm a slap and wandered away into the hot wilds of the Crimson Lake morning, leaving me to pay for her coffee.

I spent the night wrestling dreams and sheets.

Kelly on the other side of prison glass, her face appearing pocked and scratched by the indentations on my side of the barrier. Every muscle in my body ached. Adrenaline shot through me at every sound. What now? What next? I kept hoping the people who came to my cell were there to release me. Crushing disappointment every time. Guards bringing me trays of food, shoving paperwork from my lawyer through the slot. I was a man of solid stone, walking like I might crumble.

Kelly hadn't brought the baby. I was grateful for that. It was scary here.

'Sean's going to get some analysis of the CCTV happening. See if we can get me on camera at the petrol station,' I said into the warm handset. My teeth were chattering. 'He seems like a good guy. Seems like he knows what he's doing, you know?'

'Ted, the papers are saying you're going to trial.'

Kelly's tone was pleading. She was makeup-less, drawn, like she hadn't slept in days. I hadn't slept in days, either. I was absurdly reminded of those blissful few weeks when Lillian was born, when we were both obsessed with checking her breathing in the dark, silent hours. We'd sit at the kitchen table in a daze together.

'We're not going to trial, Kel.'

'But –'

'It's a big fuck-up, yes, but it's not going to go on for much longer. It's been three weeks. It's ridiculous. But it'll be over by the weekend. Sean says when we get hold of something that puts me at the petrol station at the time of the abduction, I'll be out of here. Maybe I'll try for some wrongful arrest compensation. We'll go on a holiday. I'm so fucking tired, Kelly. I want to hug you so bad.'

'The little girl chose your picture out of a photo line-up,' Kelly said. She was gripping the handset, her knuckles white. She was begging me to turn it around. I was trying. But the weight of it all was advancing towards me, and I could hardly breathe.

'Yeah,' I said. 'That happens sometimes.'

'That happens sometimes?' Kelly looked horrified.

'She's confused,' I stammered. My mouth was bone dry. 'Sean says she's confused and traumatised. She's a child. She probably does remember me from the bus stop, and she's getting me mixed up with the guy who did this.'

'But how could she –'

'See, you're not even supposed to show kids photo line-ups like that.' I shifted closer to the glass. 'When you show a kid a photo line-up, what you're basically saying is "We think the guy who did this is one of these men." So she thinks she's got to pick the guy out of the line-up. The girl would remember me from the bus stop. And she sees me in the line-up. And her traumatised mind just puts the two pieces together, even if they don't fit. Sean thinks we can have the photo line-up evidence thrown out if it ever gets to trial. But it won't, Kelly. We're not going to trial.'

'Tell me again what you said to her,' Kelly insisted. Someone in the next cubicle was yelling at their visitor, thumping the glass. The guards were snapping like dogs. I couldn't focus. Couldn't keep my thoughts in order.

'Huh?'

'The girl. What did you say to her? At the bus stop.'

I squinted, rested my forehead against my palm, tried to visualise my statement. I'd recalled what I'd said over and over, for hours, in interrogation. Now I couldn't remember any of it. My mind was dark, slippery. Nothing took hold.

'Oh, god, Kel. I don't know,' I sighed. 'I said . . . I said the rain was coming. That's it. I said there was big rain coming, and she said "Yeah." I asked if her bus was coming soon, I think. I think she said it was. And that was it.'

'Why did you ask her that?'

I stared at my wife through the glass, said nothing.

'Well?'

'What do you mean?'

'You said to the girl, "Hey, there's a big storm coming. Is your bus on its way?"'

'Yeah.'

'Why?'

'I don't know.' I shrugged. 'I wasn't really thinking. I guess I thought I should say something. We were both just standing there. Maybe I was wondering if she was going to get stuck in the rain.'

'What if she was?' Kelly said. 'What if her answer was no? That she was going to get stuck in the rain. Would you have given her a ride? Were you offering her a ride by asking?'

'No.'

'Why not?'

'Because,' – I shrugged again, helpless – 'because I'm a middle-aged man, Kelly. I don't give rides to little girls I don't know.'

'So why did you ask her in the first place?'

'I . . .'

'Why did you talk to her at all?'

I had no answer. Kelly chewed her lip, seemed to wince as something broke, or threatened to break, inside her.

'Ted, please,' she said.

'What?'

'Please just tell me you didn't do this.'

I stopped shaking. Just like that. A heat rushed over me, from the back of my neck down my arms. My eyes stung.

'What?'

Kelly cried into her fist. I flattened my hand against the glass.

'What did you just say?'

'You didn't do it. Did you?'

'How could you ask me that? You've never asked me that. In three weeks. Not once. Why are you asking me that?'

'Ted.'

'I didn't do this!'

47

I stood, gripped the iron grill above the glass with one hand. I was screaming. I'd never heard myself screaming.

'I didn't do this, Kelly! I didn't do this!'

They were dragging at me. My arms, my neck. The guards. I was losing myself. Losing all sense of where I was. I turned and grabbed the nearest guard, because he was real, because he was human, because he was near. I got hold of his shirt and held on. The cuffs came around my wrist.

'I didn't do this!'

I twisted out of the dream and grasped at the cramp in my calf. Weird things were snapping me out of sleep lately. Cramps, twitches, stabbing pains. Noises and voices that I knew weren't real. It had been the same when I first entered prison. I didn't know what my body was telling me, but I was grateful that it kept flipping these switches and cutting off the nightmares.

I went out onto the porch, into the orchestra of croaking green frogs who had invaded the small space. They perched, lumpy and wet, on the roof rafters, three lined on the rail like slick fat lumps of green clay. Only the moonlight gave them shape. I went to the box at the side of the porch and lifted back the towel, felt an immediate exhalation of warmth from within, the damp, earthy smell of birds.

Woman slept with her head tucked beneath her good wing, and the snake-like neck rose as I greeted her, the black eyes searching mine. I eased down beside her and slid my hand beneath her wing, gripped one of the fluffy bundles nestled against her side, pulled the sleeping chick out into my palms. She didn't protest. The night hours brought on a truce between us.

'I'll give it back,' I promised.

I sat in the moonlight and held the sleeping infant bird in my big palms, smoothed back the downy feathers around its small beak. The tiny creature hardly stirred.

I remembered the weight of my own child in my hands.

Dear Jake,

I'm writing to tell you how much I loved *Burn*. I know I'm late to the Last Light Chronicles; I hope you don't mind, but my mum wouldn't let me read them when they first came out and I forgot all about them in between. I loved *Burn* so much I've gone out and bought the rest of the series – I've got them all in the gold box set with the picture of Eve on the back. It's hard to know whether I should go on before I've read book one again – I read it so fast I'm sure I missed things. It's kind of sad when you find a writer you love as much as I love you, because you know some day you'll run out of books.

I'm an aspiring author myself, so when I find a great writer, I try to emulate their style. I'm unpublished, but I'm trying, and I'm up to about my thirtieth rejection letter. I know you're supposed to find your own style, your own stories, but I think if I take bits and pieces from the greats, one day I'll be great myself. I've included a short piece I wrote about Eve and Adam – I hope that's okay. I know some writers don't like that, but I am just so obsessed with you. Your two protagonists have been rattling around my mind since the first page. I had to let them out! The piece is a little bit sexy, but I'm passionate about these characters, and I hope you can experience that passion.

Maybe if you think my work has promise, you could show it to your agent. I sent some of my work to Cary myself, but he just sent me a standard rejection letter. I bet you've got plenty of those yourself! I'm not sure he even read my manuscript – I've heard they don't sometimes, particularly if they've got a heavy workload, or they're looking for something that's on trend. I think it's zombies right now. That's all anyone seems to be publishing. But I've never been someone who's 'on trend'. I'm different. Maybe if Cary knew that I knew you, he'd take my stuff more seriously.

Anyway, I've got to go and get stuck in to the books. Write back if you have the time. I really think that as fellow writers we've got a lot to offer each other.

Amanda looked like a junkie, but from what I could tell so far, she wasn't one. I sat in the car with an arm hanging out the window and a hand on the wheel, watching her, the vehicle crawling along the dirt road to South Crimson Lake at a snail's pace while she navigated her bike between rocks in the clay, just out of my reach. An emaciated spider-woman wrangling a steel horse. Now and then I let the car swerve closer to her as our words became strained by distance. Rain clouds haunted the mountains on the horizon, but there were heatwaves shimmering on the crest of the hill ahead between the cane fields.

'So you can't drive, or you won't drive?' I asked.

'I guess I probably could drive. If I tried.'

The bike was an ancient racer she'd kept immaculately clean and oiled, mustard-yellow with salmon-pink wheels. She didn't wear a helmet. A lion on her elbow glared at me as she rode. The car was an old sedan Sean had presented me with on my second day out of prison, a loaner car to move my stuff from my marital home into the motel I was staying in at the time. Kelly had our family car, the Corolla she had waited six months to be returned to her from Forensics. Sean had never asked for this loaner car back. It had come to me filled inexplicably with newspapers, warped and dried by the sun.

'You won't even ride shotgun?' I glanced at the seemingly harmless empty seat next to me.

'It's one of the ground rules. Number five, I think. Rule *five*: I *strive* to never *drive* as long as I'm *alive*.'

'This is a ridiculous rule, Amanda. Can I appeal it? It's going to put a real weight on our operations, you getting everywhere by bike.'

'There is no appeals process in place at this time. I don't do cars.' Amanda shot a glance at me, made a huffing, growling sound, maybe in frustration at the rocks, probably not. She twitched. 'Not since that night.'

That night was the night Amanda had apparently butchered her young friend, Lauren Freeman, in a car on Kissing Point, just outside Crimson Lake. Amanda and Lauren had been on their way to a party on the mountain and had parked the car down the road, along a dirt path in the thick rainforest. They'd never made it to the party. The police had found Amanda thirteen hours later, helpless, naked, yet suspiciously unscathed, in the cramped boot of the vehicle. Lauren had been curled in the back seat, her back pocked with stab wounds. There were no foot-prints around the vehicle to indicate another person had come to the spot where the girls had parked. Amanda's clothes were nearby, saturated by the overnight rain.

I watched her as she rode, tapping the side of the car with my palm to the beat of the radio. I'd done more googling of my new partner that morning, and what I learned was troubling me. Amanda had initially claimed that someone else had murdered her friend while she listened from the safety of the boot. But the lack of explanations for what had happened started quickly piling up.

For her presence in the boot of the car, she had no explanation.

For her nudity and her lack of injuries, she had no explanation.

For the total lack of physical evidence indicating a single other person at the scene of the crime, she had no explanation.

In her initial interrogations, Amanda seemed to test the waters of her own innocence carefully. She'd started by suggesting that she hadn't committed the crime and didn't know who did. Then she'd come around to the idea that she did know who it was, but wouldn't say. She'd made a brief foray into explanations that involved her blacking out or dreaming about the murder, or seeing it through the eyes of someone else. After a few days, she gave all of this up.

The idea that someone else murdered Lauren Freeman didn't make sense. Why would someone approach two women in a car on an isolated mountaintop, brutally slaughter one and leave the other untouched? But what were they doing up there in the first place, these two? Why did they park two hundred metres or more from the party, away from all the other cars, when there was plenty of room further up the mountain? Why park so deep in the bush, and not on the wide, bare roadside? Who else could have known they were there? Where the hell was the murder weapon? I realised after some time I was trying to decide if I thought she'd done it, if I thought the woman

I was looking at was some kind of fiend, the type of person who could snuff out a young life for some sick, maybe sexual, thrill. I tried to shake the line of questioning, but it returned.

The irony of fixing my sceptical gaze on Amanda Pharrell was twofold. First, I had only surface knowledge of the murder, and an entire nation had decided I was guilty with only surface knowledge of my own case. I knew what it was like to be condemned by the readers of newspapers. I didn't want to do the same to her.

I'd also spent eight months in the company of murderers, child molesters and rapists in the Silverwater Correctional Complex, and none of them had looked like fiends to me. Some of them were cuddly teddy-bear men who cried at night because they missed their mothers. I'd encountered the same thing in my time as a street cop and in the drug squad. There was no 'killer look'. There was no 'killer behaviour'. I couldn't see the truth of the matter in Amanda's face, and the logical Ted was telling me that. But I found myself still staring at her. At her downcast eyes. Why did she do it?

Could she do it again?

'How is it that someone with your kind of conviction can secure a private detective's licence?' I asked.

'By applying for one, hon.'

I squinted at her. She bumped over a large rock.

'There are disqualifying offences,' she said. 'Homicide is one of them. But if the offence occurred more than ten years ago, you can still apply, and they consider things on a case-by-case basis.'

'And they approved yours,' I snorted. 'Incredible. Was there a public outcry?'

'There's a public outcry every time I do anything. I turned up at the public pool in Smithfield a year after my release, it made the paper. *Amanda Pharrell Goes Swimming*. I was the bikini-clad butcher.' She laughed to herself. 'I like that. I like it when newspapers get colourful like that.'

'You don't take all this very seriously, do you?'

'You can't, after a while. If you don't develop a sense of humour about your own situation pretty damn quick you're going to knock yourself off.'

I thought about the night I found Woman.

'And then who'll listen to my rhymes?' she continued, grave. 'No one, that's who.'

'Your rhymes are true crimes . . . against humanity,' I said. She nearly laughed herself off her bike.

'Seriously, though,' she said. 'There'll be a healthy public outcry as soon as the local papers get wind of your presence.'

'I look forward to it,' I lied.

Amanda pulled ahead of the exposed rocks and zipped in front of me without warning, sailing down the hill. I moved to catch up and noticed red and blue lights in my rear-view mirror seconds before the patrol car blipped me.

I wasn't surprised to find the two pork chops who had ruffled my feathers at the corner store hitching their belts as they lumbered out of the vehicle. I got out and looked for Amanda, but she'd disappeared, probably into the tall, yellow sugar cane. The bigger one, Lou, slid his baton out of the sheath on his hip.

'No one told you to exit the vehicle, sir,' he said. I noted their name badges. Hench and Damford. Damford had the misfortune of being covered in acne scars from beneath his slitted eyes right down into the collar of his shirt.

'There's no speed limit on this road,' I said. 'The vehicle's in good working order. You've got no reason to stop me.'

'We don't need a reason,' Hench said, smiling. 'Routine inspection.'

'You want to conduct routine inspections, you've got to set up a road block. You can't stop random –'

'Hands on the roof!' Hench jabbed me hard in the ribs with the tip of the baton. Pain ripped up through my chest. I was winded for a second, unable to lift the arm on that side up on top of the car.

'I'll have a nice bruise from that,' I wheezed.

'You want some more?'

I really didn't. Their car was parked at an angle, the dash camera looking out over the field towards the highway. Hench took my wallet from my pocket and started taking all the cards out, flipping them into the mud. He turned it and shook the coins out, pocketed the only note, a twenty, while Damford popped open the car boot.

'What were you doing in town, sir?'

'Visiting a friend.'

'And who would that be?'

'Vicky.' I watched Damford break the rear-view mirror off its housing on the windshield. 'At the diner.'

I sighed as he took my phone from my pocket, scrolled through the recently received calls and texts. He sniggered at something.

'What?'

Hench held up the phone for me to see. There was a picture of Lillian on the screen. My daughter.

'There's a baby on here.'

'There is,' I said.

'I know you liked 'em young,' Hench said, smiling, 'but not thi–'

I tried to snatch the phone. He anticipated it, landed the baton square on my kneecap. The pain was blinding. My ears rang with it. I gripped the bone and went down. Like all cowards, Hench relented to the terror of being caught for his crime as soon as the steel cracked against the flesh. His bravado was only momentary. He tossed a glance around the field and then motioned for Damford, dropping my phone in the mud.

'See you round, mate!'

Amanda took long minutes to emerge from the cane fields, and when she did she was still looking after the police car as it rolled away, her head-twitch short and sharp like she was trying to discourage a fly from bothering her face. She made no move to help me up.

'It's fine, really,' I said. 'Don't overexert yourself.'

I sat in the driver's seat and bent and flexed my leg, felt things crunch and grind. I knew it was going to be worse tomorrow.

'I know those two cops. You've got to watch out for them.'

'Really? You don't say.'

Amanda rubbed her hands together, making the rings clink.

'Hench and Damford. Those guys are the power around here. They're the law.'

I'd never seen Amanda scared before. She rubbed her hands furiously, like they were covered in ants.

'They're a bit old for patrol, those guys, aren't they?' I said. 'They must be my age. What are they doing still out on the road?'

'I think they like it out here. They get around a lot. You see them everywhere. Watching.'

'How do they feel about you being the local private dick?' I asked.

'About the same as they feel about you being the local paedophile,' she said. 'Just try to stay out of their way.'

Amanda twitched her way over to the bike and mounted it, still looking around for the patrol car. I wiped the mud off my phone, off the picture of Lillian on the screen. I stopped myself from looking at her eyes.

We took a moment outside the house in South Crimson Lake, Amanda stretching her quads and staring at windows on the third floor, their reflection of the blue mountain range.

Crimson Lake and the houses that bordered it were hideaway hollows for people who wanted to live alone, cane farmers on properties that stretched so far that people were kept at bay by the sheer inconvenience of visiting, and tiny houses like mine buried in outcrops into the wetlands. It wouldn't have surprised me if I wasn't the only runaway in town. The land here was incredibly fertile, so most of the houses I drove by had their own personal gardens, allowing their residents to stay in for days at a time with homegrown food before having to brave it out in the company of other people. There would be moonshine stills in back sheds here. Marijuana crops nestled in the undergrowth. These were not streets that rumbled with garbage trucks in the early morning, kids laughing on their way to the bus. You came to Crimson Lake for the quiet. The shadow.

As a tourist destination, it was too far out and too wild, and the locals weren't welcoming. No one ran tours here, and the rickety wooden docks were populated with unsmiling men with hand-held fishing lines who dangled their hard, blackened feet in the water. More than once in these parts the adventurous tourists have braved Crimson Lake for a summer dip, relenting under the pressure of the humidity, figuring that crocs couldn't move from lake to lake. But the backwaters here are linked by tiny dark creeks snaking between the eucalypts that wash all manner of slithering things between the water bodies, and all it takes is a brush of something scaly against a bare shin to send the tourists packing with their tales of survival in tow.

Rich people liked the quiet and the solitude of this place. South Crimson Lake distinguished itself from Crimson Lake proper and its skulking population of shut-aways with a noticeable decrease in roadkill left lying on the asphalt to be picked at by the crows. There were paved driveways here, and a posh little cafe on the corner with alfresco dining and sprawling canvas shades. The broken-down houses, porches littered with old beer bottles, fell away. A single row of mansions bordered the national park. Huge yellow-and-red signs warned the public not to feed cassowaries crossing the road from the park to the wetlands at the end of the street, and to beware of the man-sized birds while driving. I sat in the car and fancied I could hear them deep in the jungle behind the towering houses, the yelp of something ancient in there.

Stella and Jake Scully's house was the pride of the row, a collection of blazing white blocks cut through with tinted glass walls, an infinity pool in front. I looked up and saw a teenage boy loitering at the edge of a second-floor balcony, elbow clutched into his ribs and cigarette hanging from a flopped hand. He appeared, from my vantage point, to be wearing a frayed denim vest and a beanie. I gaped at the beanie. My upper lip was sweating in the morning light.

'So you've not met the lady of the house?' I asked Amanda.

'No. It's all been over the phone until now.'

'Does she know you're bringing me in?'

'No,' Amanda said. 'Oh, I mean I called her and told her last night I'm bringing a partner with me today. But not you, specifically, no.'

'One ex-crim was enough, huh?'

'If she's prepared to accept me, she should accept you,' she mused, turning her watch around and around her wrist like she was trying to unscrew her hand. 'I'm the sexual sadist and murderer, after all. You're just some kiddie-fiddler.'

I felt a pain behind my right eye, short and sharp, like I'd been punched.

'Wow. Okay, can I suggest a ground rule to add to the list?'

'Suggestions are welcome.'

'Can we make a rule that you never use that term around me again?'

'What do you prefer? Rock spider? Bad daddy? Teddo the Peddo?'

'I prefer no casual referrals to me being a paedophile what-soever,' I said, wincing.

'Right. Got it.' She clicked her heels and saluted.

'Just stop referring to my case in every sense.'

'I'll try. I mean, I'm typically not good with rules. And I'm dead fascinated with your case. I'm so fascinated, someone should pin me in their hair and wear me to the races.'

I massaged my eyes. My brain was a lead ball rolling around my skull, bashing at the sides.

'Let's get this over with.'

I limped out of the car, deciding that if Stella Scully or her son recognised me straight off, I would leave. It was better than trying to defend my involvement this early in the game.

'So we'll go with . . . what?' Amanda asked as we got to the door.

'Collins,' I said.

Stella must have seen us approaching the house on the CCTV cameras perched all over the place like birds. She opened the door and held it for us. Her eyes followed me briefly and then settled on Amanda. I was pleased for Amanda's colourful appearance, the sun hitting the blue streaks hidden in the black of her hair and her awkward gait towards the door like the approach of some fantastic human insect. I couldn't hold a candle to her.

'Glad to finally meet you, Ms Pharrell.' Stella Scully offered her hand. Amanda stuffed her hands in her jeans and looked away. Stella was wearing a sort of white cotton shift, somewhere between a loose dress and a poncho, tied here and there to hint at her tiny waist and bony, caramel shoulders. Blonde curls and flawless skin dusted with freckles. She had the cheekbones and sculpted nose of an ex-model turned plastic surgery addict. She let Amanda pass her and I took her flaccid hand in mine, saving the rejected handshake.

'Ted Collins.'

'Pleasure.'

The foyer was enormous. Light from the windows on the second floor filtered in across the staircase, criss-crossing at a variety of angles, picking up chrome and marble fixtures. I had the distinct impression that I'd dirty the place somehow before I left, bring some of my clumsy brutishness into it without meaning to, knock something over or cover something with my greasy prints.

We walked through a sitting room, across a kitchen as big as a cruise-ship galley and into a sunroom. I took refuge in the corner of a cane lounge, away from a massive red glass sculpture on a black marble pedestal that dominated the right hand side of the room. Above towering bookshelves, the walls were lined with framed book posters. The cover of the first book of the Last Light Chronicles, *Burn*, caught my eye. Two teenage silhouettes held hands before a city in flames.

Amanda went to the bookshelves and looked at the volumes there, strummed her finger along their spines.

'So you're a new partner in this venture, are you, Mr Collins?' Stella arranged herself on the armchair adjacent to me, preening her cotton shift.

'Ted. Yes.'

'He's going to be a real hound, Stella. I can tell,' Amanda said. 'He'll sniff out that dead husband of yours before you can say "postmodernism".'

'Oh Jesus.' I shielded my eyes.

'I've found Ms Pharrell to be very direct,' Stella said. 'It's not altogether a bad thing. Most of the time.'

'I'm sure you realise she's just speculating that your husband has passed away,' I said. 'There's always a chance.'

'Well,' Stella said, 'if it does turn out that this is some sort of game, he'll want to wish he had died, I can tell you that much.'

Stella Scully picked up a glass she had hidden from my view on a small table beside her armchair. Like a trained dog, I smelled Wild Turkey. She picked up the change in my expression and raised a perfectly manicured eyebrow, jiggled the glass, made the ice sing.

'Apple juice, Ted?'

'Please.'

She went to the sideboard and poured me a short glass of Turkey, dropped a few big ice cubes in. She had the full set-up over there: ice box and pickled cherries, decanter and a canister of stirrers. There were straws and tiny serrated tongs, a chopping board as big as my palm for the limes clumped together in a bowl. Seasoned drinker. Good taste. I took the glass and inhaled its scent it for a long while.

'Why "game"?' I asked.

'I'm sorry?'

'You said "If this is some sort of game". Why would your husband's disappearance be a game?'

'He had secrets, and he played games. So in terms of men, he was nothing special.'

'You can run Ted through the last time you saw Jake,' Amanda suggested.

'Sure.' Stella gave a worn sigh. 'It's been twenty-two days. We went to bed together January twenty-first, at around ten in the evening. We'd both been drinking. I remember Jake getting up some hours later, but I didn't think much about it. I had no idea what time it was. He was always up and down throughout the night. When I woke in the morning, he wasn't there. His wallet, keys and phone were gone. I looked outside. He'd taken the Jeep, left the Jaguar in the garage.'

'You didn't get a phone call or anything during the night? Didn't hear knocking? Talking?'

'Nothing.'

'He just spontaneously got up and left?'

'Yes.' Stella swallowed her drink and smacked her lips.

'Bit odd.'

'The whole thing is rather odd, Ted.' She smiled.

'None of the missing personal items have been recovered as yet? The car?'

'No. We did a big press release and the newspapers put pictures and everything up. The only thing anyone has found was the ring.'

'Yeah. Weirder still. Amanda tells me that your husband's wedding ring was found inside a seven-foot-long saltwater crocodile.' I took my notepad from my back pocket, flipped through the pages. 'The animal had been captured and euthanised for the purpose of harvesting. It was a nuisance animal up the top end of Pine Creek. The animal was killed and butchered at Macalister's at Oak Beach. Have you or your husband ever had anything to do with either of these locations? Macalister's or Oak Beach?'

'You're not a Cairns local, Ted?' Stella asked.

'No, I'm a Sydney man.'

'Well, if you were a Cairns man, you'd know there's nothing over at Oak Beach but black tribes and swamp.' She sipped her drink. 'It's a reserve. No one goes there. And Macalister's is miles away from here. Neither of us wear croc skin. It's a very coarse leather.'

Amanda was fiddling with a box of cigars she'd taken from the bookshelf. Stella and I watched her extract one of the dark chestnut tubes from the box and sniff it with a loud, prolonged snort.

'I assume there were no remains found in the animal,' I said, trying to distract Amanda from the knick-knacks on the shelves.

'There were remains,' Amanda replied, 'but they were too degraded to know if they're human or not.' She put the cigar box back and struck a theatrical pose. 'I'm an expert on this. I've done tons of research. Indo-Pacific crocodiles, like most crocodilians, have a heart valve that bypasses the lungs, shunting blood through the aorta straight to the stomach. The blood hangs onto its carbon dioxide rather than releasing it into the lungs, and it's used to produce large amounts of highly corrosive gastric acid. They secrete ten times the gastric acid of any other animal on the planet. They can digest things other animals reject – cartilage, bone, clothes, leather . . .'

'All right.' I winced. 'Take it down a notch, David Attenborough.'

'The wedding ring was found way down in the intestinal tract,' she continued, poking her own navel. 'So it looks like we caught it after the biological material was massively degraded but before the platinum took much damage.'

'Right,' I said, nodding. 'Okay.'

'In the nick of time, you might say. Just before it could be crapped out and lost forever in the murky depths of the local wetlands.'

'You can be quiet now, Amanda,' I said.

'The remains are with the Queensland Police,' Stella said. 'I think they've moved them on to the coroner's office now. They keep telling me their tests are inconclusive. They can't separate the cell compounds. Everything is . . . chemically neutralised . . . or something. They think the guy at the coroner's office might be better than their own people. All they can really say is that the croc ate something. They can't tell me what it was.'

'Soup,' Amanda said. 'Dead croc shit is just like brown soup.'

'Amanda!'

'And there's not much Husband Soup left to examine, either.' Amanda clicked her tongue ruefully. 'Wally and his boys were just about done gutting the croc and harvesting its

66

hide when the ring fell out of its . . . well, its *ring!* By that time, Minestrone à la Scully was spread over the killing floor.'

'If your husband is alive, Stella,' I sighed, 'my vile and tactless friend and I will do what we can to find him. And if he's met his fate with this animal, whether accidentally or maliciously, then we'll try to suggest how that happened.'

'I appreciate it,' Stella said. 'You sound like you know what you're up against.'

'What's to say Jake mightn't have faked his own death by putting his wedding ring on a lump of meat and feeding it to a crocodile?' I wondered aloud. 'I mean, it sounds very Agatha Christie.'

'It sounds like a bad plan,' Amanda said. 'You'd need too much to go right for that to work. You'd need the croc to get caught. You'd need the ring to be found.'

'Right,' I said. 'Right.'

'It was a good idea, though,' Stella consoled me. 'Lateral thinking. You're a retired policeman, Ted, is that right?'

I cleared my throat and focused on Amanda, who was now playing with some golf clubs leaning in a bag by the door.

'I've done some work for law enforcement.'

'You carry yourself like a cop,' she said.

I mumbled something noncommittal. We were straying into dangerous territory. Amanda was practising her swing with a nine iron. We sat in silence watching her until she decided to take the instrument outside. She whipped the grass a couple of times and looked at the horizon as though to track the ball.

'She's an interesting choice of partner.'

'She's an interesting choice of investigator,' I said. 'You don't mind her . . . weirdness?'

'Oh, look, she can be terribly annoying, as I'm sure you've noticed.' Stella smirked. 'But she's a breath of fresh air after the police investigators I've been working with. They don't pick up the phone, and when they do they give you all that gruff newspeak rubbish about the *integrity of the case* and *investigative rigour*. You don't know if they're keeping you in the dark because they have a suspect or because they've got nothing.'

'And what about her crime?' I said. 'You don't mind that she's been convicted?'

'Look, even if I did, Amanda Pharrell is the only non-state investigator in the top end,' Stella said. 'I need someone to find my husband dead or alive or I can't file claims on our assets.'

I frowned and made some notes in my notepad, felt a strange coldness come over me.

'Oh, come on,' she laughed. 'Don't pull that face. It was hire Amanda or wait seven years for the state to declare Jake dead.'

'It's only been twenty-two days.'

'When was the last time you stopped using your phone, bank or internet accounts for three weeks?' she said. 'Jake couldn't go two days without his antidepressants. They're in the bathroom. And he hasn't filled his prescription. He's been all over the news. No sightings. Not one. My husband is dead, Mr Collins.'

'I suppose.' I sighed. 'I guess it's hard to maintain hope when it looks this bad.'

'It's impossible. And I have no confidence in the state clearing this up. The police liaisons they've sent me so far have been one lazy idiot after another.'

'It just doesn't sound like . . .' I stopped myself. Stella watched me. It didn't sound like she missed her husband, or cared if he was still alive. But as I sat there looking at my notes, I thought about Kelly. I remembered how easy it seemed to have been for her to stop loving me, her face slowly hardening in the rows of people behind the defence table, her eyes beginning to fail to meet mine by day three of the committal hearings. As the evidence grew against me so too did her hatred, blossoming slowly like a black flower, seeming to wait until I wasn't looking to unfurl, petal after petal. There were times when I glanced back into the crowd and failed to recognise her there. She changed her hair. She lost weight. She stopped calling me Ted and started calling me Edward.

I'd been in remand four weeks when she gave an interview to *60 Minutes*, distancing herself from me completely.

Maybe it hadn't been as easy as it seemed. Maybe she'd just been trying to survive, the way I was. Maybe Stella was the same. Just trying to move through the days after her husband got up out of bed and disappeared into the ether.

'What sort of man was Jake, Stella?' I asked, watching Amanda come inside and wander back to the shelves.

'He was an addictive man,' she said. 'Workaholic. Alcoholic. Shopaholic. Big boys' toys – cars and boats, gadgets.'

'Drugs?'

'When we were younger. Recreationally. Not lately. We don't like the idea of Harrison catching us.' She waved towards the foyer, the stairs. 'He's at that age.'

'How is Harrison taking all this?' I asked.

'It's hard to say.' Stella shifted in her chair, stifled a yawn. 'He's a complete arsehole.'

I scoffed, looked to Amanda to see if she'd heard.

'He's –'

'An *arsehole*,' Stella said more clearly, sipped her drink. 'It's not illegal to say that, is it? He's a teenager. He's into the whole alternative scene. Goth. Emo. Hipster. Whatever they're calling it. The kids who hate everything. Think they've got a raw deal, that no one understands them. He was grumpy and sullen before Jake went missing. He's grumpy and sullen now.'

'Is it all right if I talk to him?'

'You can talk *at* him. There's no guarantee you'll get anything back.'

'What else? Was your husband loyal to you?' I asked. 'Were you loyal to him?'

'Lately,' she said, eyeing me. 'Again, we've been well-behaved since we had Harrison. If Jake had anyone on the side, she'd need to have been pretty low maintenance.' Stella curled her feet up beneath her. 'He worked here in his office five days a week. His spare time was after work but before dinner, and the occasional Saturday night when I wasn't up for dancing.'

I looked at my papers. 'So, a pretty quiet guy.'

'Yes.'

'You said he's on antidepressants?'

'I think all writers are, aren't they?'

'But he wasn't suicidal?'

'No.'

'No major family disputes to his name? Inheritance? Insurance? Power of attorney? Trust?'

'No. He's an only child, and his parents are in aged care.'

'Was he prone to wandering in the wilderness? Taking reflective sojourns?'

'Certainly not.' She smiled. 'Jake was not the outdoors type. The reflective type, sure. But the plastic yoga mat, ocean sounds, meditation variety. Not . . . you know, the flies, ticks, sunburn variety. The most outdoorsy he gets is wandering the manicured lawns of the golf course. But if the ball goes into the bluff? Forget about it.'

I noticed the swift change from past tense to present tense. Had she righted herself for my benefit, so I wouldn't catch her referring to her husband as something gone, never to return? Or was she just naturally wavering, sometimes hoping, sometimes resigning herself?

'Right.'

I looked at the ceiling and tried to remember my training about missing persons. I'd been off the job for almost a year, and even then, it had been so long since I'd covered this stuff in the academy. I was floundering.

'What were his interactions with his followers like?' I asked. 'Any strange fans? Anyone weird him out at book launches or send him anything strange?'

'Oh, in the early days, when the books took off, we'd get the occasional weirdo calling the house or turning up to hang around the front gates,' she said. 'It's the aspiring authors who are the worst. Jake's got the ear of all the biggest publishers, so they think if they can just somehow get their work under his nose, he'll be so impressed he'll call up his people and say "Get a load of this." We had manuscripts being dumped at the front door. Bottles of wine and chocolates. We just threw them away.'

'But none of this sort of thing has happened recently?'

'Oh no. Not for years. If you ignore them completely, they go away. None of it was threatening, in any case. Just – I don't know. Desperate. There's a box of fan letters in the office,' she said. 'You're welcome to look. The police have been through them.'

'So there's nothing sinister in Jake's life that you can point to immediately? No really obvious thing? You can't tell me if your husband had any deep, dark secrets that might have caused this? Any skeletons in his closet?'

'Not that I can think of.' She shrugged.

The shrug was weird. Too casual, and I thought she knew it. I must have had 'that face' on again, because she laughed and studied her fingernails, sat smiling sadly for a moment or two.

'Look, the love went years ago, Ted. That's the honest truth,' she said. 'We were private people when we met, and the older we got, the more private we became. It seemed only natural to me that sometime, one of these days, it would all come to a quiet end. We've been coexisting here.' She gestured at the house around us. 'Sleeping in the same bed, eating at the same table, but not really *being* together. You know? He'd write. I'd play tennis. At night we'd read in bed together, saying nothing at all, until after a while we both turned off our lamps. I thought he'd find someone new, eventually, probably after Harrison was old enough to be out on his own so neither of us would be lumped with him. You understand what I'm saying, don't you? You look like a man who knows what it feels like to watch a marriage dry up.'

'I am,' I admitted.

'Well, it's not my first time.' Stella sat back in her chair. 'My daddy went the same way. A regular night. A Tuesday, I think. I can remember the sound of the door opening and closing in the hall. But I thought, with Jake, it'd be simpler than this.' She looked at Amanda. At me. 'I thought it'd be cleaner.'

•

I took a wander through the house, leaving Stella to endure Amanda chattering away on the couch about crocodilian biology. Everywhere the natural environment was on display through gaping, frameless windows, huge sheets of glass that opened onto tropical rainforest creeping up to the house on three sides. Ferns and vines, wet flowers. I peeked at the master bedroom, saw paperbacks still stacked on Jake's side of the bed: Michael Connelly and Jeffrey Archer; Danielle Steel on Stella's. Down the hall I came upon an open door and found the beanied boy sitting on the edge of an unmade bed, fiddling with a phone.

'Knock-knock.'

'Yeah?' The boy glanced up at me, gave me a cold once-over, like he was judging his chances in a fight. Teenage boys. So ready for the world to hate them.

'I'm Ted Collins. I'm a private investigator looking for your dad.'

'Well, you're not gonna find him in here.'

'You sure?' With my foot I nudged a pile of clothes as high as my knee. A stack of magazines on top of the pile slid sideways and flopped on the floor.

'Yep.'

'You speak to your dad the night he went missing?'

'Uh-huh.'

'What was he like?'

'The usual.'

'What's the usual?'

The boy shrugged.

'You guys have some kind of beef?'

Harrison squinted hard. 'I didn't feed my dad to a crocodile, if that's what you're getting at.'

'I'm not getting at anything yet.' I said.

'Whatever.'

'Why do you think your dad went out that night?'

'Dude, I've already run through all this shit with the cops,' the boy huffed at me and licked the piercing in his bottom lip. 'You guys don't share reports?'

'We're a private agency. Your mum's pretty concerned with getting him found.'

'Yeah.' The boy snorted. 'She likes money, that one.'

Harrison Scully went back to texting, and I considered that a marker of the end of the conversation. I decided to take another run at the boy when I got the chance, but downstairs I heard footsteps and knew that Amanda had finally worn Stella down. Sure enough, Amanda's voice came trailing up from below, bouncing off the high walls.

'Most people get drowned in the death roll,' she was saying. 'Or, if it's got hold of one of your limbs, the death roll will twist it off. So you're supposed to go for the eyes. Scratch them, punch them, blind the thing if you can. Distract it, before it can start to spin. Everybody says that about sharks, but with sharks it's the nose. Punch 'em in the nose. They've got these sensors, see, along the sides of their . . .'

I took a quick glance at the boy's bedroom, the posters on the walls, the clutter on the desk, cabinets, cupboards and floor. A mental snapshot. Then I left.

Amanda went through the ritual of stretching before she mounted her bike. Flexing her muscles and rolling her ankles. I sat in the driver's seat and watched her, let the heat of the vehicle drain out the open window.

'Man, that was hilarious in there.' Amanda grinned suddenly, remembering. '*Drink, Ted? Sydney man, Ted? Married, Ted?* She wants your body, that Stella. I can tell.'

Amanda did a saucy little dance on the road, rubbed her hands suggestively up over her breasts and down again. She made kissy noises at me. I didn't know whether to laugh or burst into tears.

'She did not ask me if I was married.'

'She looked at your hand.'

'You don't . . .' I sighed at the windshield. 'You can't even –'

'There was a girl in Brisbane Women's who was like that,' Amanda said. She traced a finger along her bottom lip, dropped a hip. 'Katrina. She used to flirt with the guards and get all sorts of treats. Ooh, your belt is so *thick* and *shiny*. I bet it's heavy. I bet it cracks real loud.'

I said nothing.

'No sleeping with the clients.' She stuck a finger in the air. 'Don't even *touch* the clients. Rule seventeen.'

'There are seventeen rules?'

'Pfft! At least!'

'I've only heard one to five and seventeen!' I scoffed. 'What's in between?'

'In between *five* and *seventeen* are a bunch of mysteries yet to be *seen*. You'll *glean* those rules from their smoky *screen* if you're *mean* and *keen* and *clean* and –'

'All right. All right.'

She checked the bike all over, tested the brakes. Tugged her shoelaces tight.

'You know, you're pretty chipper for someone who spent ten years in prison,' I said, as casually as I could. 'I'm not sure I'll ever get over it. And it was only eight months.'

'Oh, you'll be right, mate.'

'Are you right?' I asked. 'Really?'

'Yep.'

'I don't feel like you should be.'

'Should.' She snorted.

I pondered for a moment, looked at my own eyes in the rear-view mirror. I was not the same man I'd been before they arrested me. I would never be that person again. The underlying terror in everything would prevent that. The trial nightmares. I was never acquitted, so at any moment the Director of Public Prosecutions in Sydney could order that I be rearrested. I didn't know if anyone was still working on Claire Bingley's case. If some supersleuth was going to pop up one of these days with more evidence against me and inspire the state to take another run at me.

Even if that never happened, they might pin me for something else. Come for me in the dark, take me, charge me with a local sexual assault just because I was in the area and, living

76

alone on the edge of nowhere, I didn't have an alibi for most of my time. If these sorts of thoughts weighed on Amanda, she sure hid it well. It didn't seem like Amanda felt any lingering effects of her crime, her time behind bars. Sure, she was quirky. Bordering on annoying. The rhyming, Jesus. But she was clearly functioning – she had a good job, seemed to keep her affairs in order. Was it all a front?

'I don't get the feeling anyone really cares too much about this guy being found alive.' I nodded at the Scully house.

'His lover might.'

'His what?'

'His lover.' Amanda twitched, mounted her bike. She pedalled a few metres down the road before I started the engine and caught up to her. 'Jake Scully's got a lover. A man.'

'You're nuts,' I said. 'Where'd you get that idea?'

'The golf clubs have never been used,' Amanda said. 'Not a nick on them. Not a blade of grass on the bag, inside the bag, on the wheels, inside the wheels. No paint worn off the handles. Nothing. They still reek of new rubber. Wherever he goes when he tells her he's golfing, it's not to the golf course.'

I watched her.

'The cigar box,' she continued. 'Very pretty box. Handmade. They're a bit of an art form, popular in the seventies, coming back now with the hipster vintage thing. Pipes, too. If you don't smoke cigars, you probably wouldn't have much interest in them. The boxes.'

'You smoke cigars?' I scoffed.

'I enjoy the occasional smoke on a Sunday afternoon.' She was almost defensive. 'That's not the point. Cigar boxes can be very intricate. You pop open little compartments and slots.

Keep things in there. Secret things, if you want. Bit of coke, some pills. But mainly stuff you need for the job – matches, labels. Your guillotine or your clippers.'

She swung the bike close to me and pulled a scrap of paper out of her bra. Handed it through the window to me. I held it against the wheel as I rolled along.

Sam.

And a phone number.

'This could be his landscaper,' I said.

'It's not his landscaper.'

'It could be Samantha.'

'That's a man's handwriting right there, chump.'

'These are some pretty extreme claims, Amanda,' I said.

'Well, I don't know what to tell you.' She shrugged. 'That's the truth.'

'That's the truth, huh?'

'Yes, *indeed*! It is *decreed*: you must *concede*!'

'All right,' I sighed. 'We'll see.'

I left Amanda so I could go home and read her Scully case notes, which proved to be a fairly useless venture. The words littered about the coffee-stained paper looked as though they'd been written with a tattoo gun. Tiny, some of them mere dots and slashes. The rain came, and the little geese wandered, pecking and foraging in the lawn until a puddle filled up by the fence. I sat watching them flutter and roll and splash in it, their downy feathers becoming heavy and grey and the bones showing in their pathetic nugget wings. They were just beyond the stage where they looked like ducklings – their necks too long and beaks too short. Woman settled on the porch quite near me, and when I reached over carefully to rub the top of her head with my index finger she didn't flinch or snap. Maybe she remembered that I'd been kind to one of her children the night before. Maybe she was just tired. 'We're building a relationship, you and I,' I said. She hissed.

Beyond the case notes, Amanda had acquired all of Jake Scully's phone records. There was indeed a bunch of contact between Jake and the 'Sam' from the cigar box, showing a flurry of texts three months before Jake went missing. I could see the time of the texts, their direction, but not what they said. Sometimes the responses were only seconds apart. Long conversations that lasted for hours. Few calls were exchanged between the two men. Jake didn't want to get caught.

On the night he went missing, 21 January, the texts stopped at 8.15 pm. Jake went to bed at 10 pm, according to his wife. There was nothing after the man went to sleep. Nothing calling him out of bed in the early hours.

I examined the stills from the CCTV cameras outside the Scully house on the night he left. The tape itself had been taken into evidence by Queensland police, but we had plenty of stills. At 2.14 am Jake walked out of the house, climbed into the Jeep sitting in the driveway, and pulled out. He was a broad-shouldered man, big like me but far leaner, more triangular about his torso. Forty-one pictures showed him walking the three or four metres from the house to the Jeep and getting in it. I flipped the pages. Jake stepping out. Stepping back. Stepping out. It was a long stride. A determined stride. The fist that held the keys was clenched. He was in a hurry.

Night fell in a long, gentle stretch, the rain easing and the clouds parting onto white, then deep yellow sky. I pottered around, still getting used to the house, clearing old bricks from where they lay stacked in a pile against the side fence, shifting them around the back where they couldn't be used as missiles by the vigilantes. Since I'd boarded up all the front windows I'd had nothing from those night-time warriors. I wondered if they were regrouping, planning something else. Something worse.

The darkness found me wandering the clay roads not far from my home, following the curve of the moonlit lake between the trees, going nowhere and thinking about Jake Scully. My time in drug squad had made the rare homicides that popped up now and then pretty easy to deal with. Drug dealers invariably killed each other over three things – turf, debts and women. The big bosses killed their underlings because they skimmed off the top, got found out and didn't pay their bosses back in time. The underlings killed the big bosses because they saw what their overlords had planned for them. And regardless of rank, these loudmouthed, showy men killed each other because they rarely believed that the beautiful women who spent their time with them did so out of genuine romantic attachment. They were insecure. Short-tempered. They sat in clubs giving each other the wrong looks until someone snapped.

Where the hell did I start, now that I was responsible for finding out who killed a completely different kind of man? Jake Scully didn't have a posse of jealous, dark-eyed men following him around, opening doors for him. He wasn't a loudmouth, and he didn't seem overly concerned that his wife's attachment wasn't genuine anymore, at least by her account. Who kills a guy who lives and works in his own little world, a quiet guy, a man whose guilt and danger lay in big boys' toys and yoga retreats? Maybe Amanda was right, and Jake's books weren't his only portal into an alternate life. Maybe there was a secret lover, and with that man or woman Jake had managed to pocket a whole collection of violent pleasures I just wasn't aware of yet.

I realised I was following a light in the rainforest long after I started doing it. It was joined by the smell of wood smoke, then laughter. I emerged carefully into the thinning trees around a clearing and stuck close to a tall ghost gum as the figures around the fire solidified.

A group of teenagers swimming in the golden light, the boys knocking each other in the ribs with their elbows, shoving and snorting. Someone's phone playing music I didn't recognise. I watched, picking single words out of the chatter, amused by the painful self-consciousness of them all. Two or three sat on a log together watching their phone screens, unspeaking. Others cuddled, hands slithering between knees.

The conversation seemed to be about death. These were those sort of teens. The weary existentialists, the moody budding philosophers. I recognised the mindset. Death was the worst thing they could imagine, so it fascinated them. Their own deaths. The deaths of others. Suicide, undeath, vampires, eternal life. They couldn't possibly know how wrong they were. That so many layers of life had the potential to be worse than death.

The girls were talking about funeral songs. The boys were trying to decide whether it would be worse to drown or be burned alive. Deep stuff. There was probably some sort of wonderful irony happening here, all these human beings at their most vivid and vital so romanced by the idea of death. I listened.

And then a blonde girl stood up and threw a plastic choco-late wrapper into the flames. I backed up at the sight of her, the impossibly short shorts and long, waterbird legs. Suddenly I was back to myself, sucked into my body from the free-floating I'd been doing in the dark, back to Ted Conkaffey: child rapist. I couldn't be found around young people ever again. Young people were like poison to me now. I started to back into the dark, and stopped when I heard Harrison Scully's voice.

'You know what a croc does when it's got you? No wait, wait, wait, wait!' Harrison cut into the chatter, spread his hands out, a young god in the firelight. 'You know what they do? They don't eat you right away. They tuck your body under a log and wait till later to eat you. Wait till you're all juicy. That's got to be the worst way, dude. Being eaten by something. Feeling teeth on you.'

The teens fell silent. Snickers passed between some of the boys, determined to blow off Harrison's obvious challenge to them – his desire for them to say something just as callous about his dead dad. Harrison had the monopoly on death, in the end. He was living it. Envy on the faces around the light.

'You're fucking sick, man.'

'I'm not sick, I'm just being real. Croc took him, man. I'm telling you.'

'That's sad,' the blonde girl whined. 'I'm sad, Harry. I like your dad.'

'Shut up, bitch,' one of the boys giggled. 'Shut up with your whiny bullshit. You sound like a cat.'

'I'm *saaaaad*!' she whined. 'Harry, don't say shit like that. No more crocodile talk. They'll find him. He's fine.'

'He's not fine,' another girl said. She had her back to me, was a curvy lump on a rock beside Harrison. 'He's mud. He's mud and dirt at the bottom of a river. Croc shit between someone's toes. That's what we all become, you know. Dirt. Circle of life, baby.'

I turned my attention to the girl speaking as Harrison put his arm around her. A girlfriend. Probably who he was texting when I'd interrupted him in his bedroom, a quarter smile playing about the corner of his mouth, just a flash of it before he heard me coming. I felt a mild sort of relief, seeing the thin, lanky boy whispering in her ear, silhouetted against the flames. At least Harry had someone to support him in his grief, someone to tough-talk with him as he tried to come to terms with never seeing his father again, with never having said goodbye. The goon squad boys playing in the shadows didn't look like the emotionally supportive type, and I didn't know if Stella had anything like that in her. Harry's plump little girl-friend had shaggy goth hair she'd probably cut herself, tied up in stumpy pigtails. The ends of the pigtails were a painfully bright pink. I wondered who she was.

The trip back to the house was colder than my journey out into the night. I thought about a wild-eyed Jake Scully being tucked under a dark log by a monster crocodile. Still alive. Blind in the tea-coloured water, far from the surface.

'Mr Conkaffey, do you watch pornography?'

The sweat dripping down my jaw. Sean had told me not to sweat. Whatever you do, don't smile, and don't sweat.

'Yes, I do. A lot of men do.'

'Let's just keep the focus on you, Mr Conkaffey. We're not here about other men. We're all here about you today. About what you've done.'

'Objection.'

'Sustained. Jury, disregard the last comment.'

'Mr Conkaffey, do you recognise the DVD I'm holding here?'

The sickness was right at the back of my throat, ready. Kelly, in the stands, covering her face. The journalists had all turned towards her, assessing her, as they had been since the trial began. A pattern had begun emerging early in the trial. The prosecutor dredged up some humiliating part of my life, and the journalists noted down how Kelly reacted. My porn. My internet browser history. My ex-girlfriends. What did she know? What was a surprise? What was front-page worthy?

'Mr Con—'

'Yes, that's mine.'

'Can you read the title of this DVD for the jury, please, Mr Conkaffey?'

'Wet'n'Wild,' I sighed.

'And the girl here on the cover. How old would you say she is?'

'Jesus.' My throat closing, hot like a flaming pipe. 'I don't know. She's an adult. Look at her. I mean, she's . . . I don't know how old she is but she's an adult.'

'If you don't know how old she is, how do you know she's an adult?'

'I. You can. I mean, you can see she's –'

'Do you know who made this DVD, Mr Conkaffey?'

'I bought it in a shop on George Street. A big . . . A shop, a proper shop.'

'But you don't know who made it.'

'I didn't look.'

'So you have no idea who made this sexually explicit film, and how old its participants are – is that what you're saying, Mr Conkaffey?'

'Objection, your honour,' my barrister said. He was a short, portly guy named Gregor. Someone Sean trusted, someone familiar with the courts. 'The defendant is not on trial for child pornography. The DVD the prosecution is holding is not child pornography, in any case, even if he was. This whole line of questioning is a waste of the court's time.' Gregor's hands are on the papers in front of him, white-knuckled and damp.

'Your honour,' the prosecutor throwing his arms open, pleading, weary. 'Obviously I'm trying to decipher the defendant's sexual interests.'

'Overruled. Get to your point quickly, Mr Elba.'

'Mr Conkaffey, by your own admission, you purchased this sexually explicit DVD and others like it without knowing who made the film, its legality, or how old the participants are. Am I right?'

'They're . . . It was clear to me . . . It was clear to me when I bought the DVD that the participants were adults. They're adults having sex with adults.' I swallowed. 'That is what my sexual interests are, sir. I'm sexually interested in adult women.'

'Adult women wearing their hair in pigtails.'

'Objection!' Gregor's face becoming pink, his eyes blazing. 'The hairstyle of the girl on the cover of the DVD is of no consequence to this case!'

'She's an adult!' I pleaded. My voice broke. He'd told me never to do it. Speak calmly, directly. Never give them anything. 'You can see that, sir.'

'Can I?'

'She's . . .' I struggled. 'She's got breasts! She's –'

'So, if they've got breasts, they're old enough for you, is that right, Mr Conkaffey?'

'Objection!'

The car behind me beeped, breaking the spell. I realised I'd been holding my breath. Lake Street, behind Cairns Hospital, was baking in the early morning sun. No wind stirred the palm trees lining the side of the road.

Most of the parking spots were full. There was no shade. I got out and plucked my shirt from my chest, wondered how much sweat I'd bled out since the trial reliving those moments in the courtroom, the pot shots back and forth between lawyers, the sneering and snarling faces in the crowd. Don't look down. It seems guilty. Don't look people in the eye. It seems defiant. I'd tried to keep my eyes on the windows, the white sky above the city, and then I'd find my hands wandering, fingers pulling at each other, a tangle of aching knuckles.

Don't fidget. You'll seem nervous.

It was early, so the hospital cafe inside the automatic doors was closed. People moved in the dark of the kitchen, clattering things, opening fridges. I'd hoped to drop in and out quickly and get back to Amanda in Crimson Lake by 10 am. I wasn't expecting to get much from the morgue staff. If they still had what little trace evidence was recoverable from the croc that possibly took Jake Scully, it was unlikely they would offer me a perspective on their analysis. I had no badge to wave anymore, no ID tag, no uniform. But I needed to ask. I'd lain awake in the dim morning hours listening to the geese stirring on the porch through the open bedroom window and promised myself that if I was going to take this job with Amanda seriously, I was going to have to apply all my police processes to it. All the rigour and the structure I'd learned in the academy. It would be so easy to slip into Amanda's ways, to bumble around haphazardly on instinct, turning up for work whenever I felt like it, rummaging through the clients' belongings while they watched. Drinking on the job with Stella Scully had been a mistake. I wouldn't do that again.

I followed the barren cream hospital hallways under huge signs filled with directions to surgery wards. Right. Left. Left. Right.

I found the front counter of the Queensland Health Forensic and Scientific Services Department at the end of a long hall of sticky brown linoleum. The young woman behind the counter was picking her nails. An older woman stood at the counter with her back to me, filling in a sign-in sheet.

'Morning,' Fingernails said to me.

'Morning.'

'How can I help?'

'My name's Ted Collins.' I felt the older woman beside me glance at my face. 'I'm hoping to talk to someone about the Jake Scully case.'

'Are you with the police?'

'Not exactly.'

'Who are you with?'

'I'm not really,' – I cleared my throat – 'I'm actually not really with anyone. Well . . . I mean, I'm with my partner.' My own words were sounding very contrived, even to me. I would need to get some decent practice in at this lying business, and fast. The receptionist forgot about her nails completely and examined me. I turned profile on her. There hadn't been too many media shots of my profile. 'My partner and I are investigating the Scully disappearance independently. We've been hired by the family.'

'Mr Collins, I don't have anything down in the appoint-ment book about –'

'Yeah, I haven't made an appointment.'

'What agency are you with?'

She was looking at the phone receiver now. I backed away from the counter. How had this got so complicated so fast? Was she recognising me? Why hadn't I planned what I was going to say? There was no way I was mentioning Amanda's name. My chest was suddenly tight. If she picked up the receiver, I decided, I'd just walk away. There was no telling who she might call about the strange guy at the counter asking about the Scully case, who wasn't really with an agency and wasn't really with the police. I was deep in the bowels of the hospital. I looked at the fire escape by the entrance to the corridor.

'Kayla, it's all right,' the old woman beside me said. I watched her hand go out towards the young receptionist, white and strong and lined with blue veins. The hand of a saviour. She turned to me. 'I think I can help you, Ted.'

I followed the little woman back down the corridor towards the front of the hospital, hardly listening to her pleasantries about the humidity, the heavy afternoon rains. I was wondering if I'd just been on the edge of a panic attack. Flopping on the floor with a panic attack every time I thought someone was going to recognise me in public would not go well for our inquiries into the Scully case. You have a panic attack in public and ten people rush to your side. I imagined hearing those inevitable words from the chaos above me. *Wait a minute . . . isn't he that guy?*

Before I'd really wrestled myself from the tangle of my panicked mind, I was sitting in a chair adjacent to one occupied by the woman at an outdoor table. The staff inside at the cafe were turning on the big black coffee machine, running steam through the valves and grinding the beans.

'So, Mr Conkaffey,' the woman said, 'you've begun again.'

I paused, trying to decide if I'd really heard what I thought I had. Then I pushed my chair back and stood.

'Sit down, sit down,' the woman said. She pulled at my hand. 'I can't chase you. I don't have the knees for it.'

I sat and wiped my face with my hands. The skin felt taut and sore. The hunched, bird-like creature beside me pulled a pack of cigarettes from her coat and shook one out, put it between her thin lips. She offered me one and I took it. I hadn't smoked in years. Her hair was blazing white in the morning sun, shorn short around her huge, dangling elephant ears. Her wide lobes held blue sapphires.

'I recognised you from the papers,' she said. 'I followed it on the television, yes, and online. But the pictures in the papers. They stay with you.'

I smoked. If I just concentrated on smoking, I figured I'd be all right.

'I'm Valerie Gratteur. Val.'

I nodded.

'You okay?'

'I don't know,' I said.

'Take a minute. Let me tell you a story while you put yourself together.' The waitress came out of the cafe and set an ashtray down between us. 'One of my first cases on the job as a young medical examiner was a murder. Bludgeoning. A Kiwi woman named Kimba Sorrano. She was seventy-one. Sixteen grandchildren. Can you believe that? Each one of them more devastated by her loss than the last. This was up here, in Cairns, but the case made the papers down in Sydney. They splashed it around everywhere. Had pictures of the little ones crying in Nanna's garden. *Senseless slaughter: grandmother dies in violent home invasion.*'

I tapped my cigarette against the edge of the ashtray. Relished the warmth and familiarity of the paper roll between my fingers.

'When I got Kimba Sorrano on my table, I was relieved,' Valerie said. 'It seemed pretty open and shut to me. Her head was split right down the middle like a watermelon, and everything inside had been rattled around to sludge. The autopsy was just a formality. It was going to be a homicide – blunt force, traumatic brain injury. This was about my third case ever, so I spent a lot of time looking at Kimba. I couldn't help myself. She was such a tragic figure lying there on the slab.

Just . . . wasted. Wasted life. It used to get to me, back in the old days. But I dried my eyes eventually and started cutting.'

The waitress came and presented two coffees to us, both black, and a jug of milk. We hadn't ordered. I supposed hospital staff were assumed to need caffeine straight up in the morning hours, no matter what they did.

'So who killed Nanna?' I asked.

'One of her mules.'

'What?' I laughed. The sound was uneasy. 'Mules?'

'Kimba Sorrano had red phosphorous on her fingertips,' the old woman said, barely containing a smile. She patted her sternum with nicotine-stained fingers. 'And corrosion blisters inside her lungs. I found the phosphorous first, and when I did, I looked for the blisters. If you don't wear the right protective equipment, and you wander around in drug labs long enough, you start breathing in all the shit they use to cook the product. Classic overexposure to methamphetamine production. Kimba Sorrano was a drug lord.'

'No.'

'Yes.'

'Nanna was a narcotics queen?'

'Exactly.'

'This is insane,' I said. I felt my shoulders lowering. My heartbeat returning to normal. 'I was in drug squad for five years. I met two female drug lords. Two. They were both in their twenties. How did you even think to look for the signs?'

'Well, people think that when you do what I do, you look at the bodies and you fill in some forms and that's it. But it's far from it. I look at the body, I look at the crime scene, and I look at the artefacts leftover from the person's life before I make my decision on a cause of death. My job includes a lot of detective work. Far more detective work than my peers give me credit for. I examine photographs. I talk to the family. I spend half my work time pondering mysteries. Just like you.' She pointed at me, the accusatory grandmother with the empty cookie jar.

'So how'd you put it together?'

'Took me a while,' Valerie said. 'But I found out Kimba Sorrano worked at Cairns Airport. She was a cleaner. So I thought about it, and I realised she had access to all areas – the aircraft, the offices, the control towers, the staff areas, the bathrooms. Kimba wandered in and out through the customs barriers all day long, six days a week, wheeling her cleaning cart back and forth, back and forth.'

'Oh my lord,' I said.

'The drugs come in. She goes onto the plane to clean it. Does a sweep through, picks up the package and walks it through customs. There's no telling how long she'd been at it, but I'd suggest from the cash they found in her breadbin it would have been a while.'

'That's amazing.'

'It *is* amazing.' Val smiled, showing me her big white dentures. 'Are all your pieces back in place?'

I exhaled slowly. 'I think so.'

'So from my story, you can probably tell, I don't take things on face value. I didn't take your case on face value. Not at all. It interested me very much. From the moment I read the medical reports connected to the little girl, and then I saw your mugshot in the paper, I was hooked.'

'What do you mean?'

'I mean that the medical report said the tips of Claire Bingley's fingernails were ripped off. Every single one. That girl scratched her attacker for her dear life. And yet, not a mark on you. Not so much as a nick.'

'The prosecutors tried to explain that,' I said. 'They said I might have worn multiple layers of clothes to protect myself during the act. That theory supports the fact that there was no foreign DNA on Claire.'

'Right,' she said. 'So you wore a jacket tied up to your neck, gloves, something to protect your face and ears and eyes? You committed this act in a beekeeper's suit, did you?'

'Maybe a hazmat suit,' I mused.

She laughed. I found myself smiling. But my eyes were aching with the desire for tears. I wiped my face again, felt the beginnings of my beard.

'You're pretty cool, Dr Gratteur.'

'That's what they tell me.' The old woman blew a smoke ring over her shoulder.

'Can you tell me anything about Jake Scully?' I said, trying to get away from my own case before my nerves completely frayed.

'Jake Scully? He's dead.'

'Is he?'

'The creature didn't leave me much. What I got from the police of Jake Scully's remains, sans the crocodile stomach in which they were originally housed, could have fit into a school lunchbox. But among the mix I found a fragment of his iliac crest. The wing-shaped bit of your pelvis.' She poked me in the hip. 'If I'd found a finger bone or a tibia maybe I could have speculated that there's some chance he's still alive. But no. He is as the proverbial doornail.'

'Right.' I had momentary visions of Jake Scully dragging himself through the mangroves of some forgotten corner of the tropics, his body missing from the stomach down, trailing his own bowels. I didn't place much stock in the idea that he was out there alive somehow, either.

'Do you concur, Mr Conkaffey?'

'I concur, Dr Gratteur,' I said, and smiled. 'And I think, with a surprising amount of relief, that I'm out of a job.'

'Not necessarily. I assume Mrs Scully hired you for insurance purposes.'

'You assume correctly.'

'Well, unfortunately, I just can't say whether this was a homicide or death by other means,' she said. 'And the insurance company will want to know Mrs Scully herself didn't bump off her hubby for the cash, or if it was suicide-by-croc.'

'What's your gut tell you?'

The old doctor shrugged her shoulders. Her watery eyes gazed off towards the parking lot.

'Look, I haven't had a genuine crocodile attack victim on my table in my thirty years on the job.'

'What? This is the top end, though! Don't they happen all the time?'

'No,' she laughed. 'No, they don't. There are about five near misses every year, and two fatalities. Saltwater crocodiles are very lethargic creatures. When they do attack humans, it's for a variety of reasons – it's mating season and the big males are defending their territory, or it's aestivation season and they're stocking up for the big sleep. Maybe they've become so accustomed to humans wandering in and out of their area that they just can't help themselves. They like routine. If you wade into the water to put a boat in from the same wharf at the same time every day for a couple of weeks you might have one pull your leg out from under you – if you're in the right season. But you were asking for it, weren't you?'

'I guess so,' I said.

'Jake Scully was a big man. About your size, actually. Now, it's not unknown for crocs to take big game. They'll drag a cow into the water every now and then. But they're not voracious killers. They're lazy, and they're opportunistic. They're more about lying in the mangroves staying somewhere warm and snapping up a waterbird when it wanders too close than taking down a full-grown man.'

'Okay.'

'Most human fatalities are children. They're the right size, they won't put up much of a fight, and they're usually already in the water making a commotion when they attract the creature's attention. Now, you're telling me big Jake Scully went out that night and blindly wandered into some enormous male croc's territory, managed to hang around on the bank long enough to coax the thing out of the water to eat him? Maybe he was in the water. More likely that way. So are we to assume he went for a midnight swim? I don't know. Sounds pretty weird to me.'

'I've looked at some stills from the CCTV outside the Scully house,' I said. 'Seems to me like he walked to his car in a bit of a rush.'

'Rushing out to meet someone?'

'Maybe,' I said. 'But how did they call him out? There's no phone call to the house or his mobile. No text message or email.'

'Could the meeting have been a prior arrangement?'

'Maybe. But why the rush, then?'

'You've got me,' the doctor said, smiling. 'I can't say I'm not enjoying trying to work it out, though.'

95

'Could you murder someone with a croc?' I asked. She squinted at the sun.

'What a question.'

'Yeah,' I laughed. 'I know.'

'You'd have to train the thing,' she said. 'Go to a certain spot and feed it every day. They're not unintelligent, crocodiles. I mean, you'd have to find one first – without being eaten. They're not travellers, so if you found one, and you survived, you'd be pretty assured that it's going to be in that area again if you come back looking for it. They tend to haunt certain plots of water. So I guess you'd make a certain noise on the shoreline and throw in a chicken every day at the same time and you could train it to come over when you were around.'

'That's a lot of effort,' I said.

'It's got to be the most inconvenient and unpredictable murder weapon in the world,' she said. 'Why do it that way? Why not just use a gun or a knife or a big fat rock? Hell of a lot more assured of getting the job done.'

'Maybe you're a complete sicko and you want Jake to experience it. Being hunted. Being eaten.'

'Oh dear.' Valerie slid her eyes to me. 'You do have a dark mind, Ted.'

'Maybe Jake was shot or stabbed and thrown in, and the croc just got lucky. Picked up the corpse before anyone else could find it.'

'Could be,' she said.

I sat back and took a good look at Val while she stubbed out her cigarette. I'd heard her speak, experienced her turning my mind over completely and emptying it of all the thoughts I'd been accumulating since I saw her there at the morgue front desk. I found myself smiling at her. She tapped her cigarette packet and I nodded, and we lit two more.

'Are you working alone up here?' she asked.

'No, I've got a partner.'

'Well, that's something,' she said. 'Who is he?'

'She's Amanda Pharrell.'

'Right.' Val huffed smoke through her nose with a laugh. 'Right.'

'What's your non-face-value assessment of that one?' I asked. 'Do you know anything about her case?'

'I had Lauren Freeman on my table, yes,' Valerie said. She looked me up and down with her watery eyes. 'Whoever killed that pretty little girl hated her very much in that moment.'

'You said "whoever",' I noted.

'I did.' She smiled.

Driving back to Crimson Lake, I went through the James Cook University campus, thinking I'd stop at the Co-op and see if they had copies of Scully's books. The concrete campus was nestled in the curve of lush green hills, a secret garden of mani-cured lawns being used here and there by man-sized kangaroos as lounging spots. I parked and followed the wide pathways shaded by curved corrugated roofs, past the big glass cube of the dentistry building, where I could look in on white-jacketed students taking notes, playing with white pieces of machinery at white tables. I felt a little sad pressing between the young students returning from the cafeteria. The campus was very much like the Goulburn police academy. I remembered my youthful ambition, my keen desire to be a justice-maker.

All of that was gone now.

The air-conditioning inside the Co-op was a relief. It didn't take long to find a pile of copies of *Burn*, Scully's first, under a sign from management expressing the bookstore's dismay at the disappearance of the much-loved local author. I took a copy and weighed it in my hands, flipped through the pages. I supposed I should get them all. It was possible there were clues to Jake's vanishing in them, in any of them, but I'd always been a fast reader and wasn't intimidated. I headed down the fiction aisle and scooped up a stack from the end of the row, checked the book list in the latest one to make sure I had all four.

On the way back to the counter, I browsed the bookish things section, admiring the mugs and book cushions, the literary-themed dolls. I picked up a stuffed Edgar Allen Poe and thought about buying it for Lillian. I'd really liked Poe as a teenager. Maybe I'd encourage her to read some as she entered those people-hating years when the lure of the Gothic takes hold.

And then I remembered it was possible I wouldn't see Lillian ever again. That was the reality. Even though my charges had been dropped, people would get in the way of me seeing her while she was a child. If Kelly herself didn't step up to stop me, her parents would. All it would take is one visit from child protection officers to deem me unsafe. Officially, they'd probably say it was something about my home, its bare and hazardous state, the vigilantes who targeted it. Maybe they'd say that as a private investigator I attracted the kind of dangerous people into my life that precluded the safe care of children. If they couldn't find anything they could photograph or video or point to on paper, they'd say they found me in an agitated state when they visited and they'd order a psychological evaluation. I'd have to get a magistrate to undo any restrictions they imposed on me. It was that easy to stop someone from seeing their child. I knew. I'd seen it happen to drug dealers, their vindictive ex-wives calling in anonymous tips about the men to hotlines, taking photos of them drunk to submit to judges.

I placed the doll back on the shelf. Beyond the head of black woollen curls I spied a familiar face and locked onto it, grateful for the instant pull away from the edge of a dark place. The face was on a book cover. It was Amanda.

Murder in the Top End: The slaying of Lauren Freeman.

I put my books down and plucked the paperback from between two stacks of gangster anthologies. The cover shot of Amanda was in profile as she was led from what looked like a courthouse, wrists cuffed to a belt at the waist of her royal-blue prison tracksuit. The collarbone that peeked through the neck of the oversized jumper was untattooed. Amanda's hair was longer, blow-dried for court into a conservative bob under her chin. She had the stricken-girl, on-the-edge look of a young Joanne Lees heading towards the media circus after the disappearance of Peter Falconio. The same strangely distant eyes. I ran my fingers over the embossed lettering and felt guilty.

I turned the book over and found a picture of Lauren Freeman, Amanda's victim, on the back cover below the blurb. She was a very angular girl, a collection of sharp points to her face – the chin, the tips of the ears, the upward tilt to the corners of her eyes. She looked almost wolfish. Platinum-blonde hair dead flat on the shoulders of her white school blouse. A stark white smile offset by gorgeously sun-kissed skin. She looked like she belonged in a Surf Life Saving Queensland video, running in slow motion along a Gold Coast beach, trailing a red and yellow flag. Organic. I turned back and looked at the pale and sullen Amanda and wondered how the two girls could ever have been friends.

I put *Murder in the Top End* on top of my pile of Jake Scully books and went to the counter.

Dear Jake,

I'm not sure if you got my last letter. I wrote to you on the tenth. You're probably busy with all the fanfare around your most recent movie option. I've cut out all your interviews from the papers. Nice review in the *Times*! Woo hoo!

I'm sort of putting a scrapbook together of your writing career and have been looking back at the first articles about *Burn*. You were so excited to finally have a book out there. I read the one saying you'd written four books before *Burn* and none of them were published. Even though I'm only on my second, I share your heartbreak. My first novel was rejected by twelve publishers, and I didn't get so much as a scrap of feedback. Sometimes I wonder if they even fucking read them! I read about Stella telling you back then you'd never make it, that you needed to focus on your degree. I hear you, man. People laugh at my obsession with writing all the time. But I know I've got it. My muse is like a whole other person. So persistent. So needy. My work is great – and I'm not tooting my own trumpet. I *know* I'm good. I'm sure you knew you were good, too, back then.

I'm a lot like you used to be, Jake. I'm just mad to be who you are right now. Signing books and chatting on the radio.

You really are an inspiration to me. That eager little Jake Scully from the GenreCon panel on YouTube is gone now, and you're a lot more confident. But I can see a twinkle in your eye sometimes when I see you on *BookWeek*. I know you're not taking it all for granted. I know you won't sell out and let them make crap CGI-filled Disney movies out of the Chronicles.

I love everything about you. I taped that session you did in your house for *The Morning Show*. Sick pad! You've really made it, man. I can't tell you how proud I am of you.

If you get this letter, and the other one too, I'm wondering if you might have time to take a look at my writing. I've attached it again, just in case. I know you'll be impressed by my work. You can't fake natural talent, am I right?

When you write back, a signed copy of *Burn* would be awesome, if you don't mind. It's still my all-time favourite. I've read it seven times. I think I need a new copy, and one that's been in your hands would be a gift this young writer would treasure for all time.

There was a woman on the steps of Amanda's shop when I arrived. A potential new client, I guessed. I was more curious about the inside of the little place, so I looked past her at first through the glass panels in the door – the blinds now rolled up to reveal what lay within. On a mat just inside, two very overweight cats lay basking in the sunlight pouring in from the street, one flopped on its side, its huge belly sagging against the prickly straw of the mat. The other was curled in a roll the size of a stuffed backpack. I looked up and spied another cat sitting just outside the open upstairs window, a long ginger tail lying over the edge of the sill, twitching gently in the breeze. The rain above the distant mountains was gathering, deep blue and ominous, but it was sweltering here. I glanced at my watch as I rolled up my sleeves, my forearms already tacky with sweat.

'She doesn't come in until ten,' I said to the woman on the stoop. 'Can I help you?'

'Actually, it's you I'm looking for, Ted,' the woman said. Her red lips turned up in an unfriendly smile.

A reporter. I stopped in my tracks.

How had I not seen 'reporter' written all over this woman from the moment I stepped out of the car? The immaculate pencil skirt, the manicured nails on strong, keyboard-worn hands – one gripping a mobile phone, the other hooked around the handle of a heavy handbag. Heels. High heels in Crimson Lake.

The fact that she was waiting for me at Amanda's office was even more bad news. It wouldn't have been hard for a reporter to track down where I live. Kelly might have told her. But only Amanda and Sean knew I was working here. Or so I'd thought.

The kids on the corner across the road were watching me with interest. I took a step backwards, made a mental note to ask Amanda for a key to her cattery so that I could hide in there if I ever needed to in the future.

'I'm Fabiana Grisham.' She held out a hand. 'People call me Fab.'

'I'm busy, Ms Grisham,' I said. 'Nice to meet you.'

I turned, walked down the porch. I heard her heels coming after me.

'I just want to talk,' she said. *Here it comes. Here it comes.* The dirty great storm of public recognition whipping the palms, slashing at the cane. I gripped the front of my shirt and twisted it in my fingers as I marched towards the car. I got there and changed my mind, made an awkward sort of half-turn, looked up the street. Amanda would protect me. I imagined she'd explode into a fearless, excited ball of weirdness at any kind of threat, and I could use whatever she did as a distraction to get away. That, or pick my partner up off her feet and hurl her at the reporter before dashing away to safety. Yes, I had to find Amanda. The Shark Bar was only two blocks up.

'Are you staying in Crimson Lake, Ted?' the reporter asked. 'Are you trying to rebuild your life here?'

'How did you find me?' I asked.

'I'm from the *Herald*. We have good reach. How do the people of Crimson Lake feel about your situation, Ted? Do they know you're here?'

I wiped sweat off my brow and got into the car. Slammed the door, making the old side-view mirror rattle in its casing. Fabiana stood back and turned the recorder off on her phone, defeated, as I drove away.

Amanda skidded in the dirt on her yellow bike, kicking up a cloud of dust she seemed impressed with. She was wearing a purple sequined singlet and pale blue jeans torn at the knees. Barefoot, her toenails painted lime green beneath tattoos of hibiscus flowers. I'd had her meet me behind the town pub, one street back from the Shark Bar. She had a newspaper rolled into a tube under her arm.

'Where's the trouble, Lassie?'

I found I couldn't inhale properly. I coughed, trying to mask my terror.

'I've got a reporter on me.' I looked back towards the end of town, the post office, at the edge of the cane field. 'I don't know how but I've got a fucking reporter on me.'

'Oh.' Amanda put her newspaper down in the dirt and came over to me. She rubbed my arm too slowly, like she was feeling the strange bark of an unfamiliar tree. 'Dearie me, we've had a scare, haven't we?'

'I'm not scared, Amanda. I just don't know how she found me out.'

'Someone probably spotted you. Never know who. I mean you've had vigilantes, right? Could have been one of them. Could have been whoever told them you were here. Could have been anyone. Don't panic, Teddy Bear, one reporter is –'

'I'm not panicking.'

'One reporter's not panic-stations.'

'This is bad,' I moaned. 'This is bad.'

'Well, it was always going to happen. How long did you expect to stay on the lam? You're not Dr Richard Kimble. You were always going to get found out.'

'Stop patting me.' I shoved her hand off. 'Stop it.'

She was right. I was panicking. Gulping air. I hated that she was seeing me like this. I turned away and leaned on the car, put my chest up against it and tried to focus on the feel of the outline of the window against my sternum, the heat in the roof under my palms.

'Was she print or television?'

'Print,' I said. 'The *Herald*.'

'Gah. Who reads the *Herald*?'

'About five million people, I think.'

'Next time you see her, tell her she's got something on her face. That'll get rid of her.'

'What?'

'Tell her, "Hey, sweetheart. Hey, I don't mean to interrupt you, babe, but you got something just here."' Amanda stuck out her jaw and tapped the corner of her mouth. 'They hate that. Women. Totally undermines everything they're saying.'

I shook my head. Nothing was certain anymore. I needed to get my reeling thoughts in order. Forget about it all for a second.

'You've got eighteen thousand cats,' I said, hoping a swift right-turn in the conversation would bring my breathing back to normal.

'Eleven,' she said.

'Who has eleven cats?'

'Me.'

'I mean why? Why the hell do you have so many cats?'

'Why do you think? I rented the shop last year. A cat turned up, and it was raining, and I took her inside, and she started shooting smaller cats out of her vagina one after the other like little red cannonballs.' Amanda's face became pinched. 'It was like something from *Alien*.' She slid her fist through a circle she made of her thumb and forefinger, opened her hand and made it attack her face. 'Blargh! Disgusting!'

I stared at her. Her hand was spread on her own face, one eye peering between two fingers at me.

'So then you had eleven cats.'

'So then I had eleven cats, yes,' she confirmed.

'And you just kept them all.'

'What else was I supposed to do with them?'

'I don't know.' I shrugged, widened my eyes. 'Give them away?'

She looked at me for a moment, then leaned in close.

'Do you think,' she whispered, 'that if anyone around here *wanted* a cat, there'd be one walking about in the rain, waiting to spew ten wet pink Jelly Babies onto the first dry scrap of carpet it could find?'

I sighed. She reached up and tapped my temple with her index finger.

'Get it together, Conkaffey.'

I brushed her off again.

'Come on.' She slapped my arm. 'Enough messing around. We've got a case to solve. Did you get onto the medical examiner? Is Jake dead?'

'He's dead. Yes.'

'With *dread*, *Ted said*, Jake Scully is *dead*. He has all the lively vigour of toasted raisin *bread*.'

'Stop.'

'All right. Jump in the Ted-mobile and we'll go break the news to the family.' She swung a leg over the bike and turned the thing in front of me, cutting a nice groove in the dirt. I heard thunder over the mountains as I slid into my car.

Amanda raced ahead of me down the Scullys' street, as though we were two kids trying to get somewhere and she'd declared it a race just as she saw the finish line and stepped up her speed. It wasn't far along the palm-tree lined, wide avenue before she spotted the police car and slowed. It was a Cairns patrol car, and its brake lights were still on. I pulled to the kerb behind it and watched Amanda as she came to the driver's window, ducked her head and shamelessly checked out who was inside.

A chief super got out and adjusted his belt, said something to her. She grinned and walked the bike backwards. Then Damford and Hench emerged from the car. I felt a sudden tugging at my chest to get out and intervene, a fear that they might hurt her, so small and colourful as she was, like a little chameleon being set upon by dogs.

'. . . big lump of a man over here is my partner Ted,' Amanda was telling the chief. The old man's deeply lined face turned towards me. He recognised me. I was used to the lowering of the brows and downturn of the mouth when people took in my face.

'Can I ask your business here today, Amanda?' The chief ignored me.

'We were just about to deliver the death-o-gram to the Scullys,' she said brightly. 'We got the scoop from the medical examiner this morning. I guess you did, too, huh?'

'I'm going to ask you both to leave.' The chief looked me over once again, disdain oozing. 'I really think it would be best for everyone.'

Lou Damford and Steven Hench had their eyes locked on me. I knew I was safe from them as long as we stayed in the company of their boss. But the hunger was there. We examined each other, schoolchildren behind the teacher's back. Again I noticed how old they were for their rank. They had to be in their forties. You only stay a patrollie in your forties because you're completely incompetent, or you want to. I didn't think they were incompetent. They were too malignant. They'd have spent their careers doing what they did to me – chasing down society's outcasts and roughing them up, feeling powerful. I knew the lure of that feeling. There was nothing like standing in the middle of a busted-out crack house in full riot gear, kicking stuff over, picking up the shattered pieces of young men's lives while they wept and rolled on the floor in their cuffs. I'd never been a genuine thug as a cop. I didn't carry the role very well. But sometimes you were required to look and act tough, scare people, make them cooperate. It could get addictive. I'd known people who let it change them.

I shifted my eyes to Amanda, wondered how old these two thugs would have been when she'd committed her murder. They were probably fresh cadets. Had they been involved? Had they been the patrollies called out to check up on a car parked in the bush on Kissing Point?

'*I* really think it would be best for everyone if a pair of nice, friendly looking chums like *us* went in there and gave them the bad news,' Amanda was saying, the slap of her hand against my arm bringing me back to myself. 'You guys bashing in there with all your guns and funny hats like a bunch of stormtroopers is going to make the news ten times worse.'

'Amanda,' the chief sighed.

'*Aman-duh*,' she mocked, mirroring his hands-on-hips stance. 'Amanda what? Chief Doherty, you hate the knock-and-shock. Come on, old boy.'

'You two know each other?' I said.

'Chief Doherty was a prosecution witness at my trial,' Amanda said. 'All the cops know me. I'm a star. Notorious gangster. Smooth criminal.'

We started walking as a group towards the Scully house, Chief Doherty's voice low and unfriendly despite Amanda's playfulness. Damford and Hench's eyes were still trained on me. I cleared my throat.

'So you two know Amanda, too, then,' I said.

They didn't answer. I felt the hair rise along my forearms.

'Were you around when she was arrested?'

Still nothing. They were good at this intimidation thing. I felt sick to the stomach, kept the distance between our slow, ambling paths behind Amanda and the chief nice and wide.

As it turned out, none of us got full credit for landing the news on Stella Scully that her husband was dead. As our group turned onto the path running through the manicured front garden to the door, she opened it, and I knew the face she wore. Grave acceptance. She licked her lips and looked at us all, finally settling on me off to the side, trying not to look at her. When she spoke, it seemed she addressed her words to me.

'How did they know?' she asked.

'Hip bone,' I said. I thought it best to give it to her straight. It seemed to me like that's how she wanted it. Chief Doherty turned and gave me the kind of look that wilted killers in the interrogation room. I actually felt a pain in the middle of my face, between my eyes, like he'd punched me.

'Mrs Scully,' he said to her, 'these people aren't here with us. We did not invite them. Nor did we invite them to deliver the terrible news of your husband's death in such a callous and heartless manner.' He shook his head, glanced at me again. 'Jesus Christ, I don't know. Can we come in?'

Stella turned and wiped her eyes with her hand, then padded off through the huge foyer in her bare feet. Amanda got through the doorway. But Damford and Hench swivelled in front of me just as I stepped up, and blocked my path.

'Nice one, kiddie-fucker,' Hench sneered.

'You know, there's a bit of a ceremony to it,' Damford, the fatter one, said. 'A romance. You sit 'em down. You make 'em tea. You take your hat off. It's like foreplay.'

'You're not big on foreplay though, are you, Conkaffey?'

'Hey, she asked,' I said. 'I told her. I didn't want to make it any worse by going inside and dicking around and making tea. Drawing it out, opening the fucking envelope like we're on an awards show. I'm not even wearing a hat.'

'You're an arsehole,' Damford said.

'She hired Amanda and me in the first place because you goons fuck around too much, you know. You're doing it right now, trying to mess with me out here. Shouldn't you be in there, shining your chief's arse?'

'Are you telling us how to do our jobs now?'

'What is your problem with me?' I said. 'Is it really what I've been accused of? Because I haven't seen a kid under the age of sixteen since I got here. You say you're trying to protect this town's kids. What kids?'

'You don't think sixteen-year-olds are kids?'

'That's not what I'm saying,' I sighed. 'I'm saying I'm not a threat. And you know that.'

'No, we don't,' Hench scoffed. 'All the evidence would point otherwise, in fact.'

'If you're that worried about me, why aren't you surveilling me?'

'Who says we're not?'

'I don't think all this has anything to do with my crime,' I said. 'I think you're pissed there's another cop in town, swinging his dick around. I'm surprised you let Amanda work on your beat. Why *did* you let Amanda set up here?'

No answer. That weird, icy double stare.

'Fuck you both,' I said, turning to go. Before I could take a step, Damford grabbed my arm.

'Leave,' he said softly.

That's all he said. But the word did something to me. Got into me, like a poison cloud, crawling into my mouth and down the back of my throat, making my insides burn. I saw this man's face over mine. Felt grass under my back. Felt his fingers around my throat. I felt the threat like an all-encompassing hallucination, a phantom death. It was the impact a person feels as they freeze on the road with their eyes shut, cowering, a car sailing towards them too fast. The screech.

Damford didn't have to say 'or I'll kill you'. I knew, looking at him, that if I didn't do what he asked, the last thing I'd ever smell would be his breath.

I shrugged my arm free and backed off, my legs stiff and awkward, and retreated around the side of the house.

If I had expected there to be some large and dramatic Hollywood-style outburst from Stella at what the officers inside were telling her, I'd have been disappointed. Through the doors to the little stone courtyard where I waited, I could see across the foyer to the sitting room, a slice of the side of her delicate face. She was sitting upright, hands in her lap, listening. Emotionless, calm, the demeanour of someone taking in a lecture.

I heard a rustling behind me and turned in time to see Harrison emerging from the bushes at the edge of the rainforest, the shoulders of his black wool jumper covered in condensation. He was looking down at his phone as he walked. I cleared my throat so he didn't run into me as he headed for the door.

'Whoa,' he stopped, boots crunching in the black river stones. 'What are you doing here?'

I drew a deep breath. Glanced towards his mother inside.

'The local cops are meeting with your mum,' I struggled. 'Amanda and I . . . We . . . We came as well, but she's inside, handling it. I got shut out.'

'What are they meeting about?' he asked. He was chewing on that lip ring again, searching my eyes. The cocky kid at the fireside bragging about his father's grisly death was gone now. His whole exterior seemed to have softened. I didn't want to be the one to tell this kid his father was gone. The little arsehole I'd encountered upstairs that first day I'd visited, sure. That kid could handle it. But this one – this one looked suddenly ready to crack.

Turns out I didn't have to tell him. Like his mother, he read it off me, stripped it from my hands. He gripped the phone. Looked down at it, squeezed it, a mechanical friend he carried everywhere who somehow had no comfort to offer right now.

'I thought he'd just gone off with someone,' he murmured. 'She said he'd just run off.'

Before I knew what was happening, the boy was in my arms, his face against my chest. I hadn't meant to hug him, and he probably hadn't meant to be hugged, but as the grief ripped through his body I squeezed him tight. There was nothing else I could have done.

I glanced through the windows and saw Damford and Hench watching me from just inside the front door, one elbowing the other, gesturing, snickers. I held the child as their predatory eyes wandered over me.

You can't be an atheist in prison. If you are, you're asking for trouble. Even if you don't outwardly prescribe to a certain faith, it's advisable to at least refer to crime in the way that religions refer to it: in terms of good and evil, sin and punishment, salvation and guilt. In administrative segregation, where the crimes are violent and the victims are women, children and the elderly, exculpatory reasons for what you did sound callous. It's safer to blame your broken soul, the devil's voice in your head, than your faulty frontal lobe. And it's safer to blame God's hand, if you're innocent, than to suggest the legal system might have got it wrong. The guards don't like that kind of talk.

My mother was a guilt-ridden Catholic, but I hadn't given much thought to religion and my part in it since she died. It was when I was led into a cell for the first time, and the door closed on me, that I thought about calling out into the universe. First, to ask for help. Second, to ask why. I remember running my hand over the iron face of the inside of the cell door, thinking how many times I'd seen the front of the same door and how few times I'd seen the back of it, tossing drunks and hooligans and nightcrawlers into the station cells, dragging them out again without looking at its closed surface. I'd pushed a little at the door to see if it was really locked on me. All hope that this was a joke was now over. I heard Frankie out there in the station somewhere, crying.

I lay on the mattress that night and looked out the slit in the wall at the orange sky, a single star. I'd wondered if some voice would come. That's what happens in those stories you hear as a kid in church, when faceless apostles or whoever are thrown into dungeons, thrown in with lions, thrown into pits of fire. A voice explains to them what they're facing. Why. What they have to do to get through it, the lesson they have to learn.

Eight months in remand, and the voice never came. I heard plenty of voices, but none of them was much concerned with helping me through my ordeal. I had no idea how to make it all stop.

Amanda rode halfway to the Trinity Baptist Church without touching the handlebars of her bike, keeping pace alongside me, her arms folded and the wind whipping her short black hair now and then across her eyes. We didn't speak much. I might almost have been able to imagine she was in the car with me. She squinted at the sun, reached over and hung onto the passenger side window frame now and then. I couldn't bring the speed above thirty-five or I'd lose her. When a car came up behind us she fell back and I moved over to let it pass.

Jake Scully's Chronicles books lay scattered over the passenger seat. I'd left *Murder in the Top End* wrapped in the brown paper Co-op bag, stuffed into the glove box.

Jake's church was a small weatherboard building only metres from the banks of the Trinity Inlet, no fence at the end of the long sloping lawn before it gave way to a wall of reeds lining the water. Across the grey-black river I could see the featureless green of Admiralty Island, another barrier of mangroves hiding any access to the land.

A couple of Aboriginal kids sat on the porch of the old building, drawing lines in the mud with sticks. Amanda got off her bike and stretched her quads, pressed her toes up against the tyre of my car to stretch her calves.

'So what do we know?' I asked.

'Well, this is Jake's home church.' Amanda swept her arm across the view of the church like she was showing off a game show prize. 'He gave talks here once a week. A guest spot, just a couple of minutes at the Sunday night sermon. He would tour around bookstores and churches whenever a new book was due to come out, but he wasn't your publicity dream. He'd gotten a reputation for shyness, so mostly if you wanted to see him, you had to come here.'

'*Was* Jake shy? Do we know that?'

'I'd say it's a ruse to pay lip-service to the Christian theme in his books. You ask me? If I was fooling around with a man behind my wife's back, I wouldn't feel comfortable making too regular an appearance to talk about sin and hellfire in front of impressionable youths. Feels like the definition of hypocritical.'

'But you still have absolutely no proof Sam is a guy, do you?' I said. 'Or that he or she has any connection to our case whatsoever.'

'I do not.' Amanda winked. 'But I will soon.'

I found myself examining Amanda again. I wanted to read *Murder in the Top End* so badly. What had caused her to go off the rails so dramatically? Was she still off? Sometimes, when she thought I wasn't looking, she certainly seemed like someone with problems. The gentle head-twitching that I'd almost become accustomed to, almost didn't see anymore. The just-slightly-too-big whites of her eyes. Everything about her was like that: edging on excessive, so close to crazy that her crazy became sane, consistent enough to ignore. She was functioning. I think that's what the shrinks called it. Functional dysfunction. As long as she could still dress herself, brush her teeth, maintain a job and do the grocery shopping, what right did anyone have to question Amanda's mental health? Her potential threat? She'd done her time.

It was not as though she'd just walked out of prison, either. If she'd followed the same path I knew most convicted killers did, she'd completed pre-release programs while she was still inside. She'd been approved by the parole board and moved to a halfway house with a bunch of other female inmates on their second chance. She'd followed her curfews and listened in on the guest talks from ex-inmates on how to adjust to the outside world again, ticked off all the conditions on her re-entry report. She was certified safe for society.

Following Amanda into the church, I found myself almost envious of her, as I mentally rattled off all the help she'd received to become a part of the real world again. When your case is set aside, they take the cuffs off you and walk away. Motion dismissively towards the door, like a weary teacher sending the kids from detention out to lunch.

Get out of here. And don't. Do it. Again.

My charge had been rendered 'no billing', meaning that the state could take it up again at any time, but that right now, they couldn't pin me. They didn't want to keep pursuing the case in court and maybe find themselves with an acquitted rapist and attempted murderer on their hands. No. They wanted me to slowly boil in purgatory, just above the fires of hell, hopelessly far from the clear, clean air of the earth.

The inside of the weatherboard church had recently been lovingly lacquered, making the walls gleam pink and turquoise on one side where the light streamed in through the eastern windows. A small foyer was filled with photographs in cheap frames, a table sporting copies of a single-sheet newsletter and pamphlets on counselling services. Amanda took a quick tour of the photographs, standing on her toes to see the higher ones. I went to the corkboard, read the death and prayer notices. *Teresa Miller, dearly missed mother and wife.* In the chapel, a man with a high forehead and the rocking movements of a praying mantis had the altar. We slid into a pew at the back of the room.

'Here's the problem,' the priest was saying. 'Matthew said to them, "The harvest is plentiful. But the labourers are few! Therefore pray earnestly. Pray earnestly to the Lord of the harvest. Pray to the Lord of the harvest and send out labourers into His harvest."'

'Hallelujah!' I gave Amanda a sarcastic grin.

'No, no, we want to save our hallelujahs.' She looked around warily at the crowd, leaned in to whisper, 'Save them for the right moment.'

'I was only making fun.'

She shushed me.

'What does that mean?' the priest asked. 'I'll tell you what it means. It means those willing, and happy, and prideful in the love of the Lord are lacking, my friends. There are too few people willing to share in the harvest – in the good love – of the Lord. It takes work, it takes labour, ladies and gentlemen, to receive God's love. You know what? It's easier to be a sinner. Isn't it easy? It's so *easy* to be a sinner.'

I cast my eye around the crowd. Heads nodding in front of me, the bald and speckled heads of old men, and the shaven, styled hair of young men. Aboriginal men with arms slung around their girlfriends or wives over the back of polished pews. At the front of the congregation a collection of children knelt or lay on the floor colouring in, too young to comprehend the sermon. They sat at the feet of the preacher, who stood before a great coloured glass rendering of the crucifixion, the Lord's face upraised and mouth downturned in agony. My discomfort grew steadily, an itch in my shoulders and neck. Time passed. I sat and listened.

'But why don't people come to the harvest?' the preacher asked. 'Why don't they work for God's love? Because people love to make excuses. Some people say they sin because of their families. "I was raised that way! I know no better! I have to steal, and cheat, and submit myself to Satan's whims because my mother told me so." Some people blame society. "Oh," they say, "I have to turn away from the Lord because to be a good Christian isn't fashionable. Isn't cool. My friends won't like me." The homosexuals, they blame their *blood*. "I was born this way," they say. "Something in my blood, in my genes, in my neurons, tells me that I have to defy the will of God and lay man with man and woman with woman. That I have to stay away from the harvest."'

'Hallelujah!' Amanda shot up from her seat and thrust her fist in the air. I felt my cheeks flush with embarrassment. People turned to stare.

'Praise the Lord!'

'Amanda,' I whispered, grabbing at her, 'sit down!'

I didn't understand the desired effect of Amanda's outburst until I saw the priest, who hardly paused in his ramblings, his mouth spreading into a grin even as he spoke. He glanced at my partner, pointed at her, his long sleeve flapping with his gesture.

'Yes, sister, that's right. The homosexuals, who are perhaps our greatest excuse-makers. They tell us that their wicked desires can exist even in the smallest newborn child of God, lying in his mother's arms . . .'

'Now we wait.' Amanda smiled. The priest had been spurred on. He was on a tangent now, wandering away from the original sermon down a dark path about the homosexual as a particularly dangerous type of harvest-avoider. The people around us had also been inspired by Amanda's movement. It was almost like the spontaneous shouting of the flock was a pastime they'd only just remembered was such fun.

'He *lies* with *man* as he *lies* with *woman*.' The priest paused for effect, his face twisted in disgust. 'Is there any greater insult to God's plan?'

A movement caught my eye. A young man sliding along the back row, knocking prayer books over in his haste. He drew a packet of cigarettes from his pocket as he made for the front doors.

Gotcha, I thought.

The little girls on the front step had acquired their own colouring books now, the sticks and mud forgotten. I let the door fall closed behind me. The man from the back row was no older than twenty, seemed at least partly Indigenous Australian. Sweat stained the underarms of his red T-shirt. I gazed at the mountains, made like I was just getting air.

He looked at me. The hangdog expression of a teen caught watching porn on the school computers. I lifted the corner of my mouth in a noncommittal hello, looked at the pictures the girls had drawn in the dirt. When I glanced up, the young man was shaking the cigarette packet at me.

'Thanks.' I took one, moved closer, let him light it for me.

'No problem.'

'Jesus. When they start on about the harvest.' I smirked.

'Yeah.' He gave a sheepish grin. 'Matthew drives me fucking nuts. So repetitive. Matthew and the letters to the Corinthians. Sometimes I wish somebody would put me out of my misery.'

I laughed. Eight months in remand and I hadn't lost my cop eye. As soon as I'd laid eyes on the guy, I knew his heart wasn't in the sermon. I knew I was looking at a liar. I used to be able to spot a liar before they even entered the interrogation room, back in the old days. Before my arrest, I'd settled for knowing something was 'off' about a witness, or a suspect. I knew something was off with this kid, the way he shuffled out of the building, his head down.

'I haven't seen you here,' he said.

'No. I'm visiting. Ted.' I held out my hand.

'Ray.'

We appreciated the river curling away from us between the cane fields. The preacher's voice came through the doors in a low mumble.

'It's a nice church.' I turned and nodded at the roof, the little spire leaning against the clouds. I wasn't lying. It was cute.

'Yeah, they have cake later, after the sermon.' Ray met my eyes, possibly for the first time. 'It's good cake.'

'I've heard about the cake here,' I said.

'Really?'

'No.'

'Oh.' Ray laughed, raising deep dimples at the edges of his wide mouth.

I smiled. 'I came because I heard that writer talks here. The Chronicles guy. I was hoping to catch him on my way through. I like his books.'

'Right.' Ray's smile disappeared. He swiped at a stray black curl. 'Nah, Jake's gone missing. You mustn't have seen it. It was in the papers. He's been missing for ages. Just up and disappeared one night.'

'Disappeared? What, like, ran away, or . . .?'

'They don't know.'

'Wow,' I said.

'Yeah.'

'Shit. Shit, really? So what happened?'

'Mate, they don't have a clue.' Ray leaned in close. 'The papers have just been saying he went out one night and never came back. That was a few weeks ago, though. I mean, it's gone from the news. The police just hit a wall, I guess. I've been looking for stories about it but there are none.'

'Well.' I exhaled sharply, blew the smoke over my shoulder. 'I don't suppose you know anything. Any secrets he had or any . . . extra information? I mean, you come here.' I gestured to the church. 'You knew the guy, right?'

Ray looked at me for a moment. He took a step back.

I've never been a very good actor.

'I've told the police everything I know,' he said. His face was stiffer now. No sign of the dimples.

'I'm not the police.'

'You're someone.'

'I am someone, yes,' I said.

The door of the church hit me in the backside. Amanda squeezed out beside me, scattering the little girls sitting on the stairs, who settled again like disturbed birds.

'Oh, *Je-sus!*' she wailed. 'The Corinthians!'

Ray stamped out his cigarette on the ground and pulled a set of car keys out of his pocket. He tried to turn to leave us, but the circle of my hand around his bicep stopped him.

'Not so fast.'

'Don't touch me,' Ray snapped suddenly. A fear reaction. Words out before he could control them. 'Don't fucking touch me.'

'I'm not the police,' I said. 'Neither is she. We're working for Jake's wife. We just have a few questions about –'

'He was gay, wasn't he?' Amanda said. I scoffed. Ray didn't.

'I didn't even know the guy!'

'Yes you did,' Amanda said. 'There's a picture of you just inside the door here. Standing next to Jake. Christmas service 2013. Should we go inside and have a look?'

'No.' Ray shrugged his arm out of my grip. 'We shouldn't.'

'You're holding a copy of his second book in the picture. Did he sign it for you?'

'What do you guys want?' Ray asked. Lightning flashed above the mountains. The kid was jingling his keys.

'Some quick answers,' Amanda said.

'They better be real fucking quick,' – Ray shot a nasty look at me – 'because I'm out of here.'

'All right.' Amanda pulled up her sleeves, like a magician about to do a trick. She slapped my chest with the back of her hand. 'Watch this, Teddy. This is how they do it in the A-league.'

I felt heavy with dread.

'Jake,' Amanda said, setting her eyes on Ray. 'Was he faithful to his wife?'

'No,' Ray said.

'Unfaithful often?'

'Yes.'

'With guys?'

'Yes.'

'With you?'

'Yes.'

'Recently?'

'No.'

'Anyone outside the church know about it?'

'No.'

'Was he serious about anyone?'

'Yes.'

'Recently?'

'Yes.'

'A guy named Sam?'

'Yes.' Ray glanced at me. He found no solace in my face. I was as baffled with Amanda's technique as he was.

'Did he meet Sam within the church?'

'I don't know.'

'Do you know Sam's surname?'

'No.'

'Right.' Amanda folded her arms, satisfied. Her head twitched twice, the smile never leaving her face. 'That's about it then. Class dismissed.'

Ray gripped his keys and turned on his heel, looked me up and down once more before he left us. The little girls on the step had abandoned their colouring-in at the spectacle of Amanda's fast questions, unknowing but utterly taken with the impromptu interview in front of their church. I watched Ray get into his car.

'You're unbelievable,' I told Amanda.

'What?'

'You've just burned that witness. He's not going to help us again now.'

'What would you have done?'

'I tried to pretend I was just a Jake Scully fan,' I sighed. 'I'm not a very good actor.'

'No, you don't seem like one.'

'I do a very good bogan. I used to call up as an angry bogan looking for quick drug deals. Back in the squad.'

'I want to hear it. Do it.' She nudged me.

'No way.'

'Go on!'

'Nope.'

'Look, we don't need him anymore.' She waved at Ray's car as it pulled away. 'We need to find Sam now, see what he knows about Jake's disappearance. We'll be right, Ted.'

Amanda stopped short in the middle of the path.

'Ted. Sam. Ray. Three men. Three three-letter names. There's a bit of a triangle going on here.' She looked at the sky, as if something there would confirm it.

'Stop being weird. Tell me why Sam would know anything more about where Jake is than Ray.'

'Because Sam was a long-time partner of Jake's, not some fling.' I followed Amanda towards my car. 'Jake kept Sam's

125

phone number in a cigar box in his living room. Hidden, a little shred of evidence of his secret life that he nonetheless couldn't let go of. If Ray had been any more than a fling to Jake, he'd have hung around and given us everything he could. He'd have wanted to help.'

I wasn't sure if I believed her. I didn't like her style. I was accustomed to having a partner who discussed all strategies before we took them to the witness, laid out what we would and wouldn't say, what we'd hold back for future use. Even after I'd left, drug squad and been locked up, I never said anything unless Sean and I agreed on it. Unless we'd looked ahead to what damage it might cause.

But she'd been right about Sam. Dead right about Jake's sexuality, his infidelity, based on nothing more than a slip of paper she dug out of a cigar box. I was standing at the edge of the road, my keys in hand, staring at the grass. I came to when I realised Amanda was doing tight circles around me on the bike.

'Wake up, Ted,' she said. 'We've got sleuthing to do.'

It was raining too hard for the baby geese. They were still at the size that a good fat raindrop to the top of the head made them duck suddenly like they'd been struck by a miniature fist. So fragile, all of them. Easy to tire. Easy to trust. So that night I filled the bathtub with fifteen or twenty centimetres of water and put them all in so they could have a swim around, do something productive with themselves. Woman didn't seem to mind when I started gathering them all up in my T-shirt. She waddled unevenly to the door of the bathroom and watched us for a while, the goslings doing laps up and down the length of the tub, me sitting on the toilet lid, reading Jake Scully's first novel. The birds did a few dives and streaks across the top of the water at first, excited, their nugget wings flapping. They settled in soon and I almost forgot about them. When I looked up, Woman was gone from the doorway.

The little geese paddled up and down, tiny grey-black feet moving in wide circles. Now and then they ducked and ruffled their downy feathers, nuzzled their beaks under their wings, picked at themselves. I reached in and made a few waves, which they seemed to enjoy, splashed them. One did a full somersault, turned over so that its yellow underside showed and it kicked its wet legs in the air. I found myself smiling and drawing out my phone to take a picture as it righted itself, in case it did it again.

But who would I show such a thing to? I tapped the phone on my knee a few times, then put it away.

Jake was a good writer, and I knew that, because I'd read a lot of trash in prison. Prison books have complicated lives. They're printed in numbers estimated to sell, and when they go out to bookstores and don't sell, bookstores then have to decide what to do with them. They discount them. They shift them about and put stickers on them. Then they send them back to the publisher, if they just can't get anyone to take a chance on them. The publisher then sometimes sends them to remainder stores, where more stickers are put on them, fluorescent stickers with pen marks slashing the printed price. If they don't sell in the warehouse, it's onto the donation lot.

By the time they get to the average remand prisoner's hands, they've been read a few dozen times by other inmates. All the stickers have been peeled off through boredom, but the sticky residue remains, black with grit and grease and sporting a few stray hairs. Sometimes, because the sticky books have been in contact with other sticky books, half the cover is ripped off, leaving the title and author a mystery to the casual observer. Parts of the books that contain anything remotely sexual have been torn out to be kept as wank fodder. Sometimes, other sections will disappear – sections that describe children in detail, or murders. The cover image, where it remains, has usually been defaced in some way, incorporating more often than not the image of a giant, veined penis standing proud atop a set of impossibly spherical hairy balls.

You read these sticky, titleless, dick-plastered books anyway. You have to.

Jake's books scored points with me before I'd got far into them. I ran my fingers over their stark white pages, the embossed covers. The art was fantastic. A blazing city, a pair of windswept teens standing atop a cliff edge, looking at a wasteland. I was hooked pretty fast. I took a break for dinner, dried the goslings with a handtowel and sent them back out onto the porch with their mother. As night began to fall I was stretched on the porch sofa, starting book two, *Whisper*. The goslings returned to their box, and I pulled the towel door down over their warm little nest. Woman stayed on the porch near me but not within reach, looking irritably at the sunset between the clouds.

I felt, word by word, as though I was getting closer to Jake. The peril of his characters, to me, felt like the peril of the man whose killer I was chasing. A ghost Jake writing to me from wherever his soul now lay.

I wander in the darkness for a long time, no telling how many hours. Now and then on the horizon lights flash and pop in the various colours of evil, flame yellow and a deep blood red, as fires rage through once-quiet suburbia. I go towards the flames. My body wavers, sometimes spurred on through waves of adrenaline as memories puncture the terror. My home. My family. The gentle night hours we once slept away in peaceful dreams, and the mornings we woke unknowing what horror would one day reach us in our sanctuary. We had lived gluttonous lives. Now that happy fat, built on years of certainty, renders on the fires of a new world. A broken world. Every step I take crunches on the glass of fallen towers. Here is hell.

I'd fallen into a thick sleep full of half-whispers from my trial, responses moving on my lips, disturbing me with the foreign sound of my own voice through the layers of dream.

Do you read young adult novels, Mr Conkaffey?

I have in the past.

Do you own any?

Objection. Relevance.

Overruled.

I own some. Yes. I've got the . . . ah. The war one. The Tomorrow series.

Any others?

Um. Ah. I own Twilight. *The first Twilight book.*

Were you given these books, Mr Conkaffey?

No.

You bought them?

Yes. I bought them.

Could you tell us why you bought these books, Mr Conkaffey? These books that are directed at pre-teens?

I liked them? I mean, I liked the sound of them. I'd heard good things about them.

You like the books, did you say?

Objection, your honour. Asked and answered.

Why do you like these books so much, Mr Conkaffey?

Well, I didn't like Twilight *that much.*

Pardon me?

I didn't —

Both the protagonists of these particular series are teenage girls, are they not?

They . . . Uh, yes . . . Yes they are.

The Tomorrow series. Twilight. Little Women. The Hunger Games. Divergent. How I Live Now. *You own all of the books*

I've just listed, don't you, Mr Conkaffey? All of these books are about pre-teen girls, aren't they?

I sat up to the sound of a siren. Or what I thought was a siren. Woman was very near me, but she was strangely contorted, her head down low to the ground and her good wing up. She was making a kind of high-pitched wailing sound that fell sharply into a growl. I shook off the dream I'd been having and raked back my hair.

'Jesus! What's the matter with you?'

Woman exposed her pale grey tongue and stomped her feet. Then she righted herself and stared at me expectantly. My skin was prickling with terror. I got up and stood by the bird.

'What?'

Nothing. The bird stared at me. I lifted back the towel on the cardboard box and looked at her goslings. They were all huddled in a sleeping pile.

'You're weird,' I told Woman, and went inside.

I wasn't in there for long before the squealing, growling sound came again. I heard the bird's good wing flapping against the back door from the kitchen. A glance over the porch through the window above the couch revealed nothing. The animal stared at me, waiting for me to act. I took a shower and dressed, and by the time I'd listened to her fifth or sixth tantrum I went outside in a true huff and hustled the goose out of the corner of the porch where she stood flapping madly.

'What's wrong with yo—oh-whoa-*shit!*'

With my mouth agape, I took in the sight of the python on the roof beam, followed its thick, near-black body along the beam and around the back of the post. The creature was completely still. I backed into the goose, causing her to flap at my legs. The snake's head was flat against the timber. It might have been sleeping, but a single white eye glared sightlessly at me. Six inches from the wide head, the lean body widened into an almost spherical bump.

'Oh god,' I said. I looked at Woman. 'Oh god, no. No, no, no, no!'

My hands were shaking when I reached the box. I flung aside the towel, startling the goslings, causing them to rise to their feet all at once, alarmed soldiers. I tapped the goslings hard as I counted them, unable to control my limbs.

One, two, three, four, five, six.

I swallowed. Gulped another breath and shoved the birds into two groups.

One, two, three. Four, five, six.

They were all there.

I collapsed onto my backside and regained my breath slowly, watching Woman strut around the other side of the porch, chirping, squealing, growling. Sean had been right. She was a very good guard goose. I would have been able to hear her panic song from the front of the house. I was lucky she had continued it, even when I ignored her, or there might have been a second lump in the intruder by the time I returned home that afternoon.

I'm not a man who smiles often, and I smile at my own achievements even less. But I was wearing a great smile when I walked out of my house and onto the sunbaked road that morning carrying a two-metre diamond python I had caught with my bare hands. While Woman watched, I'd manufactured a snake catcher out of kitchen items – a sort of slipknot or noose made from a piece of twine, which I threaded through the hollow handle of a plastic broom. I'd ensnared the thing and dragged it, fat and slow and liquid, down from the roof beam and onto the porch. It had twisted and writhed a little then, the bulge in its upper body shifting, but before it could vomit up its catch, thereby making itself a lighter fugitive, I grabbed its head. I took hold of the middle in my other hand, a hard hunk of twisting muscle as thick as my arm, and lifted it. The bird watched like a quietly impressed wife as I escorted the intruder off the premises.

I know just how big my smile was when I got to the road because it dropped completely when I set eyes on the reporter. She was just shutting her car door. The snake let go of its bowels, as though in tribute to what I was feeling, and drizzled mustard-yellow muck all over my hand and forearm. I stood there, looking at the snake shit dripping off my elbow, the thing's wormy body coiling over my bicep.

Fabiana stopped before me. She looked at the snake, then at me. And then, as though neither had even mildly confused her, her big dark eyes went to the house.

Someone had hurled bright red paint across the front of the building, right over the door, the boarded-up windows, the old red bricks. It was an impressive display – dramatic, a well-chosen colour, vivid in its connotations of fresh raw meat and death. The paint had dripped, covering the bottom half of the house in hundreds of thin, glossy lines like the bars of a fiery prison. My faith in Woman the guard goose plummeted.

'Redecorating?' she asked.

'Yes,' I said. 'Trying to bring some life into the facade.'

133

Her hand was already in her handbag. I turned just in time to ruin the exclusive photograph of Ted Conkaffey out the front of his blood-spattered hovel, a huge, probably venomous snake struggling in his predatory grip. She got my shoulder, a squinting slice of my profile.

'Don't!' I snapped. She tried to aim the camera again and I twisted away. 'I don't give you permission to photograph me. You're on my property. You need my consent.'

'I'm not on your property, I'm on council land.' She pointed to her shoes, deep in the dry grass of the nature strip beyond my gate.

'You'll be sharing that council land with this snake in a minute, if you're not careful.' I lifted the snake like I was going to throw it. 'I think it's a red-bellied black.'

It clearly wasn't a red-bellied black snake. It was a very dark carpet python. But she backed up onto the dirt road anyway, in case I knew something about rare breeds of red-belly in disguise that she didn't.

'You drop the camera and I won't drop the snake.'

She tucked her camera into her bag.

'Ted, can we just talk?'

'No.' I started walking. I'd figured I'd walk the snake up the road and drop it a good distance from the house, so it might not find its way back. But seeing Fabiana made me want to make for my car. I looked at myself in the reflection of the side window, ridiculous, the snake-man of Crimson Lake thinking he can just slide the thing into the passenger seat, buckle it up, and get rolling. I turned towards town. If Fabiana followed, she followed. There was nothing I could do.

'I just want to talk. I'm not recording.'

'Bullshit.'

'What are you doing up here, Ted?' Fabiana walked beside me quickly, eyes locked on the road as her heels rolled over sharp stones in the clay.

'I'm not doing anything.'

'My sources have confirmed you're working with Amanda Pharrell. You must know Amanda is a convicted murderer. What are you doing with her? Are you in a relationship with her?'

'Is this what they teach you in a Bachelor of Journalism these days, Fabiana? How to find a non-story?'

She nearly tripped. If she went down, I was kind of glad I wouldn't be able to catch her, with my hands full of reptile.

'Oh, you're not a non-story by any means, honey,' she said as she recovered. 'People want to know what you're up to. Whether or not their town is safe from you.'

'Everyone is safe from me,' I said. 'This town, the next town. No one was ever not safe from me, and that's the point of having a trial – so you can determine whether or not someone is the someone you're not safe from or if he's just some regular dude everybody is safe from.'

'But –'

'My charges were dropped, Fabiana. You read the papers?'

'I do.'

'So right now you're just following some totally innocent guy along the side of the road on the edge of nowhere to see what he's up to,' I said. 'And the answer is nothing. Well, it's not nothing. You want the scoop, Fabiana? I'm moving a snake. That's what I'm doing. *Ted Conkaffey, innocent man, moves snake*. Great headline, babe. Top reporting.'

'You're getting quite upset.'

'No, I'm not.'

'We both know you're not innocent, Ted. Australia knows you're not innocent.'

I stopped. My hard sigh came out less aggressive than I'd wanted it to. It sounded sad. Broken over a lump in my throat. I fixed Fabiana with a glare to try to patch up my masculinity.

'You're wrong,' I said.

The reporter in her ridiculous heels stood looking at me. In my younger, more optimistic years, I might have thought her troubled gaze hid slowly darkening thoughts. That maybe something in those two words and how I'd said them, maybe something in my eyes knocked at all those closed doors in her mind and made her uncertain. But I snapped out of my optimism pretty swiftly. Journalists were never uncertain.

I walked away. She caught up.

'I'd love to be swept up in the tragedy and the drama of it all but I'm afraid I'm just too experienced for that.' She sniffed, her chin jutting. 'I'm hard news, not features.'

'I'm impressed. Really, I am.'

'I read your court reports, Ted.'

'All of them?' I asked.

'Yes, all of them.'

'So impressive.'

'The wrongly accused nice-guy act is a terribly romantic concept but I'm after facts, not fiction.'

'Uh-huh.'

'The witnesses,' she huffed. She was having trouble matching my long stride. 'You can't contest the witnesses. They were all consistent. They were all reliable.'

'I don't contest the witnesses,' I said.

'The analysis of your house? The supplementary material?'

'You mean my porn and my books?'

'Yes.'

'What about them?'

'They speak to your character,' she said. I didn't respond. She kept talking, listing things on her slender fingers as we walked along the road into a patch of rainforest. It smelled good here. Earthy. Possum crossings slashed the sky above us, net tubes that kept the animals safe from the road as they moved between the trees. I tried to spot one, but it was probably too late. We were about a kilometre from the house now. I looked back over my shoulder and tried to see it through the trees. Was it far enough for a scaly drop off? How well did snakes know their way around? I knew sucking in the details of the world around me was just me deliberately distancing myself from Fabiana's words as she rattled off sections of my trial verbatim, quoted the prosecution. I'd drifted off this way plenty of times in prison when other inmates started confiding in me about their crimes. A gentle mental wandering, fleeing from distress, from the gory details of my personal nightmare. Psychologists probably had a word for it. When I did this during the trial, the press said I looked 'bored'.

I stopped and she stopped with me, watched me crouch and place the heavy snake on the ground. I kept the beast's head pinned by a single finger as I released the body, then lifted my finger and stepped back swiftly. The snake didn't turn on me. Carpet pythons are like old men. Docile. Slow to anger. The animal tested the air with its tongue, then began slowly winding its way down towards the mangroves, cutting a path through the wet pillars of grass.

When I came back to myself, I realised Fabiana was still appreciating me. I didn't know what she hoped to see, what of my 'character' might be revealed in my letting a snake go back into the wild. I didn't care if it jarred with the character she'd read about in the court documents. Convincing her of anything wasn't going to stop people splashing paint on my doorstep or hurling bricks at my windows. I saw suddenly the futility of talking to her at all. Maybe this was what Amanda had learned in the long months after her release. That there is just no convincing some people.

'Don't walk back with me,' I told Fabiana. 'You ruin the quiet.'

She looked mildly insulted by that. I gave her a polite smile and turned back towards home.

I'd been reading about Amanda when she came walking down the stairs of Cairns train station towards the car, leading the yellow bike at her side. I watched her with interest, trying to transpose the image of my strange, annoying new friend against the Amanda her classmates testified about in interviews given to the author of *Murder in the Top End*, Eleanor Chapman.

By all accounts the teenage Amanda had been a strange and frightening creature. Like most cliché high-profile killers, the book was full of assertions about her antisocial nature, and recounts of attempts to befriend her that ended disastrously. She would apparently sabotage any fledgling friendships that might have developed between herself and a classmate by 'going off' without warning and abandoning all communication just as interaction got comfortable, refusing to speak or make eye contact with the new friend and hiding in the playground so that attempts to fix the sudden, unexplained rupture could not be made. Amanda was the wild fox who came to hang around the house warily for a few days, snatching at bits of food and cowering curiously by the edge of the woods before becoming spooked and bolting, never to be seen again.

She was quiet, but very intelligent. She would excel at written work but would fail hopelessly at any performance or group-based tasks. A teacher in her first year of high school made the mistake of surprising her by beginning to read out one of her essays to the class, at which point Amanda allegedly flipped her desk and ran out of the room.

All of this I could believe as I sat watching Amanda at the bonnet of my car, stretching her quads and calves before her ride. Amanda was an intelligent weirdo, and had probably grown up an intelligent weirdo. Her quirky confidence was something she had no doubt gained in prison. You can't go hiding and avoiding people in prison. There's nowhere to run away to. They will come for you in your cell and drag you out into the common room, interrogate you for your story, make you participate if only to torture you with interaction you don't have the stomach for. I knew this from trying to hide from my fellow inmates at Silverwater, trying to get away from their hideous murder and rape storytelling sessions on the moulded fibreglass couches in the TV room. Prisoners don't like mysterious loners. It suggests you think you're different to them. And, therefore, better.

But for all that I thought was true, there were accounts in the book that I couldn't believe. As an ex-cop and a long-time true crime reader, I'd seen the same sort of stuff plenty of times accompanying the stories of big names like H.H. Holmes and John Wayne Gacy. The obligatory childhood animal-torture story was there. A science classmate of Amanda's had told of her horror arriving for class early one morning to find the girl burning one of the classroom's pet mice alive on a desktop Bunsen burner. *She was holding it by the tail and it was twitching. I'll never forget the smell of the burning hair, the way the thing squealed. I had nightmares for years.*

I didn't believe that. It was very imaginative, very visual. I'd have given it an A in creative writing class. The Amanda I knew didn't gel with the mouse-burning Amanda. This one was apparently accommodating a small army of felines she didn't even seem to like, and from what I'd seen through the shop windows they all looked pretty well fed and cared for.

A man who had grown up in Amanda's neighbourhood but not gone to her school had recounted Amanda attacking the local corner store owner for running out of Redskins lollies. Amanda was hooked on them, and there was indeed a picture of the detached teen sucking on one at a school carnival, sitting alone at a wooden picnic table. The witness, who didn't want to be named in the book, had described pulling Amanda off the old man, whose face she had been kicking in. Amanda had apparently burst into maniacal laughter and threatened to come back and kill the guy. She'd rampaged through the store until minutes before the police arrived, knocking things off shelves and overturning baskets of fruit.

There was no account of this event from the police, however. Or the store owner, or anyone else. I didn't believe it.

Amanda came around the side of the car when she'd finished her stretches and mounted the bike she'd left leaning there. She hung her bare arms over the handlebars, squinting in the sunlight. I'd tucked *Murder in the Top End* away in the glove box long before she'd arrived, but I still felt chills imagining her finding a reason to reach through the window and open the compartment before I could stop her.

'All right, me hearty,' she said. 'Me scurvy dawg. Are ye ready to set sail?'

'We're pirates, suddenly,' I said.

'Aye.'

'Where'd you cook up this address?' I asked.

'Well, I started with the phone number, which is private, so I couldn't get details of an owner or an address. I called it a bunch of times with a genius telephone services ruse that I was sure was going to get Sam to tell me his full name, but he's not answering. Probably doesn't answer numbers he doesn't know as a rule – I'm the same. But there are precisely four Sams on the parish registry at Jake's church in Crimson Lake.' She showed me four fingers. 'I spent last night checking them out.'

'Googling them?'

'No. Three of them still live in Crimson Lake,' she said. 'So I went around to their places and snooped.'

'Surely your private investigator certification course taught you something about not being an unethical investigator, Amanda.'

'What's your point?'

'You can't go snooping around people's houses. That's my point.'

'Well, I did.' She shrugged. 'So if you want to stop crying about it like a little princess for half a minute, I can tell you I ruled those three out.'

I exhaled. 'Go on.'

She puffed her chest out with the pride of a rookie detective. 'I was pretty sure I had the winner on my first house when I opened the fridge and spied the almond milk and pomegranate–kale salad.'

'What?!'

'Almond milk and pomegranate–kale salad.' She smiled ruefully, shook her head. 'Some people.'

'You went *inside* their houses?'

'I just told you that. I'm sorry, I must have slipped into Chinese. Am I speaking Chinese?'

I covered my face.

'Computer searches and phone searches revealed nothing. I went through the second guy's filing cabinet. Very, very organised. He had a separate file for gardening-related expenses. Seed purchases and fertiliser and hoses. Look, it was a nice garden, but –'

'Amanda!'

'So the short version is we're visiting Samuel Polson today. He joined Trinity Church a few years ago. All right? This is the guy. The Sam from the phone number in the cigar box. Jake's former lover.'

I followed Amanda through the streets of Cairns towards the harbour and along the esplanade, watching for movements in the impossibly flat water that might indicate croc life. The lush city streets were overhung with palms and vines, bougainvillea and jacaranda blossoming on every corner, flowers sagging in the midday heat that would spring to life again when the afternoon rains arrived. We pulled up at a block of fifties-style apartments, pale golden brick and white trim, the mosquito screens on every window ratty and torn.

Amanda seemed to know exactly where she was going, parked the bike on the glossy green tiles by the stairs and started trekking up. She had the quiet confidence of an experienced investigator about her, of someone who'd been doing this a lot longer than the two years she actually had. It was as though any dangers she might face when she knocked on the door would be in her catalogue of experiences, from which she would simply select the appropriate response. Fight or flight. I wondered as I followed her up the stairs how many cases Amanda had taken on since her release. How successful they had been. What mistakes she had made to come to this place of contentment with the uncertain.

Maybe it wasn't experience that made her so confident. Maybe she was just crazy. It had been years on the police beat before I was that comfortable. Her fearlessness worried me.

She knocked on the door, and no one answered for a while. I decided I would let her lead – I had the feeling after we'd spoken to Ray at the church that she liked things to go that way anyway, and she was the one who had found Sam. We heard a chain being removed after a time, and the musty hall was filled with the smell of freshly cut lime.

'Yes?'

The man before us was short, and older than I'd expected. He might have been in his fifties, with a broad face and deeply lined features. He was wearing a pristine white collared shirt that looked as though it had never been sat down in. Meticulously ironed pockets and mother-of-pearl buttons.

'Mr Polson, I'm Amanda Pharrell, and this is Ted Collins.' Amanda jabbed a thumb at me. 'We're here to talk about Jake.'

Sam's ginger eyebrows met briefly in surprise. He seemed to consider telling us that he didn't know what we were talking about, but the confusion was quickly replaced by a sad, resigned smile. The man looked at me.

'So he's dead, then.'

'Why would you say something like that, Mr Polson?' Amanda snapped.

'Oh, cut the crap and come in.' He pushed open the door. 'I'll let you stay if you don't give me any of that police interrogation rubbish.'

I followed Amanda into the apartment. It was spacious and fifties-themed, in keeping with the exterior of the building. A mint green kitchen across a living room of caramel shag carpet. The last time I'd walked on any shag I'd been young enough to get away with rolling around on it, lying on my side in the woollen grass, playing with Lego. I felt a strange desire to do that now but resisted.

Mr Polson had been making himself a mojito. The thick wooden muddler was on the kitchen bench. He took the item back up again and started crushing slices of lime in the bottom of a stainless steel shaker. It was ten in the morning.

'Can I offer you guys a drink?'

'No.'

'Ye– No. No thanks.' I cleared my throat.

'Did you say you were with the police?'

'We've been hired privately by Jake's wife,' Amanda said.

'Oh, right.' Sam gave a couple of hacking laughs, poured his drink into a tall vintage crystal tumbler. 'Right. I was sure you were cops. So you'll be in a hurry then, if Stella's hired you.'

'Do you know Stella?' I asked. We followed Sam to a cane lounge set by the open balcony doors. The breeze was refreshing and made the sweat in my shirt cold against my chest and sides.

'No, not personally. Just through Jake's stories.'

'What would you call your relationship with Jake?' Amanda asked.

'A complicated friendship.' Sam smiled.

'A long one?'

'Yes.'

'A sexual one?'

'Yes,' Sam laughed, looked at me. 'This one here doesn't mess around, does she?'

Amanda raised her eyebrows at me. Gave me a smug little wiggle of her head.

'You and Jake texted a bunch of times on the night he disappeared,' I said. 'What was your conversation about?'

'Oh, it was just a catch up,' Sam said. 'You know. How's work? How's the family?'

'If you two were so familiar, why'd Jake keep your number in his cigar box?' I asked. 'Presumably if you were texting back and forth he had your number.'

'I'm sorry,' Sam shook his head. 'A cigar box?'

I explained how we'd found his phone number. He stared at his knees, deflated.

'I guess he must have kept it as a sort of memento,' he sighed. 'The first time I gave him my number, it was on a scrap of paper. I slipped it to him at a club. I came to learn later that he knew people that I knew.'

'Amanda found you through the church registry, though.' I glanced at my partner. 'Did you attend Jake's church?'

'Hell no,' Sam snorted. 'Not for masses or sermons. But the church did a lot of promotional stuff for Jake, so I signed up so I'd get the notices about his appearances. He hated people he knew going to see him talk. I'd have to sneak in the back.'

'You'd go and watch him talk?'

'I cared about him.' Sam shrugged. 'I liked to hear what he had to say about his work.'

'So yours was a romance, then?' Amanda asked.

'Maybe once. Briefly. At least, I thought so. Jake and I saw each other regularly but not exclusively.' Sam sipped his drink.

'There was a group of us. It was all very casual. When you're a man who likes the company of men and you live somewhere like Cairns, you don't get committed. You don't want to burn the other person and find yourself one down in your collection of people who understand you. You get what I mean?'

'I do,' I said.

'So you've faced a lot of discrimination up here, then?' Amanda said.

Sam leaned forward, his drink in his hand, and traced a long horizontal scar above his left eyebrow.

'Nineteen stitches,' he said. 'I was forty-five. Can you imagine that? Being bashed when you're forty-five. When was the last time you took a punch?'

There was an awkward silence while I recalled a sharp shot that had rattled my teeth not six months earlier in prison.

'He was in prison,' Amanda sniffed. I choked on my answer, coughed into my fist.

'Prison?' Sam laughed.

'She's joking,' I said. 'She means I'm from Sydney, and the streets are rough down there. That's all she means.'

'A Sydney man!'

'I am.'

'Well, welcome to 1945, Mr Collins.' Sam waved an arm to show me the land beyond the doors. 'Where fags and ethnics are the punching bag of choice for the violent drunk at the corner pub.'

'So Jake felt comfortable enough to express himself in this small community of gay men?' Amanda asked. 'He felt safe with you guys?'

'Physically and emotionally.'

'You saw him as his true self.'

'I feel like I did,' Sam said.

'How long were you together?'

'I've known Jake for about twenty years.'

'Longer than his wife, then.' I looked at Amanda.

'Yes.'

'Why did he marry Stella if he was so comfortable in your group?'

'Oh, he always had his pretend life. He'd established it long before he married Stella.' Sam sipped his drink, gazed at the horizon. 'It wasn't as though he left us to go marry her and set up the heterosexual family man facade. He'd always carried that on. His parents were big church people, and he'd maintained girlfriends throughout high school and his early working life. His dad was some government pen-pusher and he'd been set to follow. He met Stella, and she was either blind to what he was in his other life or she just ignored it. We all had that double life happening. It's Cairns. You have to protect yourself.'

'Right.'

'He started getting into the underground gay scene through a writers' group. He met my friend Clive there, and after we met, I realised Clive knew him. Jake was writing vampire porn.' Sam gave a sad laugh. 'He'd read it to me over the phone. I was pretending I could write as well but I was mainly doing it because I had a crush on him.'

'When was this?'

'Mid-nineties,' Sam said.

'And he was just going back and forth between his pretend world and you guys?' I asked.

'I think he used to tell people we were golfing buddies,' Sam grinned. 'I've never seen the guy golf in his life. I don't think he even knows which end of the club to use.'

I felt Amanda nudging me. I ignored her.

'And then he wrote that book,' Sam sighed. 'He was gone then. He'd locked the door on himself in that other world, and thrown the key out of his own reach.'

'What do you mean by that?' Amanda asked.

'Jake had written a few books before *Burn* that were never published,' Sam said. He pushed back his shirtsleeves. 'I think he wrote *Burn* as sort of a joke. He was very enamoured by apocalyptic novels, and there he was having stories about the Rapture crammed down his throat every Sunday as he sat beside Stella in church. I don't think he ever expected the book to have the reaction it did. But some big preacher in the US picked it up, one of those churches that fills football stadiums with believers. The ones who bomb abortion clinics. Christian soldiers. Suddenly it was being shown on morning evangelical television over there. Every major Christian denomination could take something from it – the extreme ones and the casual ones. They fucking loved it. It was massive. You know how those Americans are when they find something they like.'

'Wow.'

'Yeah.' Sam gulped the remains of his drink. 'Wow. It was just a fucking riot in the beginning, all of it. We all sat around and laughed about it. Jake had bought himself a convertible. A black . . . Jaguar, I think it was. And this is a guy whose shoulders drop three inches from around his ears when he walks into a room full of gay men. He was the biggest pretender I'd ever met, but before the first book he'd always been able to walk away from that. Then, the money. That book brought Jake money he'd never dreamed of. Never seen. It got serious. He had to keep going. Camera crews were setting up in his house, interviewing his parents, following him to church.'

Sam looked at his fingernails.

'In the beginning, if someone had found out about Jake's life here with us, he'd have been shunned, I suppose. Stella might have left him. And his parents might have given him a mouthful. But after that book, if people had found out what Jake was really like, there'd have been real trouble. Serious trouble.'

'Do you think what happened to Jake might have been a consequence of someone finding out that he was gay? Whether it was Stella finding out or someone else?'

Sam thought. He got up, stretched his arms above his head. 'Stella? I don't know. Someone else? Look, he had some pretty devoted fans. Some of the letters he got were weird. I don't know if he ever kept any of them.'

'Weird how?'

'Oh, Christian weird.' Sam laughed. He wandered into the kitchen. 'You know the shit that they go on with. Jake being a messenger of God. Stuff in the books being real. Imminent. He had one guy write in and ask him about his main characters, Adam and Eve. The kid insisted they were real teenagers and wanted to know where he could contact them. People were convinced Jake knew something about God that no one else knew because of the stuff he was writing.

'But he wasn't some sort of messenger. He was just taking shit right out of the Bible and reinventing it for a young audience. Adding guns. And explosions. They couldn't understand that they were just being fed the same stuff they'd been fed all their lives from their church, from their parents. It felt familiar, and it felt good, and they got hooked. The whole world got hooked. People were writing to him from Osaka. From Madrid, for Christ's sake. It wasn't a divine message. It was plagiarism, at best.'

'What was Jake like the last time you saw him?' I asked.

Sam sliced a lime carefully, his eyes downcast to his work. He thought for a long time.

'He was going a bit strange,' Sam said finally. 'The last few months. He was getting into the coke a bit too much – which was fine, I mean we all got into it a bit too much when we got together, which was getting rarer and rarer. But I got the feeling he was doing it regularly, not just when he was here. He'd said years ago that it helped him write faster. Stay focused.'

'Was he stressed? Worried?'

'I don't know. Maybe. He was finding time to get away from it all to come hang out with us, but when he did, he didn't stay long and he couldn't relax. He just seemed busy to me, not necessarily stressed. Extremely busy. All he could talk about was drafts and edits and new books and movie deals. He'd made some bad decisions, and then tied all his money up with the house and the kid's schooling. So he was cash-poor. And I think he was spending that cash in the wrong places.'

'What makes you say that?'

'He was on the phone for about three-quarters of the time he was here, last time he visited,' Sam said. 'I had an ex-boyfriend like that. I can smell a problem gambler from eight miles out. It's the coke that makes you like that, if you do it regularly enough. You start to get restless. And maybe he wanted to be the naughty boy a bit more regularly than he was.

151

It took a lot of time out of his schedule to drive up here and meet with us all. Maybe having a couple of little habits on the side made him feel like he was still winning. That the facade hadn't completely caged him.'

'Right.'

'Part of what I was texting him about the night he went missing was all of that business. I eased my way in with the casual check-in type stuff, but I was really snooping. Trying to find out if he was okay. I can show you the texts. I wanted him to know that if he got really worried, I'd lend him cash. They say never to lend friends money. But. You know.' He shrugged.

I sat back, put my arm over the end of the couch. Amanda shifted away from my hand where it hung near her arm. 'Do you know what exactly Jake was betting on?'

'He liked the horses, the dogs. Chance events, nothing that required much skill on the part of the gambler, like poker. Poker, you win, it's your doing. Horses, you win, it's divine intervention. God's hand pushing the animal along.'

'Did he say who his bookie was? Were his bookie and his dealer the same person?'

'No idea,' Sam said. 'I wish I knew.'

As Amanda sat clearing up the details with Sam, I took a phone call on the balcony from a number I didn't know. A heat haze lingered over the flat city, blurring my view of the rainforest at the edges of suburbia. I found myself smiling when I recognised the crackly voice on the other end.

'Mr Conkaffey.'

'Dr Gratteur,' I laughed. 'To what do I owe the pleasure?'

'I wish I had something pleasurable to offer you, but

152

unfortunately I'm calling to inform you that you've got a journalist on your tail,' she said. 'If you didn't know already.'

My heart sank. 'I did know.' I glanced warily at the two on the couches. 'Pretty brunette, right?'

'Right.'

'What's she doing talking to you?'

'Retracing your steps, it seems.' I heard the rumble of something in the background, a gurney being pushed past. 'Trying to find out if you're working cases.'

'You didn't –'

'Of course I bloody didn't,' Valerie scoffed. 'But I did give her a piece of my mind. I drew out the dusty old files of what was once a very profane teenage vocabulary. I was expelled from two high schools for that sass-mouth.'

'I don't doubt it. How'd she take that?'

'With the faux shock and horror of someone less important than they appear.'

'I love your work, Doctor.'

'If you get yourself in trouble,' she said, 'reach out, all right?'

'I will,' I told her. 'Thanks.'

The truth is, you never know who is going to be your ally. And when you've hit rock bottom, you'll take any outreached hand, no matter how staunchly you ever protested that you wouldn't.

I'd been in Silverwater for three months when I got into my first fight.

I looked exactly like a guy named Robert Fittich, who was in protective segregation because he was very effeminate, and had been targeted with sexual advances a number of times in general population remand. From behind, we were identical – the same broad shoulders and short, black curls, the same loping walk and big hands. From the front, Robert's face was longer and he was missing his two front teeth, and while my eyes were a dark blue his were chocolate brown. A number of times I'd wandered into the peripheral vision of guards or other inmates and been called 'Bobby'. The resemblance was so strong that another inmate had grabbed me by the arm one time and whispered about an upcoming shakedown, his eyes darting everywhere, only to land on my face and reveal I wasn't the intended recipient of the tip. I'd taken the warning with gratitude, however, and shuffled on the bits and pieces of contraband I'd been hoarding.

The problem was that Robert Fittich was getting regular oxycodone doses for back pain. Oxy is a very popular drug among heroin users behind bars who no longer have access to their drug of choice. They try to get prescriptions to take the edge off their prison detox. A guy everybody called 'Corgi' had been muscling Fittich for his oxy pills. Fittich would tongue the pill and give it to Corgi, and Corgi wouldn't beat him half to death. That was the usual arrangement, anyway. For all I knew, Fittich might have been using the oxy to pay for television privileges or Mars bars.

Fittich was transferred out one night, I don't know where. He simply disappeared. That was how it went. Charges against him might have been dropped suddenly, or he might have been called up to trial. That very morning Corgi, a wide-eyed, bobble-headed veteran junkie with no teeth at all in his upper jaw, started hassling me for oxycodone.

'I'm Ted Conkaffey,' I told him. 'You're looking for Bobby Fittich.'

Corgi told me that he was going to pull my fucking eyes out. Which would have sounded like a terrifying, unnecessarily gruesome punishment, one that might strike fear into the hearts of any ordinary man, if I hadn't heard it a hundred times already. Everybody in prison has their token threat, and the pulling out of the eyes was pretty banal as they went. 'I'm gonna kill you' just doesn't cut it in Silverwater. No one's afraid of dying.

But Corgi had it in his mind that I was Bobby Fittich. To him, there had never been two of us tall, black-haired lugs in C Pod. And when he came to me, three mornings in a row, asking for his oxy in increasingly aggressive tones, I began to worry that he might try to make good on his threat.

I didn't have to wonder long. On the fourth morning Corgi punched me square in the nose with all the force in his small body as I was coming around the corner of the chow hall. I was flattened instantly.

As an ex-street cop and a veteran on the drug squad, I know how to fight. But the surprise ambush caught me off guard, and the first shot totally crushed my nose, causing so much ruby-red blood to gush out of my head that for seconds I was tied up just dealing with that. My eyes sprouted tears, and in those terrible blind seconds Corgi jumped on my back and started punching the rear of my skull in rapid-fire blows.

A simultaneous fight at the other end of the chow hall had distracted the guards. This is how prison riots start. One fight inspires another, and because in those frantic moments when guards have to decide which fight they'll throw themselves into first, both parties can get blows in. Sometimes the guards are so distracted by the two fights that they fail to notice who, exactly, is involved in them. Get three fights going at once and people can die before anyone has a chance to do anything. On this morning, the guards all went for the other fight on the distant side of the hall. I was alone.

The hand that reached down to me in the fray belonged to Christopher Shine, an ex-firefighter who was awaiting trial on sexual assault charges on young boys dating back to before I was even born. He was a tough old guy with big arms who I knew carried a shank.

I took his hand.

I drove back to Crimson Lake along the cane-lined highways thinking about my wife, and how she'd left me. I wondered if it was fair to say that. Since my incarceration for a crime I didn't commit I'd been trying to think more openly about right and wrong, innocence and guilt and things like abandonment, and if I was trying to be as fair as possible I wasn't sure Kelly had left 'me'.

She'd received a call from Frankie one morning while she was at mothers' group, telling her to come in to the station, where she'd been sat down and told that her husband had abducted, raped and strangled a thirteen-year-old girl and left her for dead. Frankie, Davo, Morris, my friends, our weekend barbecue buddies – they didn't tell her I'd been accused of this horrific act. They told her I'd committed it. They really believed that. They'd been on the ground when the reports of the sightings of my car started coming in. They were almost as devastated as Kelly was about it.

Was it possible that I'd died then to Kelly? That I'd ceased to be the Ted she knew and had instead become Rapist Ted, someone she didn't know at all?

As always, just when I started to get a hold of the idea of forgiving Kelly, I found my knuckles were white on the steering wheel and my throat was hoarse. I missed my child. And even trying to tiptoe into the waters of that great dark lake snapped me out of my reverie. I shook my arms, rolled my shoulders and set my mind on the road ahead of me. I didn't have time to think about Lilly. It would cripple me.

My task was to pick up any evidence I could find of Jake's gambling debts or creepy fans from his wife, but before I could reach the house, I spied Jake's son Harrison sitting in a car half a block away. I picked out the silhouette of his beanie against the windscreen. I drove past and looked in on him and a similarly gothic-looking girl in the beat-up grey Datsun, both smoking. She might have been the girl from the lake, but I didn't get a good look at her. Harrison's buckled boot was hanging out the passenger-side window, tapping to music. I don't know how he found a beat in what was coming out of the car radio. As I went past with my window down, the music emitted a toneless roar of white noise.

I went around the block, and by the time I got back Harrison was heading towards the house, the girlfriend and her car gone, a paperback in his hand. He stopped when he saw me. I knew the cover of the book from my own teenage years. His eyes shot away almost as soon as they fell on me. The cocky, angry Harrison was back, and he was pissed that he'd showed me his vulnerable side, that he'd let me touch him. I didn't mind. I could play this game. Good cop, bad cop, soft kid, tough kid. I'd adapt to what he wanted.

'Oh, fuck off,' he moaned, trying to push past me.

'Your dad writes Christian fiction, so you read early Anne

Rice,' I said. I held my hands up. 'The forces of the universe become balanced.'

'Whatever,' the boy said. He went for the house. I caught up to him with my long strides.

'You're not being as rebellious as you think,' I said. 'She had a spiritual transformation recently. Her latest stuff is more in tune with –'

'Dude, why are you talking to me?' Harrison turned and lasered me in the face with his gaze. 'Anyone ever tell you the help should be seen and not heard?'

'The help?' I laughed. The kid was pretty quick. I was sure the smart mouth was more than a teenager's anger and incomprehension at losing his father. I heard the defensive bitterness of a schoolyard bullying victim in his voice. Maybe the recipient of too much parental funding and not enough parental love. His catalogue of comebacks seemed far too convenient. 'I'm here to see your mother. Is she home?'

'No.' He unlocked the door. 'So fuck –'

Stella pulled open the door as Harrison was pushing it forward, causing the boy to stumble. For a moment, mother and son were almost chest to chest, and despite the dark hair and pathetic goatee I could see the resemblance between them: short, lean creatures, their pointy faces and big eyes. Harrison slipped past her and flipped me the bird as he trudged up the stairs.

'I saw your car,' Stella said.

'Sorry, I should have called.'

'Not at all, Mr Collins. I love surprises.' She touched my arm by way of invitation and closed the door behind me.

'I'm,' – I inhaled, feeling awkward – 'I'm sorry for your loss, Stella.'

She looked at the ground for exactly three beats. It was almost as though she was counting them off in her head. The appropriate sombre pause.

'Anything I can help you with, or are you just checking up on me?'

'I'm here to have a squiz at Jake's paperwork,' I said. 'I'm looking for fan letters in particular. Do you know if he kept any?'

'Oh, *boring*.' She laughed hard. I began to analyse her walk as she led me through the foyer, towards the big sunroom where we'd first sat together. Was she drunk? I glanced at the clock. It was midday. I smiled at myself. Here I was going around keeping watch over the people of Cairns and their intoxication levels, balancing them against the time of day. I recalled the hot, wobbly moments Woman had come into my life, how difficult it had been trying to get the box of terrified geese into the back of my car. How I'd paused by the driver's door, bent double, wondering if I was going to vomit. Was it the birds that had got me sober, or was it Amanda? Here I was, also, calling myself sober. It had been mere days. And the smell of bourbon on Mrs Scully was making my shoulders tighten with desire. I was a joke.

She led me into the dead man's office and went away, came back after a while with the crystal decanter. I watched her with one eye as I rifled through Jake's drawers. She went in and out a few times, setting up a kind of picnic on the floor before the huge oak desk. Two glasses, the bourbon, some soft cheeses and expensive-looking crackers. My hunger for the spread grew in direct proportion to my trepidation at sitting on the floor and sharing it with her. I fantasised about her leaving the room again and my locking the door behind her.

Jake's papers were in a terrible mess. Classic creative type. It would take hours to organise them. I picked up things on the desk and shifted them from one side to another. Royalty statements. Cover design options in various colours and fonts. There was a large stack of printed pages bound with huge bulldog clips, an unfinished new manuscript. I flipped through, fanning my face with the paper, looking at Jake's little pencil notes to himself in the margins. I let the heavy manuscript *whump* onto the table where I had found it, the air unsettling some Post-it notes littered around the pencil tin, making them flap like feathers.

'Come have a break, detective,' Stella said.

I imagined Harrison in the upstairs bedroom, fuming, replaying that moment when his mother pulled open the door and he stumbled in front of the man he was challenging. I imagined a hundred other exchanges between the boy and his father, the big-league writer and his useless, rudderless, moody son. His typical teenage son, coming down to settle the score with the stranger-man hanging around his mother.

'I've got payment slips for advances. I've got bookshop appearance schedules. I've got . . .' I squinted at one of the sheets before me. 'Editorial notes. Any idea where he kept his fan letters?'

'I said, come. And have. A break.' Her coldness convinced me that if I didn't join her she would snap somehow. Emotionally or physically.

I went and sat awkwardly on the carpet beside her, plucked up a chip. My crunching sounded obnoxiously loud. She was wearing a dark blue cotton dress this time. Off-the-shoulder on one side, more of a complicated wrap that tangled prettily at her waist. Grecian goddess picking at grapes, bored.

My face felt hot. I gulped half a glass of bourbon. It felt like a surrender.

'Was Jake a gambling man?' I asked.

'He liked a wager.'

'Do you think he was getting to like it at a dangerous level?'

'Let's not talk about Jake.'

'Jake is why I'm here, Mrs Scully. He's the only reason I'm here.'

She laughed and made a drunken, dismissive sound with her full lips, which made me wonder if she was challenging my manhood, trying to get me to stand up to this dead and digested husband of hers who didn't want her but wouldn't let her be free. 'No one comes to Crimson Lake for work. You come here to hide or you come here to die.'

Stella ran the back of her hand up my arm. Patted the hairs against the grain, made me shiver.

'What are you hiding from?' She smiled. Her fingers on the inside of my elbow were almost painful, they were so gentle, so warm.

'Nothing,' I sighed. 'I haven't . . . I'm not . . .'

'Liar,' she whispered. 'Liar, liar, liar.'

In one smooth movement, she extended a bronze leg from the dress, slid it over my lap and slipped onto me, straddling my legs, her hips against mine. She smoothed my hair back from my forehead and breathed her bourbon perfume onto my lips.

She didn't kiss me right away. She pressed her warm forehead against mine and gathered up my hands, then put them on her waist.

'Oh god,' I said. I squeezed my eyes shut.

'I've been alone for so long,' she murmured.

I felt myself smiling at that. The morning of That Day was the last time anyone had touched me with any real desire or intimacy. That morning, at eight, I'd made love to my wife in the bedroom of our little suburban love nest, and then we'd fought, and I'd gone out 'fishing' but more accurately 'doing anything' to get away from her while she wailed at me from the middle of her bubble of helpless agony, First Baby terror. I'd watched her long enough rolling around in that cruel sphere that simultaneously protected her from anyone else under-standing her pain and guarded her from any outside assistance.

Since then I'd been hugged stiffly in consolation an amount of times I could count on my fingers, and I'd been bashed a couple of times more. Aside from being shuffled and led around by guards, I'd not been touched at any other time, and I was acutely aware of it. And now the beautiful and sinful Stella Scully was rocking her hips against mine and I was breathing against her neck and listening to the sound of her expensive cotton fabric moving against my gooseshit-stained jeans like it was the song of an ocean siren.

And then suddenly, through that glorious music, there came the voice of none other than the prosecutor in my trial.

You, a man in excess of six feet tall, one hundred and ten kilos of police-trained muscle. You picked that little girl up off the side of the road like she was a sack of potatoes and you threw her strug-gling body into your car . . .

I snapped my hands back from Stella's waist. My breath was caught in my chest.

'What is it?'

'Nothing,' I choked. I released all the air in my lungs. 'Nothing. It's okay.'

Where did that come from? I watched my big hands running over Stella's small shoulders. She was unbuttoning my shirt. Her warm, thin fingers pushing the fabric off my shoulders, kissing my neck. I gathered up a handful of her hair, tried to stay with her, the smell of her, the taste of her lips on my mouth. Why was I thinking about my trial, now of all times? When her fingers were on me, her nails running up through my hair, just when everything felt so good and so right. There into the warmth and dream came the echo of the courtroom, the whine of the microphones and the glare of the angry crowd.

'Oh, god,' Stella whispered. 'Ted. Please.'

'Please, please, please!' she begged you. 'Please don't hurt me!' she cried. But you had no mercy for her, did you, Mr Conkaffey? You drove some five full minutes with that child in the back of your car and you ignored her cries, her pleas for her mother . . .

I broke away from Stella, pushed her down underneath me, onto the rug. I swept the tray of snacks out of the way, knocked over my glass, shook my head, tried to keep my eyes on her. Stella yelped when my fingers got tangled in her hair. I laughed, apologised, pushed the wayward strands from her face.

'Stella,' I said. 'Stella. Stella. Stella.'

I tried to remind myself I was here with Stella. I was not . . .

. . . in that dark and dense bushland by the side of the highway, where you dragged the child kicking and crying from your car. And you dumped her on the bare earth like an animal, didn't you, Ted? And like an animal you tore off her clothes and you . . .

'No!' I cried. 'No! No! No!'

I was standing by the windows looking out at the lawn, my palms pressing into the sides of my head, my breath clouding the glass in front of me in painful huffs. I couldn't inhale but for what felt like the top inch of my lungs, the rest of my chest solid, filled with concrete. I gripped at my hair. 'No.'

'What the hell is wrong with you?' Stella asked.

My hands moved of their own volition, dragging down my ears, gripping at the top of my throat, squeezing. I scratched at my face, tried to claw out the visions flashing before me. Little girl on the bare earth. Little girl crying. I turned to look at Stella and found her staring at me, her face twisted in disgust. The top of her dress was unclipped at the shoulder and flopped over her waist. Her brown breasts were bared, and she was rapidly covering them up, blocking them from me with her arms.

'Get out,' she snapped.

I hesitated, trying to think of something, anything, to say.

'Get out!' she screamed.

I left.

Dear Jake,

I wonder where these letters go. They're obviously not going to you. I know you're not the kind of guy who would just accept letters from people who are devoted to you and toss them out like rubbish. Maybe they're going to that selfish piece of shit agent of yours. Hi, Cary! Mind passing this on to Jake? I got your rejection letter – really heartfelt. Thanks, mate. I'm not mad; I get it. Working with someone with so much talent must make you bitter. Make you feel like the pretender you are. Well, just remember, Cary, no matter how much you pretend, you'll never have what Jake has. Let it go. Give the man the praise he deserves.

Jake, if this ever gets to you, I wanted to tell you I saw you on *BookWeek Live*. I'd planned to go to the Cairns filming but I chickened out. Can you believe that? I just got so worked up about seeing you in the flesh, talking to you, that I stayed home, and by the time the event was over I was devastated.

The way you write about your characters, I can see that each of them is some part of you. There's Adam in you – his strength and resolve, his determination not to let any harm come to Eve. She's there within you too, Jake. Her sensitivity.

Her mistrust of the world. It's the part of her in you that I recognise the most. I can see that while she's bound with her secrets, you too are harbouring secrets of your own. How else could you know so perfectly how it feels to be the outcast, to be the one wearing the mask? Writers write because they want to create safe places. Safe worlds. I totally understand.

I get the world you've created in your books. You're unveiling the human nastiness and darkness we see every day in this country. The piggery and selfishness and greed. People are so willing to criticise each other, so ready to point out what's different and what's lacking, and they can't see through to the goodness and the talent in people who aren't beautiful and powerful and perfect. Sometimes I just marvel at people's mindlessness, their lack of civility. Sitting on the bus I look around at them, at their drooling mouths and glazed eyes. They're not like us. They don't *think*. They're miscreants. They're beasts.

I know I'm just a fan, a stranger, but I want you to know, Jake, that I can be that safe place for you to divulge your secret pains, the ones you obviously hold so tightly to your chest, lest they be taken up by the savages around us. I'm completely separate from your life – and most importantly, I respect you, Jake. I write to escape my own stupid life. You spoke on *Wake Up, America!* about feeling like an outsider at university here in Australia. Like no one understood you but your teachers. I get you, Jake. We're the same. If only you knew it. You'd feel glad you finally found me.

I've included something I've been writing lately – my own work, but it has ties to yours. It's just the first few pages of a manuscript I've been outlining about the end of the world, a world just as corrupted and desperate as the one you write about. I've included some of the landscapes and characters you use in your books. If it ends up getting published, maybe it could sell as a tie-in. I don't care if Cary reads it or not. You're better than that guy, Jake. I'm telling you.

Give my love to Stella and Harrison.

It was a tired and frazzled Ted who knocked on the door of the Beale Street office at ten the next morning. I'd had a restless night mentally replaying the incident with Stella, haunted by the things I'd thought while we touched. I hadn't had so much as a whiff of anything sexual since the morning I left home on the day that ruined my life, and now the mere suggestion of it was infected with the horrific things I'd heard at my trial. Those things I was accused of. There was a monster Ted, a me who was not me, who was very real in the minds of everyone who had attended the court. There was a very finely rendered fictitious monster Ted who savaged a small girl, who used his body as a huge and hideous weapon against her. That monster Ted wanted me to know he was still hanging around. The prosecution had created him, given him life. A taste of the world. That demon liked it here, above ground. He'd decided to stay.

I was afraid of that Ted. He'd played with my mind so easily in Jake's office. I was out of control. The images he was showing me felt real.

On the front porch that morning, I'd found a cardboard box. Wary it might be a present from the vigilantes, I'd lifted the lid off with a stick from the front yard, only to find it was filled with paperwork. Stella must have called Amanda to get my address. There were fan letters, and a thick, bound printout of Jake's bank account statement going back six months. Jake's wife might have seen something in me she didn't like – maybe felt rejected by me – but she still wanted her husband's case solved. On the morning news, they'd announced the medical examiner's ruling that Jake Scully was dead. I'd watched the brief report in the living room with my coffee, standing in my tracksuit pants and bare feet. Two goslings had wandered in through the open doors and decided the hairs on my big toes were food. They stood plucking hopelessly at them, trying to free them from the skin.

To get her life insurance money, Stella Scully would need to be able to prove Jake didn't kill himself, and she'd need the Queensland Police investigation into his death closed. Those were the only two things in the way of her payment.

Amanda opened the door wearing Batman pyjama pants and a singlet that read 'Do Not Disturb'. Four rotund felines stood around her, curious to know who was calling.

'You're not a morning person, are you?' I said. Her hair was all pushed over to one side like a freak gust of wind had taken it.

'Get in here,' she said.

I walked into a growing crowd of knee-high furry beasts, being careful not to step on any tiny toes. The room I entered was a large office with an L-shaped desk covered in stacks of paper. I put the box down on the desk and led the cats to the corner of the room, where a group of certificates was hung. Amanda's Private Investigator's licence, as well as some certificates endorsed by Brisbane Women's Correctional Facility. She'd completed her final year of high school behind bars, as well as some courses in martial arts. I raised my eyebrows.

Above the Investigator's licence was a certificate for completing an Alcoholics Anonymous program.

'I didn't know you were in AA,' I said. I'd considered joining after my first couple of weeks out of prison, but didn't like the idea of being recognised in a small group setting. Amanda was clattering things around in the kitchen. Half of the cats had followed her and the other half were rubbing themselves against my calves.

'I didn't have a problem. I hardly drink,' she said. 'I just did the course.'

'Why?' I laughed.

'You get commissary points for courses you complete at Brisbane Women's. Any courses. Those courses on the wall were the ones I found interesting. The rest are there.' She waved her hand at a stack of more certificates on the second shelf of the bookcase. I went and leafed through them. She'd completed courses in literature, biology, landscape design and psychology. There were dozens of certificates.

'You play trumpet?' I scoffed.

'I can also crochet an afghan blanket; a skill I've found incredibly useful in my everyday life.'

'This is hilarious.'

'Are you finished going through my stuff?' She had her back to me, pouring milk into two coffee mugs. A huge black cat had sprung up onto the counter beside her. She shooed the animal with her elbow as she poured.

'Get down, Nine. Nine!'

The cat persisted. She put the milk down and lifted the animal onto the floor.

'Nine?'

Amanda yawned. She pointed to the cats in turn.

'Nine. Four. Seven. That fat saggy one there is One. She's the dirty hussy who started it all.' She nudged one of the cats with her foot, a tabby who was thinner and older-looking than the rest. 'You'll discover she's a bad *mother*. Her *brother* was another *lover*, an *undercover mover* and *groover* trying to *out-manoeuvre* the other *fat cats* on his *patch*.'

'I'll take your word for it.'

'Not a lot of words rhyme with mother,' Amanda sighed reflectively. She gave me my coffee. 'What's in the box?'

'Fan letters,' I said. 'I've had a brief look, but nothing sticks out for me. A lot of it is very praising. *I love you. I love your characters. I usually read this and that, you remind me of this author and that author.*'

'Anyone accusing him of being a messiah?'

'Oh, there are a couple dripping with Bible passages.'

'No mention of feeding him to saltwater crocodiles, though.'

'Nothing that I saw. But I didn't look that closely.'

'What does the Bible say about crocodiles?' she wondered aloud. She sat down at her computer and started clicking. The cats were circling my chair like round, furry sharks, mewling for attention.

'Oh crap, there are heaps.' Amanda scrolled through the pages. 'Leviticus reckons you can't eat crocodiles because they're unclean. *Now these are to you the unclean among the swarming things which swarm on the earth: the mole, and the mouse, and the great lizard in its kinds, and the gecko, and the crocodile, and the lizard, and the sand reptile, and the chameleon.*'

'Well I'm screwed. I had three sand reptiles for breakfast.'

'No eating them, and no mating them to other animal species,' Amanda said.

'What? What the hell am I supposed to do with them then?'

'Just leave them alone, Ted.'

I folded my arms.

'In Exodus it talks about the Egyptians being in dread of the children of Israel, who were multiplying and growing mighty. The Pharaoh calls on all his people to throw Israel's newborn sons into the river.' She took on a man's voice as she read from the screen. '*Drown the Hebrew babies! Feed them to the crocodiles!*'

'Doesn't say anything about secretly gay authors,' I concluded.

'It does not,' she said. 'When Leviticus talks about man lying with man as he lies with woman, it says that he should be put to death, but it doesn't describe how.'

'This guy just didn't want anyone doing anything,' I concluded. 'I'm sure he was a real treat at dinner parties.'

'What else have you got there?'

'There's a six-month bank statement.' I showed her the pages. 'I haven't looked at it yet.'

'Well, you start going through that. I'm putting together some passages from the Chronicles books that I want to show you.'

I leant on the desk and started highlighting patterns in spending. Jake had a membership to a tiny gym at James Cook University that he paid fortnightly. I drew a thick black line through all of those, his phone and electricity bills, countless purchases at 7-Eleven and Woolworths for weekly groceries. In the month before he died, he'd bought a new keyboard online, a bunch of stationery and something from Workplace Health Online. I took the code from the purchase and punched it into Google on my phone. It was a shoulder brace to prevent slouching. Occupational hazard of an author, I imagined.

The pages in front of me were steadily turning black. There was one transaction that caught my eye, a very irregular debit to an account without a description. A personal account. I highlighted it in pink.

After the substantial royalty checks that came into the account from his agent, Cary Minnow, Jake would send an amount to the mystery account. Sometimes the amounts were very large. Sometimes they were small. They were always whole numbers. I explained the pattern to Amanda.

'The amount he's transferring isn't a regular percentage of the royalty he's putting away for tax?'

I looked at the numbers. 'No. Sometimes it's about ten per cent. Sometimes it's half. A month before he disappeared he sent nearly all the royalty payment to the mystery account. And the mystery account doesn't look like it's one of his. He has two short-term deposits and this everyday.'

'What are his savings like?'

'Pretty close to the wind for someone getting this kind of income.'

Amanda strummed her fingernails on the desk. She scratched at the scary rabbit tattoo on her hand.

'The payments are getting steadily bigger though?'

'They are.'

'If he's paying a loan shark,' she said, 'the guy might have recognised he's onto a cash cow and started steadily increasing the interest. If Jake was hooked right before he died he might have been borrowing cash to spend on games and sending the repayments back through his account.'

'But why would they kill him?' I asked. 'If he's a cash cow, and he's still making payments?'

'It's a pretty unsustainable relationship, loan shark and client. Only one person really has any fun. Maybe Jake wanted out, who knows?'

'We will, soon.'

'Let me read you these,' she said, opening Jake's second novel, *Whisper*. 'There are passages in the books, beginning in number two and continuing in books three and four, which don't really belong in the narrative. At least that's what I think. Whenever the main character Adam is alone, he starts feeling like there's a . . . a *thing* after him.'

'Go for it,' I said. One of the cats, a heavy black and white bundle of fat, stopped circling and leapt up onto my lap. It stretched along my leg, purring deeply. Amanda started to read from the book.

It's a creature without shape, a shadow that follows, always at my heels, stretching and yawning as the day draws on. It never increases its pace, but wanders silently as though on a string, this needful thing, and it gobbles up the bits of me I leave behind. Blood, thoughts, sins. I do not know where it came from, but I turn every few steps and try to discern if it is closer, and I toss and reel in terror in the night that one day I will see it closing in.

'Sounds unpleasant,' I said. Amanda switched books and started reading from *Rise*.

Sometimes I can ignore it. But it knows me, and it loves me, and a part of me feels guiltily hungry for that love. Isn't that why I have come so far? Because in a strange way I am addicted to the light that falls on me, the light that leads this Mephistopheles creature to follow, and I'm afraid that if I hid from it in the darkness I'd never find a way back to the warmth of that mountaintop glow.

'Mephistopheles. I know that name from somewhere.' I frowned. Amanda sat staring at me with her arms folded, her chin gently jutting with rhythmic twitches. 'I feel like I've heard that name before.'

'So do I.' She tapped the keys of the computer.

'Something's hunting Adam but he kind of likes it. Or at least, he doesn't do anything about it,' I said. Another cat leapt into my lap, fighting for space with the first one.

'Adam likes *the warmth* and *the glow*, which to me might be a metaphor for the giddy feelings Jake gets from his addiction,' Amanda said.

'Right.'

'In his last book, *Rapture*, he writes about the thing that's following him being so close now that he knows he's going to fall into its embrace.' She pointed to a passage in the book beside her as she scrolled through Google with her other hand. *'I've done this to myself. Flirted with glory. And now that lurching beast has come as the clock winds down to receive his happy prize.'*

'I know this,' I said.

'Mr Mistoffelees is one of the characters in *Cats*, the musical,' she said.

'*Cats*?' I gasped theatrically, pointed to the creatures all around the apartment. 'It's you! You killed Jake!'

Amanda sighed dryly, imitating my usual response to her antics.

'No, the name rings a bell for another reason. The thing coming for the dude as the clocks wind down. Mephistopheles. It's a play. A Shakespeare play? *Doctor* . . .'

'*Doctor Faustus?*'

'That's the one! The guy sells his soul,' I said. It had been more than two decades since I'd been at high school. I was proud of my memory.

'Aren't you clever?' Amanda turned her computer monitor towards me. 'Take a look at this. It's not Shakespeare, it's Christopher Marlowe. But you were close.'

On the screen was an academic article published by the *Journal of Christian Literature*. The title read 'Hell is just a frame of mind: Christopher Marlowe's *The Tragical History of the Life and Death of Doctor Faustus* and the fiction of Jake Scully'.

'Someone should give me a certificate,' I said.

'The article compares the thing that follows Adam around in the books to the devil in *Doctor Faustus* coming back at midnight to claim Faustus's soul.' Amanda glanced over the article. 'Faustus sells his soul to Lucifer for power and pleasure for a period of . . . twenty-four years. Faustus gets one of the devil's messenger boys, Mephistopheles, as a personal servant in the deal. But Faustus doesn't really use his powers for anything special. He messes around a lot. A good angel tells him to repent before the devil can take his soul. He doesn't. Time runs out.'

'I think I liked that play.' The cats had settled, one curled against my stomach, one across my knees, hot weights on my thighs.

'The article seems to suggest both the play and Jake's books explore the theme of the idiot guy who doesn't really know the power he has, who wastes his influence and his gifts, and is stalked by something that's going to come get him. Faustus and Adam are both haunted.'

'And maybe Jake himself, if we're reading it correctly.'

'Says here there are two different versions of the play,' Amanda said. 'A 1604 version and a 1616 version. In one of them, the play says it's never too late if Faustus *can* repent. In the other, it says it's never too late if Faustus *will* repent.'

'So in one version he has the power to save himself. And in the other version he doesn't.'

'Right.'

'So which was it for Jake?' I asked.

'I don't know.' She waved at my phone. 'Let's do some ringing around and find out!'

I stared at my phone for a half an hour or so. Tried to count myself down to dialling and chickened out a bunch of times. Then I just bit the bullet and called. The phone rang, and when he picked it up, Davo sniffed loudly before he spoke. He used to do that in the old days. Habit. I felt strangely sad.

'Inspector David Birch.'

'Davo, it's Ted.'

There was a silence. I heard a chair creak.

'Sorry, who?'

'It's me. It's Ted.' I could hardly breathe. 'Mate, I'm up in Queensland. I'm calling because I –'

'What the fuck do you think you're doing, calling me?' Davo's voice was suddenly low. His breath rattling in the phone mic. 'What the . . . How dare you. You fucking piece of shit.'

'Dave,' I said. 'Please. Just hear me out, all right? I need your help. I'm working on –'

The phone went dead. The trick now was to call Morris before Davo called him and warned him off helping me in any way. My hands were shaking as I scrolled through my list of contacts.

'Inspector Morris Wakefield.'

'Morris, it's Ted. Please don't hang up. Please. I'm not trying to reconnect.'

'What –'

'I'm not trying to reconnect. I'm not trying to get back into your life. I'm not causing trouble, here, Morris. I've tried Davo. I just need one small thing.'

Another long silence, the sputtering of background noises. I waited for the click, the beeping. After a few seconds I chanced speaking again.

'I'm working with an investigator up here in Queensland,' I said carefully. 'We've taken on a missing persons case. I just need a quick look at the guy's bank accounts. That's all.'

'I don't want anything to do with you, Ted. I really don't.'

'I totally understand that,' I breathed. 'I do. And I've tried to respect your wishes until now.'

'I'll help you this one time, and then you never, never contact me again. Understand? Never again.'

'Thank you. Thanks, Morris, I –'

'What's the guy's name?'

'Jake Scully.'

'Date of birth?'

I gave it. I opened my mouth to say thank you again, but the line was dead.

When I told Amanda the owner of the mystery account Jake was frequently sending money to was one Llewellyn J. Bruce, she wasn't surprised at all. She kicked off her bike and began riding like she'd known all along where we were headed. I followed her to a dock on Thomatis Creek, where she piled into a flat-bottomed airboat like she owned it, leaving me to pay the weathered old dockman for its hire. Amanda sat in the front of the thing and I drove. I took us along the creek until we reached the open water, watching the wind rip through Amanda's hair, yanking her shirt back to reveal a great yellow rose tattoo on the back of her neck. Now and then she pointed, and I saw a fat, mud-brown body slither into the water from the banks, the creature gliding out, eyes only above the water, before sinking as we passed with just a bubble or two to indicate its presence.

We pulled up at another dock somewhere south-west of where we'd started, in an inlet that I guessed was near Yarrabah. Out on the ocean the waves crashed around Rocky Island Reef, a disturbance in the calm that drew seagulls from the cliffs sheltering the bay. Amanda waited for me for a moment before trudging off into the undergrowth so fast I had to jog to keep up.

'So you know this guy, then?' I asked.

'I know *of* him,' she said. 'Stay on the trail. We're in croc country.'

I followed her along a sandy path through the mangroves until I saw the beginnings of a clearing up ahead. Where a lagoon cut into the dense forest a little camp had been assembled, two large open steel boathouses filled with assorted junk, a scattering of plastic tables and chairs, a fire pit that had blackened the earth for some metres around. The sand here was grey and sad patches of grass gripped it here and there. A troupe of dogs rushed at us as soon as we arrived and barked us into the gathering of men.

I could see who Llewellyn Bruce was right away. The others, hard men with skin mottled black and blue with ancient tattoos that had been ravaged by the sun, stood back to allow him to see us. Bruce, the largest and most tattooed of the group, licked a set of badly crowded teeth in anticipation as he assessed us.

'Do you have an appointment?' Bruce asked as Amanda came to a stop in front of him. The gathering of men gave a chuckle around us. Amanda put her hand forward, and in a move that surprised me, Bruce shook it. I guessed it was the tattoos.

'I'm Amanda Pharrell, and this is Ted Collins,' Amanda said. 'We're here for a quick chat about –'

'Drugs,' Bruce said, pointing at Amanda's face.

'No.'

'Dogs,' someone near me said. I shook my head.

'Bikes,' said someone else.

'We're here about Jake Scully,' I told Bruce. His face fell, his white goatee sagging into the folds of his bronze face.

'Oh. Nothing interesting, then.' He started walking. The crowd dissipated. A majority of the men went back to a motorcycle by the nearest shed that was partly assembled. We followed Bruce to a makeshift bar by the fire pit. 'Boring, boring, boring. No one ever surprises me anymore. Unexpected visitors. Here I was thinking the boys had remembered my birthday and got me a stripper. Shoulda known you weren't no stripper. Look at your tiny tits.'

Amanda looked at her chest. Weighed her breasts in her hands.

'They're all right. There's a good handful to them.'

'Bee stings,' Bruce sighed.

'If we could get onto the matter of the day,' I said. 'We know Jake Scully was making regular payments to you from his everyday bank account, probably for repayment of a loan. Can you confirm for us that you loaned him money?'

'No,' Bruce said. He took a huge hunting knife from behind the bar and began wiping it clean with a dirty rag.

'So you didn't loan him money?'

'I didn't say that. All I said is I won't confirm that for you. Who are you two anyway?'

'Jake's wife hired us,' Amanda said. 'We're private dicks.'

'Oh, you're dicks all right.' Bruce sniggered at his own joke, looked at the blade in the light through the palm trees. 'You think you can just wander up here from the water and knock on my door any time of day? What kind of operation do you think this is?'

'You don't have a door,' Amanda said.

'Look, we're not interested in what kind of operation this is.' I pushed Amanda aside, away from the reach of the blade. 'Jake's missing, and that's what concerns us. We hope you can shed some light on what happened.'

'*Shed some light?*' Bruce pointed the knife at my chest. 'You're a cop.'

'I used to be,' I swallowed. 'Most private detectives have some law enforcement background.'

'You look familiar.' He flipped the knife a couple of times. He was taller than me. If I tried to run, I figured his stride would outreach mine. 'You're a cop, and you look familiar. This is getting worse and worse for you two.'

'If you tell us what we want to know, we'll get out of here. Really. We're not here to give you a hard time.'

'Guh,' Bruce grunted. He stuck the knife into his belt, looked down at the dogs gathered around him, sniffing at his crusty knees. 'What kind of birthday is this?'

He walked off towards the mangroves, the little posse of dogs following him. I fell in behind, glancing back at the camp, at the men sitting around the bike, smoking, drinking beer. The sandy path led deep into the mangroves, widening at a wooden pontoon that had been beached by the side of a creek. Bruce stood in the circle of dogs for a moment before reaching down and plucking up the lowest and the fattest of the lot by a roll of its neck, a chocolate-brown half-breed that was slowly going white all over. Before I could understand what was going on, he took the knife from his belt and stuck it into the dog. I felt Amanda jolt by my side. But none of us made a sound. Not us, not the dogs. Not Bruce. The dog in his grip went limp instantly.

'In through the armpit, up into the heart,' he said, withdrawing the blade. He wiped the blood on the dog. 'It's the kindest way.'

Amanda was jamming her elbow into my ribs. In the water, centimetres below the surface, a shape had appeared, the pale, almost yellow-brown of a large croc head reflecting the light from above. There was no telling how big the animal was from the muddy depths, but the head hovering there was as long as my arm. I pulled Amanda back towards me. I guessed I would have to throw her aside if the thing leapt at us.

'Thing belonged to an old farmer near here,' Bruce said. 'The old blokes can't do it. Can't take the sight of their eyes. So they bring them out to me. I don't mind doing it.'

He turned the dead dog in his hand so that its profile was facing us. I saw the tumour hanging from the hairless flesh of the dog's underbelly, a huge growth tucked along the inside of its leg. He tossed the dog into the water. The croc beneath the surface didn't move. The corpse floated, almost on top of the creature. It was still as a stone.

'Sometimes it takes 'im a while to taste the blood,' Bruce said. He watched the croc, the dog floating. 'They're dinosaurs, these things.'

A sudden surge, a splash, and the white jaws opened and snapped at the corpse on the surface of the water. The other dogs barked and snarled. There was a flick of a tail, and then the water settled, and all clues to the savagery that lay beneath drained away. The creek was calm.

'Jake Scully was killed by a crocodile,' Amanda said.

Bruce tucked his hands into his pockets, a sliver of grey hair falling across his eyes.

'Yeah? Well, wasn't me. I take care 'a people's dogs, and the foxes when I can get 'em. Foxes are nasty things. Scare a coop full of chickens to death if they can't get through the wire. Just hang around barking till they all up and die. What a cruel thing.'

I looked at the bubbles rising from the water. The dogs watching in silence.

'Have the police come out here and spoken to you?'

'They have.'

'Why didn't you tell us that?' I said.

'Because you didn't ask.'

'So you're already under suspicion.'

'Son, the last time I wasn't under suspicion for something it was 1952.'

We fell into silence. The wind whipped the rainforest around us.

'Back in the old days,' Bruce said, 'people said I disappeared a coupla troublesome lads here and there by way of the old Wetlands Garbage Disposal. That might have been true.

But not anymore. I'm not as angry as I used to be. It's not as therapeutic.'

'So what do you do now when your customers stop paying you?'

'They don't.'

'What?' I scoffed. 'Ever?'

'Because I spent so much time back in the old days getting bad clients in touch with the beauty of nature.' He smiled, gesturing to the marshland around him, the deadly beasts hiding within it. 'I don't need to do that now. That's how a retirement plan works, my friend. You do the hard work young, so you can sit back and smile when your ball hair starts to fall out.'

He gripped a handful of his crotch and gave it a shake. Amanda laughed hard.

'What a fucking badass,' Amanda said as she climbed back into the airboat.

I boarded and watched the dogs receding through the trees, the scruffy creatures having decided that we were on our way. They did not seem disturbed at all that their number was down by one. I wondered if they were clever enough, emotional enough, to contemplate which one of them was next.

'You say "badass" like it's a good thing,' I said.

'It is.'

'The man killed a dog in front of us.'

'It was a coup de grâce,' she said. 'You saw how the thing walked. It was in pain.'

'He should have taken it to a vet and had it put down. Better yet, its owner should have taken it to a vet.'

'Last time I went to the vet, I was taking Six to have her butt looked at. She had worms. The packet of worming tablets was twelve bucks. The diagnosis, which took three minutes, was eighty.'

I drove the airboat back along the mangroves, trying to penetrate them with my eyes, seeing only darkness. Amanda sat closer to me, quietly using me as a windshield now as the wind picked up, blowing the tops of waves over the tip of the bow.

'So what do you think?' I asked. 'Worth pursuing him? His M.O. is exactly what we're looking for,' I said.

'I don't think it was him,' Amanda called over the wind. 'He's a man who doesn't waste time. Practicality is his game. Minimal effort. He didn't make that dog suffer. The thing didn't make a sound, Ted. It didn't even know what happened.'

'What's your point?'

'My point is, that if we're right about Jake's books and the darkness that was following him, we can't be right about Llewellyn, too. Llewellyn wouldn't follow Jake. He wouldn't make him feel afraid. I'd be surprised if he's left that clearing in the last ten years.'

'Well, I disagree. I like him for it.' I shrugged. 'I think there are plenty of indicators pointing right at Bruce. The money. The mode of death. Loan sharks are intimidating by nature. Just because Bruce isn't the following and haunting type doesn't mean Jake didn't feel followed or haunted by some of Bruce's threats. Maybe we're reading too much into his books and not enough into the demonstration that man just gave us.'

'You pursue Bruce further if you want to.' Amanda waved at me. 'You can have the afternoon to kick it around. I'm not wasting my time.'

I looked over my shoulder at the approaching rain. There were Aboriginal men waist-deep in the water by the mouth of the creek, fearless, pulling up nets from the muddy bottom. They paused as we passed. The water had turned a dark iron grey, dabbed with white tips as the afternoon storm followed us back down the creek.

I was bad. Sneaky, underhanded. Just plain bad.

I didn't leave Amanda at the boat ramp to spend that afternoon exploring Llewelyn Bruce and his connection to Jake further. I drove straight home and sat out the front of my paint-splashed house reading *Murder in the Top End*, so desperate to get back to the story of Amanda's case that I didn't even get out of the car before plunging in. I knew I was being a terrible partner, but I couldn't get the book out of my mind. Sitting above her in the airboat driver's seat, looking at her gazing up at me with those big doll eyes, her colourful hands gripping the ropes at either side of her, hanging on. She was almost a bright little mermaid girl taking a ride on a fisherman's boat. The patterns and shapes all over her skin made her unreal somehow. A painted, poison frog.

Was she a monster?

When the sun began to set, I found myself driving to Kissing Point, an overgrown parking lot halfway up a mountain overshadowing Crimson Lake, the slope lush with wet rainforest. I parked in one of the spaces marked with flaking, patchy yellow paint and looked at the mist rolling down into the tiny town, the creek winding through the yellow expanse of cane stretching as far as the mangroves, and then the sea. The book led me like a voice as I walked back towards the narrow road. I crossed the road and walked down the mountain until I found an overgrown side road leading into the dark.

In a small clearing approximately one hundred metres from the main road down the mountain, the popular and beautiful Lauren Freeman, seventeen years old, parked her 1989 Hyundai Sonata with the rear facing the road. In the passenger seat sat Amanda Pharrell, having been picked up by Freeman at the school that afternoon. It is believed that both girls consumed one 275 ml bottle of raspberry-flavoured Vodka Cruiser pre-mix each. Freeman's cousin's bank account would show he had purchased the alcohol the night before on his underage relative's behalf. Freeman's autopsy would reveal a blood alcohol level of 0.02 at the time of her death.

In the back of the car lay a shopping bag from Myer, taped at the top, containing a folded woollen blanket. There were various items scattered throughout the car that one might expect to find in a vehicle belonging to a teenage girl – a tube of Rimmel brand mascara, some fast food wrappers, some receipts and an old black jumper.

Amanda admitted in her trial that the girls sat talking in the car for approximately ten minutes. It was not long after both girls exited the car that she began her attack. A light rain had only just begun to fall. Amanda took the knife and plunged it into Lauren's back in the first of nine stab wounds she then inflicted upon her friend. She then undressed, leaving her clothes by . . .

I stopped reading. She then undressed? I flipped forward to the photos and looked at the pile of clothes the police found in the brush a few metres from the car, Amanda's jeans and T-shirt, her crop top, panties, socks and shoes.

Had Amanda stabbed Lauren nine times, her clothes would have been soaked in blood. The T-shirt, spread out on a stainless steel lab table in the 'exclusive photographs' section of the book, was spotless. The book claimed that the blood was washed from Amanda's clothes by the rain.

But the clothes were in a pile. Indeed, some blood, if it had fallen on the clothes, would have been washed away. However, the blood in those folds deep within the pile wouldn't. Surely some droplets would have survived, even if the clothes were drenched with rain. To me, it would only have been possible for Amanda to completely spare her clothes from Lauren's blood if she took them off *before* she stabbed the girl.

So what was Lauren doing while Amanda stripped buck naked in front of her, while she remained dressed?

And what of the Myer bag in the back seat? Why was it taped shut?

Where did the knife come from? And where did it go after the murder?

No witnesses at the party on Kissing Point testified as to having seen the murder or hearing Lauren's screams for help. The music was too loud, and the gathering of sports kids and theatre kids and almost the entire school dance team was having too much of a good time to hear the agony on the wind. When she had discarded her clothes, a naked and shivering Amanda Pharrell stood in the rain until the blood had

been washed from her skin, and then climbed into the boot of
the parked vehicle, the music from the party drifting by her
as she pulled the latch closed and sealed herself in darkness.

There was a blurred-out photograph of a naked teenage Amanda in the boot of the car, snapped at the very second she was discovered, her eyes squinting and a hand up against the morning light. There were no bruises or marks on her that I could see.

I sat down in the grass, let the book fall into my lap, and closed my eyes.

The popular and beautiful Lauren Freeman.

The nine stab wounds Amanda then inflicted upon her friend.

I flipped through the book to a photograph of Lauren Freeman. She was indeed very beautiful. Sun-golden, white-toothed, and with the chiselled cheekbones of a girl whose ancestry was full of beautiful people. There was a shot of her on a cliff top looking at the horizon, her fingers trailing absent-mindedly through the yellow hair of a Labrador standing by her side. Pretty girl on the edge of her wonderful, successful adult life. She would have been a good foot taller than Amanda.

What was this budding beauty queen doing with the socially dysfunctional teenage Amanda Pharrell? If the stories of Amanda cooking mice alive and throwing tantrums in class were true, Lauren Freeman had no business being in a car with her. Amanda couldn't simultaneously be the scary misfit her school peers represented her as *and* a member of the in-crowd.

Someone was lying.

•

I sent an email to the author of *Murder in the Top End*, Eleanor Chapman, having found her address on her website. I asked her to call me, then drove home to feed the geese. When they were locked safely away in the bathroom for the night I headed out again to try to find a bar. I'd become increasingly uncomfortable with the idea of the geese having free rein over the decidedly insecure rear porch while I was gone from the house. They could sleep there while I was inside, but I felt like they were safer from the vigilantes in the bathroom, should anyone want to wander around the back of the property to see what damage they could cause.

They made me think about my baby daughter in Sydney. Were people targeting Kelly because of me? Or had filing for divorce been enough of a gesture to keep the vengeful at bay?

I told myself I could protect the geese, and that was all. I couldn't start worrying about things I could not change. Kelly hadn't answered the phone to me in months. I couldn't call her and ask her if the two of them were safe. Strangely, I found myself hoping she had found herself a man, a new partner or boyfriend who might have come to her in the months after my arrest to try to comfort her. Then I laughed at myself for thinking that way. I'd really given up all hope of Kelly and I ever reconciling. I was already inserting macho human watchdogs into her life.

I got a strange text message on my way into Crimson Lake. It was from Amanda. She'd never texted me before. It read: *Batten down the hatches, the rains are 'ere!*

I frowned. More of her strangeness. It was indeed beginning to rain heavily, steam rising from the road. I sent back a smiley face to be safe and got out in front of the bar on the corner across from her office. I glanced at the newsagent windows before going into the bar, looking for any signs of myself. There was a little notice by the door, some hand-drawn hearts.

In memory of loyal customer Teresa Miller, sadly missed.

There were more people inside Merky's than I expected. Groups of Aboriginal men crowded around wooden booths along the walls, some men playing pool. I felt a sudden sparkle of fear in my chest that I might run into Damford and Hench here, but a quick look around told me I was safe. I wandered to the counter and sat on a stool there.

I didn't even look at the bartender. I was still staring at Amanda's strange text message. I asked for a beer, and only glanced up when seconds passed in which the man in the corner of my vision didn't move.

He was a hard-faced, elderly man, his wrinkled fingers damp with beer foam and a polishing cloth hanging on his shoulder. He just stared at me. The next customer along the bar was staring at me too.

'Just a Carlton, please?' I repeated, thinking he must have misheard me. Neither man moved. The silence and stillness behind the bar was slowly drawing the attention of other men in the room, the way that trouble will, sounding silently like a dog-whistle throughout the crowded space. In seconds, my face was burning. They knew who I was.

I was close to being sick, getting out of there and back to my car. The nausea swelled up fast. I fumbled with my keys, dropped them, climbed in. I hadn't been ready to be recognised again.

'Fucking idiot,' I seethed at myself. 'Fucking idiot.'

More and more people in Crimson Lake were going to learn about my presence in their town. I needed to remember that.

Something like a violent child-rapist moving into a small town wasn't going to stay quiet on the grapevine for long. These people lived on gossip.

I found myself driving to Holloways Beach, the tiny tourist resort nearby. The encounter at the bar in Crimson Lake had left me shaken, but a new determination I couldn't ignore was pressing at me, challenges whispered from some defiant corner of my mind. *If you can't manage to find somewhere that'll serve you a beer, what makes you think you'll continue to be able to find places that'll serve you food? What if people stop serving you petrol, Ted? What if you call an ambulance one night and they don't come?*

This beer was the marker of my very chances of survival. At least, that's how it felt in the dark of the car on that lonely stretch of cane-lined road. Palm trees began to line the horizon, and I drove into the sleepy town with my jaw clenched tight.

I marched into the first bar and ordered a beer with all the barely contained fury of a boxer about to launch into the first round. The girl behind the counter began pouring it, completely unaware. She even smiled as she gave me my change. I walked, panting, to a booth in the darkest corner and drank greedily, a small victory ruined as Fabiana Grisham slid into the seat across from me.

'I need you to get away from me,' I said.

'Dr Valerie Gratteur certainly likes you,' she said, taking a coaster from the table between us and sliding it under her glass of wine. 'She gave me absolutely nothing.'

'She probably knew she was wasting her time.'

'I don't think so,' Fabiana said. She was looking at me in a more appreciative manner than the way she had that morning at my house. Maybe something had broken in her resolve to persecute me. I didn't know or care – as many allies as I needed, I could afford to refuse this one.

'Have you been following me?' I asked. 'I'm prepared to put in a stalking charge, if that's what it takes.'

'It's a small region, Ted. There aren't that many bars, and it's beer o'clock.'

A text showed up on my phone. Amanda. *You know, cat fur is glitter for lonely people.*

Where are you? I replied.

'In her interviews with police, Claire Bingley told investigators that the man who attacked her was a policeman,' Fabiana said suddenly, all formalities put aside. 'Do you have anything you want to say about that, Ted?'

'I don't want to talk about my case with you, Fabiana.'

'Fab, please.'

I eased breath through my teeth and drank more beer. An uneasy silence passed between us, in which she waited for me to launch into my own defence, and I tried to resist doing what she wanted me to do.

'Why would she say that?' Fabiana continued. 'There's no way she could have known you were a policeman by looking at your mugshot, and you wouldn't have been in uniform when you abducted her.'

'Claire said a lot of weird things in those interviews,' I said, relenting. 'She didn't say much that made any sense. If you'd seen the tapes, and not the edited transcripts printed in the media, you'd know that.'

I'd been made to watch the tapes of Claire Bingley, my supposed victim, in the courtroom alongside the jury. I'd seen

195

them already, and hadn't wanted to see them again. Claire was a shadow of the small girl I'd glimpsed on the side of the road that awful day. The tape was recorded not long after she was released from hospital, so her face was badly bruised. Her eyes flicked and rolled around the room like she was following the path of moths fluttering near the ceiling. The eye-rolling was a post-traumatic stress disorder symptom, the prosecutor told the court. She also had night terrors and trouble eating. She barely looked at the collection of photographs in front of her, I one of the men pictured. When she spoke, she rambled and whispered.

'Deep inside the dark, into the dark, he's taking me into the dark, I can't, I'm not, Mum, Mum, there's a white dog, Mrs Anderson, I can't . . . into the . . . make sure you take your homework with you . . . into the dark, the policeman is here, he's taking me . . .'

'What did you just say?' The counsellor interviewing Claire had seized on the word. 'Did you say he was a "policeman"?'

Mrs Anderson was the name of Claire's teacher. The girl's interview with police, guided by a team of child trauma specialists, was all like this: little snippets of thoughts rushing through a broken brain. Her day with her friends. Breakfast that morning. Some of it was just fanciful mumbling about butterflies and dogs and colours. Now and then the child was lucid, and when her eyes settled and her face became composed, it was only for a few seconds before she burst into tears and collapsed into the arms of her mother sitting beside her.

Sometimes, throughout the interviews, Claire repeated what the people around her said. A clip played again and again by the prosecution was the little girl parroting the counsellor, her words fast and slurred.

Did you say he was a policeman?
Did you say he was a policeman?
Did you say he was a policeman?

I'd lost it and cried in the third hour of interview tapes. Pictures of me with my head in my hands had turned up on the cover of the *Herald* the next day under the headline 'Crocodile Tears'.

'So you don't have any real answers about why she would say that, Ted?' Fabiana asked me now.

'Is it possible she was talking about the policemen who were interviewing her? The same policemen had been doing so, in uniform, for some days at that point? Is it possible that at some time during the hours and hours she was talked to by investigators that was *unrecorded*, someone might have outright asked her if the man who did this was a policeman? Is it possible that the girl overheard her parents discussing me with investigators, maybe caught them saying something about me being a policeman?'

'I don't know.' Fabiana shrugged.

'I don't know, either. I don't know what the hell she was talking about. All I know is, she wasn't talking about me when she was talking about her attacker. Because I'm not him.'

She sat staring at me, turning her glass on the table top.

'She picked you out of a photo line-up.'

'Yes. She did. She *had* seen me,' I snapped. 'I don't know how many times I've said this. Claire *had* seen me that day by the side of the road. I've never denied that.' I sighed. My face was burning.

'You worked in the drug squad,' Fabiana said. 'That has been a point of interest for a lot of people watching this case. With drugs come drug dealers, and with drug dealers come corrupt police, lawyers, judges. Did working in the drug squad help you in any way in getting your charges dropped, Ted?'

'How could it possibly have helped me?' I asked. 'I *arrested* drug dealers. Why would they do me favours? Why would they want me back on the streets? They're not my friends.'

That wasn't strictly true. I did have friends who were drug dealers. You arrest people enough times, you begin to build a rapport. I had been arresting some of the men I encountered in my job since they were teenagers, and they'd stopped seeing it as personal after a while. When I caught them, it was because they'd fucked up, not because I was a bad person. When I'd been released from Silverwater, the first thing I had done was contact one of these wily underdogs to ask him to find me a gun. I wasn't going on the run without a gun. But the journalist didn't need to know that.

'I didn't do this,' I told Fabiana, leaning forward, looking at her eyes. 'I didn't rape Claire Bingley. I'm sick of fucking saying it.'

Fabiana was sitting back in her seat now. I looked around the bar. Luckily, we hadn't drawn any attention yet, but I wasn't going to stick around until we did. I sculled the rest of my beer.

'You're very convincing,' Fabiana said quietly. 'The way you talk. It's very convincing.'

'Great,' I said. I slammed my beer glass down and got out of there.

Amanda had texted me more nonsense when I looked at my phone in the car. More nonsensical bullshit. I called her. The background of the call was noisy, and she was already talking when the line connected.

'No, no, shut up! It's my partner. Ted? Ted! Teddy! Oh, I guess I shouldn't call you Teddy. Only *Stella* calls you *Teddy*.'

'What?' I was so furious, I realised I had bitten the inside of my cheek, my jaw grinding. 'What are you talking about? Where are you?'

'Come to O'Toole's, Ted!' she said. 'This place fucking rocks!'

O'Toole's bar was a student hangout south of James Cook University on the Captain Cook Highway. Not the usual hub of students, this was the place for the stoners and the dropouts, the booth tabletops free of textbooks and notebooks, the walls bare of special deals on jugs. I walked in and received a few looks from the bar staff and a pair of young ladies who were playing Uno over the counter.

At the back of the great room a row of pool tables stood, and I was drawn there by loud laughter. I stood and looked at Amanda for a few moments, uncomprehending.

She'd somehow metamorphosed into a teenage dream, her awkward clothes shed and her small, lean figure strapped tight into a midnight-blue dress. The dress was small, a darkness that ended in colourful tattooed fairies and temptresses and queens who cavorted over the entirety of Amanda's thighs. I hadn't seen her legs bare but they were taut from all that bike riding, calves straining in huge silver glittery heels that would have looked right at home either on the red carpet or the strip club stage. She'd tried to tame her wild black hair but it flicked and curled everywhere behind her ears and down the nape of her neck.

She was beautiful. Beautiful in a way that made me immediately on guard. All around her, young men stood and watched while she leaned over the pool table and lined up a difficult shot. She was a practised pool player. They whooped and cheered but it was obvious that their appreciation was half for her skill and half that she was there at all, that she was near, this delicious little mystery that had floated into their world.

Someone tugged my arm. The bar beside me was also crowded with guys turned on their seats to watch the gathering around the table.

'Dude, do you know who that chick is?' a kid asked.

'Huh?'

'That's *Amanda Pharrell*, man,' the kid told me, leaning in conspiratorially. 'She butchered some girl.'

'Cut her fucking head off,' another said, making cutting motions at his throat. 'Crazy, man.'

I'd had enough. I strode into the group and lifted Amanda's pool cue before she could line up her next shot.

'Ted!' she said, her eyes wide and slow as she looked up at me. 'You're here!'

'And we're leaving,' I said.

'Nah, nah, stay, Ted. Stay. Meet my new friends. This is Johnno, and Bradley, and Mickey . . .'

She plucked up a drink from a line of three short glasses on the edge of the table. She literally had a queue of drinks bought for her by the young hyenas. I grabbed her arm and she stumbled, fell against me. The one she'd called Mickey, a bronzed surfer-looking youth, pushed half-heartedly against my chest. He knew if I swung at him he was done for, and quickly backed out of my reach.

'Fuck off, man. Leave her alone.'

'She gets to decide if she goes or not,' another kid sneered.

'This isn't Feminism 101, boys,' I said. 'Back the fuck up.'

'He's my partner! He's my mate!'

'Come on.' I pulled at Amanda. 'Say bye to everyone.'

'Bye to everyone!' Amanda cried.

In the dim light of the parking lot, I realised just how drunk she was. I wondered if someone had put something in her drink. She stopped and gripped at her huge heels, seemed to want to pull them off, then thought better of it and stumbled on. She was rambling. Losing tracks of her sentences.

'In Brisbane Women's there was this girl named Manni,' she was saying. 'We were like, a pair. She . . . We . . . Because she was Manni, and I was Mandy, and our bunks were . . . We . . .'

Amanda stumbled. I tried to put an arm around her, but when my skin made contact with hers she shrank and twisted and brushed me off.

'Don't touch me!' she snapped. 'It's in the rules.'

'Are you okay?' I asked. 'Do you want to stop and take those off?'

'You gotta respect . . . the rules. Read the contract. Read the fine print.'

I stopped and watched her go for her heels again. She fell and I caught her just before she slumped onto the gravel. I swung her up into my arms and carried her like a child.

'What a mess,' I said.

'Messy messy mess,' she murmured against my neck.

I'd parked on the road just outside the parking lot. I hoisted Amanda up against my chest and popped open the passenger door, placed her gently in the seat and buckled her up. Her head lolled against the window as I shut the door, her eyes closed.

I got into the driver's seat and started the car, thinking I'd take her back to my place and put her on the couch on the porch. Or maybe in the bed. In the bed was more gentlemanly. I'd take the couch.

I was starting the engine when I realised she was awake. Amanda was slowly coming to, her eyes widening as she looked at the dashboard.

'You all right?' I asked.

'Oh no,' she said. Her hands went to the seatbelt at her chest. 'No. No. No.'

All at once she bucked against the seat, her hands hitting at the dashboard, the window, the roof. She didn't seem to know how to get out of the seatbelt. She started screaming.

'No! No! No! No!'

'It's okay!' I said, trying to grab her. 'It's all right! Amanda! Amanda! It's all right!'

She was fighting, twisting, clawing at the door in the dark, trying to find the handle. She tugged at it, found the door locked, fumbled at the window for the button.

'God, please! Please!'

She kicked at the windscreen, twisted out of the seatbelt, struggled at the door.

'Please help me!'

I got out and tore around to the passenger side. By the time I got there she'd thrown herself out the driver's door and onto the gravel. She was crawling out of the light of the car, into the grass, her whole body shaking violently.

'Amanda!'

'Not in the car. Not in the car. Not in the car,' she wailed. I tried to put my hands on her but she went into screams. *'Don't touch me!'*

I slid down against the rear tyre of my car and watched

her lying in the grass, her hands over her head and chin tucked against her chest. She lay like that, shaking and sniffling, refusing to answer me when I talked, pulling away when I reached for her hand. When she'd recovered enough to look at me I took a thin blanket from the back of the car and tried to wrap it around her, but she tore it from me and swung it over her own shoulders.

Suddenly there was a fierceness to her. Her big eyes sparkled in the light of the street lamps, ablaze with orange orbs.

'You touch me again, Ted, and I'll kill you,' she said. She pointed a finger at my face, and I felt my stomach twist.

'Amanda,' I said.

'No, shut up,' she snapped. 'I've killed. You understand? *I've killed.* I know what it feels like to rip the life out of a body. And I'll do that to you.'

The words were hot in the air, searing on my skin. I'd never feared Amanda before, but looking at her now, she was nothing of the frail little butterfly woman I'd met for the first time days before in the Shark Bar. She was a ghoul standing before me, a hollow thing, and what I saw in her hard face made me sick in an instant. She'd turned all her dark power on me, like a spider rearing in a corner, and in just the way a threatened arachnid would, she curled in on herself, twisted and crept away into the dark.

Perhaps out of a shared desire to stave off the awkwardness of the night before, neither Amanda nor I made phone contact the next day. I called Jake's agent, Cary Minnow, and managed to get through to him just before he left for a meeting.

It seemed to take precious minutes to describe to him my purpose, a speech through which he sighed and huffed.

'Oh, there were always crazy fans, mate,' Cary said. 'The bigger the writer, the more crazies. Jake got a double-whammy: the writer nuts and the religious nuts. Mixed nuts.' He laughed.

'Anyone who you worried about? Anyone make any threats?'

'Let me think. Look, the religious nuts were always upset about his mishmash of the great books. He picked and chose from here and there across a number of Christian texts. New and Old Testament, Leviticus, Genesis,' Cary said. 'Some Christians loved it. He was bringing the old, inaccessible stories to the youth of today. Some hated it, though. The characters are teenagers, so they confront all the major sins. Envy. Lust. Sometimes the characters are righteous, and sometimes they sin. We got a major global backlash when Adam and Eve had pre-marital sex in book three.'

'What do you mean, backlash?'

'Some arseholes hacked into Jake's website and trolled it,'

Cary said. 'Dumped child porn and graphic crime-scene photos all over it.'

'What?' I shook my head. 'How does that –'

'Make any sense? It doesn't,' Cary said. 'These people are lunatics.'

'When did book three come out?'

'Two years ago.'

'Right,' I sighed. 'I think I'm looking for something more recent.'

'The last thing I can think of was about this time last year,' he said. 'Some woman bought all the tickets to his book talk in Newcastle.'

'Whoa.'

'Yeah,' Cary said. 'I think there were fifty tickets. Would have cost her a bit.'

'Why did they sell all the tickets to one woman?'

'They didn't think it was just one woman,' the agent said. 'That's the sick part. She bought all of them individually. Different credit cards. Different accounts. They said she called up and did voices, even. Pretty crazy. We only got wind of the scam an hour before the talk. Jake didn't go.'

'She must have wanted a private audience with him pretty bad,' I said. 'What was she? Aspiring author?'

'Just a romantic, I think.'

'Can you remember her name?'

I got a piece of paper and wrote down Renee MacIntyre's details as Cary quoted them to me.

'You ever hear from Renee again?'

'No, no,' Cary said. 'We checked the guest lists for a while after her failed attempt at a one-on-one, but she never popped up again.'

'Right.'

'Stella would have all the fan letters, too,' Cary said. Someone spoke to him in the background of the call.

'Yeah, I'm working through them,' I said. 'I'm not seeing anything very scary.'

'All right, well I —'

'Just before you go — I know you're busy,' I said. 'Can you think of anything more recent than Renee MacIntyre? The last few months or so. Anything at all that might be helpful. An aggressive call? A strange gift?'

The line was silent. I thought he might have hung up on me.

'A fan attacked another fan at a book signing,' he said. 'Cairns, I think it was, or it might have been Brisbane. In a bookstore. You'll have to go hunting for it. The papers reported that someone got knocked out, but I was inside with Jake. We didn't hear or see any of it.'

I spent some of the morning making other calls, my hands-free hooked up while I scrubbed goose shit off the porch with a broom and some soapy water. Renee MacIntyre was a strange character — she had multiple aliases and shifted jobs and apartments every six months or so. She ran a very basic website that seemed devoted to ruining Jake's reputation, the page sprayed with multiple 'testimonies' from other fans detailing everything from his rudeness at book events to apparent sections of plagiarised text in his books. It looked like Renee had been badly scorned by Jake's refusal to turn up at the book talk she'd commandeered. There was a very angry paragraph written by a fan simply calling herself 'Rosa' that described Jake turning up drunk to a writer's festival and trying to tongue kiss her at the back of the crowd. Rosa's written style was suspiciously similar to Renee's introduction to the website.

The lead started to fail when I noticed that the Jake-hating website hadn't been updated in a year. After about three hours I finally nailed down a current address for Renee – Koh Samui, Thailand. She hadn't been back to Australia in six months. Dead end. Sometimes detective work is like that. You sit behind a desk for hours with a phone in your hand calling around in circles, putting on voices so you can call the same number multiple times and ask different questions, writing notes across your notepad. And then all of a sudden it comes to an abrupt end, and the excitement you didn't even know you'd been holding in your throat and chest melts away. I was used to doing it in a crowded bull pen, surrounded by my colleagues, friends I could roll my eyes at or eavesdrop on between calls. There was nothing between the calls now but the sound of crickets in the field across the road, the tinkling of lorikeets in the trees. My own thoughts.

As my life became more organised, I had begun to wonder about my future contact with my daughter. I wanted Sean to begin discussions with Kelly about some sort of custody arrangement. No court in the country was going to give me even fifty-fifty custody of Lillian. If the papers got hold of something like that, there'd be such a public outcry, Kelly and Lillian might be in danger. Before I knew it, they'd be standing outside the public places Kelly would let us meet, their cameras pressed up against the broad McDonald's restaurant windows, trying to get that magic snap of my baby in my arms. The only publicly respectable thing the Family Court could do was give me supervised visits in-house, and even then, I knew, they'd be analysing my conversations with Kelly, their notebooks ready, ears pricked for an aggressive tone or a snide remark.

It would be a nightmare. But it was better than nothing. My worst fear was that she would grow up without any idea of who I was. Kelly wasn't going to keep pictures of me around the house to remind Lillian who I was as she grew older. But maybe if I saw her regularly enough, even in the strained, sterilised environment of some Family Court office playroom, she'd come to accept me as a tiny part of her life.

I should have been madder about the whole situation. I should have demanded to see her, should have abused Kelly until she put the girl on the phone so I could hear her giggling and breathing, told her that I'd get a court order, make her send me pictures. But I didn't have much anger left in me after prison. Prison is full of slow-boiling, impotent anger, fury simmering behind the eyes of everyone – inmates, guards, specialists. Those brick-walled institutions are where anger comes to breed. I'd spent much of my first couple of weeks inside sitting on the edge of my bed with my head in my hands and my eyes squeezed shut, just hating, burning, pulsing with anger. I'd thrown myself against the locked door with it. I'd run my fingernails down my cheeks and neck with it. I'd screamed and cried with it. And like all fires, it ate itself up inside me until there was nothing left. It's not that I wasn't angry any more. It's just that I was ashen on the inside. Tired. I still couldn't sleep without worrying who the hell was going to walk Lillian down the aisle when she got married, or what she was going to do when all the other kids were making Father's Day cards at school.

I was aware, too, that the anger would come back one day, when I wasn't so tired and beaten. There was only so much invigorating free air I could breathe before it fuelled the little glowing embers left behind from my fall from grace. I was going to be sitting out on the back porch one day looking at the beautiful sunset over the river beyond the gates, and I was going to remember what it felt like to do something like that with my arm draped around a woman who loved me. What it was like to watch a sunset without wondering if there was someone at the front of the property now opening a can of red paint or lining up a brick.

I wasn't sure if some of this fury wasn't directed at Claire Bingley. Not so much for picking me off the photo line-up. I knew she was crazy from her ordeal. If there was anger inside me for Claire, it was not for anything she'd done or said. It was simply for having been there that day, by the side of the road, waiting for whoever took her. She should have caught the earlier bus. She should have had her parents pick her up. She should have fucking walked. Yes, I was really honest with myself, I hated Claire Bingley. I hated her for not being anywhere in the world than where she was that awful day, standing there, metres away from me, watching me as I got out of my car like a wary rabbit at the edge of the long grass. I hated her for what had happened to her. For what it had done to me.

But all of that was just craziness, too. I couldn't possibly hate Claire. None of this was her fault.

It was the man who did this to her. To us.

But who the hell was he? All I'd heard since it happened was how he was me.

Just as I was beginning to reimagine some sort of relationship with my infant daughter, how and why something like that might happen, I realised my relationship with the geese had suddenly changed. The little ones had imprinted on me. I'd learned about 'imprinting' while googling food options for the birds when they'd first come into my life. The goslings had begun to recognise me as some sort of parental figure. The fact that we were dramatically different species didn't matter – there were YouTube videos of goslings and ducklings imprinting on cats and dogs. The way they gathered around and followed their mother wherever she went in a line was now something they did to me. Because their mother was injured and couldn't move around that much, it was me they followed in a perfect row as I walked from room to room, huddling around my toes whenever I stopped. They were somehow able to anticipate my movements and get out of the way, so after an hour or so of complete terror that I would step on one of them, I forgot about the phenomenon altogether and got used to my tiny parade of followers.

They followed me out to the mailbox, where I inspected the latest work of the vigilantes. They were definitely upping their intensity. All that remained of the steel letterbox on the lawn was a charred stump. Across the road, I found more of the structure, a piece of the front, the plastic number 7 melted into a black wick. Mid-range party explosives, the type people gathered together in backyard parties and blew up feral rabbits with. They hadn't done any damage to the house at all, but this was probably an experiment. I was getting the feeling the vigilantes were young. Young enough that if I scared them they might leave me alone.

Around midday I was spurred into action, having spent

hours on the back porch with my laptop trying to find anything I could on Llewellyn Bruce and being rewarded with nothing but a dead end. In the early hours of 22 January, the night Jake went missing, Bruce and two other men were pictured in a local newspaper outside the Noki Club in Cairns as it was being raided for drugs. Turns out Bruce did leave his island hideaway at least once every ten years. It happened to be on the exact night I'd hoped he might be somewhere else.

The retired bikie enforcer is part owner in Noki and other clubs across the tropical north, and refutes claims the establishments are part of a domestic drug smuggling ring. 'I'm an old man. I have a simple life. I rarely come into the towns, so any funny business people conduct in my clubs is news to me, mate.'

I slammed the laptop closed and went for a drive to clear my head. The sky was streaked with grey cloud. Part of me hated the fact that Amanda had been right about Bruce. She was so certain about all her conclusions that it was almost as though she had one foot in the future, as though she was leading me towards solving the puzzle of Jake's disappearance, and I felt mad that she was doing it so slowly. Finding out the truth about her crime was almost, in that moment, like an act of revenge. I'd show her she couldn't keep the secrets of her past from me. I'd show her I was a worthy partner.

It was as I was standing on the porch of Lauren Freeman's house that I came to my senses. Three short-legged, silky brown dogs rushed to the door as I tapped on the screen, barking and whimpering at me through the mesh. I heard someone call out from inside that the door was open, and I went in.

What are you doing, Ted? What the hell are you trying to prove?

The house was as described in *Murder in the Top End*. I felt as though I was walking into the book's pages, as though someone would begin narrating my movements.

The hallway walls are cluttered with family photographs, a memorial walk of the Freeman clan. Light playing on the surface of the backyard pool through the far windows sparkles and dances on the glass before the faces of beloved grandfathers, grandmothers, uncles and aunts lost. Among their withered faces, a stranger sits, smiling. Someone who doesn't belong. Someone too young to belong. Their eternal beauty queen.

A short, blonde woman met me at the entrance to the living room.

'Oh! I thought you were Dynah,' she said. 'Hello there.'

'Hi,' I said. 'I'm Ted Collins. Are you, ah . . .'

'I'm Paula Freeman.'

'Lauren's mum.'

The sound of her daughter's name still darkened Paula Freeman's face. She licked her upper lip and stepped back from me, out of friendly proximity.

'Whoa, now, I don't talk to journalists, sonny. I'm sorry. I stopped talking to journalists a long time ago, you know.'

'I'm not a journalist,' I said. I didn't disguise the relief in my voice. 'I'm just, uh. I'm here because . . .'

What are you doing?

'I work for a historical section of the police,' I coughed. 'A sort of historical analytical body . . . of the police. I, uh, my job is to look at the similarities in certain sorts of cases? Violent cases. And yours, um . . .'

'Police? Oh, right! I'm sorry. I'm sorry. I didn't realise! I just get so many weirdoes turning up, you know, wanting to say things. Come in.'

She beckoned. I followed, my face flushing with guilt.

'I've gotta be careful, you know? People come. Journalists. Strange people, too. Say they saw something or they know something or that the Pharrell girl is innocent. God, if you only knew. Come in here.'

She led me into a spotless kitchen and started making me coffee before asking me if I wanted any. I slid uncomfortably onto a stool behind the kitchen island.

'I'm expecting my daughter home. Dynah. So when you knocked, I thought . . .'

'It's all right. Thank you for seeing me.'

'Here.' She thrust an instant coffee at me. She'd got it right – milk and sugar. She was frazzled, pushing back thin blonde whips from her forehead. 'Gee whiz.'

'It must be confronting, having people turn up. I'm so sorry.'

'Well, the police usually call ahead,' she laughed ruefully. 'But yes, you're right, it is. I don't go around expecting it anymore. People turn up – the electrician, the plumber, a delivery man. And then whammo! It's someone about Lauren.'

She sat down across from me, her manicured nails strumming the marble countertop.

'Lauren was pretty, see,' Paula said. 'Young and pretty – that's what gets their attention. The crime lovers. The conspiracy theorists. That JonBenét Ramsey is the perfect example. People will never let up about that kid. If she'd been a boy she'd have got half the attention.'

She sipped her coffee. I'd said almost nothing to spur her on, and now the words were tumbling out, words that had been rattling around in her mind while she was alone in the house now given cupped hands to spill into.

'They all say they were there. The amount of people who come here or write to me and say they were there that night, the night of the murder; they can't all be telling the truth,' Paula said. 'The mountain would have been crawling with people. Would have been a giant rave party rather than the small gathering of kids that it was. Just about every member of her school year claims they were there that night. That's about a hundred people.'

'Wow,' I said.

'And they each have their own versions and ideas. It's hard not to grab one of the different versions sometimes. You know? Hold onto it.'

'Why would you want to hold onto it?' I asked.

She stared into her coffee.

'Sometimes people say things that give me a kind of . . . *nicer* version of what happened,' she said. 'And it's hard not to go along with them. Because even just a little tiny bit of relief would be so good. I'd love to believe some of them.'

'What kind of nicer versions are there?'

Paula sighed. 'One girl, she called me and told me she'd seen a man in the bush with Lauren and the Pharrell girl that night. She said that the man had tried to rob the two of them. She'd investigated some robberies down in Brisbane and found there was a guy who was targeting young girls in cars. Her theory was that Lauren had been trying to protect the Pharrell girl, and it was the man, the robber, who'd killed my child.'

We paused, the two of us imagining it. The steam from our drinks intermingled before us.

'That's a nicer story, isn't it?' Paula smiled. 'Slightly. Lauren still dies. But she's a hero. There's some . . . *meaning* to what happened.'

'Right.' I nodded.

'I've heard the wildest things. That my teenage daughter was a founding member of some, some secret organisation. Some cult thing, with government ties! I got a letter saying Lauren had been killed because she was going to reveal everything about this organisation, and the Pharrell girl was just the patsy.'

'It's always the government, isn't it?' I smiled.

'Always,' she laughed. 'Lauren couldn't even get her laundry sorted out. How was she supposed to be some kind of cult leader? Another anonymous caller said she had an older boyfriend. She was into drugs. She was making porn.'

The troupe of dogs rushed from where they'd settled around our feet across the living room to the front door. I heard a car door slam outside, and footsteps on the porch. My face flushed hot again as I questioned my very purpose in the house.

'Mum?'

The girl who walked in might have been Lauren Freeman, if not for the shape of her. She was shorter and thicker than her sister, still beautiful, a curvy, sun-kissed girl in her mid-twenties. She was wearing a turquoise apron around her waist, dusty with the powder they put inside food-service gloves to keep workers' hands from getting sweaty. She was carrying a couple of shopping bags full of vegetables.

'Oh,' she said when she saw me.

'This is Tom, from the police,' Paula said.

'Ted.'

'Ted! Sorry. This is Ted. From the police.'

'Right.' Dynah looked me up and down, set her bags against the wall. 'Mum, can I talk to you? In private?'

The two women huddled in the hall. I looked at my coffee and picked out words.

'. . . see a badge?'

'This isn't the movies, Dynah . . . go around asking people to show their badges. He's in research, anyway . . . have a badge.'

The dogs around me were all pretty certain I had some goslings in my pockets. They'd made a good examination of the smell of my shoes and sat expectantly, waiting for me to produce them. I gave each a pat of consolation.

Paula disappeared into the house and Dynah came warily into the kitchen, poured herself a glass of grapefruit juice. A heavy silence lay between us as Paula bustled around in another room.

'My mum doesn't get to talk about Lauren a lot,' Dynah said eventually. Her tone was flat, almost sarcastic. She leant against the fridge and looked at me, a picture of scepticism. 'She talks *to* her a lot, but not about her.'

'She talks to her?'

'Oh, Lauren still lives here.' Dynah nodded, looking around the room. The sarcasm in her voice was thick now. 'She's *always* here.'

'You don't sound too happy about that,' I observed.

Dynah leaned on the counter before me, setting her glass down with a loud clunk.

'That's because the Lauren that my mother drags around with her,' she said, 'the one in the pictures, and the books, and the magazines – that Lauren isn't anything like the Lauren who died.'

I was surprised how candid Dynah was being with me, even as she'd just lectured her mother about speaking to strangers who came to the house. But I got the sense that her hurt over her sister's ghost was always on the tip of her tongue.

I opened my mouth to ask Dynah what she meant, but Paula came back into the room and Dynah backed off, signalling the end of our conversation.

'Ted, would you like to see Lauren's room?' Paula asked.

In a small, sunny bedroom at the back of the house another memorial lay, this one devoted to one person only. The curtains, drawn to prevent the sun from fading the unused coverlet on the bed, were thrust back as I entered, and I found myself standing in an early noughties time capsule. There was a large black-and-white poster of Leonardo DiCaprio in his teen idol days dominating the wall above the bed. The shelves over the desk were lined with CDs. *So Fresh: Hits of Summer 2004*.

Everything was as it had been at the moment Lauren left it. The desk was cluttered with colourful gel pens. There was a pile of notes in one corner, the kind high-schoolers would pass around. I picked up a paper puzzle folded into the shape of a four-petalled flower. On the surface of the petals were the words 'Blue', 'Yellow', 'Green' and 'Red'.

'They had these when I was a kid.' I smiled, showing Paula. I spread the puzzle apart, and inside found folded flaps numbered from one to eight. 'The girls used to make them. They called them chatterboxes, I think.'

'We called them fortune tellers,' she said. 'You choose a colour, then a number, and they told your fortune.'

'I don't know about the fortune bit,' I said. 'When the girls at my school used to make them they'd just be full of insults. I'd always get "You stink" or "You're a loser" or something.'

Paula sat on the bed and looked out the window. I carefully opened one of the inner flaps of the puzzle.

Lauren's fortune teller was a little harsher than those Paula and I remembered.

You're a slut.

You fucked Mr Thompson.

Your face looks like vomit.

There was one positive notation among the results inside the fortune teller puzzle. If the participant chose the number three or four, the paper told them *You will marry your true love.*

Someone had written under the words 'true love' the letters 'LD' in a different coloured pen, and had drawn a smiley face. I looked at the poster of Leonardo DiCaprio and felt sad for Lauren Freeman, cut down in that beautiful, naive time when someone might believe their true love is a Hollywood heart-throb. She was the fly in the web, adhered against lines that went back as far as her girlhood when 'true love' was real and princesses married princes, and being called a vomit-face actually hurt. The room didn't mesh with those other lines wrapped around Lauren, however. The drinker. The girl behind the wheel. The child Lauren couldn't possibly be as 'hated' as Dr Gratteur thought she'd have needed to be for someone to do what they did to her, surely. Which Lauren was real?

Dear Jake,

It must be wonderful to be a god. I don't necessarily mean a celebrity, someone who has the masses cowering and creeping along beneath them everywhere they go, although I'm sure you get your taste of that. A husband can be his wife's god. She can love him in the kind of way that gives him steering power over her whole life. She can put her neck in his hands and tell him that he can decide how long she breathes. I realise that I've made you my god, Jake. Sometimes, I can feel your fingers on my throat, pressing, taking the breath from me.

It was kind of like that, seeing you at Cairns Books on McLeod Street. It was the first time I had been in your proximity, and my throat closed at the sight of you. I was almost sick on the bus there. It wasn't just you that shocked me, but the freaks swirling around you, those happy demons putting water out for you and clicking your pen for you and standing by you like guards while the readers lined along the walls. All the fake laughter and the painful smiles. Seeing you there among the pretenders made me burn, Jake. They don't love you like I do – and the fact that they'd even pretend they do makes me so enraged. So bitter. They don't know what it's like to have been writing to you this long and receiving nothing in return. They don't know that kind of rejection.

You probably think I'm a freak. A lot of people do. A bit of fan fiction and some cheesy letters and an accidental overlooking – you're so fucking busy, after all – and now you've got me all wound up like an angry bitch in heat. Calm down, mate. Get in line. There's plenty to go around. Everybody will get their slice of Jake eventually.

They don't get it, do they? They don't get how this feels.

Our relationship isn't writer and reader. It never was. It's always been messenger and receiver. I've got yours, Jake. But all these pretenders, they're getting in the way of you receiving mine.

I've included some more writing. I know you're reading it. I don't know why you don't reply. Maybe you can't. Maybe you're frightened to see so much of yourself in me. Don't be afraid, beautiful god. I won't forsake you.

I found Amanda in my kitchen, making herself coffee. She'd said nothing about coming over, she'd just appeared, like something I'd imagined.

In the early morning hours, I'd spooked the vigilantes as they pulled up outside my house, running out there in my boxer shorts with a broom. I don't know what they'd been planning, but there had been three of them on their way out of the car, and all three had jumped back in at the sight of me. I hadn't noted any details about them, or the vehicle. I'd had a restless night thinking about Dynah Freeman's words.

That Lauren isn't anything like the Lauren who died.

'You have geese,' Amanda said as I padded into the kitchen in my cotton robe.

'I do.'

'I would never have picked you as a bird man.'

'Neither would I,' I said, looking out the windows at them huddled on the porch. 'They were kind of an accident. Like your cats.'

'Between us, we could start a farm.'

'Geese, cats, man-eating gators. A little food chain all of our own.'

She cringed at the taste of my coffee. Looked tired. Though it had been a day since I'd seen her at her most vulnerable, she still didn't seem right. She had the worn and slightly frazzled face of a woman who'd had her foundations shaken, who'd momentarily lost her grip on the handlebars and swerved towards the side of the road. When she noticed me watching her too closely she perked up and started jabbering on about Brisbane Women's Correctional as she always did, with the nostalgic warmth of someone talking about high school summer holidays.

It was strange that Amanda had had prison friends. That she even called them 'friends', and remembered them with affection. Because whatever Hollywood-inspired expectations I'd had about making friends in prison, I knew almost straight away that it was impossible. Prison is full of criminals, who can and will sell out anyone around for even the smallest comfort. It's better to have the thicker mattress than a friend. It's better to have extended TV time than a friend. It's better to move down to a less secure section than to have a friend. In all situations, making sacrifices so you can make a friend isn't worth it. You do get close to people so that as a group you can take or protect these small advantages and comforts from other groups of people, but the people in your group aren't your 'friends'. Inside the group, it's only a matter of time before those advantages have to be divided, and then it's every man for himself.

The other difficulty that comes with making friends in prison is the overwhelming number of jailhouse snitches. Another prisoner gets you talking for a couple of hours, and slowly, carefully, they extract as many accurate details from your life as they can. Where you lived. What car you drove. Your wife's name. After a couple of days of this, they start to pick at you for details about your supposed crime. What you'd done that morning. What you were wearing when it happened. They pair that with what they read in the paper and go straight to the police with a story about your quiet confession to them in the corner of the chow hall. They've got just enough real-world details about you to make it sound credible. They cut a deal for a reduced sentence, or a transfer, or an extra goddamn blanket, in return for testifying against you.

Prisons are jungles. Madhouses. And here was Amanda telling me about long, emotional chats with her dorm-mates at night in Brisbane Women's Correctional. Little girls at a slumber party playing truth or dare, blankets spread out on the concrete floor.

When the goslings saw me through the open door to the porch they came rushing to me in a straight line and gathered around my feet.

'They're imprinted,' Amanda said, looking up.

'Yeah.'

We both watched them.

'Amanda, can we talk about –'

'No,' she said.

'I should have guessed,' I sighed.

'We can talk about that,' she said, pointing to a folder on the tabletop. 'That's the police report on the assault at the bookshop on McLeod Street in Cairns where Jake was doing a reading. They've also emailed me the CCTV.'

'Let's have a look,' I said.

We loaded up four video files from Amanda's email. The footage was soundless. On the porch, the geese gathered around our feet as we watched the first video – a roof-mounted shot that followed Jake from a taxi into the front doors of the bookstore. There was a queue of about fifty people outside the building, books tucked under arms and heads down in embarrassment and glee as the big man got out of the white cab.

'He really is like some kind of rock star,' I said.

'He sure is. Look at this chick. She's just about peeing her pants.'

Amanda tapped the screen, where a young girl was gushing over Jake as he tried to enter the building. She grabbed at his hand as he went by, and another man gave her a quiet talking to once Jake was inside.

'That's Cary, the agent,' Amanda said.

We played the video back a second time, but didn't note anything interesting. We shifted to the second video, which was a rolling composite of four cameras within the store. The cameras would record for ten seconds before flipping to the next camera in the sequence.

Jake walked into the store and was set up at the table by a huddle of bookstore staff, who poured him water, arranged books at his side and generally twittered and flapped all about him like excited birds. The big man seemed to take the attention in his stride. Through the windows, the crowd stood watching, waiting to be let inside.

'Imagine having that kind of power,' I said. 'Everybody rushing around after you. Following you everywhere. Looking up to you.'

'The geese rush around after you,' she said.

'They look up at me, too, I guess.' I stared down at the goslings, most of whom had fallen asleep on my toes. 'It's a long way up.'

'Who's this guy?' Amanda asked, pointing at the screen again. The crowd had been let in. She'd singled out a man in a baseball cap at the edge of the crowd, not in the queue but loitering between the bookshelves near the gathering. He was dressed in a black jacket with the collar turned up, and seemed like a short, lean man, but aside from that I could not tell a thing about him from the footage. He played with some of the books in the aisle and glanced now and then at Jake.

I turned to the police report.

14:19:47 Young male suspect identified after incident by bookstore staff appears between bookshelves near book signing table. Witnesses 2 and 3 suggest suspect was talking/mumbling to himself. Specific words not heard. Witness 2 suggests tone was aggressive.

'I like to mumble aggressively to myself in bookstores,' Amanda said. 'What the hell's wrong with that?'

'Stalkers should be seen and not heard,' I said.

'You think he's a stalker?'

'I don't know.' I sighed, watching the man pacing the aisle, disappearing and reappearing on the screen. 'He's certainly agitated.'

14:24:13 Suspect is recorded damaging bookstore property.

I watched as the man in the aisle stuck his fingers in between a pair of books and swept sideways, knocking a dozen or so books off the shelf in one dramatic sweep. He did the same to the left, leaving a handful of books on the very centre of the shelves, standing alone.

'He's making a mess.'

'What's the betting those are Jake's books,' Amanda said. 'He's swept the books around Jake's series onto the floor, leaving only the Chronicles on the shelf.'

The man in the video crouched and seemed to grip at his head for a moment. None of the store staff had noticed the books falling, the man gripping at himself. A couple of fans in the queue were watching, but they didn't seem to want to sacrifice their places in the line to meet their favourite author to report some crazy guy in the aisles.

As we opened the third video, we spotted the man walking quickly out of the store.

14:32:02 Suspect leaves bookstore.

'And this is the assault,' Amanda said, opening the fourth video. The man in the cap exited the store and turned left, away from the queue of Jake Scully fans, seemingly wanting to leave the scene altogether. I watched as his feet came to a halt at the very edge of the image, before another pair of feet. Someone got in his way. The two pairs of feet stayed steady for a moment, before the man's left leg shifted back into a fighting stance. There was a struggle, and the two reappeared on the screen, a woman fallen, the man on top of her. Amanda shifted in her seat as we watched the man raise his elbow high before his fist swung down into the woman's face, once, twice, before he got up and ran off screen.

The queue of fans broke apart, surrounding the woman. The screen was flooded with people.

14:32:59 Suspect assaults Patricia Dorrell with fist.

'Have we got notes on Patricia's statement?' I shuffled through the papers. Amanda plucked out a blue witness statement in messy, patrol-cop handwriting.

'*I stopped the man as he was walking by and asked him what the event at the bookstore was,*' I read aloud. '*He said it was a signing with Jake Scully. I asked him who Jake Scully was, and he grabbed me by the arms and threw me onto the ground. I was punched twice and knocked unconscious.*'

'Hmm,' Amanda said. 'Superfan can't handle people not knowing who his hero is.'

'This doesn't feel right,' I said.

'What?'

'Well what kind of superfan is he if he can't even approach the author himself?' I said. 'He skirted around the back of the bookshelves to get out of the store. At no time did he come any closer than, what, five metres from Jake? Jake never even noticed him.'

'So?'

'So shouldn't he be like, *Oh! Jake! I love you!*'

I waved at an imaginary Jake. Amanda had a little smirk at my fan impression. I felt my face grow red.

'Shut up. You know what I mean.'

'Maybe that's the point,' she said. 'Maybe Jake not noticing him is the whole point. I mean he's an angry guy, isn't he? We can see that. Maybe he's angry at Jake. Angry enough to kill him. Was Jake in the practice of writing back to fans who wrote him?'

'I've looked through the fan letters Stella found in his office. From what I can see, he wrote back to fans in the beginning of his career,' I said. 'Some fans he even maintained a friendly correspondence with. But that was back when he was newly published, when being a celebrity of sorts had novelty. Around the time book two hit the US, he had to stop with the fan letters. There were so many.'

'The fan letters in the box, are they all there is?' Amanda asked.

'No, no, those are just the hard copies. Cary linked me into Jake's email account. There are hundreds in there. I've had a quick glance at them but I'll obviously have to look more closely.'

Woman, who had settled near us at the steps to the backyard, rose and limped a couple of steps on her braced leg. She opened her great wings and dropped her head, and again came that strange half-barking, half-growling I'd heard once before.

'What's up with Mother Goose?'

'She did this the other day,' I said. I got up and looked around the roof beams. 'There was a snake. She knew about it long before I did.'

Amanda leapt out of her seat as three loud bangs sounded from the front of the house. I'd thought the vigilantes would leave me alone during the day, but as I stood listening, I wondered if I was wrong. There were footsteps on my hardwood floor, and then a voice sounded from inside.

'Hellooo,' he called. 'Anybody home?'

Amanda seemed to recognise the voice. She ducked down quickly and started gathering up the little geese. I watched in confusion as she shepherded them back towards their house at the corner of the porch and shoved them all inside, pulling the towel down as a door. She even pushed Woman back into that corner. The big bird gave her no resistance.

Constable Lou Damford stepped from the hall into my kitchen. I felt a ripple of electricity through my chest, rage and humiliation.

'What the fuck?' I said. 'I didn't invite you in.'

'We called out,' Hench said, appearing beside his partner. 'We called and called and made ourselves plain at the front door. No one answered. We made the executive decision to force entry, in case anyone inside was in danger.'

'You did not call,' I said. 'We'd have heard you from back here.'

I walked into the kitchen and looked down the hall. The front door was off its hinges, lying flat on the floor.

'Steve's been hoarse.' Damford smiled, his acne scars stretching. 'Possible he wasn't loud enough.'

'What the hell are you doing here?'

'We've had reports from neighbours that your letterbox was blown apart by explosives. Ownership of explosives in the domestic environment, including fireworks and bomb-making paraphernalia, is a crime, mate.' He tucked his thumbs into his belt. 'We've been approved for a search of these premises.'

The smaller one, Hench, took a piece of paper out of his breast pocket and flung it into the sink. I looked back at Amanda. She was standing almost as a guard of my geese, one foot positioned in front of the door to their little house, her other foot pinning Woman into the corner of the porch. She wasn't looking at us. Her eyes were fixed on the floor.

'Why would I blow up my own letterbox?' I sighed, knowing it was useless but unable to stop myself. 'Why would someone . . . Urgh. Just forget it.'

'We won't be long,' Damford said, wandering past me to the sink. 'I'm sure we won't find anything. I'll just have a quick check under here.'

He took the dish rack by its side and tipped the dishes, glasses and cutlery standing in it onto the floor. The shattering noises set Woman squawking again.

'I'll look in here,' Hench said cheerfully, opening the fridge. He started scooping jars off of the top shelf and onto the tiles so that they smashed in sprays of vibrant colour across my kitchen floor. He picked up the milk bottle, unscrewed it, and poured the contents into the mess.

'You guys knock yourself out,' I said, wandering back to the porch. 'I'll be out back.'

I went to my seat on the porch while the Crimson Lake police trashed my house, telling myself it wasn't the worst thing that had happened to me that month. As I sat waiting for them to finish, it was Amanda's behaviour that got my attention. She slowly sank into a crouch beside Woman, and in time put an arm around the great bird, even stroking the huge white feathers of her good wing with the tips of her fingers. Woman didn't snap at her, but remained alert, giving an anguished squeak every now and then at the sounds that came from inside. Amanda's gaze was on the horizon. Her eyes were sad.

I was going to get something on these pricks. Amanda skulked away quietly in the middle of the officers' onslaught on my place. When Damford and Hench were finished, and I heard them walk out the front door, I dragged my laptop over and started looking around the internet for signs of them.

There wasn't much, which wasn't surprising. They weren't the most photogenic characters in the entire world. I found an article from the Holloways Beach rugby team that mentioned a good try just on half-time by Hench. The mud-spattered officer looked even more threatening drenched in sweat, high-fiving another player. It was the high-five guys give after a particularly sick joke, or a pub fight. The kind gang rapists use to tag each other in. Unwholesome desires in the eyes. Malice.

The article said Hench was forty-three. There was another article buried deep about a group of cadets joining up in Cairns, pictures of them getting on the bus down to Goulburn Academy. No pictures, but their names. Hench, seventeen. Damford, nineteen.

Two constables. Both in their early forties. In over twenty years of service, they'd never moved up a single rank. There were two possible reasons for this. One, they were incredibly badly behaved, and hadn't been taken up for the multiple promotional opportunities that must, by sheer service time alone, have come their way. If they were that bad on the job, they must have been connected – had family in the force that kept them from being discharged altogether. Was I to believe that both of them had protection from upstairs?

The only other explanation was that I'd been right in my early musings – these guys wanted to stay in patrol. They wanted to throw their weight around. Drive fast cars and kick down doors without wide-eyed, shivering probationary constables following them. While they occupied the space for patrol officers assigned to Crimson Lake, no new recruits could be posted there. It was their turf.

There was one more article that caught my attention. It was a small piece on a yachting blog that noted Damford's purchase of a very slick speed cruiser, navy blue, *The Eel*. I liked the name of the boat. I thought it suited the guy perfectly. There was a picture of Damford shaking hands awkwardly with the previous owner, his face turned away from the camera. I didn't know anything about boats. Idly, I copied the name of the boat and its type and punched them into the search engine, just messing around now, my search over.

The old advertisement for the boat was still up on the yacht broker's website. Jersey Boat Sales had listed the vessel for $79,999. A big red *SOLD* banner was plastered proudly over the image of the low, sharp boat.

That was an awful lot of play money for a constable. I went back to the original photograph of Damford and the boat-seller, the half-grip handshake and the back quarter of the man's face, all I could see as he seemed to reactively cower from the lens as the flash burst.

It took about six hours to clean the house after the officers had left. They'd done a solid job of destroying my things, but I also went overboard trying to remove the stain of their actions from the house and thus cleanse my own psyche. I even took the untouched plates and cups down from the shelves and gave them a going over in the sink. I had to know that some surfaces, particularly those I ate from and slept in, were newly clean.

Sean emailed me while I was re-hanging the door to tell me Kelly wasn't up for any sort of physical custody of Lillian, as expected, but she had sent through a bunch of photographs of my child as a kind of piecemeal gesture to keep me quiet. I knelt down on the floor in the hall and opened the attachment, and there, sitting at my old kitchen table – the one we'd purchased on an abysmal trip to Ikea as a new couple – was my infant daughter. I wasn't ready for how old she looked. She had enough hair now for a tiny jet-black ponytail. She was grinning, and in her open mouth I saw what I thought might have been the beginnings of a tooth. I zoomed in on the photograph and felt my face break into a wide smile. Her first tooth.

There was a knock at the door. I was so lost in my grief that I pulled it open before I'd arranged my face. Fabiana got a full-frontal glimpse of my downturned mouth and wet eyes before I realised what I'd done and turned away, swiped at my cheeks.

'Are you . . . okay?' she asked.

'I'm fine, I'm fine. It's bleach. I'm using bleach.' I walked away from her as fast as I could. I felt my back teeth grind together as her heels sounded on the hall floorboards.

'That wasn't an invitation to come in,' I called, taking refuge at the kitchen window.

'Well you should have shut the door, then.'

'I'd have thought you'd have had enough doors slammed in your face to know when the intention is there, Fab.'

'What is it?' she asked. 'Bad news?'

'No.' I wiped my nose on the back of my hand. 'Everything's fine. Is there something I can help you with?'

'Coffee?' she said.

'I'm out.'

'Tea, then.'

'I'm outta that, too.'

'Look, I didn't come here to harass you, Ted. I come in peace today.'

'I don't care what you come in.' I thrust open the cupboard doors. 'I'm out of tea and coffee. I had . . . visitors. They . . . *used* . . . everything.'

She looked at the shelf where Hench or his miscreant partner had aimed his sweeping arm at all the glass he could find, taking out the olive oil, some tomato sauce and the bachelor's liquid gold – a bottle of soy sauce. Her eyes fell to the very bottom shelf, where I'd lined up a couple of bottles of cheap wine.

•

When I asked myself what the hell I was doing sitting down on my back steps with this woman and some wine, I wondered if it was just that Hench and Damford's earlier attack had stripped the resistance from me. Those animals in uniform, or the vigilantes who came in the night, or the inevitability of the news that I was floating around in the town's bloodstream like a malignant cell spreading – one of them, all of them, had broken any resolve I'd mustered since leaving prison. But I had to admit, also, that there was something about Fabiana herself that intrigued me, if only that the rage I felt around her was something new to feel, something different to the quiet terror that had been my only friend since my arrest. There was something familiar about this kind of hurt. I remembered it from my time inside. Felt comfortably enveloped by it, like the fence at the bottom of the property.

'Do you get crocs here?' She motioned to the cyclone fencing in the distance as though she'd read my mind. The fading sunlight caught the red of the wine in her glass and some of the same colour woven into her dark hair, making her seem almost witch-like, a fire beauty. I looked away.

'I haven't seen any. But I hear them barking. Growling.'

She hardly seemed to be listening.

'Why don't you take me through that day, Ted?' she said suddenly.

'What?'

'That day. Why don't we talk about it?'

The anger turned, rolled.

'Because I don't have to,' I said, almost sneered. 'I don't have to do anything, Fabiana. I didn't have to let you in here. In fact, I don't know why I did. I think I might be going nuts. I'm tired. I'm tired of all of this.'

'Just give up, then,' she said. 'Stop hiding. Stop running. Tell me everything.'

'I'd be wasting my time with you,' I said.

'Well, I don't know.' She shrugged, rubbed her knees uncomfortably. 'I don't know if you're wasting it with me anymore.'

She didn't seem like the kind of woman who was frequently lost for words. And yet she was struggling before me, unsure where to look.

'You mean you might actually be coming around to the idea that I'm telling the truth?' I scoffed. 'I thought you said you worked for the *Herald*.'

'I've been looking into the case,' she said. 'Really looking into it. I listened to that woman, Valerie, when she gave me an earful about you and told me to check out your arrest photographs. How there wasn't a nick on you, and her theory about defensive wounds. I have to admit that some things about the case don't make any sense. She told me to go and investigate a man named Trevor Fuller.'

'The silent witness.' I leaned back against the sun-warmed porch. It was so like Valerie to be right on the money like that. 'Uh-huh.'

'I haven't been able to find much on him.'

'There isn't much.' I sipped my wine. 'Not under "Fuller" anyway. He has a couple of previous names, but after the trial he changed it again. Homeless people are always changing their names, trying to stay fresh in the police records every time they're arrested. During the trial he was Trevor Finch. But he was never called to the stand. We didn't get that far before they ruled no billing. His evidence was never heard.'

'What did Trevor know about you?' Fabiana asked.

'It's not what he knew, it's what he saw,' I sighed. I was sinking. Being drawn down deep into the bowels of my recollections of that day, into the miles and miles of police reports, into the hours and hours of interrogation video in which I tried to account for every second of that day, before, during, and after that awful moment when I laid eyes on Claire Bingley by the side of the road, not having any idea how very bad ever doing so was going to be for me.

Tick, tick, tick. The seconds going by.

12.47 pm. Marilyn Hope and Sally Hope drive past, seeing my car turn and stop suddenly in the bus stop.

12.48 pm. Gary Fisher drives past, seeing me with the back passenger door open.

12.48 pm. Michael Lee-Reynolds drives past, seeing me with the back passenger door open, my body half in, half out of the vehicle as I mess around in the back seat.

12.49 pm. Jessica and Diana Harper drive past, seeing me talking to Claire Bingley.

12.50 pm. Two more carloads of witnesses see me wave at the girl.

'And then what?' Fabiana was saying. I was sweating, wiping my palms on my damp forehead, trying to stop it dripping in my eyes. There was no sign of a storm on the mountains, meaning tomorrow's would be big, the land humidity-choked and gasping.

'Twelve-fifty, I drove off,' I said. 'I took the highway to the 7-Eleven, about twelve minutes up the road, and I bought bait.'

'There were no cameras inside that service station,' Fabiana said.

'No.'

'Why not?'

'It had only just become a 7-Eleven.' I rubbed my eyes. I was so tired of telling these stories. 'Before that, it had just been a privately owned station. The 7-Eleven was planning to refurbish it and add cameras to the interior. They had cameras on the outside of the building.'

'Why didn't your purchase of bait show up on the sales for the day?'

It was difficult not to scream that I'd answered these questions a hundred times already. Once I'd bitten back the sound, I eased air through my teeth.

'The guy's EFTPOS system was down,' I said. 'I took a bottle of water and the bait to the counter. I had a five dollar note for the water, but not enough for it *and* the bait. I asked to pay on EFTPOS, and the guy told me it wasn't working. He looked at the note in my hand and said not to worry about paying for the bait. Just to take it.'

'That seems unusual to me,' Fabiana said carefully. '7-Eleven is a big chain company. You'd think every item would be accounted for, leaving underling employees like that guy unable to just give stuff away.'

'The bait was a couple of bucks. And he didn't seem too interested in the job, if I'm honest. Pretty disinterested in life in general. Maybe the takings hadn't switched over to the big chain yet. Maybe this guy was leftover from when the station was privately owned, and he was used to doing things like that. I don't know. We never got to cross-examine him.'

'So you buy the water and get the bait. So far, you're invisible. Your purchases don't show up, and the guy doesn't remember you. He's disinterested.'

'There was a phone call, I think.' I frowned. 'In the middle of all this. While I was being served. He was distracted.'

'Distracted and disinterested,' she said.

'Right.'

'And accustomed to giving away small stuff. The guy doesn't ring the purchase in, which accounts for why it's not on the takings for the day.'

'No, he just took the cash.'

'So why didn't you show up on the exterior CCTV?'

I smirked ruefully. 'Because I walked in and walked out through the camera's blind spots.'

Fabiana stared at me. I knew how this sounded. I'd known how it sounded from the very start. As far-fetched as they came. But that was the story. I couldn't change it.

'The CCTV cameras covered the petrol pumps,' I said, demonstrating with my hands. 'They pointed straight out from the roof of the building. I parked around the side of the building and walked in underneath them. The road leading up to the petrol station curves away sharply from the driveway. So you don't see me. At all.'

'That's incredibly unlucky,' she said, trying to swallow her scepticism.

'You're telling me.'

'So you park and go into the store, and Trevor Fuller comes in after you?' She turned towards me, seemed to scooch a little closer.

'No, he never entered the store,' I said. 'He was hanging around outside. I don't know what he was doing. He might have been going through the bins there for food. They throw out a lot of outdated stuff from the convection ovens. He did appear on the cameras briefly, wandering around.'

'Trevor Fuller is long-term homeless. He had a couple of drug arrests back in the nineties under his various other names, and was treated at a psychiatric clinic in Kings Cross in 2009.'

'Yep. Hence me being completely unable to use him as a witness at trial, even if the whole thing hadn't have fallen apart before I could have,' I sighed. 'I have one witness in the whole world who proves me innocent. And he's a fucking homeless loon.'

I sculled the rest of my wine and poured myself more. When I offered her some, she refused.

'What exactly did Trevor Fuller say he saw?'

'He told police he saw me. I came around the corner on him really quick and he thought I was going to jump him, he said. He remembered me when he saw me on the news at a homeless shelter.'

'Did he see your car?'

'Yes.'

'Did he see *into* your car?'

I paused, watching her.

'Why?' I asked. 'What? So he doesn't see that Claire Bingley's not in there, tied up on the back seat or something?'

'I never said "tied up".'

'Stop.' I found my fist clenched against my forehead. 'Just stop. I don't know why we're talking like this. It always ends up the same way.'

We sat in a painful silence for a minute or so. She wanted to speak a couple of times, but before the sound could come from her lips she settled back again and turned away from me. I felt the flames licking up my insides.

'I like the Trevor Fuller line of inquiry,' I said. 'Okay? I like the feeling that I almost had a witness. That I almost had someone who could save me. You going and saying that even if he was the best, most credible witness in the country, it doesn't mean anything because he didn't see into the back of the car – that just ruins my day, all right? And it's been pretty shitty already so far.'

'Well, I'm sorry,' she said. I was surprised by it. I shuffled on the step.

'You left the bus stop at twelve-fifty,' Fabiana continued after a time, looking at my eyes. 'Claire was gone, vanished, when her bus drove past two minutes later.'

'Yep.'

'What if the times are wrong?' Fabiana said.

'What do you mean?'

'The first witness, Sally Hope, said it was twelve-forty-seven exactly when her mum drove past you,' Fabiana said. 'Sally reported that she remembered the exact time because she glanced at the clock in the car and calculated that they had thirteen minutes to get to her dance lesson. But what if she was wrong? But what if the clock in their car was off? And what if the bus's clock was out, too? Let's say that, across the twelve witnesses who account for your activity at the bus stop, they're all a little bit out. We can double the time, if you like, say the time between you leaving and Claire being gone was four minutes, not two.'

'Okay.' I shrugged. 'So what?'

'It means that he was *there*,' Fabiana said. 'It means he was no more than four minutes from that very spot when you got into your car and drove away. Minus from that the time it takes to get out of the car, walk up and grab the girl. Put her in his car, get back in. There's not a lot of time. He was nearby – very nearby – when you were there.'

'Four minutes. He could have driven up, seen her and grabbed her in that time,' I said. 'Or –'

'Or he was already there, watching, when you arrived,' she

said. 'He might have been about to pounce. He might have paused when you turned up so suddenly and unexpectedly. And when you moved on . . .'

The sweat had spread across my shoulder blades. I felt a trickle running down my spine.

'What do you remember about that moment? The minutes before?' she asked. 'Did you see anything? Hear anything? Do you remember any other cars parked nearby?'

I looked at the mountains. It was too much, all of it. I needed to finish it now. I stood and took the bottle from the porch, signifying the end of our conversation.

'Only her,' I said. 'All I remember is the girl.'

Fresh sheets usually put me right to sleep. But there was no sleeping after Fabiana left. The shrill seconds before I'd arrived at the bus stop played over and over in my mind as I lay in the dark.

I'd been thinking about the fight with Kelly. Arguing with her in my mind, the turning circle of blame always coming back to me, because she'd just had a baby and was slowly going out of her mind. No one in the house had been sleeping. I'd been clumsy on the job with exhaustion, filling in forms wrong, getting perps mixed up. On my days off I slept too much and didn't contribute around the household. Didn't hold her enough. Didn't talk to her enough.

At midnight I got up and dressed, checked on the sleeping geese and went out the front door. The cane field was alive with creatures fluttering and buzzing in the moonlight, a good helping of tiny winged things inspecting me, drawn in by my body heat, as I stood at the roadside looking. I went to the low brick wall at the front of the house and sat there listening to the sounds of the night, a truck's horn on a distant highway and the noise of night birds in the rainforest further down the road. The air was still thick with humidity, and a light sweat began at my temples.

It was an hour before I saw lights on the road. I crept behind the wall and crouched, watched as the lights went out just a hundred metres from where I hid. The vigilantes. The ridiculous hope I'd held that they might arrive flourished in my chest, and I was almost smiling as the car rolled past, gravel and dirt crumbling under its tyres. Datsun Bluebird, grey. There were four or five figures inside. The car rolled past without stopping, trying to see if all the lights were out. They were.

As the car moved on to turn around before the forest, I crept out from behind the wall and shuffled into the dark by a bush, my skin alive now and ticking with my heartbeat. The car returned, faster this time, rolling as fast as a man might jog. I saw the back passenger window roll down, the one behind the driver, and I rose to my feet as a girl leaned out the window.

'Kiddie fucker!' she screamed, and lit the fuse of a glowing red firecracker. Her face was lit candy-pink by the flames as she hurled the rocket towards my front porch. I recognised her.

'Hey!' I yelled. I had no real plan, and my lack of preparation showed when the car swerved back onto the road and headed straight for me. 'Hey! Hey! Hey!'

'Oh fuck!' one of the teens yelled. I bashed the bonnet with my hands as the vehicle flew by, but the dust it kicked up as it roared into the night blinded me, so I couldn't run after it. I stood coughing in the dark, the sulphur smell of the firecrackers on my tongue.

I congratulated myself on my sleuthing skills as I sat in my car on a stretch of dirt on the east side of Crimson Lake, watching Harrison Scully and another tall, lanky boy wander into view at the exact moment I'd predicted. I'd made a few broad assumptions to find Harrison here in this moment. First, I'd assumed that, rather than attending the nearest state high school at Smithfield, up north, Jake's heterosexual Christian charade probably required that the kid be enrolled at either St Agnes School or the Crimson Lake Christian College, both located south on highway 91. I'd assumed Harrison would catch the bus rather than get his girlfriend to drive him, being so wrapped up in his own angry masculinity that such a gesture would have been refused outright. I'd assumed that, rather than eating breakfast at home and risking having to engage in conversation with his mother, Harrison was the kind of kid who'd grab an Ice Break and a bag of chips on the walk to the bus stop, detouring through the town with a friend rather than going to school directly. And now here he was, walking around the corner of the Crimson Lake Post office, a beaten-up denim bag slung over his shoulder and iced coffee in hand. Genius.

'Harry,' I said as I got out of the car. The boy turned and looked at me, almost unrecognising, before telling his friend to go ahead. No sign of the gentle Harrison Scully again. This guy was all aggression. I walked up and stood in the wet grass, and the angular young man squinted at me from beneath his beanie.

'Harry?' he sneered.

'Sorry. Harrison then.'

'What do you want now?' He started walking.

'I actually wanted to know if you were with your girlfriend last night,' I said.

'What girlfriend?'

'The girl with the shaggy hair. Pink pigtails. You know the one.'

'Dude, what the fuck?' he sighed. 'Jesus, why are you so obsessed with me?'

I laughed. 'I'm not obsessed with you. I'm trying to get a message to your girlfriend. And maybe to you. She's been driving by and chucking shit at my house with a bunch of goons. It's getting really boring.'

Harrison stopped and pulled a deeply sceptical face. I stopped with him.

'Yeah,' I said.

'Why would they be chucking shit at your house?'

I chewed my lips. Maybe this had been a bad idea. My stomach started to sink.

'Her older brother was talking about this paedophile guy who lives down by the lake,' Harrison said. 'He heard the guy moved to town from Sydney to try to hide from the police. I know they were talking about going and scaring the dude. But they said he was, like, an old man or something.'

I rubbed my face, looked away.

'You're not –'

'No, I'm not,' I said. 'I might have the wrong crew of goons.'

'That's funny.' Harrison cracked a rare grin. 'People chucking shit at your house. Like is it literally shit, or –?'

'No. Firecrackers. Paint.'

'That's hilarious.'

'Yeah. Hilarious.'

'What other people do in their own time isn't any of my business,' the boy said. 'So you can fuck off with your messages for her. I suggest you stay away from her altogether.'

'You suggest that, do you?'

'Hell yes,' he said and looked me up and down, mostly up. 'Don't be a fool, bro.'

'I'll try not to be,' I said. 'What's your girlfriend's name?'

Harrison twitched, just once, with tension. I suppose he might have thought I really would stick to my job, stay away from him and the girl. But all the bravado in front of his lanky friend, who was watching closely from afar, was completely lost on me. It was no longer a joke. I really was getting too deep into his secret little world.

'She's not my girlfriend,' he said. 'I don't know her name.'

The boy walked off, his head down and shoulders up. When he got to his friend, the other boy looked back at me with concern, like he knew I'd just given Harrison a good spooking.

Amanda rode her yellow bike down the wide stone stairs of Cairns train station, pulling it alongside my car and almost causing a homeless man with a shopping trolley full of bags to lose his load in order to avoid a collision. Her smile was spread wide, so I knew we were at another peak in the rollercoaster of her emotions.

'Of all the places we could go to pursue a killer, a bookstore is probably one of the best.' She grinned. 'Right?'

'There are worse places,' I yawned.

We took the backstreets north through the city, pausing in our conversations to cross major roads, Amanda zipping between the cars as a colourful blur while I waited for traffic lights. She was very good on the bike. Bored waiting for me, she did wheelies and jumps in alleyways, impressing the men lying there on newspapers, stained with sweat and sun-bronzed in every shade of brown.

Our plan was to hit Cairns Books and talk to any of the staff who might have seen or known the attacker who attended Jake's book signing. I'd gone through the fan letters again, discarding everything written by women, trying to find the rage and restlessness I'd seen in the man in the CCTV footage in the words on the pages. For the most part, what anger there was in the fan letters was of a spiritually righteous type. They were trying to teach Jake where he'd gone wrong by messing with the scriptures, trying to show him the 'light'. It was a spitting-from-the-pulpit anger. Not the punching-women-in-the-street kind.

Amanda put a hand on the side of the car as I caught up to her, letting the vehicle's momentum pull her along. I put an elbow on the windowsill.

'The victim of the street assault,' I said. 'You think the fan hit her because she didn't know who Jake was?'

'First she asks the guy what the event is,' Amanda says. 'He's happy to answer that. It's only when she asks him who Jake Scully is that she gets clocked.'

'Why would this superfan hurt Jake if he loved him so much?' I mused. 'I mean, let's play it out. The guy loves Jake so madly he's sent into a rage by anyone who doesn't know who he is. Jake becomes a kind of obsession. He makes contact with Jake somehow and lures him out one night so that he can confront him. Things go wrong. Jake ends up as croc food.'

'How does he lure him out?' Amanda frowned.

'Before that – how does he make contact? I'm not seeing him in the fan letters. I'm not seeing him in the phone records. Does he know him?' I asked. Amanda was silent, weaving the bike around clumps of grass that had risen up between the cracks in the alley floor, the humidity bringing the insatiable wild to the concrete sprawl.

'I did think the hoodie was weird,' Amanda said. 'It's Cairns. Who wears a hoodie? You'd only bear that kind of heat because you're afraid you're going to be recognised.'

'By Jake?'

247

'Maybe. What about Cary?' Amanda glanced at me. 'What about one of the bookstore staff? Jake's publisher from Sydney was there. Maybe the fan was some kind of aspiring author. Those wannabe writer types are all fucking crazy.'

'What makes you say that?'

'There was one in my dorm for a while at Brisbane Women's. Frieda, think her name was. Or Freddie? Some publisher had taken an interest in one of her early pieces, and the girl got the idea that she was just sort of waiting for the woman at the publishing house to say yes to one of her manuscripts. You know what young people are like. She lets her imagination run away with her and she starts telling people she's practically under contract. Then she's got a verbal contract. Then it's a signed contract. For years, this chick's been writing, starting one novel after another after another. She sends the woman the first thirty thousand words of a book and the woman says, "Oh that's great, honey. That's great. Not publishing quality, but you're getting there."'

'How frustrating,' I said.

'Frieda sucks it up, tells her friends and family it was a misunderstanding – the publisher's accepted her for a mentorship, not actual publication. Still bullshit, but it saves face, right? And it maintains the fantasy. She feels like she's getting closer and closer all the time. After a couple of years, Frieda's, like, seven or eight manuscripts in with this woman. They've been in communication since Frieda left high school. And then the woman leaves the publishing company. Snap, just like that, she decides to be a stay-at-home mum instead.'

'Oh no,' I said.

'Yeah. She passes Frieda on to another guy at the publishing house, but the first manuscript the guy gets? He says it's shit. "Naive hack-job with no real plot." Frieda used to go around the dorm mumbling that to herself. *Naive hack-job with no real plot. Naive hack-job with no real plot.*'

'Oh dear.'

'Make matters worse,' – Amanda twitched – 'Frieda's still obsessed with the old publisher. Starts following her new blog about parenting. Ex-publisher turned yummy mummy is writing about one of her kids, how she encourages the kid even when he's failing at something terribly. She says she used to do it when she worked in publishing. That sometimes people's work was so bad, there was no point in trying to teach them anything. She just tried to make them feel good. *That's great, honey. That's great. Keep trying!*'

'Frieda didn't take it well?'

'Not at all.'

'So what happened?' I asked.

'Frieda went round to the yummy mummy's house and did a hack job,' Amanda said. 'Lost the plot.'

'Were the kids all right?' I asked.

'Nope.'

'Jesus.' I leant back in the car, looked at the road ahead of me. 'Over *books*.'

'Books are something else, I think,' Amanda said. 'They're, like, your guts. You scoop out your own guts and you give them to someone on a plate and they turn their nose up. And then there you are. Hollow. Gutless. At least, that's how I imagine it to be. I've never written anything.'

'You're very visual,' I said. 'Maybe you should write something.'

'Ode to Ted!' She raised a finger in the air. 'There once was a man from Sydney . . .'

'I think that's a limerick.'

'Whose lips! Were as red! As a kidney!'

'I think you're getting worse,' I sighed. 'Is it possible you're actually getting worse?'

A car pulled in to the alleyway ahead of us, turning off the main road awkwardly between two parked cars. I slammed on the brakes, though there was plenty of distance between us, wondering if it was me who was going down the one-way street the wrong way. Before I could wonder aloud, Amanda had walked her bike back to my window and stood looking ahead, her lips pursed.

'That's Damford and Hench,' she said, glancing behind her at the mouth of the alley. 'Reverse back.'

'What?' I said. 'I can't. Wha– . . . How do you know it's them?'

The car rolling towards us was a white Jeep. But as I looked closely, I could see the outline of the two cops' uniforms as the windscreen fell into shadow.

'Fuck,' I said.

'There's time,' Amanda said.

'No.' I put the car into park and got out. 'You go to the bookstore. I'll meet you there. I'm not spending my life running from these fucks.'

I don't know what got a hold of me, but it was something totally beyond logic. The sound of Amanda's bike ticking away towards the road behind us snapped me out of that momentary violent fantasy, and I stood fully awake and afraid by the open car as the Jeep stopped a metre or so away. I glanced into the car to try to see if I had any weapons to my name, but there was nothing there – an empty cardboard box that had held some of my things when I moved, and some papers scattered about.

I'd known cops during my time in the force who would hound criminals like this. The first few appearances look like chance meetings, but after a time, the cops I knew would begin to pop up in the perp's life at places and times they couldn't possibly have known about. Finding me in Cairns, hunting me down in a non-police vehicle was a move meant to show me that I was on their minds. That whenever we met, it was planned, and there was nowhere I could go that they wouldn't find me.

Try sleeping at night when you know that. When you know that they're always over your shoulder somewhere. Watching.

Because I'd begun to think of them as 'piggies' from the moment we'd met, it was hard not to apply animal characteristics to their movements, to see as absurd the way they waddled unevenly, like they were accustomed to all fours. Lou Damford, with his deep acne scars, walked towards me with the familiarity of a friend.

'Empty your pockets and put your hands on the roof of the car.'

'No,' I said.

His partner Steven laughed. 'Don't be a stupid fuck,' he said.

'Is that an undercover police vehicle?' I asked, nodding in the direction of their car. 'Does it have a dash camera?'

'No,' Damford said, smiling. 'It doesn't.'

'Then you're not on police business.'

Damford flicked out his baton, the one I'd copped in the knee a few days earlier. I felt the muscles in my legs tighten, my fingers tuck into fists.

'You're going to submit to a search, or you're going to get hurt.'

'I think I'm going to get hurt anyway,' I said.

Damford swung the baton at me, missed as I stepped back towards my car. I put my hands up, frightened by the weight he'd put behind the swing.

'I'm complying,' I said. I put my hands on the car. 'I'm complying.'

Hench popped open the front passenger door and started rifling through the contents of the car, grabbing papers and glancing over them before he threw them into the alleyway. Damford put his baton away and started frisking me, his hard, flat hands slapping at my shoulder blades.

'What the fuck do you guys want? Huh?' I said. 'What do you actually want from me?'

'We want what all *real* cops want,' Hench said, patting down my sides. 'We want safe streets, and happy women and children.'

'Real cops?' I said. 'So you're upset with who I am, but extra insulted that I used to be one of you.'

'*Murder in the Top End,*' Damford said, lifting the book from the glove box and showing his partner over the roof of the car. The two exchanged a meaningful look, as though finding the book only confirmed something they'd suspected all along. What it was, I didn't know. The two knew I'd been working with Amanda. They'd seen her in my company. Twice.

'What's your problem with Amanda?'

'What do you think, arsehole? She's a fucking butcher.'

'You knew she was a killer before I turned up,' I said. 'What's your problem with her and me?'

'Shut the fuck up.' Hench jabbed me in the back, right in the kidneys.

'Just search the car and fuck off then,' I said.

'See, the thing about your crime, Ted, is that your re-offence stats are out of this world,' Hench murmured, working his way up my legs. 'Untreated child rapists with a propensity towards violence, like you, have a sixty per cent recidivism rate.'

'I had no idea you were such a scholar,' I said.

'Means you're more likely to do it again than not,' he said, his hands at my hips. 'You have sexual stimulus in your life, the chances are even higher. Now, if we were to find you with material sexually stimulating for a man with your tastes . . .'

'What are these, Ted?' Damford asked from across the vehicle, holding up a copy of *Rise*, Jake Scully's third book, with the teenage girl on the cover. He tapped the book. 'How old's this girl?'

'I notice that Amanda Pharrell has an interesting sort of body type for a full-grown woman,' Hench said, his hands still lingering at my hips. 'She's particularly . . . underdeveloped. Wouldn't you say, Ted?'

I eased air through my teeth.

'She's got no tits, is what I'm saying.' Hench slid his hands around my hips and gathered a handful of my crotch. He squeezed, his breath in my ear. 'Does she get you hard, Ted?'

I tried to shift sideways, and Hench's hands rose swiftly, tucked under my arms and pulled me back. I lost balance, turned just in time to cop his knee in my chin. My teeth sank into my bottom lip. I staggered, going down on one knee, trying to squirm away from him.

'There's no fucking dash cam,' I said. 'There's nothing stopping me from fighting back.'

253

'You go ahead and try.' Hench smiled as his partner rounded the car behind me.

I must have been unconscious for less than an hour, because it wasn't Amanda who found me. A waitress from a restaurant further up the alley had noticed me while she was emptying the bins, noticed my good pair of shoes sticking out from behind my car. I woke to the sensation of her pressing a tea towel to my face and calling back to her colleagues.

'Get an ambulance!'

'No, don't.' I reached into my mouth, touched a gap at the back of my jaw where a tooth had been. 'Don't call anyone.'

They'll recognise you in a hospital. They'll call the police if the injuries are bad.

How bad was it?

My head was swimming. I clawed my way up the shifting concrete and tried to sit, felt my ribs crunch. Could I drive? Blood rattled in my throat.

'You need an ambulance, mate. You're mincemeat.'

I examined my blood-soaked hands. The skin was off all of my knuckles. Had I got some good shots in? I hoped so.

'Get my phone.' I waved up the alleyway. 'It's . . . It's up there somewhere. They threw it. Get it and give it to me. I know who to call.'

I had little memory of Dr Gratteur coming for me, or the ride in her car to Cairns Hospital. My first truly vivid memories were of lying flat looking at the wispy old woman as she sat sewing a gash on my forearm, the curved needle tugging at the flesh as she pulled the wound closed. I thought I was on a bed, but as I watched I noticed my numb fingers lay in a strange trench that ran the length of the table. I shifted my head and felt steel under me.

'Is this an autopsy table?' I asked. Valerie glanced at me.

'It is.'

'Lauren Freeman might have lain here,' I whispered. Letting my eyes fall closed was glorious.

'Well! Believe it or not, that's actually one of the least crazy things you've said in the last hour or so.' The doctor stood, her stool squeaking on the floor. 'Might be time for more yummy yummy drugs, I think.'

She fiddled with an IV line in my other arm. I stretched and heard my knees pop, had flashes of them being knocked from beneath me. A dull ache infected everything.

'Do the police know I'm here?' I asked.

'You told me it was the police who did this to you.'

'No, yes. But. Do the other police –'

'No one knows you're here,' she replied.

'Except me,' a voice said. I heard heels on the tiled floor. 'Jesus Christ, Ted, what the fuck happened?'

A warm hand on my forehead. I opened my eyes and found my vision had blurred. I shifted up, trying to decide which colourful shape was Valerie and which was Fabiana.

'I'd love to know how you got in here,' Valerie said.

'I've switched sides,' Fabiana told her. 'Or at least I'm not . . . I'm not sure anymore. I'm neutral. Look, I'm not going to be a pain in the arse. I just wanted to know if he's all right.'

'How did you find out I was here?' I asked.

'I have my ways. Couple of waitresses reported to cops in Cairns that a big guy with black hair had been beaten. Said some old woman picked him up before the ambulance could get there. You weren't answering your phone. It didn't take a genius.'

'Old woman?' Valerie snorted.

'Who did this to you?' Fabiana helped me as I struggled to sit up. 'I want to know names. We'll get the details down in time for the nightly news in Sydney. This is *bullshit*.'

'Are you daft, girl? Why do you think he's here?' Valerie snapped. 'He's here because he can't even go to a public fucking hospital right now or someone will recognise him. If you put a word of this in the news I'll smack that lipstick right off your face.'

'This is absolutely appalling! His charges have been dropped. He can't be treated like this!'

'Well, excuse me if I don't go falling down in admiration at your crusade for justice, honey,' Valerie said. 'Let me remind you that you were in here mere days ago trying to hang him in the town square.'

'Can you stop?' I said. 'I just want to go home. Please take me home.'

'Even if he was guilty, I wouldn't stand by and let a man be beaten in the street like a fucking dog,' Fabiana said.

'I don't know.' Valerie shrugged. 'It makes great news.'

'Stop.' I grabbed the closest blurry shape, which turned out to be Fabiana. 'Just get me home.'

Dear Jake,

Yesterday I went on a scouting tour. Do you know why? Because I wanted to know what it's like to have so much to lose.

I've never had much to lose, myself. I don't count material things, even though you've got that beautiful house stuffed pretty full of useless junk, it looks like. Lots of modern art. That's all Stella's doing, I imagine. No, what I'm talking about is the walls and structures we build inside ourselves. Most people start doing it from the very beginning, when they're children. Your parents help you put down the basics. The slab. The floorboards. The tiles. Your self-confidence. Your strength. The essentials, like how to give and receive love. You've got all that going. I watched you in the evening with the boy and your trophy wife, and though he's clearly a failure waiting to happen and she's got all the inner complexity of a schoolkid's lunchbox, you love them. You are capable of that.

My foundations are crumbled and broken. I don't know if I was born this way or what. I don't trust anyone. I go about the world tucked into myself, hateful. I'm like a spider in a hole. It's cold in here.

You. You have nice strong foundations. On top of them you've built walls, and a roof to keep out the rain. I bet you feel safe. I bet it's a happy brain you've got in that handsome skull. Built strong.

I like destroying things. I always have. I like taking things apart and seeing how they work. When I was a kid I liked to break toys with my hands. I'd rip up teddies and pull the heads off dolls. Some toys were tough, I had to get Daddy's hammer out to smash 'em up. As I sat in the dark last night looking up at your glorious house, watching you go from room to room, I thought about tearing you apart, Jake. Striking first at your confidence. Then at your strength. What if I threatened the people you love, Jake? How long would it take you to crack?

What if I went into your house and stabbed your pretty little goth boy in his bed, Jake? Would he drop the tough-guy facade and cry out for his papa?

What's it gonna take to get your attention?

I listened to the tapping for a long time before I ventured to lift my head from the pillow and look down at the end of the bed. It was Amanda sitting there working on her laptop, stopping now and then only to curl wisps of her wild hair around her long fingers. The bedside table was littered with crumpled pill packets. I rolled over slightly, took one, and pulled it back into the darkness beneath the sheet with me, popping the capsules out in the dark.

'Are you awake?' she asked.

'Mmm-hmm.'

The whole bed shuddered as she leapt from the bottom to the pillow beside me, the motion setting off all my aches and pains at once.

'Finally! Jesus! It's been three days!'

'No,' I groaned. 'Surely not.'

She snuggled under the sheets. I lay looking at her, querying the kind of woman who recoiled from my touch like she'd been burned but who would happily sneak under my sheets, presumably with no idea what I was wearing underneath them. I checked. I was wearing pyjama pants. My ribs were taped, and the gash in my left arm had been wrapped tightly in cotton. I had no idea what my face looked like, but it didn't feel good.

'Get ready for the download,' Amanda said.

'I'm ready.'

'One.' She held up a finger. 'None of the bookstore staff recognised the angry fan from the book launch. But one of the ladies who worked there helpfully mentioned that she thought the guy was young, and had dark hair in a ponytail.'

'All right,' I said.

'Two,' Amanda said, 'the street on which Cairns Books lies isn't the most secure street in the entire world. But there are some CCTV cameras on it. I contacted a pool supplies shop a few blocks down from the bookstore and asked them to go back through their footage and see if they could see the guy. Took them a whole day.'

'What did they find?'

'They found the guy.'

'And?'

'And he walked right by the store. Hood up. Completely useless.'

'Why did you bother telling me about it, then?' I frowned.

'Because I think you should be aware of every nuance of my independent, solo and entirely one-man investigation in the time you've been lying here like a half-chewed slug,' she said. 'I've been working my arse off. How can you appreciate that unless you know every –'

'All right, all right, all right.'

'Three,' she continued, wary of being interrupted again, 'I also obtained useless shots of the guy walking by a liquor store and a shoe shop.'

'You're truly wondrous.'

'And then I got *this brilliant shot* of him from outside the train station!' she wailed in triumph, turning the laptop towards me. I stared at the long face of a man in his early twenties, his eyes downcast to a mobile phone, the hood of his jacket around his shoulders.

'Lo! There stands our foe!' she trumpeted.

'The villain, unmasked!' I joined in for once. 'So who is he?'

'No idea.' Amanda snuggled down against the pillows. 'I was just going through some of the Last Light Chronicles Fan Club profiles on Facebook to see if anyone looks similar.'

I lay back against the soft bed and watched her scrolling through the profile pictures on the screen. Now and then she stopped when a name appeared beside a blank picture, taking the meagre information from the profile and the name itself to do a Google search for photographs of the individual. It was painstaking work, but she seemed to do it on autopilot, her eyes not wavering from the screen, her face set. I tossed and turned and slept a little, and she never moved but for her fingers on the keys, tapping robotically.

I only realised I was dozing off again when I was awakened by her quiet 'Huh.'

'What?'

'I've been going through photos from all Jake's reading events on the Facebook pages of various booksellers,' she said. 'What do you think about this guy?'

She showed me a picture of Jake sitting at a desk beside what looked like a theatre stage, his broad back a mass of grey wool at the bottom of the picture. At the corner of the frame was a young man with a long face, brooding eyes hidden beneath a heavy brow. One arm lay limp at his side, the other clutching it awkwardly. He was standing apart from the men and women swamping the table.

He was younger in the picture than he was in the CCTV footage.

'Looks pretty similar,' I said. 'Can you get any other angles?'

Amanda clicked through and stopped on another crowded picture, the same theatre space now being used as a cocktail party setting.

'Is that Jake?' Amanda pointed to the uppermost edge of the picture. The same grey wool jumper. The young man with the ponytail. Jake appeared to be whispering in the kid's ear.

'How can we find out who that kid is?' I asked.

'Maybe he's been tagged.' Amanda went back to the original photograph, swept the pointer over the faces in the crowd. Names flickered and disappeared. None appeared for the ponytailed man.

'Start writing to those other people. See if you can find someone who knows him. We'll see if his name is in the fan letters.'

I closed my eyes, tried to remember something about the three days I'd lost in slumber. I had vague recollections of Amanda being there. I remembered wandering out into the hall, shivering, the sheet clutched around me, spying her at the kitchen table on her laptop in the middle of the night. Amanda standing outside the toilet talking to me while I tried to remain upright, too exhausted to be embarrassed by the sounds of my pissing, too drugged to hang on to what she was saying. There was also a deeply troubling memory of going to the crack in the boarded-up windows in the early morning or late afternoon and seeing Amanda outside on the nature strip, talking to Damford and Hench.

I knew the memory was real because the Amanda of my mind was a bright, excited, tirelessly cheerful character. And I'd been shocked by how subdued she was, standing there before the two chubby, dark-eyed officers. She was staring at her feet, listening to them lecture her. Threaten her. She wasn't the eternal child I knew. She looked her age.

What had they been talking about?

A car engine revved outside. Amanda and I turned and looked at the doorway. On the back porch, I heard Woman begin to squawk as the revving increased, higher and higher, the spray of gravel.

'What the fuck is that?'

'I don't know. It's not vigilantes. They don't come during the day.'

I got out of the bed, and all my pains came to life at once, my hips clicking and ribs crunching and head swirling. I gripped my way to the front room, Amanda following. She took one crack in the side of the boarded up window, and I took the other.

There was a green sedan on the road, revving and revving, the driver now and then dropping the car into drive and spraying clay and rocks. My hands were shaking as I held onto the wood, trying to see the faces in the car. They were all adult men.

'These aren't the ones,' I told Amanda. 'The usual ones.'

'You're gonna die, Ted Conkaffey!' the man in the passenger seat hollered. 'You're gonna die, you piece of shit!'

'Well!' Amanda sighed. 'That's not very ni–'

Gunshots popped at the front of the house, and I heard the bullets tear into the boards on the window in the other room. I glimpsed the shooter in the back seat, sweeping his aim across the house.

'Get down!' I cried.

Amanda hit the floor before I did. I sank into a painful crouch then fell on my stomach as bullets tore through the boarded windows, showering us in splinters.

The car roared away and I rolled onto my back, looking up at the beams of light filtering through the holes. There were eight or nine, a crooked gold ladder leading towards the ceiling. Amanda was lying on her stomach looking at me, her hands, covered in woodchips, splayed out in front of her.

'That was the most exciting thing I've been through in . . .' She paused, considered. 'Weeks, at least.'

'I can't say I share your enthusiasm.' I dragged myself to my feet. My knees felt wobbly. 'I'll feed the geese and lock them up, you get your things. Let's get out of here, at least for a while.'

I told Amanda I'd meet her at her office, that I had an errand to run. But in truth I wanted to be alone to try to get my head around the idea that someone had just shot at my house. Thoughts whizzed through my mind as I wound the car aimlessly through the cane plantations, going nowhere.

I was so lucky I didn't live with my wife and child anymore.

I needed to call the police.

The police had almost killed me three days earlier.

I needed to get my geese out of there. They weren't safe.

The last thought caused the tingle in my nose that comes before tears, but the emotion didn't go further than that. I couldn't lose it now. Not over geese. But I couldn't deny that Woman and her babies had provided a great relief for me in my days in Crimson Lake, both by taking the place of my lost child and by reminding me that I wasn't the most helpless creature around – that in fact there was danger and terror all around, and that if these birds could survive, I could too. I'd enjoyed sitting on the porch in the mornings and looking at them, remembering them huddled in the cardboard box I'd taken them to the vet in, their feathers fluffed with raw, primal fear. Their lives, literally, in my hands. Whatever had happened to bring them to my door, it had ended. Maybe one day, like them, I'd be rescued from this.

I stopped at the side of the road and held my head. The fires inside were swelling, swirling. This was getting dangerous. I felt all my injuries come alive at once as the anger ripped through me. Anger at Damford and Hench, anger at the hillbillies shooting at my house, anger at that snide little shit Harrison Scully. A kid who'd hurl himself, sobbing, against my chest and demand physical consolation one second and look at me like I was a piece of trash the next, talk down to me in the street like he was a full-grown man.

When I was a kid and an adult asked for me something, I fucking gave it. Because that's what you did. Adults were adults, no matter who they were. Their word ruled. You didn't consider what they could or couldn't do to you and weigh your options.

I realised I was staring through the windscreen in a daze, my phone in my fingers. Before I could stop myself, I was googling the local state school. I was going to find Harrison's girlfriend before she and her vigilante friends spread news of my presence in town any further. Already, it seemed, they'd let some rather dangerous characters know what I'd been accused of and where I lived. If they kept going, I'd have a mob on my doorstep in days. Maybe I could put the fear of god into her somehow. Maybe if I rattled her a bit I could stem the leak. Part of me knew it was futile. But I was so shaken by the shooting that I needed a mission, right now, a project to focus me, stop me from falling off the edge.

I looked through the listings of state schools around Crimson Lake and clicked on the first one. My hands were shaking as I selected the number. I cleared my tight throat, stretched my neck as the receptionist came on the line.

'Thorn Crest State School, Marian speaking.'

'How ya goin', Marian. M'name's Ted Collins. I'm a contractor with the Department of Transport and Main Roads, workin' up on State Route 91 here. I'm sorry to bother ya,' I said, and sniffed. 'But I'm doing some stuff here on the roadside and there's a bunch of schoolkids in a Datsun Bluebird making absolute arses of themselves right on the edge of the turnoff.'

'Oh dear.'

'Yeah, look I don't mean to be a snitch.' I sniffed again. 'But I've asked them to move on and they just told me to fuck off, basically.'

'My god,' Marian the receptionist sighed. 'Where's this?'

'Up on the highway. Turnoff near Pickering Street. The ringleader of this group's a young girl with black and pink hair. Pigtails. These lot are smoking up a chimney in their bloody school uniforms and all.'

'Pink hair?' Marian perked up. 'Oh no, that doesn't sound like one of our girls. We've got the strictest dress code here in the whole region.'

'Really?'

'Yes indeed. Our uniform policies are of the highest standard. We take great pride in our students' appearance, in their representation of the school. We have forty-three students in the secondary school, and none of them have coloured hair. Are you sure they were school students?'

I hung up on Marian and dialled Smithfield State, Bringley State and Rosetta State schools. My temperature was starting to fall. I leant against the window as I told my story to the receptionist, Greg, at Hoffman State High School.

'Right,' Greg snapped suddenly. 'That sounds like that bloody Zoe Miller again.'

'Sorry,' I sat up. 'Who?'

'Jessie,' Greg the receptionist was saying in the background of the call, 'Jessie, ring Carmel, will you? Zoe Miller and those boys are off smoking on the side of the highway. Mr Collins? Mr Collins, I'm still here. Thank you for your call. We'll send our day officer out to retrieve the students.'

'Okay, thank –'

He hung up on me.

I drove, consumed with unexpected guilt at having pulled the wool over the eyes of a bunch of hardworking school receptionists and probably landing Zoe Miller in trouble she didn't deserve, all so I could chase her down and mouth off to her for letting my cat out of the bag. It was a stupid thing to do. I squeezed the steering wheel, tense. She was a kid. What did I think I was doing? I was getting reckless now, trying to protect my secret, trying to get to the bottom of things that really had nothing to do with my search for Jake Scully's killer. I needed to focus. Stay on the job. Exercise caution.

I saw Dynah Freeman standing by the side of the road and forgot all about caution.

Dynah was waiting at the bus stop at the far end of Crimson Lake, in a group of people her own age, I presumed heading in the direction of the university for afternoon classes.

I jogged painfully towards the bus stop just as the bus was arriving. Dynah saw me coming, and her reaction wasn't one of overwhelming pleasure to see me.

'Just two minutes.' I held up some fingers. 'Three, max.'

'This is my bus.'

'I'll pay for a cab,' I said. Dynah's friends exchanged meaningful glances with her, asking her to give them some sort of signal if she was in trouble. She seemed to consider it.

'I'm fine. He's a friend of my mum's,' she told her friends, waving them off. The same brooding look I'd seen on her before came over her as she watched the bus roll away. She'd probably taken on the look at her sister's funeral, and now it was a mask that came down every time someone mentioned the girl. She must have worn it for every Christmas. Every birthday.

'Cigarette?' she asked, slipping one from a packet. I took one, just to be social. 'What the fuck happened to you?'

'Car accident,' I said. 'I'm all right.'

'I wasn't concerned.' She snorted.

'I kind of felt like, at your mother's place, you had something more to say to me about your sister,' I said.

'Why don't you just ask Amanda what happened?' Dynah asked, searching my eyes. 'I hear you're working with her.'

'Where did you hear that?'

'It's a small town.' She exhaled smoke. 'You take a shit, everybody knows about it.'

I contemplated what this meant, whether she was closed off to me now as a tiny window into Lauren's world, into what caused her to be in a car with Amanda that night, the popular girl and the school weirdo, parked alone in the dark.

'People like to keep me updated on what she's doing,' Dynah said. 'It's weird. I don't know why they think it helps. I can't stop them. They text: *I saw Amanda here. I saw Amanda there.* Someone said they saw her with some big guy, black hair. Sounded familiar.'

'I don't know what to say.' I shrugged.

'What are you two up to?' Dynah asked. 'Trying to prove her innocent? She going after wrongful incarceration compensation or something?'

'No.' I squinted in the midday sun. 'No. She doesn't know I'm looking at her case at all.'

'So you're looking at the case?'

I'd come to the bus stop full of questions for Dynah, and now I felt like I was under fire. Her gaze tugged at me.

'I don't really know. I guess I just got curious,' I said. 'She's

268

a weird creature. I can't decide whether she's dangerous or hilarious.'

'Uh-huh. She's pretty funny.'

'No, I mean,' – my face was burning – 'I mean in terms of her personality, not, um, her deeds.'

'Yep.'

'And then you said Lauren wasn't the girl everyone thought she was.'

'Yeah.' Dynah sniffed. 'She wasn't. So what? What difference does it make what kind of girl she was? You know, I spend a lot of my time shovelling dirt onto Lauren's grave. And just when I think I'm done, people like you come along and start digging her up again.'

'I'm sorry.' I found I couldn't look at her. 'I shouldn't have bothered you with it.'

'S'all right.' She sighed, after a time. 'It's not like it hasn't happened before.'

There was a man near my car. I mightn't have noticed him had I not been avoiding eye contact with Dynah, ashamed of disturbing her sister's memory so blatantly just to get away from my own troubles. The man bent and lifted a huge black camera, and started snapping.

'Oh, fuck!' I held a hand up to my face.

'What?'

'Nothing, nothing. Thanks, Dynah. Thanks.' I turned and started walking away, towards the man with the camera, then remembered I'd offered Dynah cab money and started walking back. I stopped short, horrified at the idea of the cameraman getting shots of me giving a young woman cash on the side of the street.

'Urgh.' I gave a pained expression. 'I know I promised you cab money.'

'Damn straight,' she said.

'I'm. Right now, I just, uh . . .'

'Just go.' She waved me away. 'Douchebag.'

I walked up on the guy by my car with barely contained fury. He was a thin man with dark curls and a short, grey beard. He continued snapping. Media.

'Take one more photo of me and I'll feed you that fucking thing,' I said.

He lowered the camera and grinned, flipped a switch on top of the camera, probably going to video.

'Blonde girls and bus stops, Ted Conkaffey,' he said. 'You just can't help yourself, can you?'

'I'm getting in my car, and I'm leaving.' I gave him a wide berth as I made my way to the driver's side door, so he couldn't get me with any cameraman brutality claims.

'No fun,' he laughed.

'How did you find me?' I asked, one foot in the car. 'Please, just tell me that.'

'What? You haven't seen the footage yet?' he said. 'Oh my god, this is priceless. Can I film you watching it on my phone? Get your reaction? Seriously, mate, I'll pay you for the privilege.'

He started coming around the car. My nerve failed and I got in, slammed the door and locked it.

'It's all over the news,' he said, swiping at his phone. 'You're gonna love this!'

I started the car and drove away.

•

I found Amanda at her desk with those red reading glasses on again, the usual crowd of felines greeting me at the door, meowing. I closed the door and checked the street, but there were no other reporters. My knees were weak as I went around the desk and shooed her out of the chair.

'What? What's wrong with you?'

I couldn't answer. My fingers were numb as I typed my own name into a Google search. The first things that came up were videos. All with the same thumbnail image.

Me. Sitting on my back porch.

'Jesus,' I whispered. 'Jesus. Jesus.'

'What?' Amanda crouched beside me, watching the screen as I clicked play.

Why don't you take me through that day, Ted?

What?

That day. Why don't we talk about it?

'Oh my god.' There was terror in my voice. 'Why would she do this?'

'Who?' Amanda asked.

'Fabiana, the journalist.' I pointed at the screen. 'That's my back porch. She must have had a hidden camera on her, and she's filmed our whole conversation.'

I scrolled up and read the headline over the video. *Secret defence witness in Conkaffey case goes unheard.*

'In his first public appearance since his charges were dropped, Ted Conkaffey has revealed details of a witness never heard at trial who may complicate public perception of his guilt,' Amanda read aloud. 'A weathered, bearded Conkaffey spoke to *Sydney Morning Herald* reporter Fabiana Grisham about the possibility that the thirteen-year-old victim's real attacker was in the same area when he was witnessed approaching the teen.'

'It wasn't a public appearance!' I moaned. 'It wasn't an interview. I was tricked.'

'That sneaky slut!' Amanda thumped the table. 'When she comes around apologising I'm gonna kick her right in the taco.'

'I'm dead,' I said, scrolling through the articles. 'I'm totally dead.'

Every major newspaper was covering it. There was an old mugshot of me on the front of *The Age*, the page covered with quotes from the video.

'I almost had someone who could save me,' Conkaffey laments.

I scrolled down and looked over the reader comments, all 1432 of them.

Jerry34: Anyone who believes this piece of shit deserves to die. The justice system is fucked.

Littlebittykitty: Palm trees in the background. Looks like Conkaffey's moved north????

S8888er: Wood love to no where this is! Bring back the death penalty!

JaybeBaybe92: The people should rise up and hunt down this rapist dog.

Amanda got up and stretched, shoved a cat off the keyboard.

'You never know, Ted,' she said. 'It might change the game for you. Or it might be the beginning of the end. All I know is, these things don't last forever. Believe me.' She nudged at me, trying to take her chair back. 'In any case, I'm bored with your troubles. I want to keep hunting this superfan.'

'I can't concentrate on the Scully case.' I flopped onto the floor and held my head in my hands. 'I can't even breathe. Jesus Christ, doesn't anything scare you anymore?'

'Not really,' she said brightly, her eyes following her mouse pointer around the screen.

'They're going to hunt me down and burn me at the stake!'

'Barbecued partner,' she said. 'That's an interesting idea. Ted roast. Ted toast. Post-roast, Ted is a ghost!'

'Amanda, please.'

'Who will *host* this *boastful roast*?'

'Amanda!'

'You've got a gun, haven't you?' She glanced at me, not really seeing. 'You'll be fine. Just go outside and wave it around if a crowd gathers. That always works.'

'Don't tell me you've got a gun,' I said.

'I have some pretty impressive replicas,' she said. 'They go bang and everything.'

The cats seemed to sense my distress, and a couple actually rubbed themselves against me. Amanda fell back into the trance that the screen induced, hunting around Facebook for the ponytailed fan. I wavered between wanting to call Fabiana to abuse her, and the fear that she might record whatever I said, that any contact with her from then on would be poison.

It was becoming clear to me that moving to a tiny town on the edge of nowhere hadn't been the best decision I could have made in wanting to escape my crime. I should have stayed in the city, hiding in the crowds, moving short distances now and then when I was discovered, like a bird in the canopy. The photographer who had confronted me as I stood with Dynah must have seen the palm trees and the marshlands in the video, as well as the old Queenslander architecture of my house, and made a wild guess that I'd fled to Cairns. From there, a determined media veteran might have started asking around the city if anyone could confirm I was up here. It's possible someone had contacted Kelly, and she'd given me away. Or maybe my lawyer's files had been hacked. Maybe Zoe Miller and her little group of vigilantes had spread the news of my presence further than I knew. Either way, at least two journalists had hunted me down. It didn't seem like a huge leap for the ordinary man to do so. For *many* ordinary men.

'All right.' Amanda clicked her fingers loudly in my face. 'Snap out of it, man. I've got a response here from one of the Scully fans.'

I dragged myself to the edge of the desk and hung on, my chin resting on my hands. My entire body felt like lead. It was a major effort to lift my eyes to the screen.

'I've written to this chick asking her about the guy in the photo.' Amanda pointed. 'I think she's the president of the fan club. She's written back. *Hi Amanda, The guy in the photograph is one of our Brisbane chapter members, Ormund Smitt. He's a bit of a strange character, that one, and doesn't always answer when contacted. Good luck in your search! God bless you and yours.* Aww, how nice. She blessed us. Do you feel blessed?'

'No.'

'Interesting comment – he's a bit strange. That's not a very Christian thing to say. She's colouring my perception of him before I've even spoken to the guy.'

'He must be really strange, then, for her to have spoken out of turn.'

'Let's hope so!' Amanda rubbed her hands together.

'Ormund Smitt,' I said. 'Does he have a Facebook?'

'No.' Amanda tapped away at the keys. 'Too mainstream, probably. I'll search around and see if he has a website . . . He does. He *does* have a website.'

I dragged a chair beside her and climbed into it. When she clicked on Ormund Smitt's website, DarkWorldRising.com, the screen fell dark and a loading symbol popped up in the middle of the screen.

'Now this is exciting,' Amanda said.

'Our world is growing dark,' a young man's voice came through the speakers, low and sinister. 'Around us, signs of the coming judgement are everywhere . . .'

Images began to flood the screen as dark music swelled. I recognised the track from one of the more recent Batman movies. Still shots of the hijacked planes hitting the World Trade Center floated by. The people falling. Refugees fleeing Syria in boats. Princess Diana's wrecked car in the Pont de l'Alma tunnel. The ominous music was in tune with the images. They were in no order of content or chronology. A picture of an empty bathtub spattered with blood floated over a shot of O.J. Simpson being arrested.

'Recognising the signs takes great skill and light,' the voice continued. 'It takes a trained mind to push away the blindness enforced on us from birth.'

Amanda watched as the introduction video came to its end with dire warnings of the fall of man, a smile playing about the corners of her mouth. When the video finally finished she fell into fits of laughter, rocking in her chair, her arms around herself.

'That was amazing!' she howled. 'Let's watch it again!'

'Let's focus on the task at hand,' I said over her giggles, snatching the mouse away from her. 'We're trying to solve a murder, not entertain you.'

'Oh, lord,' she moaned in glee, wiping tears from her eyes. 'O.J. Simpson . . .'

I had a quick read of the 'About' section of the website. It seemed mainly devoted to interpreting news and current affairs as biblical signs of the beginning of the end of the world. The most recent piece seemed to be on the refugee crisis in Syria. Warnings from the book of Genesis that man would have nowhere to run to escape his sinful past flashed on the screen in red. The whole website looked very 1990s, with moving pictures and plenty of capitalisation for emphasis.

'Let's see if we can get in contact,' I said.

I wrote a quick email to Ormund, telling him I wanted to speak to him about Jake Scully and nothing more. While I waited, I looked around the internet trying to find any information I could on the man. Aside from the pictures on the fan club Facebook page, there was little to show of him. Amanda sat on the floor among the cats, not patting them but allowing them to walk over her lap now and then as she made calls to contacts about our suspect – police, other PIs based in Sydney, someone she seemed to know at the Registry of Births, Deaths and Marriages.

'He has one assault charge from 2013,' she said. 'Similar sort of incident. He knocked out another Jake Scully fan at a writers' festival for asking the wrong question at a meet-and-greet.'

'How old is this guy?'

'He's twenty-four.'

I heard a car door slam in the street and found myself tense over the keyboard, my shoulders high. When no one knocked at the door to the office after a few moments, I breathed easy again.

I was about to submit to my fears and go to the windows, look out and see if there was a mob assembling, readying themselves to come for me. But the email icon on Amanda's screen started flashing, and a message popped up.

'Oh my god.' She threw the cats out of her lap and slid into the chair beside me. 'It's him! It's Captain Punch-a-Lot!'

The email contained a single word: *Skype?*

Amanda switched over to Skype and sent Ormund a call. I changed chairs with her and shifted back into the shadows. The last thing I wanted was for the guy to recognise me from the day's news coverage and can the whole thing.

When Ormund's camera window opened, there appeared on the screen a thin young man wearing a black mask cut in half just below the nose. It looked to me like a Guy Fawkes mask that had been painted from its original black-and-white to straight black, the narrow, high eyebrows caught in the light of Ormund's laptop. His mouth was thin-lipped, pursed in concentration. In the background, a concrete room, probably a garage. I saw Amanda's cheeks lift as a smile crept over her face, and I kicked her chair before she could start laughing.

'This is serious,' I murmured.

'Are you there?' Ormund asked.

'We're here. This is Amanda. Ted's hiding in the shadows here.' She waved a hand at me. 'Thanks for hooking up with us.'

'What do you want?' Ormund spat. He obviously didn't like being bothered in the middle of his computer time. I noted some action figures on the desk, a can of Red Bull by the keyboard and some scattered bits and pieces of rubbish at the corners of the screen. A gamer? The response time from my email to linking up on Skype certainly suggested Ormund had already been sitting at the screen or nearby when he read my words.

'Well, as you know, my partner and I are investigating the death of Jake Scully,' Amanda said. 'We've been on the case for –'

'Your email said as much,' Ormund sneered. 'Whenever you start a sentence with "As you know", you're wasting someone's time, just so you know. And right now it's mine.'

Amanda twitched, glancing back at me.

'Well!' she said laughingly. 'My apologies!'

'You're also wasting my time if you're here trying to investigate Jake's death.' Ormund wiped his nose on the back of his hand, making the mask rise slightly into his fluffy hair. 'Jake isn't dead. He left all his things behind, and he's in hiding.'

'Oh, really?' Amanda said. 'Well, that's interesting. Do you, ah . . . Do you know where he is? Because a pathologist in Cairns has got one of his hip bones and we're thinking he might like it back.'

I reached over and took the mouse from Amanda, launched her screen video program and clicked the 'record' icon at the bottom of the screen. Ormund laughed, adjusted his mask.

'If you think that's really Jake's bone, it mightn't even be worth continuing this conversation, because apparently you've got your head stuck in the sand.' Ormund sighed dramatically, looking away from the screen, bored. 'I haven't got the time to explain the whole thing to you.'

Amanda muted the microphone and turned to me.

'It must be exhausting to be this narcissistic,' she said. 'I'm nowhere near this narcissistic, am I?'

I smiled. She clicked the microphone back on.

'I'm a very busy person,' Ormund continued. 'If you'd bothered to read any of the hundreds of articles I've written about the Last Light Chronicles and the Australian government, you'd have some idea of what's really going on.'

Amanda clicked the microphone off. 'It's always the bloody

government with these people,' she said. She clicked it back on again.

'Look, Ted and I are very concerned about Jake,' Amanda told Ormund. 'We really like the guy. Ted here's a big fan of the books, aren't you, Ted?' She slapped my chest. 'He's been crying into his beard for weeks, wondering what the hell happened. Why don't you fill us two idiots in on what's really going on.'

Ormund sighed dramatically again. Behind him, I could see a set of concrete stairs ascending above a row of shelves. Someone walked across the doorway and back again, and I heard a fridge door slam. Probably the guy's mother. I took an inventory of the room. Tools. Boxes. Rows of Xbox games. It was definitely a basement. This guy was the former clichéd oily teen who'd now grown roots into his parents' house, a boy-man his parents would only be rid of when they stopped paying for his gaming subscriptions. It might have been funny if it wasn't so frighteningly similar to the stories of some very dangerous people who'd also been obsessed with the government, conspiracies, the end of the world. I thought about Anders Breivik in Norway, the mother who had grieved for him when he was hauled away to prison.

'People think Jake started signalling the end of days in the Last Light Chronicles, but the truth is, he was writing about it long before that,' Ormund said. 'All of his early writings are online, and most people disregard their importance because as a writer he was just finding his feet.'

'Vampire porn,' Amanda laughed. 'Wasn't he writing vampire porn?'

'Urgh.' Ormund slapped the mask over his eyes. 'See, this is why I don't talk to people like you. Gothic fiction began some of the most cherished erotic conventions in modern literature. Do you even read?'

'So Jake was signalling the beginning of the end back then, too,' I cut in, before Amanda lost us all the cooperation Ormund was willing to give.

'He was trying to find a way to tell people that society is going to fall,' Ormund said. 'If you'd done any of your homework, you'd know Jake's father was Assistant Deputy Director of Operations for the Office of National Assessments. They work closely with ASIO.'

'Spies!' Amanda clapped.

'Jesus, you're an idiot,' Ormund said. 'He wasn't working with spies. He was working in national security. He found out that things are coming to an end, and when he tried to bring Jake into the business, Jake learned it too. He wanted to warn everyone.'

'So why didn't he just put it out there plainly?' Amanda asked. 'Grab a megaphone. *Attention, everyone! The end is nigh!*'

'How has that worked out for other people who have done that?' Ormund asked, his head tilted curiously.

'Not, uh . . . not very well.'

'Jake didn't want to be seen as crazy, and he also didn't want to be disappeared for exposing government secrets.'

'So he put it in fiction,' I said. 'So that only the cleverest readers would be able to figure it out.'

'The biblical references are like clues,' Ormund said. 'They tell us when the end will come, how, and what we can do if we want to survive it.'

'And what do they say?' Amanda asked. 'How can we survive it?'

Ormund laughed. 'I don't think fools like you deserve to know.'

Amanda looked at me, chewing her lips to prevent them from stretching into a smile.

'Towards the end of the Last Light Chronicles, Jake talks about a dark thing pursuing him,' Ormund said. 'He writes about feeling haunted.'

'We noticed that too!' Amanda held up her hand for a high-five. I reciprocated begrudgingly.

'Jake knew he'd pissed off enough people with the Chronicles. His warnings about the end of days were becoming more and more blatant, until he was forced into hiding. The truth is, Jake was trying to give us a chance. He wanted to make sure only the right people would be able to decipher the code in his works and make it to the next world. And if you aren't capable of that, I'm not going to give you a free ticket in. Jake is a good man. He's likely shared what he knows with some people who really don't deserve it. His pathetic, loser agent and his ridiculous family. When the end comes, only those who can really be trusted should be prepared.'

'All right then,' Amanda sighed. 'You don't have to tell us the secret password to the spaceship to the new world. Just tell us where Jake's hiding. Because we've been hired to do a job, and we need to get paid.'

Ormund snorted in disgust and reached towards the screen. He slammed his laptop closed, and the chat window went blank.

'That,' Amanda said, 'was some crazy shit.'

'Very entertaining.'

'You said it, mate!'

'What do you think?' I asked. 'Anything there?'

'Well, we know he has a rage problem,' she mused. 'And he's deeper into Jake than anyone we've met so far. I'm not ruling him out. Maybe he met Jake, confronted him with all these wild accusations about the end of days and government conspiracies and Jake ruined his little fantasy by telling him what we're both thinking – that he's a dick and he's wrong about everything. Maybe his great messiah Jake Scully just turned out to be some dude who writes stories and not the key to Ormund's dream.'

'Ormund didn't say anything about Jake being gay, either,' I noted. 'If he's trying to prove to us fools that he knows what Jake was *really* up to, what he was *really* like, why didn't he mention Jake's biggest secret?'

'Either he doesn't know,' Amanda said, 'or he's not happy about it. Thinks it's a lie planted by the government. Like the hip bone.'

'I'd be interested to see this earlier writing of Jake's,' I said. 'Ormund said it was all available online.'

Amanda started scouring the internet, looking for Jake's works. My phone rang in my pocket, a number I didn't recognise.

'Hello?'

'Mr Collins,' a voice said. 'This is Eleanor Chapman.'

I coughed. Amanda looked at me.

'Oh, hi! Hi.'

'You sent me an email asking about my book, *Murder in the Top End*.'

'I did,' I said. 'Let me just get somewhere more private.'

I held my hand over the phone and mouthed 'my lawyer' to Amanda. Forgetting my terror of being out in the open while the Australian media bandied my photograph about, I went out the front door and stood in the street.

'What's your interest in the case?' Eleanor asked. 'No one has contacted me in a long time.'

'Oh, I'm a fellow true crime author. I'm working on a . . . um . . . a compilation book of young Australian killers? It's my first work. I'm thinking I'm going to feature the Lauren Freeman murder in one of the first chapters. Your book is very good. It's been very helpful.'

'Well, thank you.' Eleanor laughed. 'The book did very well. It's a good story.'

'Really chilling.' I glanced inside the glass panel in the door to see Amanda at the computer. 'What's that they say? Every parent's worst nightmare?'

'Some of the detectives who worked on that case ended up leaving the force,' Eleanor said, sighing. 'Couldn't handle it.'

'I bet.'

'So what specifically can I help you with?'

'Well, look, I'm sort of hoping to start each chapter with a breakdown of the victim and what they were like,' I said. 'You've got a bit about Lauren in the book but there are still some things I don't know about her.'

'Oh, yes,' Eleanor said, 'that was my only regret about that work. There was only so much I could get. The closer you write a true crime book to the time of the murder, the better it'll sell – but the harder it is to get anyone to talk to you. The victim's family is all choked up and the killer's family is still scrounging around for a narrative they can live with.'

'There wasn't much in the book about Amanda's family, either,' I said.

'Not much to tell there. Daddy was a loudmouth drunk covered in tattoos who had almost nothing to do with the family. Died of a heart attack when Amanda was six. Mother completely shut up shop after the murder. Gave a very colourless, brief character witness statement at the hearing through her lawyer. Amanda pled guilty straight away, as you know, so there wasn't so much a trial as a series of committal and plea hearings. But a good testimony by Mum in person might have knocked a few years off the sentence.'

'Wow,' I said.

'I don't think mummy and daughter were ever that close. Amanda was always a bit of a wanderer. Free spirit. You couldn't pull her down from the clouds.'

'A bit strange that she would be such close friends with Lauren Freeman, then,' I said. 'I've visited the Freemans and they seem very buttoned-up.'

'Oh, they are,' Eleanor said. 'They were, at least. Lauren was that typical girl-next-door. If she'd been American she would have been captain of the cheerleading team. Prefect in primary school. Teacher's pet. She had such opportunity ahead of her. Her sister was absolutely crushed by the death. Dianne, was it?'

'Dynah.'

'I think there might have been some tension there, little-sister jealousy. The two girls had some roaring fight the week before the murder and Dynah had scratched Lauren on the face. When the wound had to be accounted for in the autopsy findings, and the mother had to ask Dynah if that's what had truly happened, the girl just broke down. I was there, doing interviews. It was one of the most awful things I've ever seen. Kids. They do stupid things. She probably still regrets it to this day.'

'So, uh.' I chewed my lips, trying to think how best to word my inquiry. 'Look, you just mentioned Lauren would have been a cheerleader in the US . . . I mean, I've watched a lot of these true crime documentaries and when the cheerleader gets killed they always find she's got some kind of dark secret . . . I hope I'm not being disrespectful here. You know, how she's always got a secret drug habit, or she's a bit too flirty with the English teacher . . .'

'I think I know what you're getting at.' Eleanor laughed.

'Was there anything you didn't mention in the book that you found out at the time? Anything that might have been best left unrevealed – things being so tense and all?'

'Absolutely not,' she said. 'Believe me, I dug around. I would have loved for this thing to have been more than just a freak accident, some psycho goth kid going nuts. But Lauren was just an angel. She was a genuinely good kid.'

'And you still stand by that reasoning for the murder?' I said. 'That it was just a *psycho goth kid going nuts*?'

'I do,' she said. 'I took one look at Amanda Pharrell at her first hearing. I knew there was nothing in there. She was cold as ice. Lauren tried to do a good thing, to bring this little weirdo kid to a party she would never have been invited to otherwise, and Amanda just snapped.'

I looked in the window at Amanda again. She was patting one of the fat cats with her bare foot.

'I'm a bit confused about the murder weapon,' I said. 'In the book, you go through the autopsy report and you say that it was probably a ten- or twelve-centimetre pocket knife. Did you ever find out where that knife came from? Did anyone ever ask why it wasn't found at the crime scene?'

'I'm sorry, I'm afraid I'm going to have to go, Mr Collins. I've got a meeting I've got to prepare for very soon.'

'They searched the bush for the knife with metal detectors and never found it,' I continued. 'I mean, what did she do with it?'

'Email me through any other questions you have, and I'll try to answer them as best I can,' Eleanor said. I heard the sound of a car door in the background of the call. She paused, thinking. 'I think I might have some old photos somewhere, some pictures that didn't make it into the book. There aren't any more of Amanda, but there are some of Lauren. I mean, you're not planning to speak to Amanda herself for this project, are you?'

'Umm. I hadn't decided yet.'

'Don't. If I can offer you any advice at all, it's that you shouldn't bother. She's a master manipulator, that one. She'll just mess with your head and it'll only ruin the integrity of the work. Stay away from Amanda Pharrell.'

I felt a zing of pain through my chest. I was remembering something from days earlier, the very words vibrating through my ear canals, shaking loose a vision of myself on my back in the alleyway in Cairns. Lou Damford was standing over me, a handful of my shirt in his hand, his feet on either side of my chest. I remember his fist in the air, caught in the hot white light of the sun.

Stay away from Amanda Pharrell, he'd said.

Dear Jake,

You had yourself a nice little self-examination session this morning, didn't you? From the steep rise at the side of the house, if you clamber onto the big rock there, you can see right into the ensuite window. You probably didn't worry about this too much when you designed the house, did you? Who would take the trouble to cut through the rainforest off Danbury Road, following the lights in the dark like gold beacons? Who would risk losing their whole foot in the soft, wet soil, to be scraped by lush prickly leaves and rained upon by dew from the canopies to catch a glimpse of Jake Scully at the full-length mirror, combing his hair back, looking into his own eyes? I watched you there this morning, tilting back your head and searching beneath your jawline for imperfections, plucking at the fine hairs between your dark brows, turning and trying to decide if you are fatter than when Stella married you, if all that sitting around clattering at the keys has made you soft.

Of course, you're not fatter. You keep yourself beautiful not only for your wife but for your occasional lovers. Yes, I know about Ray. I know about the boys you pick up in clubs when you can make it down to Melbourne and Sydney. I watched you this morning running your fingers down your taut belly and into the dark hairs around your cock and I wondered if you were thinking about those young men while your wife slept in the other room. I first got a hint of your other tastes watching you in the downstairs office, when you flicked over after the tiny black words stopped crawling across the screen so you could watch men fuck for a while like some blank-faced supervisor.

It's getting harder and harder not to spend all my time watching you. Just like when I read your books, you take me away, even when you don't know you're doing it. I watch you write. I watch you shower. I watch you fuck your wife. I've stood in your presence while you sleep. I've sat in your chair behind your big bad desk and pretended to be you. I've touched you through your things. I'm the ghost that haunts you.

I watch you open letters from fans. As I suspected, you hardly see them. You've only got eyes for yourself.

I'm a dark satellite orbiting you, my golden, warm sun. I can only be seen when you shadow me. You grow cold for a second, and you look out.

Hi there, beauty.

I left Amanda trying to find Jake Scully's original works online. Most of the places that hosted the stories were membership-only fan clubs that seemed very selective about who they let into their group. It seemed we'd have to wait until the hosts, who were all in the United States, woke up and went online to see if we could make it in. Amanda sat creating profiles for herself, and sometimes me, if the group was mostly male-looking avatars. She'd profess her undying love and admiration of Jake, and even hint now and then that she didn't believe he was dead, before sending her messages off.

I, on the other hand, was completely useless. I sat trying not to google myself on my phone, and every now and then relenting and looking at images and headlines before quickly closing them again. Pictures of me and Dynah were already hitting the likes of the *Daily Mail* and news.com.au. They'd blurred Dynah's image, thankfully. The journalist who'd caught me at the bus stop must have approached her and questioned her, but the blurred face meant she hadn't allowed him permission to use her image. It probably meant that she now knew who I was, however. At least Amanda, if she went online, wouldn't see me with the sister of her murder victim.

Battered and bruised Conkaffey back on the prowl, one headline read.

Bus-stop accused hunts blondes in Far North.

I scrutinised the image of myself. My face was only in profile, and with the black eye and swollen bottom lip it was possible Stella Scully wouldn't recognise me. But if Harrison saw the article, he'd likely make the connection between the old-man paedophile his girlfriend and her friends had been harassing, and the questions I'd asked him on his way to school. In time I became too restless and lied to Amanda, told her I'd do a round trip and check out Ormund Smitt's home address, see if I could chat to the kid face to face. His home address was easy enough for Amanda to track down with the limited databases she'd been allowed into as a licensed private detective. I felt some of the dread lift as I slid into my car. If I was moving, surely the vigilantes, angry townspeople and rabid journalists would find me harder to catch.

'Remember,' Amanda called as I left, 'when they come for you with their pitchforks and flaming torches, don't run up any windmills. It's a stupid idea.'

Valerie Gratteur's North Cairns home backed onto the water, the balcony that encircled the entire upper floor providing views of Smiths Creek on two sides. The cyclone fencing that kept crocs off her property was artfully hidden in the brush, which cleared for a small jetty locked off with a gate. The front garden was lush with peach-coloured bougainvillea that Valerie was pulling at as I arrived, trying to stop it creeping up the banister of the long front steps. I parked in the drive and said nothing. I was afraid that if I opened my mouth I'd cry.

She came over as I unloaded the cardboard box from the back seat and set it on the warm bonnet. She peeled off a gardening glove and pulled back one cardboard flap just enough to see Woman's curious black eye.

'How many chicks?'

I cleared my throat. 'There are six.'

She rubbed my arm with her small hand and looked up at me in the fading light. I felt pathetic. A grown man on the edge of a breakdown over a bunch of geese. I laughed at the thought, swallowed the ache at the back of my throat.

'They'll love it here.'

'I know.' I nodded. 'I know. They're fucking geese, I mean, Jesus. Pull yourself together, man.'

'I've seen the news,' she said. 'It's not just the geese.'

I followed her inside with a bag of feed and set it on the kitchen counter while she tended to the birds. It felt a lot like the day I packed a few of my meagre possessions into the car at my house in Sydney, trying to decide what I would really need to begin again, what I could stand to leave behind until Kelly and I made some kind of arrangement about the divorce. She hadn't been there. The hardest part had been trying to decide which of Lillian's things I'd take with me to keep me company until I saw her again. I didn't know how long it would be. I'd walked around the nursery touching her things, the knitted bunnies and cotton onesies and little girls' books. I'd thought it might be best to take something that smelled like her, but I didn't like the idea of depriving her of anything. In the end it had been too hard. I left the room just as it was.

I don't know when Kelly stopped believing me. She'd asked me the question. I guess I shouldn't have been surprised that she did. In the first days, the early days, it must have been important for her to decide which camp she was in. Hard times were ahead. All her friends would look at the evidence in the newspaper and abandon her if she stood by me. People would yell at her on the way to court. If she had any doubts, she'd put on a good show in the first days when the charges were laid out before me. We'd both sat through exhausting interrogations about that fateful Sunday at the bus stop. What we'd been fighting about that morning. How regularly I went fishing. What sort of equipment I used. How often we had sex. Whether we'd had sex that morning.

When what I was being accused of was finally painted for Kelly in all of its intricacies, she'd stopped yelling and howling at my colleagues in outrage and begun to listen to them. I think it was Frankie who'd read through the proposed timeline with Kelly. She trusted Frankie. And Frankie couldn't keep believing me.

Even if she'd stopped believing after the first few weeks, Kelly had still put her hand up against the glass and told me how horrified she was by it all and how hard we were going to fight and who she was going to hire, whether we could afford it or not.

She'd dragged Lillian into the prison with her, the tiny child in the pram in the visiting room, big men on tiny stools leaning over to get a glimpse of that small, chubby face and my wife slamming the sunshade shut in disgust.

I think it was about four months in when she missed a visit, and then another, and then when she finally came all she could talk about was how much weight I'd lost and how I needed to see a doctor. And then she stopped putting her hand on the glass so that her fingers matched mine.

She never really told me she didn't believe me. She just stopped scheduling visits. It was Sean who'd sat me down and told me we were getting a divorce. I should have known from the moment she asked me if I did it, mere days after my arrest, that it would come to this.

You didn't do it. Did you?

I watched Valerie pottering about in her kitchen and wondered if she was about to ask me. Outside the huge windows, beyond the balcony rail, lorikeets played in the trees, within arm's reach of the porch. There were panels of stained glass in some of the windows. The red sunset was rolling through them, one slice at a time, making rainbows on my shirt. Valerie put a coffee before me and, despite the heat, the warmth coming through the china into the palms of my hands was comforting. It had been cold that day when I'd packed my life up and left my wife and baby in Sydney. There was a little of that cold still lingering all around me, in my bones, a draft I could never find the source of.

When Valerie spoke, I winced.

'She didn't do it. Did she?'

'Who?'

'Amanda.'

'Oh.' I shook my head, tried to clear my tangled thoughts. 'Oh, I don't know. She did something, that's for sure. The girl's messed up.'

I told Valerie about my night at the pub with Amanda. How she'd looked at me, her eyes cat-like and sparkling in the dark, and told me she'd kill me.

'You stab someone nine times in the back . . .' Valerie mused quietly, sipping her tea. 'Why?'

'Because you hate them? Because they betrayed you?'

She waved a dismissive hand. 'That's an old crime-show load of bullshit.'

I laughed. It was still weird, hearing someone so old and so prim-looking dropping curse words like they were the time of day.

'It is,' she continued. '*The betrayer gets stabbed in the back.* What a load of arse. "Excuse me, mate. You slept with my girl-friend. I'm gonna stab you. Turn around a minute, will you?"'

'You're the seasoned pathologist. You tell me.'

'I haven't seen a lot of backstabbings,' Valerie said. 'But I have seen a lot of stabbings. And in my experience you either stab someone once, twice, or twenty-five-fucking-thousand times.'

I laughed again. The pain in my throat was easing. I could see the geese walking hesitantly along the porch through the glass door.

'That seems like a strange rule,' I said.

'Once? You're in a fight. You're waving a knife around. You lunge, and you think "Holy shit, did I just stab him? Fuck! I just stabbed the guy!" After which, you promptly run off.'

'Okay.' I nodded.

'Twice?' She held up two fingers. 'Well, that's when you've accidentally got him, but you think "Well, shit, I've just stabbed the guy. Better give him one more so he stays down while I hightail it."'

'And the "twenty-five-fucking-thousand times" one?' I asked.

'Well, that's when you're so hopped-up on rage or drugs you don't realise you've stabbed him at all,' she said. 'You're slashing and poking physically but mentally you're off with the fairies. I've heard of coppers coming in on bloody scenes where the perp is still stabbing and yelling at the victim and the victim is fucking *long* dead. Skin spotted with holes like a red leopard.'

'Hmm.'

'Most of the time the stabbing goes on because the victim won't stop moving. Gets the death twitches. Urges the stabber on.'

'Right,' I sighed.

'So nine times?' She looked back at me. 'And in the back? That's weird.'

'What are you thinking?' I asked.

'I'm thinking whoever stabbed Lauren Freeman was going for twenty-five-fucking-thousand times,' Valerie said. 'But was interrupted.'

'That makes zero sense with the logistics of the scene,' I said. 'You don't have what you need for that to work. No one there but Lauren and Amanda. No drugs. No apparent rage.'

'So the logistics of the scene make no sense, then,' Valerie said.

Our conversation was interrupted by a loud chiming on my phone. An email from Eleanor Chapman. I opened the attachment and scrolled through the pictures of Lauren, the golden girl on a beach. At a party. Cuddling between sister and mother on a crowded bus. Sitting alone on a park bench.

A message came through from Amanda as I was staring at the screen.

Meet me at the Scullys'.

At the car, I said goodbye to Valerie and thanked her for taking care of my birds. A gentle wind was rising, cutting through the thick humidity, and I wondered if the rains were finally on their way.

'When the rain finally comes, it'll be big,' she said, looking at the mountains. Her short white hair was tossed up by the wind so that it flared behind her ears, making her look like an ancient elf. I got into the car and watched her go inside, but before I turned on the ignition I remembered something from the email. I opened it again and scrolled to the bottom picture, an image of Lauren sitting on a park bench. The image was narrower than it should have been, like the picture it had been scanned from had been cut in half.

On Lauren's right shoulder, a man's hand could be seen emerging from around her neck, dangling at her breast.

Dear Jake,

When I was a boy my mother got me a small brown dachs-
hund. It was completely out of the blue. I hadn't spoken of
any desire for an animal, but something got into her, the desire
for a single magical Disney Christmas moment in my childhood. So she put the dog into a long, blue box with a ribbon
and presented it to me. A life to call my own. That's what the
animal was from the outset, very much a *life* – its fur prickled
and shivered with life and even as it slept in a warm, soft bundle
the life crept through it visibly, the quickly thumping heart
and pulsing veins and rising and falling belly, pink as a piglet.

   Something happened to me whenever I was around the
creature. My teeth would grit. I felt, from the very first
moment I looked at it, the distinct snapping shut of my jaws
and the painful pressure of my front teeth as they were forced
into each other. The pressure carried on through my jaw and
neck, and it was all I could do to keep it from travelling down
my arms and into my hands, causing me to squeeze the life
from the thing. In time the gritting and grinding of my teeth
did bleed down into my body, and I found myself holding
the little dog under my chin, pushing the bone down into its

skull, knowing I was hurting it but unable to stop. I loved it so much I could have bitten it. I could have eaten it. It was dangerous, furious love.

And isn't that what all those corny true crime documentaries talk about? Lovers who become so consumed with the object of their desire that they just burst and strangle them one day. Wring the essence from them. Draw them into their own chests, crush them into their hearts, a human key that slots so nicely into a keyhole left hollow and gaping too long. When we fuck and hug and hold each other, are we trying to do the same thing? To draw ourselves into each other?

Don't you see that all the time on the news? In the wake of some crisis, people zinging together like magnets, locking chest to chest and cheek to cheek. Snap. Click.

I want to put you inside me, Jake, and see if you fit. See if you fill the emptiness there. Maybe if I hurl your human body into the abyss in my heart, you'll only tumble and clatter against the sides of me like a stone down a mineshaft. Maybe I'll have to take everything you are, your child, your wife, your house, your things, your writing, and hurl them into me too.

I'm a vortex. I only know how to eat things.

Amanda was waiting for me outside the Scully house, her shirt damp with sweat from the ride. The hot wind was licking at the palm trees by the side of the road.

'They've got cyclone warnings on the news,' she said. 'If it's big enough, it might eclipse you being in town altogether.'

'I can only hope,' I said. 'You can tell them it picked me up and took me away to Oz.'

'Have you heard from that journalist?'

'Yes.' Fabiana had tried to call me a number of times on the drive to and from Valerie's. I'd not picked up. 'I haven't got time for that right now. The damage is done. I'm going to put my head down and focus on this investigation, and hopefully when I come up again it'll all be over.'

She looked at me with what might have been tenderness, or pity, or just the quiet and empty gaze of a half-mad murderer. Maybe I'd been projecting emotions like pity and sadness onto Amanda all along. Talking about the stabbing murder of Lauren Freeman with Valerie had left me mildly sick inside, visions rising now and then of the huge knife plunging into the lean muscle of her back.

The girl wasn't made of meat. To stab her in the back would have been hard. It would have taken a lot of fury. There were bones to worry about. Ribs and wide, protective shoulder blades. It would have taken a strength the little woman before me could hardly have possessed as a teenager. Unless she was so chock-full of adrenaline that she was almost possessed.

We went to the door and Stella flung it open before we could knock. She was wrapped in a fluffy white robe that had red wine-stains on the cuffs. Even the unshakeable Amanda seemed taken aback.

'*You.*' She pointed at my face. 'You fucking liar.'

'Uh-oh,' Amanda said.

Stella wiped at the mascara smudged under her eyes. 'No wonder you wouldn't touch me. You're a fucking paedophile. He's a paedophile!' she wailed at Amanda, her words slurred. 'Did you know?'

'Yeah. I knew.'

'You *knew?*' Stella's arms hung at her sides.

'Well, not that he's a paedo at *heart*, but that he's accused of it, sure.' Amanda almost laughed. 'I mean, what are accusations?'

'I'm outta here.' I turned on my heel.

'Stay.' Amanda grabbed at me. 'Stay, Ted. Jesus, Stella, you want to find your husband or not? What does it matter to you what they're saying about Ted? It's got nothing to do with our case. We're almost there.'

'Our case?' Stella snapped. '*There is no case.* You're insane, and this is over.'

'What?' Amanda reeled.

'People like this are subhuman.' Stella flung her hand at me, a few sobs sneaking out of her. 'Can't you see? Oh my god, you can't, can you? You're so fucked up by your own weird fucking existence, you've got no sense of –'

'Look, we're close.' Amanda wasn't grasping the situation. She began listing on her fingers. 'We have a very good suspect. We have some stuff we need to check on from Cary. We –'

'You fucking freak,' Stella said.

Amanda's mouth closed slowly.

'You freak. Of course you don't get it. How could you? You're a freak too, just like him.'

Amanda's face had lost all of its emotion. It was hard. Her stare fixed. The hairs on the back of my neck stood on end, and I started walking back up the path towards her.

'Amanda, don't!'

She leapt at the woman in the doorway, her reaching arms sandwiched in the crack of the door as Stella desperately shoved it shut. Amanda wriggled, twisted, tried to force her way into the gap. I wrapped an arm around her middle and hurled myself backwards, but the strength in her was incredible. She actually seemed to weigh double. Her limbs were hard as steel.

'We're not giving up this case, you stupid bitch!' she yelled. 'It's ours now, you understand? It's ours now!'

She struggled free of my arms and kicked over a potted palm, smashing the terracotta pot on the edge of the stone steps. She whirled around, and I found myself ducking away, afraid she was going to take a swing at me.

'We're not freaks, Ted,' she snapped, jabbing her finger at me. 'No matter what we've done, you and I are not freaks.'

It was hard to know the safest thing to do. As I drove home, thoughts of the best course of action flitted through my mind, but I never seemed to lock on to the perfect solution to my problem. Should I flee again? Go back to Sydney, ask Sean if I could stay at his place for a while? While I was sleeping on my lawyer's couch, what would happen to all my things back here in Crimson Lake? Would the vigilantes burn down the house if I left it completely? They'd certainly go after Amanda to try to find me. Was it fair, leaving her to explain where I had gone?

I was chewing my nails as I turned onto the clay road leading to my house. There were people at the side of the road opposite the property. I recognised the journalist who had snapped pictures of me with Dynah Freeman at the bus stop, and a couple of other people I assumed to be his colleagues, standing by their car. As I pulled in to the driveway I noticed shadows further up the street, faceless forms protected from the light by the overhanging vines of the rainforest. Two female police officers were on my property, standing by the edge of the front porch, watching me park. Were these two in league with Damford and Hench? Were they here to arrest me? I couldn't see them offering me a beat-down right in front of the press, but as I emerged from my vehicle I felt all the old wounds awakening.

'Ted Conkaffey?' one of them asked.

'Yep,' I said.

The two women took a moment to assess me, taking in the size and shape of my body, the earnestness they perceived in my face. Did I look like a man who was capable of what I was accused? I tried to discover the results of their assessment, but these two had closed faces. I glanced at their name badges. Taylor and Sweeney, Holloways Beach regional.

'Are you here to take me in?'

'No,' Sweeney said. 'We're here to protect you.'

'Oh.' I was genuinely shocked. 'Well, that's nice. For me. I guess you two drew the short straws down at the station, did you?'

'I don't know,' Taylor said. She looked me up and down again, adjusted her belt. 'I just don't know anymore.'

The three of us stood awkwardly together and looked at the media across the street, none having really determined where we stood with each other. The creaking leather of their boots and the coppery smell of their guns and equipment made me feel good, and for a moment I shut my eyes and tried to imagine I was back in Sydney in police headquarters, listening to young street cops clomp by my desk in their huge, heavy boots.

'What's with the silent witness?' Sweeney said. Taylor slapped her on the arm, a reprimand. They'd obviously agreed not to get into my case with me, should I make an appearance that night. Maybe they'd been told specifically not to.

'Fuller? He saw me at the petrol station. But they didn't let him make a statement.'

'Why?'

'He was a drunk,' I said. 'A homeless drunk. Mental health issues. We were going to fight for his credibility as a witness but they ruled no billing before we could.'

Sweeney squinted, scratched her neck uncomfortably. For a while, we listened to the frogs croaking in the marshland at the back of the property.

'Why didn't anyone see you fishing?' She persisted. 'I read that no one saw you on the pier.'

'I was there.' I shrugged. 'I was there for about an hour and a half. Maybe two.'

'Hey, we're not here to talk about this.' Taylor put her hands out, double stop signs for her partner and me. 'We're here to make sure no one comes onto the property. Your guilt or innocence is not of any interest to us, Mr Conkaffey.'

'It's of interest to me,' Sweeney said quietly. I gave her a grateful smile and started up the porch towards the house. There were five burst water balloons on the porch near the boarded-up windows. I smelled piss. That was a new one. I stood wondering about the mechanics of getting urine into tiny water balloons, the perils of transporting them to their target without them exploding and soaking everything with the fetid smell.

'Detectives Damford and Hench,' Taylor said suddenly, stopping me at the door. 'Do you know those guys?'

I felt my fingers lock onto the doorknob, the keys painful in my other hand.

'Know them?'

'Yeah. Like, have you had dealings with them in the past? I know they've given you a hard time since you moved here, but was there something before that?'

'No,' I said. 'We've only come into contact since I arrived. Why do you ask?'

Taylor shrugged. Both cops turned back towards the road, hands on their belts.

'Really.' I let the door handle go. 'Please, tell me. Why do you ask that?'

The two officers ignored me. I walked inside, a new sense of trouble stirring in my veins.

The night was full of voices. I lay on my side on the bed and listened to the rise and fall of the officers' words as journalists and locals tested the boundaries of my property. Sometimes red and blue lights flashed against the windows and ceiling. I fancied I could smell the piss on the porch even from the back bedroom, but I seemed to get used to it after a while. At all hours, there were gawkers rolling past the property, stopping to look, chatting to protesters who stood out the front.

Officer Taylor's question bothered me. It was likely she and her partner had been brought in from another jurisdiction to cover my house because Damford and Hench were unwilling to do it, or were too consumed with their other duties in Crimson Lake. Maybe Taylor had wondered why the two men hadn't been assigned to me. How much other crime could there be in such a tiny town?

The voices continued in the dark.

'Move along. Move along, sir.'

'Is he in there?'

'Get off the fence, ma'am.'

'We don't want that guy in our town.'

'Move that car off the grass. This is private property. Return to your vehicle and go home.'

'She was *thir*-teen! How do you guys sleep at night?'

'You're here protecting a fucking rapist pig. You should be out there chasing them down, not watching over them as they sleep.'

'Return to your vehicle, sir, and go home.'

Revving engines. At midnight I thought about making the two officers coffee, but when I peered through the crack in the window boards it was two new officers, a man and a woman, and I didn't know if they'd be as gentle with me as the previous ones. I was about to go out and cuddle the geese, then I remembered they weren't there.

I was drifting back to sleep in the cool blue hours of the early morning when I was awakened by a sick feeling in my stomach and the strange sense that I'd heard a sharp noise, a metallic scraping. My thoughts turned to the back of the property. There wasn't anyone protecting the back, and although any intruders would have to walk along fifty or sixty metres of unprotected, croc-infested land to get to my gate, I thought it wasn't that much of a stretch for someone who was willing to come all the way out to my property to confront the police.

I grabbed a torch, crept to the back porch and pushed the door open quietly, holding my breath. Even the frogs were quiet. In the bushes, the low ticking of crickets and grasshoppers, and off in the distance that terrible sound – the cough-like barking of crocs calling to each other across the black water.

I was listening to things so far away that when the cough sounded from near the car it jolted my whole body. I'd moved the vehicle around the back of the property at the request of the first set of protective officers.

'Hey!' I clicked the torch and blasted it into the dark. 'Hey!'

Two figures rose from where they'd been crouching at the front wheel. I clutched at the back of my shorts.

'I've got a gun.'

I didn't. But I made a note to myself that if this happened again, it might be a good idea to be armed with more than just a torch. As I came around the side of the car, my light beam picked up two pale, youthful faces, one of them half-hidden beneath a black woollen beanie. Harrison shoved something into his pocket.

I gave a little bitter laugh. Harrison and his girlfriend Zoe stepped back, blinking in the light.

'We were going to slash your tyres,' the boy said. The admission came quickly, seemed to tumble out of his mouth. It was a weird thing to say. I put it down to shock.

'I can see that. Is this about your dad, or is it about the news?' I asked Harrison.

'It's about you being a monster,' the girl sneered. This was the first time I was getting a close-up look at Zoe Miller. Under her pale foundation, I could see she was hiding a good spattering of dark brown freckles over her nose and pierced cheeks. Freckles weren't very goth. She had all the confidence Harrison usually had, the cocky malice he carried around, which seemed to have fled completely in the torchlight. 'We found out what you did, you sick fuck.'

'And I found out who you are, Zoe Miller,' I said. I drew a breath to continue, to ask her what her parents thought about her throwing firecrackers at people's houses in the middle of the night, driving around with boys in the early morning hours. But the look on the two kids' faces now was enough. They glanced at each other, and now both were genuinely scared.

I knew her name. Why was that so terrifying?

'We're going,' Harrison grabbed her arm. 'Zoe, go. Go.'

'No way,' I said, sidestepping to block their path. 'You're giving me the knife. Hand it over. You're not leaving here with a weapon in your possession.'

The two teenagers stared at me. I took a step forward, backing them against the fence.

'The knife.' I gestured to Harrison's pocket where I'd seen him stash the weapon. 'Hand it over.'

'No.'

'Hand it over.'

'Fuck you!'

I dropped the torch, reached out and grabbed the kid by the shoulder and hood of his thin jacket, my big hand gathering up so much fabric in one go that his shirt lifted over his belly, pulled up into his armpits. I dug into his pocket and grabbed the rubber handle of the knife.

'Get off me! Get the fuck off me, man!'

The teens lunged at me. I was shoved back into the verandah rail. They fled towards the back of the property. I heard the jangle of the diamond wire just as the two officers from out the front came racing down the side of the house, alerted to the commotion.

I picked up the torch and shone it on the tool in my hands. It wasn't a knife.

Ormund Smitt lived with his mother in a wide, low house on the suburban outskirts of Cairns, the grass on the extensive property close-cropped to stop snakes traversing the lawn from the little clusters of palm trees between properties. I kind of loved Ormund's shameless cliché 'gamer' lifestyle, the angry young man who remained pale and wan from sitting for long hours in the basement of his house when everyone else in Cairns was sun-scorched just from checking the mailbox. Young defiance seemed to be a regimented thing, the embittered scowl like a mask, the skilful touch-typing from years in chat rooms and forums a prerequisite for membership. Ormund Smitt's pale, lank hair and Harrison Scully's inexplicable beanie were part of a uniform that had a distinct message: an unapologetic 'fuck you' to everyone.

They knew themselves. Perhaps that was what I admired about people like Ormund Smitt. I'd known myself as a cop. I had a uniform. A skill set. A message. Who the hell was I now?

I sat in the car halfway down the block from Smitt's house and watched Amanda hiding in the shade of the palms by the side of the road, her bike leaning against a tree. She was straight-backed, sitting in the lotus position, her eyes closed and her chin against her chest. Already, I supposed, I'd taken on some of the behaviours I needed for membership in the pariah clan. I wasn't covered in tattoos, but I'd altered my appearance – the thick, dark beard was still a shock to me in the bathroom mirror each morning. I'd surrounded myself, albeit accidentally, with a brood of helpless animals – instantly becoming the commander of a group of lives simultaneously worse off than, and accepting of, me. While Amanda had her twitches and moods, I didn't sleep, hardly ate, and was deeply paranoid.

As I was watching Amanda in the dappled sunlight, appreciating our strange kinship, she suddenly snapped out of her meditative state and crawled to the window of the car, kneeling on the grass.

'I'm over this,' she said. 'Let's spook this kook.'

She took a phone I hadn't seen before out of her back pocket, an older-style flip phone which snapped open with a satisfying crack. She began typing, her tongue wedged between her front teeth, and when she was finished she looked up with a satisfied smile.

'What did you do?'

She looked at the phone. 'I got Ormund's number from one of my contacts at Telstra. I just texted him: *We know you're talking to police and investigators about Jake Scully. We'd like you to understand that this is not a good idea.*'

'I like it.' I made an appreciative face, glanced contemplatively into the distance. 'It's authoritative, stern, yet vague. What are you hoping for, exactly?'

'I'm hoping he shits his pants thinking it's the Illuminati, the corrupt government shadow masters who've driven Jake underground for revealing the secrets of the apocalypse.' She watched her phone. 'Maybe I should have encrypted it.'

We waited, Amanda twitching gently. She took a tissue out of her pocket eventually and bit off a corner, munched the fragment of paper with her canine teeth. When the phone beeped she gave a sharp laugh, rocking backwards onto her heels.

'*Who is this?*' she read, launching forward to reply.

'*Just back away, Smitt,*' she read out as she typed.

'You're going to give this kid nightmares,' I said.

There was silence from Ormund. An hour passed. Amanda stared expectantly at the house. I wasn't sure exactly what she hoped to see or hear, whether she expected Ormund's terror at her prank to inspire any physical action. But she had been right about Sam and Ray, and she'd proved herself far more proficient in internet-based investigation than me. I was willing to sit by the side of the road with her for a few hours and hope for something. Part of me knew this willingness was made of things like fear of the men and women outside my house, and dread of the dark hours I would have to spend there that night.

When my phone beeped, Amanda jolted with excitement, only to flop on the grass morosely when she realised the message was mine. It was from Kelly.

60 Minutes called again.

I found myself actually gripping at my chest, the sharp pains in the muscles around my heart fluttering at the sight of her name on the screen. She hadn't answered any attempt at communication from me since I left Sydney. The screen above her text was crowded with messages from me, most of them late-night and long.

Kelly had given a *60 Minutes* interview in the dreadful last days of my trial, ignoring Sean's pleas with her about jeopardising my case. The interview was legally approved on the basis that Kelly herself wouldn't comment on the trial proceedings at all, but would answer questions on what sort of father and husband I'd been and what our home life had been like. But the program had been titled *Married to Evil*, and it was edited to catch her at her most vulnerable – when she didn't think she was being filmed, staring off across an empty highway near our home, sighing while she rocked our crying child. Wife abandoned. Wife confused. Wife betrayed.

I don't think the interview did anything bad for my image. I think at that time my image was as bad as it could possibly be, and the idea that what I'd done to Claire Bingley had also left my wife in the lurch wasn't worth the hype.

Still, my fingers were shaking as I texted back.

Are you going to talk?

There was a pause, and then she replied.

I don't know. I thought it had all gone quiet. But that video has stirred it all up again. People are always asking me if I knew. This might be a good chance to say I didn't.

I'd seen an article on a crime blog in the early days after my release when I was still furiously googling my name every night to see what new horrors had been added to my personal history online. The headline had been *Protecting a Predator?*. The author wondered how any wife could not know her husband was a child sexual predator, and had used our marriage as its case study. It was pure trash and speculation, containing plenty of scary black-and-white shots of me being led into court. But it was perfectly timed, going viral right alongside news of my no-billing. People wondered, had she known?

When I didn't reply, she texted again.

If you could stay out of the press for a while, that'd be great.

•

Kelly's texts got the fire into me, a painful restless stirring my mother used to call 'ants in the pants'. I had the unconscious inkling that if I just kept moving, somehow I'd stay one step ahead of what was troubling me. I left Amanda outside Ormund Smitt's house, sitting in the shade peeling a twig down to strands. I told her I'd bring back lunch, but not where I was going or why I was going alone. She didn't ask. Probably knew how I felt.

Here was the problem. Violent paedophiles were not like me. They didn't look like me, and they didn't act like me. And that made me even more frightening to the public than the ones who fit the bill perfectly.

I defied all the societal assumptions about the paedophile. The violent paedophile does what he does for a number of reasons, according to Joe Average. He's old and broken, for starters. The stock-character paedophile is an elderly man whose wife has died or divorced him or gone off to residential care, leaving him alone in a small shadowy house adorned with all the trust symbols kids associate with their grandparents – the rosebushes out front, the glass jars of old-fashioned candies in the kitchen, the friendly dog he walks daily. The old man was probably stained with his unsavoury tastes six decades ago, serving as an altar boy at some nameless suburban church, pouring holy water in some deathly silent back room under the predatory gaze of a withered priest. Since then, he's kept this trauma secret, and his dark desires have been sated by his wife. Suddenly she's gone, and the little band of neighbourhood kiddies that used to trail around behind her still come to visit.

Aside from his elderly, secretive and trauma-based aspects, the stock-character paedophile has plenty of poster boys who have added to his warning-sign list. Maybe he's the greasy, hunched Dennis Ferguson type who horrifies the public with his angry defiance, licking his lips, twitching, batting angrily at the cameras outside the halfway house where he hunkers down. Maybe he's the crazy-eyed Jimmy Savile type, chugging on huge phallic cigars and grinning with long teeth from behind the lenses of rose-tinted glasses, untouchable, rich, spidery in his movements.

He's not me, that's for sure. The picture I provided for the public was not any of those things. I had a nice upbringing in the Western suburbs of Sydney. I was never sexually or physically abused. The Ted Conkaffey who graced the front pages of the newspapers was tall, powerfully built, late thirties, and leaning towards handsome. I was gainfully employed, married, with a baby daughter. I'd passed psych evaluations to qualify as a police officer, so no secret underlying neurological misfire explained what I had apparently done. I didn't have especially more or less to do with small children. I had one of my own, of course, but aside from spending time with Lillian I didn't hang around parks or playgrounds looking at or talking to small children, and I had never had cause to invite any into my home, either while my wife was there or when she wasn't. I hadn't sought employment that would give me access to children. I hadn't tried to charm my way into positions in which I got them alone in quiet rooms, caring for, entertaining, teaching or counselling them.

I bunked the paedophile trend in every possible way, and that frightened people. The Australian public had convinced themselves that they knew what child sexual predators looked and sounded and smelled like. They thought they had a handle on things. And then along comes Ted Conkaffey. A wholly new, and more sophisticated, breed of monster.

Who could possibly have seen through such an innovative disguise?

My wife.

Surely she'd seen something. Heard something. This sort of twisted, depraved appetite didn't just manifest instantly at the sight of a kid standing alone on the side of the road. It must have been something I'd been hiding for a long time. Maybe all my life. Surely I'd revealed my true self to Kelly at some point in our eight-year marriage – made a strange comment while drunk, left some questionable internet searches in my browser history, got a little handsy with the neighbour's kid in the backyard pool one Saturday afternoon.

At the end of the day, the true test of Kelly's culpability in my crime had to have been the arrival of our daughter. Surely when Kelly gave birth to Lillian and I'd held the warm, struggling infant in my big hands for the first time, some primal maternal alert had pinged.

These dark thoughts completely took me over, so that when I eventually wriggled out of their grasp I found myself parked in the main street of Holloways Beach, my hands on the wheel, staring straight ahead with my jaw clamped shut. Two women seated in the outdoor area just beside my car window were staring at me, wondering perhaps what had got me so rigid with thought. I jumped out of the car and walked quickly away from them before they could recognise me.

I'd recognised Dynah's turquoise apron the first time I met her in the Freemans' kitchen from a cafe called 'Starfish' on the main drag at Holloways Beach. The footpath was littered so tightly with tables that I had to slide sideways between people enjoying their lunches. The occasional upwards glance from diners sent minor electric shocks through me. Did they recognise me? What would they do if they did?

I found Dynah ringing up bills at the counter. It was only when she looked up at me with those tired, world-worn eyes that I realised how incredibly rude I was being, just barging in here hoping to pick on her again about her long-dead sister.

She glanced sideways at her manager. It was a look that told me instantly that not only had she seen the news, but that she was going to tell him exactly what she'd seen and exactly how that related to the big, bearded guy at the counter.

'Please.' I held my hands up. 'Please don't.'

'What do you want?' she said.

'I'll order.' I glanced at the huge chalkboards behind her. 'I don't want to cause you any trouble. I'll get a chicken sandwich and a ham and cheese. Take away.'

She rang up the food reluctantly. The hand that darted out for my money was swift, frightened. I went to a table at the side of the room to wait, and when she brought the food out in a carry bag she surprised me by sliding into the seat across from me, reaching out and grabbing my hand, her touch hard, unkind.

'You need to let this fucking thing go,' she said, leaning close so that I could see the fury in her eyes. 'You've got enough troubles of your own right now, mate.'

I took out my phone and opened the email from Eleanor Chapman. I put it on the table before us and pointed to the photograph of Lauren Freeman, the one with the mysterious hand hanging over her shoulder.

'Whose hand is that?'

'Jesus Christ, are you even listening to me?' Dynah snapped. She shook her head ruefully. 'No wonder you're in such a fucking mess. You're a complete dumbass. Mate, you're all over the news. They're saying you tried to kill some kid down in Sydney.'

'Yeah.' I nodded, still holding the phone. 'That's what they're saying.'

'So what are you doing coming after me? I'd be hiding somewhere safe, if I was you.'

'Well, there's more to my story than the official version, Dynah,' I said. 'I think you can tell that, or you wouldn't be speaking to me right now. I think you're a good judge of character. And you know what? So am I. And I think there's more to your sister's story than the official version, too.'

She sighed at me. Glanced at the doorway to the kitchen, where the manager was watching carefully. He'd probably given her five minutes to clear up whatever the problem was with her mysterious visitor and then get the hell back to work. Time was running out.

'I've been reading *Murder in the Top End*,' I said. 'And a couple of things about it bother me. First, it paints a picture of Amanda Pharrell as being a complete weirdo. A freak. Now, I'm all right with that. She *is* a complete weirdo, and she would have been back then. Maybe not the sinister and violent kind of weird described in the book, but certainly not normal.'

'So what's your problem, then?' Dynah asked.

'My problem is that the book gives no account whatsoever of Amanda suffering any bullying while she was at school,' I said. 'Think about it. The girl's bananas. A loner. Her dad's an alcoholic and her mother wants nothing to do with her.

She's a dreamer. A social outcast. So why didn't the popular girls make her life a living hell?'

Dynah sat staring at me, her arms folded over her chest.

'My second problem is with your sister,' I said. 'She's stunning. Clever. Athletic. I mean, she's *dead*, and half the people she went to school with are still claiming to have been her best friend. She's got the whole cohort twisted around her little finger even from beyond the grave.'

Dynah said nothing.

'So why no boyfriend?' I asked. 'No mention of any boyfriends whatsoever. That's what bothers me the most, you know? I mean, plenty about this bothers me, don't get me wrong. There's the totally ludicrous notion that a girl like Lauren and someone like Amanda might be parked in the bush together not far from a school party just, what, having a chat? Painting each other's nails? They're saying she and Amanda arrived at the party together, shared a pre-party drink, planned to go off together and have a good night in full view of all Lauren's school buddies. And yet there's no evidence whatsoever to suggest Lauren even looked at Amanda once before that night. That they'd ever even had a casual relationship. Spoken. Passed notes. Been over to each other's houses. So Lauren's going to drive her to the party? With no concern at all for what that might do to her social status?'

Dynah sighed heavily.

'But no boyfriend?' I scoffed. 'Come on. A girl like Lauren would have had a *queue* of potential –'

'There was no one else there,' Dynah said. She stood up fast, towered over me at the table. 'There was no one else there, all right? Just leave it alone. Leave the fucking thing alone.'

'I wasn't asking –'

I stood, but the manager was coming around the counter, obviously noting his employee's distress. Dynah wiped at her eyes. I showed her the photograph of her sister again, and the arm hanging over Lauren's shoulder.

'Who is this guy?' I asked, one eye on the approaching manager. 'A friend? A teacher? Why was the relationship secret?'

'He had nothing to do with it,' Dynah spat. She whirled around and almost knocked her manager over, the guy trudging towards me to give me what I deserved.

I didn't get what I deserved. But I had what I needed.

I sat for long hours in the car down the block from Ormund Smitt's house while Amanda whipped the young man into a paranoid frenzy. She was having far too much fun with the situation. Now and then she lay back on the grass and giggled at what she was writing, thumbs dancing over the buttons, pretending to be some government ghouls in an icy office block somewhere putting their strategy together to bring Ormund down. It was frightening how easily she could tap into the boy's ludicrous terrors. And how much she seemed to be entertained by that terror.

When I couldn't stand it any longer, I asked what she was saying.

'I was texting that we know that Ormund knows where Jake is, and that we're going to get him to tell us, even if it means using our old-school torture methods.'

'I feel faintly queasy about how unethical this is,' I said, leaning my arm on the car door. 'What happens if you convince this kid that all his conspiracy theories are true, and top-secret agents are going to come waterboard his arse –'

'*When* I convince him of that,' she grinned.

'*When* you do,' I sighed, 'and it turns out he doesn't have a clue what happened to Jake?'

'If he's innocent, we'll have wasted an afternoon, and provided a lonely young man with plenty of wank material for him and his end-of-the-world cronies.' She sat up, picked blades of grass from her spiky hair. 'Ted, I've known people like this. There are plenty of them in jail. Conspiracy theorists. Paranoid delusionals. Psychics and mediums. They concoct these stupid theories because they're lonely, and they want to feel important. Imagine if the world really was going to end, and you were the only person with the special intellect necessary to divine that information from a bunch of otherwise innocuous books. What a way to stick it to the big boys who picked on you in high school.'

'I suppose.' I glanced at the house through the fading sunlight.

'And imagine then that someone actually comes out of the woodwork and confirms it for you – Yes, Ormund, you discovered our secret. September 11 *was* a stunt by the US government. There *was* a shooter on the grassy knoll. The rapture *is* coming, and Jake Scully *did* know. We're not happy about it, but we're admitting it. You were *right all along, Ormund.*'

She slid down onto her side, reading another message back from the boy.

'He loves it,' she said. 'Deep down inside.'

I looked up as I heard a screen door bang, and the willowy figure of Ormund Smitt emerged from his house. He shouted something back through the door, then marched purposefully towards his car, giving a cursory glance up and down the street. He bent and looked under the engine before getting in, searched up to the end of the car. For what? Bombs? Tracking devices? The cruelty of the situation weighed on me. This kid was obviously crazy.

'Lee Harvey Oswald,' I murmured.

'Huh?'

'The shooter on the grassy knoll. It reminded me. Lee Harvey Oswald said he didn't shoot JFK. He said he was just a patsy. A crazy patsy for whoever really wanted Kennedy dead.'

'Start the car.' Amanda was slapping my arm. 'Ormund's on the move. Keep on him. If I lose you, call me when you end up where you're going.'

I started the engine at the same time as our target. Ormund pulled what was probably his mother's blue Tarago out of the driveway and took off down the street.

While I was following Ormund, and the sun dipped below the mountains, Fabiana called me again. I'd been ignoring her calls, but now I had something to focus on, something to do with my hands while I spoke to her. I was feeling reckless. I answered the call and pressed the speaker.

'Can I help you?'

'I didn't think you'd pick up,' she said after a long stretch of silence, in which she must have been regaining her composure. 'Ted, I'm sorry. What I did was –'

'Illegal? Unethical? A complete betrayal of trust?' I said.

'All of those things.' She sighed.

'Mean. It was strangely mean. You didn't seem like that kind of person when I first met you. Although, maybe I was just kidding myself.'

'Ted,' Fabiana breathed, 'listen. I've been . . . I've been so mixed up over this case. They sent me up here to hunt down a predator and squeeze something out of him. Either some hideously lit snapshots or, better yet, a videoed stream of abuse for the front page of the website. But you're not anything like what I expected you to be. You're . . . You're . . .'

'Gentle?' I said.

'Well.' She considered, laughed in spite of herself. 'Yes.'

'Gentle, handsome, tall,' I said. 'A young guy. A nice guy. Good to women. Good to animals. All my bills are paid. All the tea towels in my kitchen are neatly folded.'

'Yes.'

'Well, that's lovely,' I said, trying to contain the anger in my voice. 'How about you stop thinking about what a great guy I am, and start focusing on my *actual fucking case*?'

There was silence while she thought about my words. The Tarago slipped between the cars ahead of me, turning off towards the coast.

'I'd like to think that if I was the hunchbacked old fiend with the crazy eyes you'd been expecting, you'd still have pursued my innocence by having a look at the evidence. I don't want people supporting me because I'm relatable. I want them supporting me because I'm innocent.'

'You're so angry. What's happened?' she asked. Her voice was smaller. A little hurt.

I drove in silence. The phone on the dashboard shone, the call live. I considered just hanging up. But as I breathed, long and low, I started calming down. The exhaustion rushed up again, tried to douse the flames.

'People are hassling my wife.' I rubbed my face with one hand, gripped the wheel with the other. 'It's hard. Okay, she abandoned me. But she never had anything to do with this. This happened to her as much as it happened to me, and she doesn't deserve the hassle. I'm trying to bury myself in my work to get away from it all, but people are turning up at my house now. It's scary.'

'Listen,' she said again, 'can I meet you tonight?'

'No,' I laughed. 'Absolutely not.'

'I won't be recording you.'

'Why the hell else would you want to meet with me?'

'Because I believe you, Ted.' I heard the strain in her voice. 'And other people are starting to believe you too. I know it hurts. I know what I did was wrong. But that video has made a few people out there start to challenge what they think they know about you. I think we can do more. I think there's a chance you won't have to live like this forever.'

I held onto the steering wheel, tried to believe her. I didn't.

'Would you just give me a few minutes to talk?'

I looked at the phone on the dashboard, the blue people mover ahead of me on the highway off ramp heading into the lush forest lining the grey streak of ocean in the distance.

I used my phone to drop a pin and sent the map to Amanda. I assumed she'd take a back route through the bush to try to catch up to Ormund and me. Ormund parked the car by the side of the road and I stopped just out of his line of sight, slipping out into the bush and tucking my gun into the back of my jeans. There was a part of me that was still sceptical about Ormund's involvement in Jake's disappearance. The kid seemed like a true delusional when we'd talked to him on Skype, someone so caught up in their fantasy world they hardly seemed capable of operating in the real one. But underestimating him would be a mistake. Thunder cracked overhead as I followed the narrow-shouldered young man down a trail into the mangroves.

We were deep in croc country now. The air was thick with the sickly sweet smell of pythons, and now and then in the distance I heard what might have been a croc bark, the huge reptiles waking for the twilight hunt, calling to each other across the water. Between the trees I glimpsed the creek, but it was a long way off, parallel to us as we made our way through the bush. Now and then Ormund stopped to look into the growing darkness, a hand reaching out absent-mindedly, plucking the seeded heads off reeds at the edge of the path. I crouched and waited, wiped sweat from my brow with the edge of my T-shirt. I needed the rain. When it began to mist I licked it off my upper lip, grateful.

Without any kind of warning I suddenly became aware of Amanda. She appeared behind me like a ghost, hands by her sides, an eyebrow raised in questioning. I pointed up the path at Ormund. She was walking towards me as though on eggshells, still panting from her frantic ride, her jeans sprayed with mud up to her mid-thighs and hair slicked back with sweat.

We followed Ormund for a half an hour. Everything ached, my battered legs tired on the uneven ground. Before long, the mangroves opened onto the creek bank. There, the young man began to peel away the palm fronds and clinging vines covering a large, square object.

I raised my gun and stepped out of the bush into the clearing.

'Get down,' I said. 'Down on the ground, Smitt.'

Ormund whirled around and looked at me. His face was set, eyes glimmering in the fading light, the fear and guilt of a young son caught in his father's office. He seemed not to see the gun at all.

'I won't tell you where he is.' Ormund was shivering. He seemed suddenly, impossibly small.

'We know where he is, Ormund,' I said 'He's dead. You were obsessed with him. You led him out here in the middle of the night somehow and you killed him.'

The young man snorted, looked away.

'Were you in communication with Jake?' I asked. 'Did he say something you didn't like?'

Ormund seemed to decide to rush at me and set his feet, his eyes blazing. I shifted my weight and he thought better of it, backed up against the car.

'Why did you do it, Ormund?' I asked.

'You couldn't possibly understand it all.' Ormund shivered, mumbled something I couldn't hear. 'You couldn't possibly . . .'

He glanced at Amanda, back at me, and then turned and bolted for the water.

'Fuck!' Amanda cried, half in frustration, half in amusement. 'He's going for the creek!'

We shouted for the boy to stop, but he sprinted into the water, arms forward, crashing through the muddy brown creek like a child would at the beach. Amanda didn't slow as we ran to the bank. I put an arm out and held her back.

'It's not worth it.' I looked up and down the bank, tried to spot any crocs there, sliding on their fat bellies into the water after the boy.

I realised I was panting, my lungs clamped tight against my ribs, as we watched Ormund swim towards the opposite bank. What would I see if he was taken? A sickening splash. An arm reaching. And then the red stillness of the water. I couldn't watch. I covered my face with my hands and turned away, shoved fingers into my ears.

'God, no, please,' I moaned. I didn't want to hear the scream. 'Please. Please.'

'He made it.' Amanda laughed beside me after a time, slapping me hard in the arm. 'The crazy fucker made it.'

The vines that Ormund had pulled down from the trees around Jake's car had not died. Like all jungle plants, they were too hardy, too strong, their furry fingers suctioning to the windows and doors, the leaves continuing to uncurl across the glass and inside the wheel mount. If we hadn't found the vehicle, I knew the rainforest would have eaten it completely in time, wrapped its tentacles around its windows and doors and drawn it into itself, the way an octopus pulls a struggling crab into its sucking mouth. We stripped away the vines, shoved back the palm fronds, their razor edges digging at our hands. The inside of the car was dark. I pulled open the driver's side door and flicked the switch of the roof light.

No light. The battery was dead. The smell was of mould and takeaway. I remembered Stella telling me that Jake had been an addictive man. The back seat was covered in discarded fast-food bags scrunched and tossed over the driver's shoulder. Discarded receipts for bets on greyhounds. Guilty pleasures. Secrets he refused to bring home.

There were no keys in the ignition. Amanda appeared at the murky front passenger-side door and popped it open, digging around in the glove box, the very tips of her fingers pushing the papers aside to avoid leaving prints.

'So this is the spot,' Amanda said. 'Ormund lured him out here. Maybe confronted him with his theory about the books, the end-of-the-world secret Jake had hidden inside them. Maybe Jake disagreed, told Ormund his theory was bullshit. That the books were just books. Ormund killed him, and dumped him in the creek. Some fat croc came along and disposed of the corpse.'

'I don't know,' I sighed, rummaging through the lolly wrappers in the centre console. 'Lured him out here how? There was no email. No text. No phone call.'

I left the car and did a walk-around, pulling down vines, looking for a bullet hole or streak of blood, something to indicate there'd been a struggle between the two men and Jake had come off second best. I crouched and looked for the glint of a shell casing using the flashlight on my phone. There was none. There were no torn branches besides those which covered the car. There were no bloody disturbed rocks. No flattened areas of reeds.

'What are these?' Amanda said.

She was leaning over the passenger seat, holding a wad of papers. The sheets were dry and cracked, crumpled from being folded and shoved down the side of the driver's seat. She spread them out on the centre console.

'Fan letters.' I looked through the pages. 'These are new. I haven't seen these.'

'They weren't part of the collection at the house?'

'No.' I glanced quickly over the text. 'No. These are different.'

I was starting to get a sinking feeling as I read over the words. The letters got longer and longer.

I am just so obsessed with you.

I can't tell you how proud I am of you.

We're the same. If only you knew it. You'd feel glad you finally found me.

'Look.' I showed Amanda. 'These didn't come by mail. They're emails. Printed emails.'

The hair on the back of my neck was rising. I trembled as I read.

It must be wonderful to be a god.

You probably think I'm a freak.

What if I threatened the people you love, Jake?

What's it gonna take to get your attention?

'Why didn't Cary alert us to these?' Amanda was looking at one of the later pages. 'These are twisted.'

'That's not Jake's regular email address.' I pointed to the top of the page. 'This must be the old one. An old email address, from the old website, where you can access all Jake's previous works. Makes sense. Ormund would have been a Jake Scully fan before he was famous. He'd have written to him on the old address. Cary mustn't have known about it.'

'Superfan,' Amanda whispered, her eyes wild with excitement.

'Let's shut this up and call the police,' I said, closing the driver's door. 'We don't want to contaminate it any further. We'll let them know what we found and tip them off about Smitt.'

'We're taking these.' Amanda shoved the letters into my hand. 'We've done too much hard work to let the boys in blue take all the credit.'

Dear Jake,

Have you ever thought about what it must be like to be your characters? To be picked up and shuffled about the game board so unwillingly. To be tortured, taken, cast away when their usefulness dries up. Do you ever feel sorry for them? Do you even know how brutally your fingers work them, how hard you pump their jaws to make them talk, your little puppets jabbering about? While you play with your crew, your main posse of favourites, characters like me wait in the shadows to be picked up, again and again. I've never felt your god's grip around my waist. I think about it all the time.

Raising characters must be something of what it's like to raise a child. All those years of careful moulding. Intentions. Dreams. What was it like when your son Harrison stopped being your puppet and started wandering about on his own, spouting out words you'd never given him to say? I watched you sitting with him in the courtyard yesterday, reaching out and trying to touch him, your aching face as he pulled away. You made him, and now he's out of your control. His fate is not yours to write, even as your fingers tap frantically at the keys, trying to get him back in the cage again.

Maybe this is the beginning of the end. You lost control of one character. Maybe you'll start to lose tendrils of plot. Did God mean for his son to die? Or was that the result of all the wayward characters he'd created running amok over the page? What might happen if some waiting shadow you'd grown so accustomed to ignoring suddenly struck out and changed the game? What if I was to steal one of your favourites away?

Everybody loves a good twist, right?

My street was full of people. A television broadcast van was parked at an angle in the cane field, camera guys filming a man in a suit across the road, my house in the background of the shot, gold lights shining through huge softboxes on stands. A small knot of people had simply come to watch, neutral, their arms folded and faces cast in shadows. The rest were dipping in and out of the shot, bent white cardboard signs hastily put together, wobbling as their holders chanted. I stopped my car in the dark at the end of the street and read the signs, listened to the voices on the wind.

Justice for Claire.

Keep our children safe.

Burn, Ted, burn.

I gripped the wheel and watched them. They couldn't be there all night. No one was that committed. When the cameras had their shots, surely the crowd would disperse. I leaned back in the driver's seat and started tapping at my phone. These people weren't going to stop my work. They could stop me going home, but they would not take away my only distraction – the hunt for Ormund Smitt, the inescapable desire to wrap up what had happened to Jake in a neat package of truth. There were things I could hold on to. Jake was one of them. I could pretend that resolving his case would resolve mine. I'd engaged in some pretty solid delusions in my life. This was not going to be any different.

I called a yawning and begrudging Cary and had him give me access to Jake's old email account, the one he'd started as a young writer with big dreams and little recognition. Cary seemed less than impressed that we'd found Jake's car. I guessed he knew Jake was dead, like everyone else, and the circumstances weren't going to make a difference to his relationship with the writer going forward. Jake was gone. How he went was for everyone else to figure out.

'That account's a decade old,' he told me, pots and pans clattering in the background of the call. 'The police have already looked through it. There's nothing of interest in there.'

'You're wrong,' I said. 'I won't say much, because the police might want to keep things about the discovery of Jake's car a secret. But we've got reason to believe the old email account was still active.'

'It was a fan, was it?' Cary seemed to perk up. 'My god. One of the readers?'

'Thanks for the login details,' I said. 'I can't say any more.'

I opened Jake's account and looked through the emails. Ormund's were the only recently received messages in the inbox. I scrolled through the last message, the one that talked about Harrison and Jake sitting in the courtyard of their house, the older man trying to reason with the wayward boy.

You made him, and now he's out of your control.

Someone walked by my car door in the dark, startling me. I hunched down, pressed the phone against my chest. It was suddenly much darker than it had been when I'd arrived. When the stranger had gone, I tapped the screen awake again.

There was one email in the 'deleted' folder. I opened it up and looked at the subject header.

Re: Your inquiry, Sugarbell Ranch.

Another passer-by in the dark. I wasn't safe here. I ditched the car in the rainforest and walked through the bush to the mangroves, fumbling along in the dark, trying not to think about crocodiles. Spider webs caught in my outstretched hands and palms sliced at my forearms as I made my way to the gate. When I emerged into the backyard, a police officer stepped out from the dark at the side of the house. Sweeney, one of the two patrollies who had protected my house the night before. My shoes were full of muddy water and the bottoms of my jeans were wet.

'Oh,' she said. 'It's you.'

I went to the tap at the side of the porch and took off my shoes and socks, rinsed the stinking mud away, put my feet under the stream and rubbed dirt from between my toes.

'Are you guys on all night again?' I asked.

'Someone will watch the house until this all blows over,' she said, watching me wash the cuffs of my jeans. 'The protective detail sheet says twelve days. If you're still being hounded after that, the chief might extend.'

I could hear the chanting at the front of the house from where we stood. We stared awkwardly at each other, listening.

Keep our children safe!
Don't wait till it's too late!

'Safe doesn't rhyme with late,' I said. Sweeney looked at me like I was mad. I felt lonely for Amanda suddenly. She would have appreciated my attention to rhymes, and my painful attempt to throw cheer into a situation most people recognised as unredeemable. Nothing was too strange or too awkward when said in the presence of Amanda. The cop walked away.

I went to the bedroom and sat on the floor by the crack in the window and listened to the news reports. A man in a suit stood on the grass off to the side of the crowd, a microphone in hand, going through pre-recorded crosses for *A Current Affair*. He recorded some interviews with locals for a longer piece, trying out a number of introductions the editors could choose from later when they put the exclusive together.

'A town in terror,' he said, nodding and raising his chin sharply to catch the light. 'The quiet, tropical community of Crimson Lake, where the only threat to youngsters is usually the steamy summer heat. It's a place where families feel safe, and the friendly local farmers are always there to lend each other a helping hand. Well, no more.'

The cameras dipped. A woman stepped out from the shadows.

'Good one, Mike.' She took a card from a guy standing behind the camera and replaced it with another, stepped away from the shot. 'Go again in three, two . . .'

'In the quiet town of Crimson Lake, a terror is lurking,' the suited guy said, jutting his square jaw. 'This small tropical community, where the only threat to youngsters is usually . . .'

I couldn't listen anymore. I thought I'd have a couple of Wild Turkeys on the back porch, try to lull myself into a false sense of calm while I worked through the emails Amanda and I had found in Jake's car. As I turned into the hall, however, I glanced back towards the front door and noticed a slice of light.

The door was ajar. My stomach plummeted. I went to the door and pulled it open, looked out at the two female cops standing on the edge of the porch. They heard it creak and turned around.

'Did you two come in here?' I asked.

'What?'

'This door was unlatched,' I said. 'Has anyone been in here today? Since I've been gone?'

'No. Go back inside, Mr Conkaffey, before the crowd sees you.'

I shut the door with a growing sense of dread. I knew I'd locked the door when I left that morning to spy on Ormund Smitt. I went to the bedroom and counted off the meagre things there – the laptop, my boxes of papers. I went into the kitchen and picked my phone up off the bench. Everything seemed just how I'd left it, but the electric feeling creeping up my arms told me that something wasn't right. The phone buzzed in my hand, startling me so that I dropped it on the tiles.

'Hello?'

'Ted? It's Francine.'

I felt light-headed. Everything was wrong. I hadn't talked to Little Frankie since my pre-arrest questioning, since she'd left my interrogation and I'd heard her crying in the office, begging our colleagues to tell her that it wasn't true.

'Hi,' I said, trying to think of something to fill the awful silence. 'Hi.'

'I, uh . . .' Frankie sighed exasperatedly.

'Did Kelly ask you to call?'

'No,' she said. 'Why would she ask me to call?'

'Oh, *60 Minutes* is after her again. That's all.'

'No I'm, um, I'm actually calling because I'm wondering if you can tell me if you know a couple of guys.' She shuffled a paper. 'An L. Damford and a S. Hench?'

I gripped a chair by the kitchen table, crawled into its seat.

'Why are you asking me that?'

'They're from your area. They've put in a couple of requests for warrants to search your place. A friend from the Queensland force told me. Gossip, you know. The requests have been knocked back, but they keep coming. I'm wondering if, uh . . .' She fell quiet. I hung onto the phone. 'If they're after you. With all the news, and everything. You know?'

'They are,' I said. 'Those guys are after me. It's not just about my case. It's deeper. They . . . I've got a partner. They don't want me working with her.'

Across the miles between us, we listened to each other's breathing, saying nothing. Outside, the chanting changed. I couldn't make out the words.

'It was hard to know if I should warn you,' she said.

'I'm grateful that you did,' I told her. I thought about all the conversations I'd had with her in my mind since my arrest. The nights I'd lain awake in prison trying to explain to her that I was innocent. That I was sorry. That I missed her. I missed them all – those hard-nosed cops I used to call my brothers and sisters, the tired faces I passed when I came on shift, the drunken louts I celebrated with at the station Christmas party.

Before I could say any of that now, Frankie hung up on me.

Panic. As raw and as real as a heat burning through me, crawling up my throat, pulsing in my ears. I put the phone down on the kitchen table and went to the front room. I dumped the box of possessions there onto the floor. Picked up paperbacks and flipped through them. Shoved clothes out of the way. When I found nothing, I went to the bedroom, tore the sheets off the bed, crouched low and lifted the mattress, leaned it against the wall, ran my hand over the back of it, looking for slits or holes. I'd forgotten all about my injuries now. The pain didn't matter. Panic had eclipsed it.

Damford and Hench wanted an official reason to come into my house. They wanted approval. A piece of paper to hold in the air. They'd never bothered with it before. They'd been in and out of my house on no more approval than their own.

There was only one reason I could think of for getting the search approved. They knew they'd find something this time.

When I noticed Fabiana Grisham standing in the doorway of the bedroom, I hardly acknowledged her. She wasn't the immediate threat.

'The front door was unlocked. What the hell are you doing?'

'There's going to be a search,' I said. I tore out the drawer of the dresser and dumped its contents on the bed. 'They've planted something.'

She fell silent, watching me. I was aware of the fact that she was very dressed-down, that she'd slapped on a soft white cotton dress to deal with the heat and her long hair was up in a high ponytail, off her sweaty neck. I was also aware that she looked amazing, but I couldn't seem to fix my eyes on her. They wandered frantically over the room, then the ensuite. I ran in there and opened the cupboards, ran my hands up under the sink in case something was taped there.

'Ted,' she said. She was suddenly close, her hands on my arms. 'Ted, you're panicking. You're going crazy.'

335

I pushed her away and bent over the toilet, running my hands over the dusty back of the cistern. *Look everywhere*, I thought. *Look up*. I went back to the bedroom, pulled the mattress back onto the bed and stood on it, ran my hands over the tops of the ceiling fan blades. I knew from my time in drug squad how creative people could be when they wanted to hide something very important. Drug dealers pulled away pieces of the skirting board, taped things beneath chairs, sewed things into the sides of mattresses. The possibilities were endless. I reminded myself to check all the pockets of my clothes. My shoes. To look in the pipes behind the washing machine.

Fabiana stood watching me from the door of the ensuite.

I hadn't forgiven her. But enemy assistance in the middle of a crisis is better than none at all.

'You can stare at me or you can help,' I said.

She thought about it for a little while, then she went to the kitchen. I could hear her shoving things around under the sink. I joined her in time, lifting and shifting all the pantry contents from one side of the wide shelves to the other. I stood on a chair and checked the ceiling fans there, then went out onto the porch and pulled apart the cane lounge.

I came across my gun sitting in the top draw of my dresser. Held it for a few seconds and felt the old pull backwards, the lure of silence. Escape button. It would be so simple to get out of this trap.

At about midnight, I'd finished searching under the porch with a flashlight. I stood tapping it against my palm in the dark backyard, trying to think. She walked down the stairs with a couple of glasses of wine, her lean body silhouetted through the cotton dress in the lights from the kitchen. I was filthy and drenched in sweat. Cane toads scurried from her across the wet lawn as she came towards me. We stood barefoot, looking at the moonlit water between the trees.

'There's a group on the internet called *Innocent Ted*,' she said quietly. 'They started up after the interview footage. They're trying to get a written statement from Trevor Fuller to release on the blog. They're also trying to see if they can access phone tower pings in the area on that day. See who else was around.'

'Who are these people?' I asked.

She shrugged. 'They're just people. Strangers who believe you.'

I stared at the water, aware that she was watching me. She wanted me to tell her that I forgave her. But I didn't. I didn't have it in me at that particular moment. There was only panic. Only the rushing visions of what might come. The search. The discovery. The arrest. The cell.

Right back where I started. Back behind the wire.

Fabiana reached out and took my hand, gave it a squeeze. I looked down at it, unsure if I could meet her eyes. I hadn't realised until that moment, but the chanting at the front of the house had stopped. I could hear quiet laughter now and then from the cops, but their soft voices were the only human sound. Fabiana and I might have been two normal people standing in their yard, enjoying the heat of the night. It was the first time I'd been so close to normality since my release.

The panic eased as I fell into the fantasy. Yes, that was the answer. Forget completely about everything. Ignore what Fabiana had done. Ignore the people on the road. Ignore the undeniable idea that everything was about to end and grab desperately onto the illusion. I was an emotionless passenger calmly drinking scotch in the cruise ship bar, even as the floor tilted beneath me and the cold water rose around my ankles.

'You're not alone, Ted,' Fabiana said.

I let go of her hand, reached up and took her soft cheek.

I pretended I was someone else and I kissed her.

DT. SGT LEIGHTON: This is Detective Sergeant Anthony Leighton of the Crimson Lake Police Beat, badge number 477177. I'm sitting with Detective Sergeant Veronica Prince, and our interview is in relation to the investigation into the murder of Lauren Jessica Freeman, seventeen, of Crimson Lake. The time is 09.49 on the morning of 11 February 2004. Detective Sergeant Prince, would you confirm your presence.

DT. SGT PRINCE: Veronica Prince, badge number 481911.

DT. SGT LEIGHTON: Amanda, would you state your name, address and birth date for the recording.

PHARRELL: Um. It's Amanda Pharrell. Amanda Joy Pharrell. Tuesday, first December 1986 was the day I was born. Um.

DT. SGT LEIGHTON: Your address?

PHARRELL: 14 Possum Place, Crimson Lake. The white house.

DT. SGT LEIGHTON: Amanda, this is our second interview. At the end of our last interview, we had started talking about your relationship with the victim, Lauren Freeman.

PHARRELL: Yep.

DT. SGT LEIGHTON: I wanted to go back into that, and have a chat about why you accepted the ride from Lauren last

Wednesday night, on the night she was killed. Can you tell me if you and Lauren were friends?

PHARRELL: Were we friends?

DT. SGT LEIGHTON: Yes.

PHARRELL: Um. No. Not really. I mean we weren't *not* friends. I don't have many friends. I don't –

DT. SGT LEIGHTON: Maybe you could get into why you accepted the ride. Why you were headed to the party together.

PHARRELL: Well, she said there was a party on. At Kissing Point. I don't mind going to things, like parties and things, if I get asked. Some parties they don't ask people, like there aren't invitations and things –

DT. SGT LEIGHTON: Amanda –

PHARRELL: I mean, I think it must be lame to make invitations to things now. Maybe invitations are something only kids do. I've never had a party. I don't know. I never know what's right.

DT. SGT LEIGHTON: But did Lauren ask you to come along to the party with her? Did she say something like, 'Hey, come along with me to this night?' That the two of you would go together?

PHARRELL: Well, no, it wasn't her party.

DT. SGT PRINCE: Look, we're trying to shed some light on why Lauren asked you to go with her in the first place, Amanda. People are telling us, and you're telling us, that the two of you weren't friends.

PHARRELL: She threw a pencil at me once.

DT. SGT LEIGHTON: I'm sorry?

PHARRELL: In primary school. Year Five, I think. We both had Ms Grace. Lauren threw a pencil at me. I mean, everyone

340

was throwing pencils at me, and she joined in, but I don't think she'd have remembered it now, if you asked her. If she was alive.

DT. SGT LEIGHTON: Is that why you did what you did?

PHARRELL: Did what?

DT. SGT LEIGHTON: Is that why you stabbed her, Amanda? I'm asking if you stabbed her because there were things from your past, like when she threw the pencil at you in Year Five, that made you angry at her. Is that why you stabbed her?

PHARRELL: (inaudible)

DT. SGT LEIGHTON: If we can just understand why this happened, Amanda, it would be so much easier on everyone. On Lauren's family. I mean, there might be a reason why you did what you did. There might have been something –

PHARRELL: When can I go home? I'm so tired. I'd really like to go home soon.

DT. SGT LEIGHTON: Is there someone else who might understand, and be able to explain better the relationship between you and Lauren? Did you ever tell anyone how you felt about Lauren?

DT. SGT PRINCE: It's okay to hate someone, Amanda. Everybody hates someone. Did you hate Lauren? Did Lauren maybe try to take you to the party as a way of saying sorry for whatever she'd done?

PHARRELL: I'm sure she was a really nice girl.

DT. SGT LEIGHTON: (inaudible)

DT. SGT PRINCE: I might take a break, Tony. This is pretty heavy for me.

DT. SGT LEIGHTON: Interview suspended at –

PHARRELL: Her family will probably miss her heaps.

We woke to the sound of a bang against the boards on the front windows. A hurled lump of brick, probably. There were plenty of voices outside, but cutting through them was the yelling of one of the protective officers.

'Hey! Do that again and I'll book you, mate!'

Fabiana had been curled on her side, turned away from me. She rolled over and buried her face in my shoulder. I lay staring at the ceiling, barely remembering what we'd done. I'd gone away, recoiled into myself, let another Ted that was not Ted come out and take over my brain. I had the sense that I'd done this before, that there was another me in there who could handle trauma and terror better than I could. Maybe that's how I'd dealt with my job all those years, with dead babies in drug dens and dealers' wives lying on soiled mattresses with their throats cut. The Other Ted didn't give a shit. He was an ordinary guy. A guy without troubles. A guy who wasn't in danger. An invincible guy.

Whoever he was, Other Ted was gone now, and all the hurt that the regular me felt panged through me. Fabiana held me. But I didn't hold her. I hadn't forgotten what she'd done. I sat up and scratched my scalp awake.

Determined to stay asleep, Fabiana latched onto me as a kind of anchor to dreamland, her arm coming around my stomach and legs entwining with mine.

'This is one committed mob,' she sighed when none of her manoeuvres worked.

'I don't think there'd be half as many if *A Current Affair* wasn't there,' I said. 'Angry mobs love that show. Coffee?'

'I think I'm going to need it,' she said.

I padded into the kitchen and stopped to survey the yard, half-expecting some devastation from the vigilantes there. I'd chained the back gate, but it looked like someone had at least pushed on it experimentally, bent the top of the wire fence trying to get through. The cops probably chased them away.

I took the coffee off the shelf and set two mugs on the counter. I felt generally wretched. I'd fallen into Fabiana and her attraction to me as a last-ditch effort to escape my reality. Now that the spell was broken, I wanted to scream at her for feeding me to the dogs with that goddamn video. Images of the night before pushed at me. I thought I liked her. But I really didn't like what she'd done to me.

How to tell her that I never wanted to see her again, but that I didn't want her to leave?

When Fabiana entered the kitchen I had paused, staring at the dry brown grounds in the open jar.

'Y'all right?'

There was a tiny plastic triangle sticking out of the top of the coffee grinds, a translucent mountain jutting from chocolate-coloured boulders. I reached in and took the peak between my thumb and forefinger, pulled gently. The grinds shifted, collapsing, sinking. I pulled again, and the bag began to emerge from the jar.

'Oh my god,' I said. Fabiana pushed in beside me.

The photographs in the little zip-lock bag were curled to fit into the jar. I tipped the jar into the sink and pulled the bag out, flattened the photographs on the counter. There was a stack of them, five or six polaroids. I knew what they were without having to look very closely.

'Oh shit.' Fabiana snatched the bag off me and held it up to her nose. 'Jesus. Jesus!'

There was a pounding at the front door. I recognised Hench's voice above the crowd. I watched in numb terror as Fabiana shoved the bag with the photos in the front of her underpants, pulling down the T-shirt of mine that she'd borrowed to wear so that it hung at the top of her thighs.

Damford and Hench didn't wait for me to go and open the door. It made a good show for the crowd to kick the door in, again. There was a cheer from the front of the house. The two officers walked in and took in the scene before them.

The coffee grounds all over the sink. Fabiana standing there beside me, her hair mussed and her fingers grabbing nervously at the neck of her T-shirt. This was not what they had planned. Hench took his baton out of his belt.

'Hands up, Conkaffey. We've got a warrant for a site search.'

He poked me in the belly, not hard. Not like he had on other occasions. The two didn't know what to make of Fabiana. She was too clean, too beautiful to be a prostitute I'd brought home from Cairns. But what woman in her right mind would have anything to do with me right now? What the hell was I doing entertaining women when I had the mob at my door calling for my lynching?

'Search the house,' I said. 'You won't find anything.'

'Not now.' Hench looked distastefully at the sink. He slipped a finger into the waistband of my boxers and made the elastic snap. 'Looks like we were seconds too late, eh, Ted? Get your shirt off. Put your hands on the sink.'

'Does your warrant include a body search?' Fabiana piped up. She went to the kitchen table and sat down. I winced, thinking the zip-lock plastic was going to crumple loudly in her pants. But it didn't make a sound. 'I bet it doesn't. I bet it's premises only.'

They turned on her like dogs.

'What's your name, miss?'

'I don't have to give you my name.'

'Huh,' Damford sneered. 'Spoken like a true criminal piece of shit. You know who this guy here is? This is Ted Conkaffey, honey. You heard that name?'

'I have.'

'Then you'll know your boyfriend here usually likes 'em a lot younger than you. Like twenty years younger. That's not a problem?'

'Can you just get on with what you're doing and leave?' I stepped away from Hench, out of the swing of his baton. He pushed over the milk carton at his side so that it tipped and fell on the floor, vomiting milk under the fridge.

'Whoops.'

Damford was looking at Fabiana, trying to decide if she was hiding the photographs. It was clear we'd only just found the photographs mere seconds before they'd come in. They were either on me, or they were on her. Hench gave me an experimental nudge with his hip as he passed me while walking to the cupboard, trying to make the baggie crackle in my waistband or crotch. He opened the cupboard, looked around. Opened the drawers and shuffled loudly through the cutlery.

'You won't find anything,' I repeated slowly. I caught the fat officer's eye. 'Believe me.'

Damford and Hench knocked a few more things over on their way out, stopped and looked through the door at my bedroom. But they knew that this time, for the first time, I'd won. When I shut the front door behind them, the sickness in my stomach made itself known. I went back into the kitchen, where Fabiana had placed the pictures on the table, her role as my saviour now ended.

I opened the bag and carefully laid out the six photographs, each of them curved from being inside the coffee jar. They were all the same pose, but the girls were different. They were each lying on their back on different surfaces; two on beds, one on the carpet of what looked like a cluttered bedroom, one across the back seat of a car, two on couches. Each of the girls had an arm raised and hanging over their eyes, an elbow jutting upwards, shielding their identities. They were naked, their knobbly teenage knees splayed and milk-white bodies stretched tight. Gaping grotesquely in the light of the flash.

I found Fabiana standing in the bedroom, looking at her hands. The look she gave me was that of a woman who didn't know if she'd done the right thing.

I sat in the car outside the Starfish cafe, shifting through the fan letters from Jake Scully's car in my hands. I could hardly concentrate on them. Until now, I'd been trying to leave my gun at home, but the journalists and the vigilantes were making me nervous, so I'd started carrying it down the back of my jeans. The storm seemed to be bringing with it all the terrible energy of both cases, Amanda's and mine. Hard truths were coming. On the radio, every half hour a news brief mentioned that the police had found Jake's car and were putting it through forensic testing. They mentioned Smitt, saying police wanted to question the young man in relation to the famous writer's disappearance. The radio hosts kept directing people to the Crime Stoppers website, where pictures of Smitt were being displayed. His mother had already submitted herself to police. Didn't know where the young man was. Didn't know anything about the case.

I didn't doubt that the letters to Jake were from Smitt. They had his natural arrogance, his patronising eloquence. There was a fire crackling behind the words as I worked through the first five letters. A barely contained desperation to have the older man meet his eye, just once. And that familiar hurt when he wouldn't. The wounded pride of an ignored child, confused when their uniqueness isn't recognised. Face in the crowd, beaming, waiting.

I watched the words slowly darkening, darkening. When Dynah arrived at the cafe, keys in hand, I had to wrench myself up out of that black and horrid world Smitt had created and into the light of day again. Smitt's universe was so dark, and so deep, and I knew somewhere down there Jake Scully's body was swirling. The animal that had taken him had just been the vehicle. I was sure there was a bottom to the swamp, but only Ormund himself knew where it was and what lurked there.

I put down Smitt's letters to Jake and picked up the photographs from the coffee jar in my kitchen. The little girls lost.

Dynah stopped and watched me as I got out of the car. There was a flicker of a defeated smile about her lips as I came towards her. The beginnings of tears in her eyes.

•

The wind was whipping the palm trees when I left the Starfish cafe, and as I pulled open the car door the handle was yanked hard from my hand by the approaching storm. I looked at the mountains and found the sky above them an angry dark blue, lightning flashing over the top of the range. There was no rain here yet but the ground seemed to know it was coming, the asphalt already steaming. Creatures in the gardens behind the buildings on the main street were calling out. There would be no customers for Dynah that afternoon. She'd stand in the dark kitchen looking out, watching the gutters flood.

I sat in the car for a long time, staring at the letters in the passenger seat, wondering if I should go now and find Amanda and tell her that I knew everything. My head was pounding. I turned the car around and headed towards Crimson Lake. Dynah's words were ringing in my mind. My thoughts were tangled up in teenage voices, images of bodies sprawled, eyes hidden, horrified, downturned mouths as their images were captured.

When I arrived at the small office in Beale Street there were two journalists standing on the wooden stairs drinking coffee from mugs I recognised as Amanda's. She'd made our pursuers coffee, but not warmed to them enough to invite them inside. That was Amanda: halfway between one seat of logic and another. The two men looked at me as I locked the car and put the zip-lock bag with the pictures of the naked girls in the back pocket of my jeans. I didn't worry about being caught with them now. They'd come out soon enough. The men at the door studied my face, tried to assess whether I'd respond to their questions even before I'd made it up the path.

'Just one comment,' the journalist on the right said, holding his mug out like a friendly hand. 'Anything, Ted.'

'No comment, mate,' I said as I pushed past.

Amanda was standing in the kitchen with her own mug of coffee, stirring slowly, her unseeing eyes settled on the chocolate-brown liquid going round and round. She seemed like the weather outside, a storm slowly building, and I wondered absurdly if she knew what I had just learned about her from Dynah. If she could somehow hear Dynah's voice in my head, rambling away, the horrific web of images she spun there. I went to the desk and sat down, looked at the computer screen, which showed a live blog with updates on the search for Ormund Smitt. Police had attended the local hardware store where he worked as a cashier and were conducting interviews there. There were no signs of the young man. I shifted things around the desk, not knowing where to begin. Amanda was still stirring the coffee in the kitchen, her eyes glazed.

'Amanda,' I said.

'Yes.'

'Amanda, I know. I know what happened. At Kissing Point.'

There was silence. I was holding a stack of papers, just needing to have something to hold onto while I blasted my partner's world apart. I didn't even know what they were. Printouts of screenshots from Ormund's website. Emails from Cary. Copies of the fan letters we found in Jake's car. But their weight in my fingers was reassuring. I repeated what I'd said, but Amanda didn't react. The stirring had taken on a momentum of its own, soundless. Three cats were sitting rigidly on the kitchen floor looking up at their motion-trapped master and wondering how to break the spell.

I'd had enough of this. My resolve snapped. I had too many questions for her, and those questions pulsed at the back of my throat, painful and heavy, things I could no longer ignore. I planned to go to her. Shake her. But it was as I set the papers on the table with a breezy *whump* that I realised our mistake. I looked at the stack of printed pages. Heard the sound of them hitting the table rattling, echoing through my brain. The sound made my whole body jolt.

'Oh my god,' I said

Amanda finally came alive, her head turning to me, giving a twitch.

'What?'

'We gotta go,' I said, stumbling back into the bookcase behind the desk. I grabbed my keys from the tabletop. 'Get the bike. We've got to go to the Scully place right now!'

Stella Scully's car was parked in the driveway of the huge house nestled into the rainforest. I parked behind it and looked up the street towards where I knew Amanda would emerge between the walls of cane, watching lightning crack over the yellow plains. The horizon was streaked with black. Whatever was coming was going to flatten the marshlands and bring the muddy waters bubbling up around the houses on the banks. I felt a wave of gratitude to Valerie Gratteur, knowing that my geese were safe inside her sturdy Queenslander closer to Cairns. The waters at the end of my property were going to swell, and I didn't know what I'd find creeping around my house with the vigilantes whenever I returned.

I couldn't wait for Amanda, not with what I knew, what I'd realised as I set those heavy papers on the desk in her office. What that sound triggered in me.

The thick, dull *whump* of the pages onto the desk. The weight of them. I'd thought about writers and their words, about the words on the pages being stroked and held by readers, about how precious those words become. How they'd tortured Ormund Smitt. How they'd stirred and stirred inside him until they created a monster.

I jogged to the front door and banged hard on it, pumped the doorbell, looked inside the glass panel at the cold and dark foyer. I saw no one. I walked back up the drive and looked at Harrison's balcony, at the upstairs windows reflecting the coming storm. Without calling again I took a rock from the front garden and pitched it hard at the glass beside the door. The panel shattered inward, spraying glass over the tiles. An alarm system started squealing. I unlocked the door and pushed my way through, mashed the control panel with my palm as I passed, trying in vain to shut off the noise.

'Stella?' I called, running into the dining room. I did a circuit of the kitchen, the big laundry room, came around the sitting room towards the office where she'd put her hands on my chest, tried to draw my body into hers. My face was aflame. Half painful humiliation, half desire to find her now, to make things right by ensuring she was safe. 'Stella!'

I found her on the rug on the floor, curled on her side, more little plates of biscuits and snacks laid out all around her like she'd never left that moment, the two of us together. There was an empty bottle of champagne lying on its side in the curve of her body. I dropped onto my knees and pushed the golden curls that had fallen in her face away from her cheeks. She was very warm, but stiff as a board. I tried to pull her arm, twist her onto her back, but she seemed to be resisting me.

'Is she all right?'

Amanda came in behind me, her hair speckled with rain and her neck red with exertion. She knelt and pushed her fingers into Stella's neck.

'She's hardly breathing,' I said. I shoved the bottle and plates out of the way. 'Sit her up. Stella? Can you hear me?'

I heard a sound and grabbed my gun out of my jeans, whirled around and found Harrison standing in the doorway. His face was passive, his eyes wandering from his mother to me, to Amanda as she ignored him and pulled the unconscious woman onto her side, lifted her chin, and started to dial for an ambulance on her phone. Zoe appeared behind him, more curious, a wary dog caught doing something it shouldn't have, uncertain if punishment was to come. I flicked the gun at the two teenagers, trying to usher them into the room, but they merely jolted, almost indignant at my aim.

'Get in here,' I said. 'Both of you.'

Harrison sidestepped into the room, pulling at the edges of his beanie so that the hem rested over his eyebrows. The girl remained in the doorway. I could see their minds working, silent zings of information, questions, passing between them on invisible lines. Neither seemed to be able to decide whether to stay or run. Their legs were set slightly too wide apart.

'What has she had?' I asked. 'Harrison, what have you given her?'

'Rohypnol,' the girl answered for him.

'How many?'

'Twelve.'

Harrison stared at the ground, at his black and white shoes, the pen lines around the sole, doodled grinning faces with fangs.

I stood, kept the gun on the boy. Amanda was watching me from where she knelt beside Stella, her fingers still on the woman's neck, feeling that heart pump slowly, slowly beneath the caramel skin. She murmured to the operator, her voice low, fast, her eyes flicking between Stella and the standoff in the room.

'This is Zoe Miller,' I told Amanda. 'Six months ago, her mother Teresa Miller died in a car accident. Only it wasn't an accident. Was it? When I found you two down the side of my house, beside my car, in the night, you said you were trying to slash my tyres.'

I could hardly breathe. My chest was tight as a drum.

'I thought that was weird,' I said. 'Harrison. How you just blurted it out. "We were going to slash your tyres." Why would you say that? Because you didn't want me to know what you were really up to. You didn't want me to know you were actually going after my brake cable, just like you did to Zoe's mother. That's why you brought the wire cutters. That's why you didn't have a knife.'

Zoe smirked bitterly. Harrison watched me.

I moved a couple of steps around the desk. I didn't want to frighten the girl out of the doorway, but I didn't want to lose the boy, either. He was standing by the golf clubs, his head down, eyes finding his partner now and then, communicating.

'That's why you didn't want me to know your girlfriend's name, Harrison,' I continued, watching the boy. 'Because if I knew her mother was dead, I'd wonder what the chances were of two innocent kids losing a parent each in the space of six months. I've been looking at her mother's name written all over this town. Teresa Miller, dearly missed. Teresa Miller, lost too soon. You knew we'd drill down and look at everything, and you sure didn't want us looking at that.'

'This guy.' Harrison gave an indignant laugh, shaking his head. 'Fuck.'

'It's not a bad plan,' Amanda commented, her voice quiet. 'Zoe's mother gets killed in a freak car accident. Harrison's dad gets knocked off by a crazy fan. Two parents down. Two to go.'

'Six months,' I said. 'Just enough time for people to miss the connection. You wait a couple of years and then . . . what? Whose turn was it next?'

'It was going to be my dad next.' Zoe's bottom lip was restless. She looked like she wanted to scream. Or cry. She pointed to Stella. 'But she . . . She hired you fucking losers.'

The girl sobbed hard, five or six times, holding the sleeves of her long black T-shirt against her mouth. Harrison was staring at me, his head dipped. The stud in his bottom lip was twisting back and forth as he worried it with his teeth.

'Those letters.' Amanda snorted a small, angry laugh. 'They weren't from Ormund Smitt. They were from you. You dummied up a bunch of crazy shit and emailed it to your dad. Got him all paranoid. Made threats against . . . against *yourself*.'

'Shut up,' Harrison snapped. The panic was eating at him. I could see it creeping up his skin, making his neck flush red, his jaw burning. 'All you've got so far are fucking theories. Who's going to believe some fucking kiddie-fiddler and his murderer girlfriend when you bring them this bullshit?'

'It's in the letters,' I said. 'It's all in the letters. They were beautifully written. Very clever. You got the batshit crazy superfan voice down just right. And by letting Ormund know where your dad's car was, you tied him into the whole mess.

Of course, you knew he was going to visit the car. Put his prints and fibres all over it. How could he not? Your dad was Ormund's whole life. His purpose. His secret mission. You had any number of obsessives to choose from. But you chose a local. Someone who might have lured Jake into the waterways.'

I suddenly felt exhausted. All the planning that had gone into this. The cold, long hours of planning.

'But you went too far. The last letters were too much. You wrote as Ormund wandering around the house like a ghost. *I watch you shower. I watch you fuck your wife. I've sat in your chair behind your big bad desk and pretended to be you.*'

I shook my head.

'Ormund Smitt never sat behind this desk,' I said.

I reached out and picked up the manuscript on the desk, the first page layered with a thin sheet of dust. I waved the paper stack so that the pages flopped over my hand. I'd only remembered the manuscript as I sat at Amanda's office just minutes before, as I felt the weight of the papers there flip from my fingers and flop on the table. If I'd not remembered . . . I trembled. If I'd not remembered the manuscript . . .

'New book,' I said. 'Jake must have been about halfway through. Your plan – you had it just about right. It's plausible an obsessive, dangerous freak like Ormund Smitt might have written those weird letters to your dad. But there's no way the same obsessive, dangerous freak would have left this here. If he was really getting into the house, watching him, watching you, he'd have taken this manuscript. He'd have at least had a look, and mentioned it in the letters. No sick, obsessed, murderous fan is going to leave a writer's *brand-new unfinished manuscript* untouched on the desk like it means nothing.'

355

'Fuck you.' Harrison scoffed again. 'What the fuck do you know about it? About any of it?'

'That's why there was no phone call. No message calling Jake out into night. The last letters told Jake the superfan was coming for his son. Jake must have been worried about what Ormund would do to you, Harrison. And then you wake him up in the middle of the night and you say you've got a message, telling you to come out and meet him. *Dad, some guy online wants to meet me by the river. He says he's got to talk to me about you. I'm scared.* Jake goes instead, thinking he's going to finally confront the guy. Get him away from his son.'

'This is so fucked up.' Zoe was crying hard now. But when she took her hands down from her face, I could see there were no tears. 'Harry? Harry, we're so fucked. They know everything. We're so fucked!'

'We're fine.' Harrison's voice trembled. 'It's okay, baby. It's okay.'

'You're not fine,' I said. 'Amanda's going to wait for the ambulance, and you two are coming with me.'

Harrison yanked the golf club he'd been holding behind his back out of the bag, the whole bag clattering to the floor, spilling golf balls. He swung the shining club once, twice, and then hurled the whole thing at me. It turned end over end and smashed into the framed book poster behind the desk.

I was never going to shoot him. I'd never really held the aim right on him. Even as he revealed himself, before me, even as I saw the denial fall and the stupid, reckless, hateful kid who'd murdered his own father emerged from behind the mask, I had no intention of shooting Harrison. All I wanted to do was contain them, because in Harrison's face I could see the sick

356

grey pallor of a young mind slowly burning, and I knew he was losing all hope. He was losing all control. He was far more dangerous to himself now than I could ever be. But by the time I'd ducked out of the way of the golf club and straightened up, the two teenagers were gone.

I ran out of the house and turned left up the street, past the sign warning of cassowaries crossing the wide, warm road. The rain was falling in soft diagonal sheets, hitting the asphalt and rising again in curling plumes of steam. Up ahead, at the corner, I saw the two running side by side. I set off in a sprint and heard Zoe squeal as she turned and spotted me.

They disappeared into the lush undergrowth, two black rabbits sliding in the wet mulch. It seemed an age before I reached the place where they had entered. There was no sign of them but for their footprints in the earth. I slid and stumbled down into the rainforest, grabbing at furry vines, grateful for the animal path as it eventually evened out onto a flat. My mouth was hanging open, thick air pumping through my lungs. There was no rain here. The frogs were deafening, a deep, consistent roar.

I ran for ten minutes on nothing but the thought that they must have turned left, where the forest was thinner and lighter, and not right, back towards the house. My jeans were soaked from ferns hanging across the narrow path, slashing at my thighs. I looked back a couple of times but saw no sign of Amanda. When I called out for the two teenagers, nothing answered but the rush of sound from the living things around me.

By the time the storm was above us I was sure I'd lost them. But I turned a corner sharply and Zoe stood there by a tree, those long sleeves still in her mouth, one canine tooth worrying at a loose thread. The rain had smeared her mascara down her cheeks in two thin streams. I slid to a stop and grabbed her by the shoulders.

'We're so fucked!' she was howling.

'Where is he?' I asked.

'We killed my mum.' She swallowed hard and searched my eyes, her breath hitching over shuddering sobs. 'We killed my fucking mum! Oh my god, we killed my mum!'

'Where is Harrison going?' I shook her. 'Tell me before he hurts someone else!'

I wanted to slap her. Nothing was coming out of her but moans. It was a shivering and howling girl who pushed her way into my arms. I held her despite everything – what she had done, my desire to catch her partner, the shameful feeling of a girl's body against mine with all that I had been accused of, with all the horrific images my mind had been filled with since the trial. I thought it was safest to hold her, to smooth down her scraggily pink hair, to tell her she was all right, just in case she really was as helpless as she seemed and those were not crocodile tears on her cheeks.

I knew I was wrong when I felt the knife in my back.

Her first shot was badly played. She drove the kitchen knife up into my shoulder blade, the tip penetrating my back no more than a few centimetres before it hit bone. She must have taken it from the Scully house. I could feel the sharpness of the blade. I tightened my arms around her, and she tried again, stabbing frantically at my back, hitting that bone again and again. I threw her onto the ground, shocked, hurting, and she rose up again like a snake and embedded the whole blade in my right thigh.

Thunder crashed overhead. I yelled in pain, pulled the knife out of my leg, balled a fist, and punched the girl in the face. She sagged onto the ground at my feet, her head on my shoe.

'Shit!' I yelled, grabbing at the wound in my leg. The impact had felt like an insect sting, but as my head cleared the pain shook through my upper leg and hip, dull and heavy and red. The blood was coming fast. I slipped the knife into my pocket and limped on, growling, the leg suddenly seeming to weigh as much as my whole body.

I left Zoe there in the dark and headed along the path, calling for the boy. The path led downward, and soon I spied the muddy river between the trees, and the beginnings of thick, twisted mangroves. I slowed, keeping an eye out for movement. There was no sign of Amanda behind me. I stopped, drawing my gun, when I saw the boy between the trees.

He stood on the end of a long, high pier, a thing designed for high tide, resting on thin legs a couple of metres above the water. Though I called his name as I emerged from the forest into the light rain, he didn't turn. The beanie was dripping thin streams of water onto his narrow shoulders, his black T-shirt hanging crookedly. In his hand, he held a long stick, which he tapped rapidly against the edge of the pier. I kept the gun on him and looked up towards the trees, hearing a rustling but unable to tell if it was my partner or his.

'Harrison,' I said, taking my first steps onto the pier. 'I want you to turn around and put your hands on your head.'

The pier might have been fifteen metres long. I could smell fish guts reinvigorated by the rain. While I edged closer, the boy kept tapping, rapping the stick all along the edges of the boards. I didn't know what he was doing until he gave a couple of short, hard grunts, like he was trying to clear a blockage from his throat. I knew that noise. He was calling them. He was making the bark of a crocodile.

Every muscle in my body was taut. I searched the muddy, black water, but nothing moved beneath the low ripples of the rain.

'Harrison,' I said. He looked at me. Defiant. The world was crashing down, and Harrison Scully was doing all he could to resist bowing out, letting the fantasy take him over. Giving in to the Harrison that was not Harrison deep down inside.

'Why did you do this?' I asked. I inched closer. 'Whose idea was it?'

He tapped the stick on the edge of the pier. At first I thought he wouldn't answer. But in time the words came.

'It was only going to be Teresa, at first,' he said. He shook his head. 'Zoe's mum, she . . . she was all over us. She did not want us to be together, right from the start. Man, it was . . . It was scary, how much she hated us. The idea of us. Like we were the worst thing she could ever imagine. Zoe wanted to run away. But she's just a kid. I knew that wouldn't cut it. We needed to stay. We needed to change the situation.'

The child before me shivered in the rain. The irony of him calling Zoe a kid struck me. He looked so small. His shoulders were turned inward, like the bony wings of a bird.

'Try to imagine,' Harrison struggled, words half-forming on his lips. 'Try to imagine what it might be like for a person to be your god. Like, a real person. Not just any real person, either, but a selfish idiot who can't even control his own wife.

361

Try to imagine what it must be like to be another person's slave. *I was his slave*,' Harrison thumped his own chest. Looked off, dazed.

'Harry –'

'He was going to send me away. It's like, we got rid of Zoe's mum, and my dad picks up the vendetta against us right where Teresa left off. We were cursed. All we wanted was to be together, and we killed someone for it. That should have been enough. He had no interest in me. None. And then he grabs at this one little thing he doesn't like and thinks he'll stick his nose in and break us apart.'

I watched the boy panting, seething. His shoulders shaking with rage, thin beneath his drenched shirt.

'I cut the cable,' Harrison said. 'But I asked her first. I made sure.'

'You killed Zoe's mother,' I said. 'The two of you. And nothing happened. You got away with it.'

'Exactly.' Harrison looked at me, wild-eyed. 'Exactly. Nothing happened. Nothing fucking happened. There was the funeral. The wake. Everybody cried. Everybody went home. Zoe and me, we went home *together*. It was . . . It was . . .'

Harrison held his arms out, begging, pleading with me to understand.

'It was great,' I finished.

'It was great!' Harrison laughed, broke into sobs. 'We're so fucked up. You understand? Zoe and me are so fucked up that *we killed her mother and it was great.*'

The boy sobbed hard. Flexed the stick, paced up and down the tiny end of the pier.

'Harrison.' I shifted closer again.

'And with Teresa dead, and it being so great, we had to wonder, didn't we? Why not do them all?' He swallowed hard. 'It was so easy. It was so great. Why not have all the funerals? Why not have all the wakes? We started playing around with the idea. Just fucking around, you know? Zoe's dad's a pig. Just a . . . a human pig. But then my dad starts on us about being together. About being young and stupid. And I knew we had Teresa all over again. That he was just going to pick at us and pick at us until we couldn't take it anymore. He'd written to this rehabilitation ranch for troubled youths. Can you believe that? He wanted to put me on a six-month program for being with my fucking girlfriend.'

He was pleading with me now. He needed me to understand.

'In two years, we could be rid of them all,' he said. 'And Zoe and me, we could take over the lives they'd left behind. They weren't using them. They were wandering around the enormous fucking empty house avoiding each other, trying not to run into each other on the stairs. What was the point? What was the point of it all? Why should we have let them go on being our fucking gods when it was so easy to make it stop?'

Amanda suddenly thundered out of the bush behind me and skidded to a halt at my side, her sneakers sliding on the slick wet wood.

'Whoa!' She grabbed at my arm. 'Nearly went over that time! You okay, boss? You're covered in blood.'

'I'm fine.' I glanced at her. 'Did you pass Zoe?'

'Out like a light.'

'Harrison?' I said. 'Harrison, I want you to put your hands up.'

The boy wasn't done. He was staring at the water, the stick in his fists. Half his mind was swirling in the rage-filled memory of what he and his girlfriend had done. He made those barking noises again. Spun around and looked at me, stopped me in my tracks.

'It was so easy,' he said.

Amanda took a couple of steps forward but I grabbed her arm and dragged her back as something flicked across the top of the water a few metres out from the end of the pier. Harrison turned towards us, still tapping that long stick, his face spread wide in a smile.

'You want to meet my pet?' he asked.

'Holy fuckballs.' Amanda's voice beside me was small and uncertain. 'I'm not sure our fee covers this.'

'Harrison, come slowly towards us,' I said. 'We can talk more about what happened when you get off the pier.'

The kid ignored me. He was the defiant schoolchild who wouldn't come in from the rain, who made a show of himself in front of the students gathered inside the classroom. Lost in his own little world. There was another flicker of movement by the end leg of the pier, and Harrison leaned over the rickety wooden rail, waving the stick from side to side. I didn't know whether to scream at the kid or bargain with him. As I watched, a black lump of something rose from the surface of the water, shimmering with rain. A snout or an eye. I couldn't tell. All I knew was that it was alive.

'Don't do this, Harry,' I said. 'If you jump into the water, I can't come in after you.'

Harrison Scully looked at me. He seemed to forget Amanda was there. My partner pulled out her own gun, the replica, an enormous silver Smith and Wesson revolver so big in her hands it was almost comical. I watched her flip open the barrel of the revolver, check the bullets inside. I didn't know replicas had moveable barrels. Her face was set. Emotionless.

'We just want to be free,' Harrison said. 'You get it, right?'

I flinched at the blast. I'd taken my eyes off Amanda for a second, and in that time she'd raised the gun and shot Harrison in the upper body. It was no replica. The boy flew backwards and landed on the end of the pier.

'Amanda!'

'I don't have the stomach for much more of this,' she said. She marched towards the end of the pier and, as she neared the boy, her foot seemed to disappear right through the surface of the wood, like magic. The boards were sawn right down the middle, wedged together at the centre over a sheer drop. A trap. The same trap Harrison had led Jake through, that fateful night, in the dark hours when he lured his father out of bed with phoney threats from a stranger. I was seeing Amanda fall through the pier, and I was seeing Jake falling too, grabbing at the air, screaming, his eyes rising to the boy at the end of the pier, who turned, who was not a stranger, not a threat, but his own child.

I was seeing Jake trying to grip the wood, sliding, disappearing into the depths where a predator waited, a wild thing tamed by his very own son.

Amanda fell out of sight before I could scream her name. Her gun clattered on the boards in front of the hole.

'Amanda! Amanda!' I ran to the edge of where she'd fallen, but as I came to the opening and fell on my knees I heard Harrison getting to his feet. He was bleeding. I tried to lift my gun, but he clicked the hammer of Amanda's gun back with a sickening snap.

'Don't,' he said.

The boards flopped downward on their thick nails, the wedges that had kept them upright fallen into the muddy water. There was no sign of Amanda. The water below me swirled. I thought I heard a scream, but it might have been the storm raging all around us. Rain ran down the back of my head and along my jaw in a steady stream. My stomach was twisted in a hard knot.

'Put the gun down,' Harrison said.

I did as I was told.

'Please. Please. She's my partner,' I breathed, wanting to fall forward into the hole, to go after her, whatever that meant. The hands that held Amanda's gun on me were shaking. I chanced a look up into Harrison's eyes and saw the uncertainty there, the terror.

'I'm not your dad,' I said. 'You don't know me. I don't deserve to die. My partner doesn't deserve to die. Put the gun down.'

I fancied I could hear the springs in the trigger as the boy squeezed. My skin was alive with horror at the thought of a bullet plunging through me. The barrel of the gun was locked on my right eye. The boy wasn't answering. I took a chance.

'You're not going to shoot me with the safety on,' I said.

Harrison turned the gun just slightly to look at the side of it, altering the aim from my eye to the space beside my left ear. That was all I needed. I launched my body at his legs, clearing the hole in front of me and falling on the boards at the end of the pier. The gun roared. We slid, limbs scrambling, the edge of the pier sickeningly near. My body moved with a will of its own, the wounds in my back and legs forgotten, my own partner forgotten, hands grabbing Harrison's arms as he clawed at me. He twisted, slipped between my legs, tried to shove me over the edge of the pier. I gave a heavy swing that glanced off the shoulder where Amanda's bullet had landed, sending him sprawling on the boards.

I thought I'd won. I was sure Amanda's gun had fallen into the river when I launched myself at the boy, but as I stood and went to him he spun around, lifting the pistol, and fired at me point-blank. Missing my head by mere centimetres, the bullet whipping past my right ear.

The gunshot deafened me, started a ringing up in my ears like a fire alarm. I knocked the gun out of the boy's hand in a desperate swipe and fell on him. His hands were at my waist, and they found the knife Zoe had stabbed me with. I grabbed the boy's wrist before he could plunge it into my neck and turned the blade downward, away from me. My elbow slipped out from under me as the boy kicked upwards. The knife plunged into his throat, the handle embedded just under his jaw.

'Idiot,' I seethed, pulling the blade out, half talking to the boy and half talking to myself. 'Fucking idiot.'

'Oh god.' The boy gurgled, grabbed at his bloody throat, coughed as he felt the warm blood rushing between his fingers. 'Oh god, I'm dying. I'm dying.'

'You're not dying.' I ripped off my wet shirt and bunched it up, stuffed it onto the wound. The boy's hands were trembling as they came around mine, holding the shirt. A child's fear, the defiant murderer gone. 'But my partner probably is. So I'm leaving you here and going to find her.'

'No, no, no,' he coughed, gripping madly at the shirt. He reached for me. 'I'm dying!'

I could hear sirens on the other side of the hill. The ambulance had come for Stella. They'd see the cars, the door open. I hoped some neighbours had heard the gunshots and would send officers down into the bush. I hoped Zoe was still unconscious there, and hadn't fled. These were short, frantic thoughts as I leapt over the gap in the pier and jogged back towards the mangroves. My real mission was to find Amanda. That was all that counted. Two stupid children had murdered one of their parents each. No one else could die.

I ran along the grey beach, scanning the waters, looking for some sign of Amanda. I kept an eye on the edge of the forest, shuddering to a stop now and then as I fancied I saw movement in the long grass.

'Amanda!' I called. I ran back to the pier and started the other way along the tiny, muddy beach. 'Amanda!'

As I ran, I remembered what Dynah had told me. I saw Amanda's crime before my very eyes as I searched and called and hoped she wasn't dead.

'This is dumb,' twelve-year-old Dynah said from the back seat of Lauren's car. 'We ought to just go home.'

Her older sister ignored her, eyes on the road, now and then letting a hand drift to her flat-ironed hair and run the length of the strands to their tips. Lauren always touched her hair when she was nervous, so that sometimes if something really important was coming up, like a dance recital at school or a public speaking assignment, she'd make the ends all greasy. Dynah suspected that Lauren's nervousness was the key to her perfect performances, at the school, at home, in front of her friends. Dynah never seemed to be able to reach that peak of anxious energy. When Dynah had to talk in front of a crowd, or when she was invited to an important party, she started feeling sick, and then tired, and then she bailed out. That was her way.

She was feeling sick now, because she knew what was going to happen when they reached the meeting point. She huffed and folded her arms over her chest, tried to keep her eyes focused on the rainforest passing by the windows as the car climbed into the dark towards Kissing Point. Dynah didn't know the girl in the seat in front of her, Amanda. But she seemed like a stupid choice for the Special Project. Lauren and the boys needed girls for the Special Project who wouldn't go blabbering on to everyone about

369

it, and this Amanda girl hadn't shut up from the moment she got into the car. Dynah rubbed her belly and tried to breathe.

'How many people are going to this thing?' Amanda was asking. 'Twenty? Thirty? Who organised it? Is Troy Ledwidge going to be there? He's scary, that Troy Ledwidge. Someone told me he lives alone. He's seventeen and he lives alone.'

'You don't leave enough time between your questions for people to answer,' Lauren laughed uncomfortably. 'You're hyper-active, girl. Chill out!'

'I just can't believe you invited me. I'm so excited to be invited. Ha! That rhymes. I'm so *excited* to be *invited*. I've never been to one of these before. I know there was a really good party after the social last year. Did you go to that?'

'What? Oh. Oh yeah, some people went down to the beach, I guess.' Lauren cleared her throat, shifted upward in the driver's seat.

'We should go home.' Dynah kicked her sister's seat.

'So, Amanda,' Lauren said, 'we're just going to park a bit out of the way and then walk up to the party. Sound good? We don't want to get the car stuck up there when everyone tries to leave.'

Dynah fidgeted. The way Lauren said 'So, Amanda' was just the way she'd said 'So, Dynah' the first time she'd asked her to be a part of the Special Project. Sweetly, gently, as though she was asking a minor favour for which there'd be a huge reward. So Dyyyyynah . . . So Amaaaanda . . . Almost as though she was sacrificing herself, giving the opportunity over to her more deserving friend. As though the winner in the exchange was really going to be Amanda herself, and Lauren was just oh so kind for giving up her spot.

The car pulled off the main road and rumbled down a narrow dirt path, stopped in the clearing behind a thick row of trees. The girls got out. Dynah could hear music on the wind. Amanda finished the Cruiser she'd been sipping and put it in the car's centre console.

'So I've actually got a surprise for you, yeah?' Lauren said, sliding her fingers down the length of her hair. 'I've brought along a dress for you to wear to the party. It's in the back seat. Dynah, get it out, would you?'

Dynah reached into the back seat and pulled out the Myer bag. Chucked it on the ground beside the car's tyre. It flopped on its side but didn't open. The tape across the top of the bag kept it shut. Dynah knew there wasn't really a dress inside. Just an old blanket to pad the bag out. A lie. Dynah thought lies were just about the worst thing in the world, and then here was a special kind of lie, one that could be held in your hands. An object. Amanda was just about vibrating with excitement. She could hear the older girl's teeth chattering.

'I can hear the music,' Amanda said, looking towards the tops of the trees, as though the sound from the party up the road could be seen floating by, musical notes illuminated against the clouds. 'I can't believe this.'

'You can't wear that.' Lauren looked at Amanda's jeans, her stripy shirt. 'Take your clothes off, and we'll get you changed, yeah?'

In the dim glow of the car's interior lights, Dynah watched Amanda strip down to her underpants and bra. It was a pink crop-top from Kmart. Dynah had started on one of those, but even she'd graduated to an A-cup underwire bra by now. Amanda's body was thin and lean, the milk-white of skin that rarely saw sun. Dynah didn't know much about the girl, but she must have been a weirdo if Lauren had chosen her for the Special Project. Someone who wouldn't matter. Someone who wouldn't be believed. Like her. No one would have believed Dynah, even if she snitched. She knew that.

Amanda stood in the clearing in her tiny underpants in front of the two girls, rubbing her long, spidery arms. Dynah swallowed back the sickness in her throat.

'Okay.' Lauren looked towards the trees as the sound of the men's footsteps emerged through the dull sound of the distant music. 'Now don't panic, yeah?'

Lou and Steve emerged from the bush. They were both in their patrol uniforms. Dynah had heard Lauren talking to her boyfriend Lou that afternoon on the kitchen phone, whispering, asking him when his shift would end. She'd doodled 'LD' on the chalkboard by the fridge, then quickly rubbed it out so their mother didn't see. Lauren thought she was so amazing, dating someone outside school. A fully grown man. And a cop, too. It was exciting. It was so *dangerous*. Dynah had suffered through questioning on the way to school a bunch of times, Lauren's friends pursuing her, poking her, trying to get details. Who was he? Was he really in his thirties? Were the handcuffs real? Lauren had said that when Dynah grew up, maybe she could go out with his friend, Steve. Dynah crept to the car, the familiar tremors starting in her limbs.

'Hello, ladies,' Lou said, smiling.

'Police.' Amanda's face was void of emotion. She looked at Lauren. 'It's the police.'

'Here's the thing,' Lauren said brightly. 'Lou's my boyfriend, okay? And he's got a Special Project going. We just need you to play along. This is a really big favour for us, Amanda. Okay? It's a really special, really important project, and we just need you to do what we say.'

'Aren't we going to the party?' Amanda's hands crept to her chest, gripped the cloth bra. 'Aren't we –'

'Sure,' Lauren said. 'Sure we are. You want to be friends, right? Don't you want to be my friend? Well, you can just do me this favour, and then we'll be friends.'

Amanda looked at Dynah. The child cringed.

'We'll be really fast,' Lauren said, nudging Lou. 'Don't hurt her, okay? Just do what you've got to do and we'll get out of here.'

'Take your pants off,' Steve said, coming towards Amanda. Dynah watched as the officer grabbed the lanky teenager's arms, Lauren's boyfriend tugging the girl's underpants off. 'You're going to lie on the ground, and we're just gonna snap a few shots.'

'Put her on the back seat,' Lou said. 'We'll use the light of the car.'

Dynah couldn't hold her tears in anymore. She went to the edge of the clearing, listened to Amanda's cries of confusion and protest. The girl was frightened. Dynah had been frightened, her first time. She cried into her hands, and in time felt her sister's hand on her shoulder.

'It's fine, Dy, it's fine,' Lauren said. 'God, it's not a big deal. They're just photos.'

'Why couldn't they just have pictures of me and you and leave it at that?'

'You're too little to understand. The pictures are really important. They're using the pictures to get very important people to do what they say,' Lauren soothed. 'And the more pictures they have, the more they can say, "Well, you're in big trouble now, Mister. You have to do what we want."'

'Who are these people?' Dynah said. 'Why do they . . . How come they don't . . .'

'It's called blackmail,' Lauren said carefully.

'I don't like it!'

'It doesn't have to be forever,' Lauren whispered. 'They're going to use the pictures to get some money. It's a really good plan. No one gets hurt. They're really smart, Lou and Steve. You're too young. You don't get it. It's not a big deal. Lou says we might get married one day. You could be the bridesmaid. Would you like to be my bridesmaid?'

Amanda was fighting the two men in the open doorway of the car. All of a sudden the fight seemed to go out of her, and Steve grabbed the girl's arm, pulled it across her eyes. Amanda's right knee was shaking. The burst of the camera flash reflected off the dark trees around them.

The men came back to the middle of the clearing, and Lauren joined them. Dynah couldn't seem to walk properly. All her limbs were stiff with fear. When she joined the group, Steve reached down and touched her ear, and the little girl reeled away from him.

'Good shots,' Lou said, putting his arm around Lauren's shoulder. 'She's a skinny minnie. She won't say anything, will she?'

'No, she's the school weirdo.' Lauren took a packet of cigarettes from Lou's pocket. 'She's a total freak. No one would believe her, even if she did.'

'You're not going to say anything either, are you, pretty one?' Steve said, giving Dynah's bicep a squeeze. His grip tightened until Dynah's arm ached, but the ugly smile never left the big man. 'You wouldn't tell on us, would you?'

'Listen, why don't we go up to the party?' Lou said. 'I'll take you up to the party. Dynah, you come with us. Steve will drive Amanda home.'

'No.' Lauren shrugged Lou off. 'We don't want to leave her alone.'

'She won't be alone. She'll be with me. She'll be fine.' Steve adjusted his belt. 'I'll take care of her.'

Dynah grabbed at her older sister's arm. 'Don't leave her alone with him, Lauren.'

'What? What am I going to do? I wouldn't hurt her.'

'Come on, both of you.' Lou took Dynah's wrist, slid his arm back around Lauren's shoulders. He winked at his partner. 'She'll be fine! He's a police officer, aren't you, Stevie?'

Steve took a pocket knife from a pouch on the back of his belt. He flicked it open in the light of the car with a snap.

'I just want to show her my new toy.' Steve flashed the blade in front of Dynah. 'Pretty, huh?'

'Come on.' Lou tugged Dynah, pushed her sister along. 'Let's go.'

'Lauren,' Dynah begged.

'Come on, Dynah.' Lauren smiled uneasily. 'It's fine.'

'Please.' Dynah looked back at the car through the trees. She saw Steve approaching the car, Amanda's feet still hanging over the back seat out the open door. 'Lauren, we can't leave her.'

Her older sister and her police officer boyfriend walked ahead up the dirt path towards the main road. Dynah followed them, hugging herself tightly, a light rain beginning to fall. The sobs rippled up through her. All she wanted to do was go home.

She stopped walking. Lauren seemed to sense it, and turned around. The sisters' eyes met in the dark.

'We can't,' Dynah said. She turned and ran back towards the clearing.

'Dynah!' Lauren was furious now. 'Dynah! Fucking leave it!'

Dynah sprinted back along the path. When she got to the car, Steve was lying with his legs out of the open door, his arms on the back seat, Amanda beneath him. Dynah kicked him hard in the leg and pulled at his hips.

'What the fuck?'

'Dynah, leave them alone!' Lauren grabbed at her sister, pushed her away. 'You're such a fucking drag! Jesus!'

'Lou, control these bitches, would you?' Steve grabbed at his open belt, pushed Dynah hard so that she fell on her backside on the dirt. Lou was there, grabbing at her. 'Fuck! Get them out of here.'

Dynah wondered, for years after that night, if Amanda's movements were soundless, or if she was just too frightened for her mind to register the noises that the stabbing surely made in those frantic last seconds of her sister's life. Though she couldn't hear, she did see Amanda rise up from the back seat of the car, a black silhouette against the gold interior lights, the knife in her hand. Lauren jolted a couple of times as the knife entered her back. Amanda hammered the knife in quickly, a few manic jabs, but when Lauren fell Dynah could see that Amanda wasn't really aiming at the girl at all. She was just stabbing at the first thing she came into contact with, the first figure her body recognised. Amanda hadn't meant to stab Lauren. She'd just taken Steve's knife from the seat beside her, got up, and started stabbing.

There was a moment of blind terror before the sounds of those around her returned to Dynah's ears. Steve was howling, gripping his hair, looking at Lauren on the ground lying flat near Dynah's feet. Lou grabbed Amanda and threw her into the side of the car, knocking the knife from her fingers. He grabbed the bloody tool and looked up at his partner.

'Go, Steve,' Lou said. 'Run! Take Dynah with you. I'll clean up here.'

I knew I'd found Amanda when I started to see blood in the sand. I followed the trail until it became a long dragging smear, sideways along the waterline and then directly up to the edge of the trees. Amanda had collapsed there on top of a small log, her head and shoulder flopped back over it, eyes staring at the sky. I thought she was dead. The worst of her injuries seemed to be in her legs, long open gashes, one leg of her jeans completely torn off, exposing bloodied flesh. The blood was incredible. It soaked her from neck to waist. I rushed up and gathered her in my arms, folded her and lifted her against my chest.

To my surprise, one cold hand gripped at my chest hairs.

'You're shirtless,' she breathed. Her head lolled against my shoulder. There was blood on her lip.

'Hang on, Amanda,' I said. 'Hang on.'

'Strip . . .' she whispered. Tried to laugh. 'Stripper.'

I ran towards the pier. There were two police officers there, seeing to Harrison. They saw me and pointed towards the hill. There were no paramedics on the trails. I'd have to run to the ambulance up on the road. My wounded leg was numb. I ran higher and higher through the bush, seeing glimpses of the road in the distance. My feet sank in the soft mulch. I knelt and rested against a tree for a moment, gathered Amanda up tighter against me. There were teeth marks in the arm beneath my fingers, a row of holes in the tattoos where the beast had clamped down on her.

'I know about Kissing Point,' I told her. If she was going to die in my arms, she was going to know that I understood what had happened. That I wasn't going to let Steven Hench and Lou Damford get away with what they had done to Amanda. To Lauren. To Dynah. To all the little girls they'd managed to wrangle in front of their cameras, to snap in their impossibly innocent, naked forms.

I'd stood in my kitchen that day and looked at the six photographs. They'd removed the one of a frightened teenage Amanda from the collection, thinking I'd probably recognise the back seat of Lauren's car from the crime-scene photographs in *Murder in the Top End*. That maybe I'd recognise Amanda herself, her sharp jaw and spidery limbs. But they couldn't have anticipated that I'd recognise Dynah Freeman. Dynah looked about twelve years old in the photograph. She'd been biting her lips, suppressing tears. I could almost hear her sister convincing her to just do this strange favour for her older boyfriend and not, under threat of violence, to tell anyone. They were only photos, she'd told the child. It was no big deal.

I'd sat with Dynah Freeman, now an adult, in the empty cafe and listened to her cries. Listened to her describe that night, when her older sister had asked her to come along, thinking Amanda was more likely to buy into the whole arrangement if Lauren's goofy little sister was in the back seat. The promise of a cool party with a popular girl. A pretty new dress.

Dynah hadn't ever spoken to Damford and Hench again. She saw them around town. They saw her. She saw Amanda, knew that the older woman was crazy. She didn't know exactly what Lou Damford and Steven Hench had used those photographs for, but she could guess. They bullied powerful men. They blackmailed people for money. A handful of dirty pictures of young girls had probably opened hundreds of doors for the two men over the years. They planted them in men's houses. In their bedrooms. In their offices. Then they turned up and discovered them and started making their demands. It wasn't even about money, Dynah knew, though she could tell there was plenty of that floating around the two men. It was about power. The raw animal power they'd exhibited on that night, two grown men and three girls tangled up in the dark of the rainforest, the girls helpless but to do the men's bidding. Dynah had grabbed Steve's legs and hips, tried to drag him off Amanda's tiny body beneath him on the seat of the car. He hadn't budged. Dead weight. The adult Dynah knew Steve Hench was as unmoveable and untouchable to the men he manipulated as he'd been to her that night.

I sat against the tree in the storm and held my partner and told her I would get the men who had done this to her. Unconsciousness was threatening her. Amanda's head rolled against my arm. But I wouldn't let her sleep. Not yet. I needed to know.

'Why didn't you ever tell anyone?' I asked her. I squeezed her body against mine, tried to shake her awake. 'Why did you let them take you to jail?'

Amanda looked up at me. Her eyes were closing.

'Because I was happy there,' she said.

EPILOGUE

She pressed her shoe against the front tyre of the bike, dug her heel into the dirt and leaned forward. Pain rippled up through the scarred and lumpy muscles of her calf, receding slowly into a warm ache. She breathed, felt the sun on the back of her neck. Amanda swung her leg over the bike and pushed off, just as a light, misty rain began to fall.

Amanda watched as the raindrops began to catch in the fine hairs over her tattooed arms, stretched forward and gripping the curved handlebars tight. Her arms were unfamiliar to her. From the moment the policemen had snapped those pictures of her on the back seat of Lauren's car all those years ago, Amanda had felt the desire to cover up her skin. She'd started getting tattooed in prison, hand-poke designs from another inmate, a woman swift with a sewing needle and ink collected from pens stolen from the administration office. She'd started with a crooked bluebird on her hip. As picture upon picture and layer upon layer of flowers and beetles and ladies and animals climbed up her legs and arms and chest, she'd felt her naked and vulnerable self covered, protected. The policemen had exposed her. Laid her bare. She'd never wanted to be bare again. Not an inch of her.

She'd gotten used to her coloured and shaded arms. But now the pink cracks and slashes the crocodile's jaws had made in her had taken some of her protective layers away. She was still flesh underneath. Pink scar-tissue, the colour of the inside of a cat's ear. There were rows of holes in some places, where the beast had clamped down on her. Other parts of her body were cracked with pale lightning where she'd been shaken by the monster, rolled in the water. She was a broken vase put back together, and the new pink skin reminded her of her old body, the one Damford and Hench had defiled. But that wasn't so terrifying now. She'd had time in hospital to watch the cracks forming. She could accept them.

Amanda pedalled between the high walls of cane along the muddy road, glancing up at the swallows that marked her way on the wires, like sentinels against the grey sky. She remembered sitting in her hospital bed and watching Dynah Freeman giving a press conference on the television in the corner of the room, leaning around a group of nurses who had gathered to watch the coverage. She'd seen footage of Damford and Hench being arrested at their houses, seen Dynah crying as she sat at the table beneath a huge photograph of her dead sister's smiling face. It had only been twelve hours since some police detectives Amanda didn't know came to her bedside to ask her about the night in the rainforest. They'd told her Dynah's version of the story, asked her if it was true. If Steven Hench and Lou Damford had taken those pictures of her. If Steven Hench had lain on top of her. If he'd touched her. If he'd raped her. They'd shown her a photocopy of a picture of her child self.

Amanda had looked at her scarred arms. Ran her fingertips along the new lines. Fault lines in the story she'd told herself all these years. That she was a killer. That underneath her skin, the truth would be forever trapped. It was out now. Dynah had let it all out.

Journalists had come to the hospital. She'd accepted their visits. They'd told her about Ormund Smitt, about the counselling he was getting now, the stuff he was still writing online about Jake and the government and the secret societies. They'd told her about Stella waking up from her coma on an upper floor of the same hospital, about the tests being done to see if she'd received any brain damage from the drugs her child had given her. The journalists had wanted to know about Lauren Freeman even more than they wanted to know about the two teenage killers she and Ted had put away. No one knew what headline to apply. *Scully case solved, son behind bars. Teen lovers' murder plot leaves two parents dead.* Amanda had been so used to those scribblers and their funny little notebooks, how they looked at her like a dangerous predator. No one knew how to look at her now. Was she a victim? Was she a monster? Was she a crime-solving detective hero? Amanda didn't mind the confusion. She kind of liked confusing people.

She turned the handlebars and took a detour through Beale Street, past the Shark Bar, where Vicky was washing the front windows. Amanda let the bike roll through the gravel outside her office, where the new sign hanging above the door was gleaming in the fresh rain. Conkaffey & Pharrell. Ted had wanted to add 'Investigations', but Amanda had suffered enough adding anything at all to the shopfront. She didn't like change. Announcements, proclamations, exclamations. '"Investigations" is a label,' she'd told Ted as he sat at her bedside, showing her the sign design on his phone. 'It'll limit us. It'll tell people investigations is all we do.'

'It *is* all we do,' her partner had said. God, the man lacked vision.

She rode through the cane fields and through the tunnels of rainforest made by the road, looking out for cassowaries, the wind in her short hair. In time Amanda turned onto the road that led to Ted's house and rolled to the brick fence, hopped off and walked her bike along the side through the short grass. From the back of her jeans, Amanda drew an envelope folded in half.

When she reached the corner of the house she saw him. He was lying on the lawn, propped up on his elbows in the afternoon sun, his long legs spread before him. By the fence at the bottom of the property, six grey geese wandered in a loose pack, pecking at the grass. It hadn't rained here yet. His eyes were closed against the golden light. It had only been three days since Ted had visited her at the hospital, but he'd changed again. Each time he'd appeared at her bedside, Amanda had noticed something different. He'd put on some weight. He'd spent some time outside, and his skin was darker. Today, the beard was gone. He'd told her that the vigilante attacks had stopped. He sometimes heard cars driving by late at night, slowing as they passed, curious. But there'd been no more bricks, fireworks, piss. No more crowds. It was quiet.

The journalist probably helped. Fabiana was gone now. She'd taken what she wanted from Ted – a cause, a mission, something to write about. After the interview about the silent witness had appeared in the news, the *Innocent Ted* group had formed around a blog site, and Fabiana was now their spokeswoman back in Sydney. Amanda had watched videos of the woman online from her hospital bed, read through the hundreds and hundreds of reader comments. At first, Fabiana had received a barrage of abuse online for putting up the interview video, and things had got worse when the public realised that she and Ted were briefly lovers. People said she was 'betraying all women' by shacking up with a 'monster'. They'd compared her to women who marry serial killers in prison. There were comments on the blog posts that begged her not to have children with Ted, because they'd surely be the next victims of his sickness. She'd appeared on a number of morning talk shows with a whole lot of stoic dignity. She didn't respond to the death threats she received online. She said that her mission in life now was fighting for Ted, so she didn't have time for that kind of rubbish, not with her increased obligations at the paper and her new part-time battle for justice. In time, the comments had started changing. The questions grew. There'd been no sign of Ted himself on the internet. The big man had let the journalist go about her business of rescuing his reputation. Amanda was glad. The woman owed him that. And more.

Amanda lifted the envelope to her lips now. Nibbled the corner thoughtfully. A large white goose had approached her from the side of the house and now stood taking her in, its beady eyes questioning, as Amanda was questioning.

Inside the envelope were printed pages, screenshots of her investigation into the white dog. Amanda had become interested in the mentions of the white dog in Claire Bingley's interview tapes, which she had watched over and over again since Ted came into her life. The little girl who Ted was accused of attacking was deeply traumatised, and yes, she had said many strange things in the hours and hours she was recorded and questioned about what happened to her. But in total, Amanda had counted three times that a white dog was mentioned. The girl first spoke of a white dog in her hospital interview. She mentioned it next when she was interviewed by a trauma counsellor. And just once, in an interview conducted at the Parramatta police headquarters, Amanda swore the girl mumbled 'dog' when she was left alone in the room with the recorder.

It was enough for Amanda. She'd taken the clue and run.

What she'd brought with her today were three pieces of paper. First, there was a photocopy of a page of a Mount Annan local newspaper, the issue dated four days before Claire Bingley was abducted. In the 'Freebies' section, an ad had listed a medium-sized cross-breed white dog, free to good home, 'moving to England and cannot take her with us'. On the back of the page, Amanda had made notes from her conversation with the posters of the ad. She'd called the couple who'd owned the dog from her hospital bed and talked to them in the quiet of the night, listening to the sounds of a London morning in the background of the call. Though they didn't remember much about the man who'd taken their dog, they did remember his dark blue ute.

Amanda had started looking for a dark blue ute in all the evidence she could find about the moment Claire was abducted, and her search had led her to the second piece of paper in the envelope. It was a screenshot she had obtained from the CCTV camera of a homewares store in Camden Park, eight kilometres from the spot where Claire Bingley was abducted. She'd started with cameras near Mount Annan, where the child had been abducted, and spiralled out. The only reason the owners of the store had kept the tape for the day Claire Bingley was abducted was because they'd been robbed the day after, and their cash register had been stolen, so the tape for the entire week had been entered into the police records. The image Amanda found was of a blue ute waiting at the traffic lights outside the store, the shadowed figure of a man sitting in the driver's seat. At the edge of the passenger-side window, two tiny triangles were visible. With the quality of the video, and the distance of the shot, it was possible that the two white triangles in the window of the ute were flashes of light, reflections of the shopfront or the sun pouring between the buildings.

But Amanda didn't think so. She thought they were the pointy ears of a medium-sized, white dog.

The final piece of paper in the envelope was another screenshot, this one taken from the security camera outside the Yagoona RSPCA shelter. As a matter of course, the RSPCA keep screenshots of all members of the public they catch dumping animals at their shelter gates. In the picture, a man was tying the leash of a medium-sized white dog to the gates of the centre. The man in the picture was bent at the waist, his face hidden. It was the best picture the camera had yielded. When the animal rescue staff had arrived the following morning, they'd found the dog there, his front left paw fractured.

Amanda could see Claire Bingley standing at the bus stop when she closed her eyes. The little girl turning from watching

Ted's car drive away at the sound of a yelp in the bush behind the bus stop. A white dog in the dark, shadowy brush, limping on its paw, whimpering in pain. What child wouldn't go to an animal in distress?

Amanda stood at the corner of Ted's house now and wondered. She knew that the few months she had been tracking down the man with the white dog were a good indication of how likely it was that she would eventually catch him. She was a good investigator, and her prison time had taught her the kind of quiet patience it took to find a monster as skilful, and as slippery, as the man with the blue ute seemed to be. But Amanda also knew that if she kept going, if she gave the information to Ted, and together they hunted down Claire Bingley's attacker, she would lose him.

If Ted cleared his name completely, she'd be alone again. There'd be no reason for him to stay in the prison he'd built himself beside the dark waters of Crimson Lake. And Amanda kind of enjoyed having Ted around, even though he wasn't often up for her games, and he couldn't rhyme to save his life.

He made her happy. And she hadn't been this happy since they threw her in prison for the first time all those years ago, the remand centre where she'd waited to go on trial. She'd stood in the doorway to the dorm with her toothbrush and soap and toilet paper ration and watched as the occupants of this strange new concrete wonderland awakened to her presence. She'd watched them emerging from their blankets, leaning around the corners of their bunks, examining her. Suddenly, her shaking had stopped.

She'd recognised them.

These were the broken dolls. The weirdoes. The freaks.

These were the people she'd belonged with all her life. She'd finally found them. She'd finally found her place.

She'd felt that same sense of homecoming when the big man appeared in the Shark Bar doorway, trying to contain his worry, trying to hide his face. Here was another outsider. Here was one of her people.

Amanda took a deep breath and squeezed the envelope tight. As she stepped forward into the sunlight, the man on the grass noticed her. Ted turned and smiled as she made her way over.

She'd just have to trust him, she guessed.

ACKNOWLEDGEMENTS

Some people think that writers sit alone in quiet, private offices coming up with ideas that rush seamlessly from the brain to the computer keys, perfect waves of words ready to be packaged for consumption. Maybe there's a writer out there somewhere for whom this is true, but I can tell you one thing for sure – it isn't me.

Long before I got to that quiet private office, I studied under some very skilled creative writing teachers, Dr Ros Petelin, Dr Kim Wilkins, Dr Camilla Nelson, Dr Gary Crew, Dr Ross Watkins and James Forsyth among them. Working with the hilarious and warm-hearted James Patterson has been a crash course in fast-paced crime, and I'm so grateful to him for it.

Gaby Naher took a collection of the certainly less than perfect words I'd produced and decided she'd fight for their space in the world, and Bev Cousins soon joined her. Without these two courageous women, my stories would never have left the room.

The meticulous Kathryn Knight edits my work, and the tenacious Jess Malpass finds opportunities for me to talk to people about it. The world over, more people put my work in the hands of readers with love and support I could never have hoped for. Thomas Wörtche in Germany, Selina Walker and Susan Sandon in the UK, and Lisa Gallagher, Michaela Hamilton and Kristin Sevick in the US are among them.

And just beyond the office door is my wonderful husband, who's always there when the words won't come. Tim, you are a delight in my life. I'm so lucky I found you.

If you enjoyed *Crimson Lake*, read on for
an exclusive extract from Candice Fox's
prize-winning novel.

HADES

A dark, compelling and original thriller
that will have you spellbound
from its atmospheric opening pages
to its shocking climax.

PROLOGUE

As soon as the stranger set the bundle on the floor, Hades could tell it was the body of a child. It was curled on its side and wrapped in a worn blue sheet secured with duct tape around the neck, waist and knees. One tiny pearl-coloured foot poked out from the hem, limp on his sticky linoleum. Hades leaned against the counter of his cramped, cluttered kitchen and stared at that little foot. The stranger shifted uneasily in the doorway, drew a cigarette from a packet and pulled out some matches. The man they called Hades lifted his eyes briefly to the stranger's thin angled face.

'Don't smoke in my house.'

The stranger had been told how to get to Hades' place but not about its bewildering, frightening character. Beyond the iron gates of the Utulla tip, on the ragged edge of the Western suburbs, lay a gravel road leading through mountains of trash to a hill that blocked out the sky, black and imposing, guarded by stars. A crown of trees and scrub on top of the hill obscured all view of the small wooden shack. The stranger had driven with painful care past piles of rubbish as high as apartment buildings crawling with every manner of night creature – owls, cats and rodents picking and shifting through old milk cartons and bags of rotting meat. Luminescent eyes peered from the cabins of burned-out car shells and from beneath sheets of twisted corrugated iron.

Farther along the gravel path, the stranger began to encounter a new breed of watchful beast. Creatures made from warped scraps of metal and pieces of discarded machinery lined the road – a broken washing machine beaten and buckled into the figure of a snarling lion, a series of bicycles woven together and curled and stretched into the body of a grazing flamingo. In the light of the moon, the animals with their kitchen-utensil feathers and Coke-bottle eyes seemed tense and ready. When the stranger entered the house he was a little relieved to be away from them and their attention. The relief evaporated when he laid eyes on the man they called the Lord of the Underworld.

Hades was standing in the corner of the kitchen when the stranger entered, as though he'd known he was coming. He had not moved from there, his furry arms folded over his barrel chest. Cold heavy-lidded eyes fixed on the bundle in the stranger's arms. There was a Walther PP handgun with a silencer on the disordered bench beside him by a half-empty glass of scotch. Hades' grey hair looked neat atop his thick skull. He was squat and bulky like an ox, power and rage barely contained in the painful closeness of the kitchen.

The air inside the little house seemed pressed tight by the trees, a dark dome licking and stroking the hot air through the windows. Hades' kitchen was adorned with things he had salvaged from the dump. Ornate bottles and jars of every conceivable colour hung by fishing line from the ceiling, strange cutting and slicing implements were nailed like weapons to the walls. There were china fish and pieces of plastic fruit and a stuffed yellow ferret coiled, sleeping, in a basket by the foot of the door, jars of things there seemed no sense in keeping – coloured marbles and lens-less spectacles and bottle caps in their thousands – and lines of dolls' heads along the window-sill, some with eyes and some without, gaping mouths smiling, howling, crying. Through the door to the tiny living room, a wall crammed with tattered paperbacks was visible, the books lying and standing in every position from the unpolished floor-boards to the mould-spotted ceiling.

The stranger writhed in the silence. Wanted to look at every-thing but afraid of what he might see. Night birds moaned in the trees outside the mismatched stained-glass windows.

'Do you, uh . . .' The stranger worked the back of his neck with his fingernails. 'Do you want me to go and get the other one?'

Hades said nothing for a long time. His eyes were locked on the body of the child in the worn blue sheet.

'Tell me how this happened.'

The stranger felt new sweat tickle at his temples.

'Look,' he sighed, 'I was told there'd be no questions. I was told I could just come and drop them off and . . .'

'You were told wrong.'

One of Hades' chubby fingers tapped his left bicep slowly,

as though counting off time. The stranger fingered the cigarette he had failed to light, drawing it to his lips, remembered the warning. He slipped it into his pocket and stared at the bundle on the floor, at the shape of the girl's small head tucked against her chest.

'It was supposed to be the most perfect, perfect thing,' the stranger said, shaking his head at the body. 'It was all Benny's idea. He saw a newspaper story about this guy, Tenor I think his name was, this crazy scientist dude. He'd just copped a fat wad of cash for some thing he was working on with skin cancer or sunburn or some shit like that. Benny got obsessed with the guy, kept bringing us newspaper clippings. He showed us a picture of the guy and his little wife and his two kiddies and said the family was mega-rich already and he was just adding his new dosh to a big stinking pile.'

The stranger drew a long breath that inflated his narrow chest. Hades watched, unmoving.

'We'd got word that the family was going to be alone at their holiday house in Long Jetty. So we drove up there, the six of us, to rattle their cage and take the babies – just for a bit, you know, not for long. It was going to be the easiest job, man. Bust in, bust out, keep them for a couple of days and then organise an exchange. We weren't gonna do nothing with them. I'd even borrowed some games they could play while they stayed with us.'

Hades opened one of the drawers beside him and extracted a notepad and pen. From where he stood, he slapped them onto the small table by the side wall.

'These others,' he said, 'write down their names. And your own.'

The stranger began to protest, but Hades was silent. The stranger sat on the plastic chair by the table, his fingers trembling, and began to write names on the paper. His handwriting was childlike and crooked, smeared.

'Everything just went wrong so fast,' he murmured as he wrote, holding the paper steady with his long white fingers. 'Benny got the idea that the dude was giving him the eye like he was gonna do something stupid. I wasn't paying attention. The woman was screaming and crying and carrying on and someone clocked her and the kids were struggling. Benny blew the parents away. He just . . . he pumped them and pumped them till his gun was flat. He was always so fucking trigger happy. He was always so fucking ready for a fight.'

The stranger seemed stirred by some emotion, letting air out of his chest slowly through his teeth. He stared at the names he had written on the paper. Hades watched.

'One minute everything was fine. The next thing I know we're on the road with the kids in the boot and no one to sell them to. We started talking about getting rid of them and someone said they knew you and . . .' The stranger shrugged and wiped his nose on his hand.

For the first time since the stranger had arrived, Hades left the corner of the kitchen. He seemed larger and more menacing somehow, his oversized, calloused hands godly as they cradled the tiny notepad, tearing off the page with the names. The stranger sat, defeated, in the plastic chair. He didn't raise his eyes as Hades folded the small square of paper, slipping it into his pocket. He didn't notice as the older man took up the pistol, actioned it and flicked the safety off.

'It was an accident,' the stranger murmured, his bloodshot eyes brimming with tears as he stared, lips parted, at the body in the bundle. 'Everything was going so well.'

The man named Hades put two bullets into the stranger. The stranger's confused eyes fixed on Hades, his hands grabbing at the holes in his body. Hades put the gun back on the counter and lifted the scotch to his lips. The night birds had stopped their moaning and only the sound of the stranger dying filled the air.

Hades set the glass down with a sigh and began to trace the dump yards around the hill with his mind, searching for the best place for the body of the stranger and, somewhere separate, somewhere fitting, to bury the bodies of the little ones. There was a place he knew behind the sorting centre where a tree had sprung up between the piles of garbage – the twisted and gnarled thing sometimes produced little pink flowers. He would bury the children there together and dig the stranger in somewhere, anywhere, with the dozens of rapists, killers and thieves who littered the grounds of the dump. Hades closed his eyes. Too many strangers were coming to his dump these nights with their bundles of lost lives. He would have to put the word out that no new clients were welcome. The ones he knew, his regular clients, brought him the bodies of evil ones. But these strangers. He shook his head. These strangers kept bringing innocents.

Hades set his empty glass on the counter by his gun. His eyes wandered across the cracked floor to the small pearl foot of the dead girl.

It was then that he noticed the toes were clenched.

1

I figured I'd struck it lucky when I first laid eyes on Eden Archer. She was sitting by the window with her back to me. I could just see a slice of her angular face when she surveyed the circle of men around her. It seemed to be some kind of counselling session, probably about the man I was replacing, Eden's late partner. Some of the men in the circle were grey-faced and sullen, like they were only just keeping their emotions in check. The psychologist himself looked as if someone had just stolen his last zack.

Eden, on the other hand, was quietly contemplative. She had a flick-blade in her right hand, visible only to me, and she was sliding it open and shut with her thumb. I ran my eyes over her long black braid and licked my teeth. I knew her type, had encountered plenty in the academy. No friends, no interest in having a mess around in the male dorms on quiet weekends when the officers were away. She could run in those three-inch heels, no doubt about that. The forty-dollar manicure was her third this month but she would break a rat's neck if she found it in her pantry. I liked the look of her. I liked the way she breathed, slow and calm, while the officers around her tried not to fall to pieces.

I stood there at the mirrored glass, half-listening to Captain James blab on about the loss of Doyle to the Sydney Metro Homicide Squad and what it had done to morale. The counselling session broke up and Eden slipped her knife into her belt. The white cotton top clung to her carefully sculpted figure. Her eyes were big and dark, downcast to the carpet as she walked through the door towards me.

'Eden.' The captain motioned at me. 'Frank Bennett, your new partner.'

I grinned and shook her hand. It was warm and hard in mine.

'Condolences,' I said. 'I heard Doyle was a great guy.' I'd also heard Eden had come back with his blood mist all over her face, bits of his brain on her shirt.

'You've got big shoes to fill.' She nodded. Her voice was as flat as a tack.

She half-smiled in a tired kind of way, as if my turning up to be her partner was just another annoyance in what had been a long and shitty morning. Her eyes met mine for the briefest of seconds before she walked away.

Captain James showed me to my spot in the bull-pit. The desk had been stripped of Doyle's personal belongings. It was chipped and bare, save for a black plastic telephone and a laptop port. A number of people looked up from their desks as I entered. I figured they'd introduce themselves in time. A group of men and women by the coffee station gave me the once-over and then turned inward to compare their assessments. They held mugs with slogans like 'Beware of the Twilight Fan' and 'World's Biggest Asshole' printed on the side.

My mother had been a wildlife warrior, the kind who would stop and fish around in the pouches of kangaroo corpses for joeys and scrape half-squashed birds off the road to give them pleasant deaths or fix them. One morning she brought me home a box of baby owls to care for, three in all, abandoned by their mother. The men and women in the office made me think of those owls, the way they clustered into a corner of the shoebox when I'd opened it, the way their eyes howled black and empty with terror.

I was keen to get talking to people here. There were some exciting cases happening and this assignment was very much a step up for me. My last department at North Sydney had been mainly Asian gangland crime. It was all very straightforward and repetitive – territorial drive-bys and executions and restaurant hold-ups, fathers beaten and young girls terrorised into silence. I knew from the media hype and word around my old office that Sydney Metro were looking for an eleven-year-old girl who'd gone missing and was probably dead somewhere. And I'd heard another rumour that someone here had worked on the Ivan Milat backpacker murders in the 1990s. I wanted to unpack my stuff quickly and go looking for some war tales.

Eden sat on the edge of my desk as I opened my plastic tub and began sorting my stuff into drawers. She cleared her throat once and looked around uncomfortably, avoiding my glance.

'Married?' she asked.

'Twice.'

'Kids?'

'Ha!'

She glanced at me, turning the silver watch on her wrist round and round. I sat down in Doyle's chair. It had been warmed by the morning sun pouring in through the windows high above us. I knew this and yet my skin crawled with the idea that he might have been sitting here, moments earlier, talking on the phone or checking his emails.

'Why'd you take this job?'

I could smell her as I bent down and lifted my backpack from the floor. She smelt expensive. Flash leather boots hugging her calves, boutique perfume on her throat. I told myself she was probably late twenties and that women that age looked for guys a bit older – and the ten years or so I had on her didn't necessarily make me a creep. I told myself she wouldn't notice the grey coming in from my temples.

'I lost a partner too. Been alone for six months now.'

'Sorry.' Again that flatness in her voice. 'On the job?'

'No. Suicide.'

A man approached us, circled the desk and then sat down beside Eden, one leg up on the desktop, facing me. There was a large ugly scar the length of his right temple running into his hairline like white lightning. It pulled up the corner of his eye. Eden looked at him with that embarrassed half-smile.

'Frankie, right?' he grinned, flashing white canines.

'Frank.'

'Eric.' He gripped my hand and pumped it. 'This one gets too much for you to handle, you just let me know, uh?' He elbowed Eden hard in the ribs. Obnoxious. She smirked.

'I'm sure I'll be fine.'

I began to pack my things away faster. Eric reached into the tub beside him and pulled out a folder.

'This your service record?'

I reached for the manila folder he was holding. He tugged it away.

'Yeah, thanks, I'll have it back.' I felt my tongue stick to the roof of my mouth. Eden sat watching. Eric stood back and flicked through the papers.

'Oh, look at this. North Sydney Homicide. Asian gangs. You speak Korean? Mandarin? Says here under disciplinary history you got a serious DUI on the way to work.' He laughed. 'On the *way* to work, Frankie. You got a problem with that? You like to drink?'

I snatched the folder from him. His wide hand thundered on my shoulder.

'I'm just giving you a hard time.'

I ignored him and he wandered back to the group of owls. He jerked his thumb towards me and said something and the owls stared. Eden was watching my face. I scratched my neck as the heat crept down my chest.

'Fucking jerk.' I shook my head.

'Yeah.' She smiled, a full-size, bright white flash. 'He's good at that.'

FIND OUT WHAT HAPPENS NEXT…

HADES

OUT 21 SEPTEMBER 2017

AVAILABLE TO PRE-ORDER NOW